River is a classic tale of longing—a quest story that takes
its young heroine on a magical journey
backwards through time and across the globe.
As young Emily tumbles mysteriously
from one decade to the next,
from Brooklyn to Melbourne,
from South Africa to Lithuania,
she meets a long line of strong female ancestors,
and witnesses their trials and triumphs
at moments that send their lives
in astonishing and unpredictable directions.
If you've ever wondered what your mother
or grandmother or great-grandmother
went through when she was young,
this richly-imagined story travels the river
of time to a past that shows us who we are now.

—**Kate Manning**, author of *My Notorious Life*

RIVER

GUERNICA WORLD EDITIONS 21

RIVER

Shira Nayman

GUERNICA
World
EDITIONS

TORONTO—CHICAGO—BUFFALO—LANCASTER (U.K.)
2020

Michael Mirolla, general editor
Margo LaPierre, editor
Cover design: Allen Jomoc Jr.
Interior layout: Jill Ronsley, suneditwrite.com
Guernica Editions Inc.
287 Templemead Drive, Hamilton (ON), Canada L8W 2W4
2250 Military Road, Tonawanda, N.Y. 14150-6000 U.S.A.
www.guernicaeditions.com

Distributors:
Independent Publishers Group (IPG)
600 North Pulaski Road, Chicago IL 60624
University of Toronto Press Distribution,
5201 Dufferin Street, Toronto (ON), Canada M3H 5T8
Gazelle Book Services, White Cross Mills
High Town, Lancaster LA1 4XS U.K.

First edition.
Printed in Canada.

Legal Deposit—First Quarter
Library of Congress Catalog Card Number: 2019946621
Library and Archives Canada Cataloguing in Publication
Title: River / Shira Nayman.
Names: Nayman, Shira, 1960- author.
Description: Series statement: Guernica world editions ; 21
Identifiers: Canadiana (print) 20190154942 | Canadiana (ebook)
20190155035 | ISBN 9781771834575
(softcover) | ISBN 9781771834582 (EPUB) | ISBN 9781771834599 (Kindle)
Classification: LCC PS3614.A96 R58 2020 | DDC 813/.6—dc23

For my parents,
Doreen Nayman (née Shapiro) and Jack Nayman, z"l,
and my children, Juliana and Lucas
—the river of generations,
flowing into one another, eternally—

It began in mystery, and it will end in mystery,
but what a savage and beautiful
country lies in between.
—Diane Ackerman

PROLOGUE

THE WHIR OF ENGINES VIBRATED in my bones as the plane tilted upward. The skies separated invisibly, releasing us from the world left behind. This was the first time Ray and I were travelling together to Australia, where my mother had grown up. As a child, I'd spent a few summers there with my grandmother. The last time, when I was fourteen, my brother, Billy, and I had gone on our own. I have few memories from that difficult, hurly-burly summer.

Now, I was going to visit Grandma, who had been unwell for some years. We'd had the sad news that she was in the final stages of her illness and didn't have long to live.

Ray didn't love flying, and it was such a long journey—twenty-four hours in the air.

"I can go on my own, truly," I'd said.

Ray had laid his hand on my belly. "I wouldn't dream of that. I want to meet your grandmother and see where you stayed as a child. And I want to be with my girls."

When I'd gone for the ultrasound, we'd nodded *yes* when the technician had asked if we wanted to know the baby's gender.

Now, as the plane pulled away from the ground, I squeezed Ray's hand. I looked down at our intertwined fingers, a tight sphere, strong as rock. I closed my eyes and an image swam into view—the most beautiful face I'd ever seen, a little girl with curly brown hair and dark green eyes, the color of her skin halfway between Ray's and mine.

Twenty-four hours of flying changes you, setting you back down on the earth's crust subtly reborn. I felt unwell throughout the flight—fits of nausea, and unpleasant cramping. I was just entering my second trimester, and I reminded myself that the doctor had said it was perfectly safe to fly. The last few hours of the flight, while Ray slumbered, leaning up against the shuttered porthole, I was intensely and uncomfortably alert. I couldn't wait for the flight to be over.

The lights finally came on and the pilot announced we were beginning our descent. I felt a rush of relief. Ray stirred. I leaned over to kiss his cheek. I had known, when I sighted Ray across the room five years earlier, a week after my twenty-third birthday, that I would marry him. Our eyes had met, and as he walked toward me, I'd had the uncanny feeling that I could see the air around him—currents of shimmering color, liquid blues and burnt shades of orange—aware of a pungent feeling of his history. Something about that history within him seemed to connect with the history within me. *Yes,* I thought that very first day. *I know him, and I always have.*

Ray opened his eyes. I loved catching him on the edge of wakefulness, when his eyes were bountifully open to me.

"We're landing," I said.

* * *

Uncle Michael met us at the airport. He gave us both bear hugs.

"About bloody time you kids came to visit—now I get to show you around!" he said to Ray, grinning broadly.

Uncle Michael had met Ray at our wedding in Brooklyn; he was happy we were now in Melbourne on his own home turf.

"How's Grandma?" I asked.

His smile was snuffed. "Not too good, I'm afraid," he said. "But she's so excited about seeing you, and meeting Ray. I can't tell you …"

We drove directly to the nursing home. Uncle Michael gave Ray a steady stream of explanation all the way in, pointing out the different architectural styles—Victorian houses with filigreed wrought iron fences and awnings; sedate Edwardian buildings with broad arches and wild gardens. As we approached the city center, Uncle Michael pointed out the most prominent skyscrapers: Premier Tower, Eureka Tower, and Australia 108, still under construction, which would rise to 1039 feet.

We pulled off the freeway.

"When we were kids, Melbourne was a bit of a backwater. There was none of this. Last time your mum was here, she said she hardly recognized the place."

I wondered how it all looked to Ray's eyes; he was a long way from where he grew up, in suburban Atlanta, part of a sprawling African American family. I could hardly imagine what his childhood must have been like; I'd grown up far away from all relatives outside of our little island of four. Ray sat in the passenger seat beside Uncle Michael, looking intently out of the window, the bright Melbourne light pouring in through the windshield. I wondered what he was thinking.

As we approached the Spencer Street Bridge, the Yarra River came into view, glimmering faintly in the morning light. In the weeks leading up to our trip, Ray had done some research on Melbourne and the surrounding areas. He'd learned that Melbourne had been built on the fertile land around the Yarra that for more than forty thousand years had been home to the Wurundjeri people of the Kulin nation. We were both looking forward to visiting the Koorie Heritage Trust, dedicated to the culture and history of the country's First Nations.

"Fun fact," Uncle Michael said, as we merged onto the bridge. "When they began digging in 1927 to build this bridge, they ran into trouble, twenty meters down. Red gum stump that took them three weeks to remove. Turned out to be eight thousand years old! There's a big number. You have to think about the people who were here at that time. A lot of us Westerners—when we think of ancient cultures, we come up with Homer's Greece and the Roman Empire. But Australia is home to the oldest continuous culture on earth."

Uncle Michael turned to the back seat for a moment to cast me a glance. "Sorry, guys. You probably know all this yourself."

"I've done a bit of reading," Ray said. "But barely scraped the surface. It's all new and interesting to me, Mike."

"The latest research suggests that the Aboriginal peoples are descendants from the first people to leave Africa, seventy-five thousand years ago. Emily, I remember when your mum and dad went to see the Kakadu cave paintings in Arnhem Land—those are about forty thousand years old. Boggles the mind, right?"

"My family also left Africa," Ray said. "Not quite so long ago, though. And not exactly by choice."

"Yeah, bloody awful," Uncle Michael said. "Colonizers the world over—" he muttered. "They started it, and we kept it going. It's a national disgrace here, same as over in the United States."

The nursing home sat on a park, with patches of tailored lawn, carefully tended flower beds, and mature trees spreading shade just where it was needed. Grandma loved flora of all kinds; I'm sure she adored sitting on the porch I could see facing directly onto the park.

The entry foyer opened onto a large living room. A dozen or so residents were seated around a fireplace alight with gas flames, involved in a discussion being run by a staff member. Several called out greetings, others smiled. We passed through a narrow room where less able residents sat in wheelchairs or reclined on daybeds, some tended to by helpers, others alone and looking forlorn. I felt a rising panic—I could hardly imagine Grandma, my beloved, vibrant, oh-so-energetic Grandma here, rather than in her house, the house I'd known and loved and realized in that moment I would never see again.

Auntie Liora emerged from the dining room.

"Darlings!" she said, embracing first me and then Ray. "I can't tell you how excited Grandma is to see you."

I could see the worry in her face.

"How's your mum?" she asked.

I could feel my face doing its squirrely thing, rushing up into a tree to hide among the leaves. A stiff smile pulled at my lips.

"Not so bad, this time," I said.

"Three weeks into the chemo …"

I nodded.

"Well, she's a trouper, no doubt about it. Best mum in the world."

I smiled. "Well, one of them. You're another."

She squeezed my hand and together we made our way down a long corridor. At the end of it, Uncle Michael paused before the door to the left.

"Remember," he said, "she may look different, but she's still Grandma."

The panic turned to a hard knot that sat in my throat. I managed to nod. Uncle Michael rearranged his features back to the cheerful expression I associated with him. He opened the door.

Grandma sat propped up in a hospital-style bed in the corner of a bright L-shaped room. Her tiny frame, the size of a slight teenager's, came as a tremendous shock. I recalled the photograph I'd once seen of her as a girl of fourteen, slender as a reed, her wavy, dark hair caught by a breeze, a wistful and yet determined look on her face as she peered into the future. She'd returned to the size she was when still a girl, though now, her freshly styled hair was white and her cheeks sunken. She wore an elegant bed jacket in shades of mauve; a matching hand-painted silk scarf was draped around her neck. Her face broke into the brightest smile, though not before I had registered the expression of endurance and eyes deep with pain. The same look I'd seen in my own mother's face during her long bouts with chemotherapy treatments.

"Emily! Ray!" She reached out her hand.

Many familiar objects leapt to my eyes: the portrait of Grandpa Jack, whom I never met since he died before I was born; another of my great-grandmother Sarah who had presided fiercely over Grandma's difficult childhood in South Africa. The shiny brass samovar originally from Lithuania, and the beautiful small sculpture of a mother and daughter that Grandma had made decades ago in a pottery class. Grandma's talents had always seemed boundless to me; everything she touched turned to beauty.

"Darling," she said, "how lovely of you to come."

I took her delicate hand and leaned in to kiss her. Her familiar scent, milky and sweet.

5

"Ray," she said, "I'm so happy to lay eyes on you in person."

Grandma had been too unwell to travel to New York for the wedding. She'd spoken to Ray on video chat, but this was her first time meeting him for real.

Ray kissed Grandma on the cheek.

Now, Grandma turned her full attention to me.

"Mama wanted so much to come," I said.

The clench line hardened along Grandma's jaw, and she tried to hide the sorrow in her eyes.

"Well, you're here for her, too," she said softly. "I spoke to her an hour ago. She sends her love, of course. And she's doing so much better!"

I nodded, wiped away the tear that had trickled down.

"And you, my darling. How are you feeling? You're really very tiny—I can hardly see the bump!"

I removed my coat and pulled my sweater around my belly.

"There she is," Grandma said, her eyes twinkling. "I'm so eager to meet her."

Grandma would likely not live to meet the baby. But her face was full-wattage joy—she certainly was not allowing any such thought.

Within moments, Grandma and Ray were chatting away. Grandma wanted to know *everything!* All about his work, and family—the name of every sibling, aunt, uncle, cousin, and grandparent, all four of whom were, miraculously to me, still living. I'd only ever had Grandma, and she lived a world away.

In between visits to Grandma, Ray and I explored Melbourne and the surrounds—a visit to the Healesville animal sanctuary, and also Phillip Island, where at sunset, we saw a thousand tiny fairy penguins emerge from the sea, blanketing the wide white sands before waddling into hundreds of burrows hidden around the scrubby vegetation abutting the beach. I took Ray to places Mama and Grandma had taken me as a child—the aquarium, the planetarium, and the Victorian Hopetoun

Tea Rooms in the Parisian-style Block Arcade. There we sampled their famous vanilla slice, similar to what we called a napoleon, but with less cream and a distinctive two-inch-thick yellow custard. Ray loved the friendly "Aussie" way—broad, relaxed smiles that seemed to match the broad, relaxed sound of the accent, the dropped consonants, elongated vowels, and habit of shortening nouns into flippant half-words—bicky for biscuit, Chrissie for Christmas, arvo (afternoon), cuppa (cup of tea), chocky (chocolate), and my personal favorite, the composite chocky bicky! Wherever we went, it was *G'day mate,* and people interested in striking up a conversation once they caught wind of our American accents—*Luv ya accent!*

The day we spent at the Koorie Heritage Trust felt complicated. If we were here to travel around Australia, rather than to visit Grandma, we could have immersed ourselves in the culture and history of Australia's First Nations. Visiting the Koorie Trust, while wonderful in some ways, also felt frustrating, like we were looking through a tiny peephole onto a wafer-thin sliver of an unimaginably rich domain. We stood for some time looking at the scar tree; Aboriginal peoples would remove sections of bark to make shields or canoes in ways that allowed the tree to stay alive, leaving scars that the tree would then grow around, resulting in unusual markings and shapes. Sometimes, an artist would decorate the open scar tissue, further transforming the wound. Some scar trees held special spiritual significance.

We took our time walking through the gallery spaces, pausing in a room hung with paintings. One caught my eye and held me spellbound: *Exile,* by an artist named Lin Onus, who I read was an Aboriginal-Scottish Australian painter. The painting showed a youth walking alone on a path through a wide field, dwarfed by a vast sky hung with a low white sun. High in the sky, darkening the top quarter of the canvas, the cloud was a roiling sea, deepening with blue smoke and dabs of orange fire, shading to darkness up by the frame. The youth was carrying a small can with a handle, what the Aussies call a "billy," a tin used for heating water over a fire.

Though his carriage was upright and dignified, he gave the impression of being slightly stooped, as if the sky were a burden he must shoulder as he made his way to an uncertain destination, carrying only a small tin.

* * *

Grandma's decline accelerated. On the last day of our two-week trip, I arrived at the nursing home to find her dozing. I sat by her bedside, listening to her breathing, which seemed newly shallow and clipped. I gazed at her face, my mind traveling back to the many weeks I'd spent in her home, the house my mother grew up in: the conversations over endless cups of tea, trips to the city and to the countryside, and to concerts, the ballet, and on one occasion, to see the Melbourne production of *The Lion King,* which Grandma had loved with the same overblown child's enthusiasm that my little brother, Billy, and I had both felt.

I took her hand. Her eyes fluttered open.

"There you are, my darling." A muted version of her electric smile rose like a pale sun on her face. "You have no idea what your visit has meant to me. Spending time with you, getting to know Ray."

I chatted to her a little about our adventures—told her how much Ray had enjoyed the vanilla slice at the Hopetoun Tea Rooms.

"You always loved those," she said. "We also called them napoleons in South Africa, same as you Americans."

Something flickered within me, as it seemed, also, to flicker within her.

"But you knew that, didn't you," she said. Then: "Help me, darling—" She gestured for me to help her sit up in bed. She had become so thin and frail, helping her up felt like helping to move a child.

"I just love Ray," she said, her eyes pale, as if the color were leaking away. "He's your *bashert.*"

"*Bashert?*" I asked. My Australian relatives would sometimes use words from their Jewish culture, words I didn't know, since I had been raised without religion, and an ocean away from them.

"Soul mate, life mate," Grandma said. "He's—well, he's everything. Kind, honorable, creative, smart. And he loves you fully, I can see that. For who you are. And who wouldn't!"

She tilted her head, then gently sang, *"To know, know, know you, is to love, love, love you."* She'd sung that to Billy and me when we were young. Her trained singing voice astonishingly still held some power.

"He has the right values," she added. "How I wish I could meet his family. His mother, father, grandparents, and of course his brother and sisters. I always thought marriage was partly a clash of family cultures—but not for you, Emily! Seems like a beautiful merging."

Ray's family had in fact embraced me. I'd loved becoming part of their rowdy, opinionated, loving, sometimes contentious brood.

"And he's been blessed with your family, too. It may be small, at least the American contingent. But there is no finer."

Grandma closed her eyes. Talking was clearly tiring her. For a minute, her breathing slowed, and I wondered if she'd fallen back asleep, but then her eyes again snapped open.

"I understood," she said, something urgent, now, in her tone.

"What did you understand, Grandma?"

"What happened. That summer. The last time you were here. Such a long time ago … you were only fourteen."

I felt a curdling of old anxiety, a feeling that somewhere along the way I'd put to rest.

"You see, after you left, I thought a lot about—well, everything. And I realized something. All these years I've wanted to say something to you about it … I never found the right moment. You were so involved in building your life—as it should be. I didn't want to bring up—well—"

"What, Grandma? What didn't you want to bring up?"

"The past."

She raised her hand with some effort and gestured to her bedside table. "Open the drawer."

The drawer was filled with little boxes, trays, and soft pouches, in which she kept jewelry, everything neatly arranged. Grandma's bedside drawer had always looked just like this.

"All the way in the back," she said. "The little blue pouch."

I retrieved the pouch, made of silky blue fabric in a floral design.

"Go ahead, open it," Grandma said.

I opened the zipper and withdrew a tiny china plate that looked like it was from a child's tea set. It flashed with a familiarity that felt personal.

"I've always wanted you to have this. Ever since I was a girl myself. It's yours, after all."

"What do you mean, Grandma? What do you mean that it's—mine?"

"It's been yours for a very long time. And then you left it here, all those years ago. I don't think you meant to, but you did."

I had no memory of the little plate, though it did seem oddly familiar. Was Grandma confused?

"Thank you, Grandma," I said, turning it over in my hands, noting the delicate border of miniature roses. "I will treasure it."

"Maybe now is the right time," Grandma said, her voice a whisper. "To talk about it. About what happened. You see I remembered it myself, remembered it from when I was fourteen." She took in another of those shallow breaths that frightened me. "From when we were both fourteen, all the way back. *I remembered everything.*"

Her eyes went milky and I felt a spear of alarm. I could feel her spirit lightening, disappearing somewhere, and then, her eyelids closed and her breathing steadied and I realized that this time, she had fallen back asleep.

I sat there for a very long time, Grandma's soft hand in mine, listening to her erratic, shallow breathing, as fragmented images leapt about within. I didn't know what to make of all this—and yet I also knew that it was coming back. A piece of myself I'd long ago hidden away. The light disappeared as night emerged and the shadows elongated.

Grandma did not stir when Ray knocked on the door and then entered, nor when I extricated my hand and planted a kiss on her downy cheek and whispered into her ear, "I love you, Grandma. I'm so grateful you are my Grandma."

I drew away. Tears spilled from my eyes.

It all came back, every little bit.

We were leaving early in the morning and I knew there would be no sleep.

Ray and I stayed up through the night. It wasn't so much that I needed to tell him everything. It was more that I needed to reclaim it for myself.

CHAPTER ONE

THE SUMMER I TURNED FOURTEEN was a time of extremes. Excitement and fear, fun times and peril, togetherness and wrenching apart.

Mama and Papa had talked about the cross-country trip for as long as I could remember; the big family adventure had existed in the distant future, like a shining North Star. I think I didn't quite expect it to happen. Then, that Friday evening before our final week of school, they announced their plan. Mama looked secretive and happy as she cooked our favorite meal of salmon and fried rice. She stood by the stove, framed by the picture window that looked out onto our small Brooklyn back yard. The overgrown yew trees, scraggly against the darkening sky, hugged the clubhouse we'd built for Billy, with its cedar-shingled sides, pitched-tar roof, and tiny double-paned windows we'd bought at Home Depot. Mama looked small by the window, which came as a jolt—my mama, who had always been larger than life to me, with her electric energy and heightened good cheer. The cooking fan hummed and the blue tile above the stove twinkled. I glanced around the loft-like space—Papa on his computer at the kitchen table, Billy drawing at the kiddie table in the corner, under the leaves of the ficus tree Mama had planted when Billy was born that now reached almost to the ceiling.

"Want to help, Billy?" I asked, and he jumped up from his chair.

"I do the napkins!" he said. "And how 'bout the forks and spoons?"

"You can crack open the eggs when you're done," Mama said. She always put the little ribbons of fried egg into the rice last so that they'd be fresh and fluffy. Billy grinned so widely his lips seemed to disappear. He loved cracking the eggs.

With everything ready, Papa put away his computer and we sat down to eat. Billy offered one of his original versions of grace—*Thank you, Universe, for this wonderful life.*

Papa smiled. "You got that right, Billy," he said, looking back and forth between my face and Billy's. "Tell you what, kids—It's happening! From sea to shining sea!"

I knew immediately what he meant. "Our trip!" I said to Billy. "The Great Big Ride across our Great Big Country!"

Billy was a sponge for whatever emotion was coursing through our family. He jumped up from his seat, "Oh boy! Oh boy!" and did a little happy dance, nose crinkling with joy.

All that weekend, our apartment was a frenzy of duffel bags and guidebooks, things being searched for, lists being made. Papa taped a huge map of the United States onto the dining room wall and we all had to say one place we most wanted to go.

"Where's SeaWorld?" Billy asked, peering anxiously at the map from his perch on the dining room chair.

"SeaWorld isn't on the map," I said.

"I gonna see the whales. Dolphins, too," he said with five-year-old determination. Papa wrote *SeaWorld* in red magic marker right over *Orlando* in Florida, adding *NASA,* his own choice, nearby in black.

"The Pacific," Mama said.

That's when I noticed something new in her face—a gray shade in her skin that seemed part mood and part sky and felt like a cold wind, brewing with storm.

"What is it, Mama?" I asked, scanning her face. Her eyes creased with smile and her features relaxed, but the blue-gray was still there and it sent a shiver of panic through me.

"I've always loved the ocean, you know that," she said, "and the Pacific joins my new home to my old one." Mama had come from Australia to the United States to go to graduate school and then stayed when she met Papa. "If you stand on the cliffs at Santa Cruz, you can hear the seagulls singing 'Waltzing Matilda.'"

She knew my question was about the strangeness in her face, not about why she wanted to see the Pacific. But her smile told me to leave it alone—to look at the map with the rest of the family, to tumble into the excitement of planning our America-sized journey.

We packed way too much stuff; it wouldn't fit in the trunk of our old bomb of a car, a 2000 Nissan Maxima we'd recently bought with eighty thousand miles already on it.

None of us wanted to weed belongings, and we were all eager to get on the road.

"Here," Mama said, reaching for several plastic containers packed with toys, CDs, and board games, "I'll just stack them on my lap."

No one stopped to think of what that would mean—Mama sitting for three thousand miles on the way there, and three thousand more on the way back, her lap piled with stuff. We just had our eyes on the road, itching to feel it peeling away beneath us.

"Up, up, and away!" Papa said as he wheedled his way out of our tight parking spot, a half block from the Brooklyn brownstone I'd lived in since coming home from the hospital two days after my birth. I craned my neck to look behind at the chocolate-colored facade. I fixed on the second-floor window to the right, my bedroom, which I pictured sitting empty.

"I'll be back soon," I whispered, picturing the white four-poster bed we'd bought at IKEA, with its red flower-print comforter and mass of cushy pillows. I saw my collection of plush animals—scraggly bear, bright blue whale, silky flamingo, and the rest of my nighttime lovables. My arms ached to hold them; my whole body ached to be back where I belonged, in our lively, open, wonderful home.

But I also ached to spread my arms and run out into the world, to feel new air on my face, to plunge into unknown territory and unexpected adventures.

* * *

We'd planned a journey that didn't make a lot of practical sense but was true to everyone's passions and wishes.

"That's the fun of it," Mama had said.

It was one of her favorite sayings. She'd said it when she opened the bucket of flour she kept for us to play with when we were little. Billy and I and the kitchen floor would end up covered in white powder and Mama would clap her flour-covered hands and we'd watch as the snowy white billowed in the air then fell softly to the floor.

I had the feeling that this vast country of ours, which had always been a fuzzy mystery to me, would begin to come into focus.

The first part of the drive involved a zigzag, heading north and east to Rhode Island to visit the oldest synagogue in the United States—Mama's choice—then south to Orlando to hit NASA—on Papa's list, as well as mine, and SeaWorld—pure Billy. Next stop would be the Belle Meade Plantation, and then Elvis's Graceland and Sun Studio. How tantalizing it all felt in anticipation, each place we talked about an entire and exotic world promising riches of delight.

I had not, however, imagined the extremes. Poverty, like nothing I'd ever seen before: skinny kids in ragged clothing standing stock-still at the edge of the trailer park, peering through the chain link at our car cruising by. Heat so intense that the moment we stepped from the air-conditioned lobby of the Hampton Inn into the parking lot, we were covered head to toe in a layer of sweat. And stretches of straight, flat road cutting through high green cornstalks on both sides: *nature's curtains,* Mama said.

We would make it to the impressive antebellum Belle Meade Plantation in Tennessee, where we almost stayed one night, before everything ruptured. Instead of continuing across the vast landscape to the other *shining sea* where Mama might have put her toes into the Pacific Ocean, as she'd hoped, the trip would come to a rude halt, Billy and I flung into an adventure of a different kind.

* * *

The minute we got out of Brooklyn, I opened my notebook and began drawing columns for things we were going to count. *Churches, animals* (with number estimates of livestock), *town halls, libraries, schools.*

Strapped into his car seat, Billy craned his head my way. "What you writing, Sis?" he asked. I read aloud what I'd written.

We settled into our "serious watching," staring out the window to start collecting our visual finds.

Snacks appeared every now and then, along with a juice box or metal flask of water, passed back by Mama, who was in charge of the food. The car sparkled with happiness; we were a family who loved road trips.

We were fond of visiting churches on our travels. I loved the vaulted spaces, with their cold stone and soaring steeples: the way the air felt, the baptism wells and banks of candles to commemorate the dead, the organ pipes and carved pews baked with the scent of frankincense and myrrh. The Touro Synagogue in Newport, Rhode Island, felt altogether different—an imposing rectangular building with nothing vaulted about it. The interior was grand, rather than lofty: an open rectangle with a balcony running all the way around, supported by twelve enormous columns representing the twelve tribes of Israel, each carved from a single tree. In the center of the room, an elaborately carved podium draped in gold brocade dominated a square stage edged with banisters; above the stage, massive candelabras hung down from the ornate ceiling.

We sat on the old wooden seats and Papa read from the informational pamphlet.

"The Touro Synagogue is the oldest synagogue in the United States. Building was completed in 1763."

We heard about the ups and downs of the Jewish community through the Revolutionary War, when the British used the synagogue as a hospital and meeting house, and on into the Civil War, when most of the Jewish community fled. I was intrigued when Papa got to the part about George Washington visiting Newport in 1790 to rally support for his Bill of Rights, three months after Rhode Island joined the union.

"As part of the welcoming ceremonies for the president of the United States," Papa read, "Moses Mendes Seixas, then president of the synagogue congregation, was given the honor of addressing George Washington. Seixas raised the issue of religious liberties and the separation of church and state. Later, Washington quoted Seixas's thoughts in stating the new government's support of First Amendment rights."

"How astounding!" Papa said. "This small community apparently had an important impact on the drafting of our constitution."

"Who knew!" Mama said.

"Look at this, Sis." Billy had wandered over to where a plaque was affixed to the wall. "Go on, read it!" he said.

"Okay, here comes your reading machine." I joined him by the wall.

"In 1790, the congregation received a letter from President George Washington that said, 'The government of the United States gives to bigotry no sanction, to persecution no assistance.' The letter, sent before the Bill of Rights was ratified, is held up as an affirmation of the fledgling government's commitment to religious liberty."

Papa took a stab at explaining what I'd just read to Billy.

Mama pointed to the podium. "That's the bimah," she said. "It really is beautiful."

"Where's the organ?" Billy asked, craning his head around.

"Synagogues don't have organs," Mama replied.

"Where's *Jesusonthecross?*" Billy said it as one word, scanning the walls.

"No Jesus either," Mama said. Then added, "Wouldn't it be fun to stay for a service?"

"Today's Thursday—we could stay an extra day and go for Friday night service," Papa said.

Mama's face flushed with happiness. I found this confusing. Though Mama was Jewish and had had a "full-on Jewish upbringing"—the words she used whenever anyone asked—our lives had been shorn of organized religion. Papa had been raised without any religion, his father having been low-key generically Christian, and his mother, from Iceland, raised as an atheist.

"Good idea," Billy said. "Maybe if we come to the synagogue I could be *whole* Jewish instead of just *half* Jewish."

"What's wrong with being half Jewish?" Papa asked with a smile. "That way you get to be two things, instead of just one!"

"Elias is whole Jewish. He told me so," Billy said. Elias was one of Billy's friends from kindergarten. "That means you get to sing the special Itsy Bitsy Spider. Maybe that's what they do at the bimah, Mama, right? Sing the special song."

"What's the special Itsy Bitsy Spider song?" Mama asked.

"The one with the naughty word in it. *Bum*."

Mama and Papa both laughed. Billy looked offended.

"Elias told me about it! They're having it this summer!"

"Having what, darling?"

"Elias's older brother. He's having his *Bum Itsy*. You know," Billy put his fingers in the walking spider shape and sang out in his piping voice, "*Itsy **bum**itsy spider, climbed up the water spout*."

"Who told you about the song?" Papa asked.

"Nobody told me about the song. I figured that part out myself."

Mama explained that Billy had misunderstood. She told him the words *Bar Mitzvah* and tried to tell him what that was all about.

"Well, then, I want to do that. The *Bar—Mitzvah*. So I wanna get *whole Jewish* for that."

"You could do it if you wanted to," Mama said, growing serious. "First of all, even if you were what you call *half Jewish* you could have a Bar Mitzvah. But according to Jewish law, you *are* in fact *whole Jewish*, since in the Jewish tradition, if your mother is Jewish, you are as *whole Jewish* as you can get."

This made Billy happy. "I'll tell Elias when we get back. That I'm just the same as him."

That night, Billy went to bed feeling cranky and hot. I awoke after midnight to hear my parents' worried voices.

"A hundred and five," Mama said, bustling about, getting things into a bag.

Since he had been an infant, Billy had spiked high fevers.

Mama saw I was awake. "Emily, we're taking him to the emergency room. You stay and get some sleep. Emergency rooms are hard. . And I don't want you picking anything up there—all that sickness."

I'd been to the ER quite a few times as a tagalong—on occasion because of Billy's fever spikes, but also because of what the doctor called Billy's "catastrophic nose bleeds," not to mention the time Billy got seventeen stitches after a fall. Scary, that's how I'd always found it. No fun at all.

"Okay, I'll stay," I said, sleepily aware of a small spear of panic starting somewhere in the pit of my stomach.

"We have our cell phones," Mama said. "You need to dial nine to get an outside line. And there's someone at the front desk if you need anything." Mama gave me a hasty kiss. Papa scooped Billy into his arms, and then they were gone.

I fell into a hazy half-sleep, rattled by the odd nighttime hotel sounds I hadn't noticed before: the muffled, clattery clash of the ice machine in the alcove outside our door; an intermittent soft beep that came from the smoke detector; the buzzy drone of a TV from the next room. I slipped in and out of troubled dreams involving Billy in dangerous situations, his dear face looming and fading as I ran and tumbled and tried to catch hold of his hand. In the midst of it, I bolted upright in bed, suddenly alert. A knife of fluorescent light beamed in through a crack in the blackout curtain.

My heart pounded and I mouthed a prayer for Billy. *Please, God, whoever you are, wherever you are, take care of my little brother.* I repeated the prayer, twice, three times, waiting for the spread of calm. Instead, anxiety bloomed; something was troubling me, beneath my concern for Billy. He always recovered quickly from his fevers, and deep inside, I knew he was going to be just fine. Why, then, this terrible foreboding that was growing by the minute? My mother's face swam into my mind's eye: no sparkle in her eyes, no warm, affirming smile. A different Mama: that blue-gray skin tone deepened, and ashy circles appeared under dull eyes.

"Mama!" I called out into the empty room. "What's wrong?"

But the Mama in my mind's eye remained silent, nothing but an almost imperceptible shaking of her head.

The agitation in my legs and arms made it impossible to stay in bed. I jumped up and quickly changed from my pajamas into my clothes; so restless, I felt I was jumping out of my skin. I needed to move. I thought I'd walk around the lobby—or maybe even take a quick walk outside. The thought of looking up at the stars comforted me.

I slipped the hotel key card into my pocket and opened the door. The hallway was silent; the soft sounds of my footsteps on the carpet were soothing. I willed my still-pounding heart to slow to the rhythm of my steps and within minutes, I was once again breathing calmly and in command of my wayward emotions.

I also knew where I was going and what I had to do.

Passing by the front desk, the young woman on duty flashed me a look of concern.

"May I help you, miss?"

"I have to go meet my parents," I said. My voice sounded surprisingly assured. "They took my brother to the ER."

"Of course, I talked to them as they were leaving. I hope your brother is doing better," the woman said.

"Can you call me a taxi?" I asked.

"Actually, there's one outside. The guy who dropped your parents off. He came right back—the hotel is his main station. We've known him for years. He's very trustworthy."

She accompanied me outside and waved down the driveway for the taxi.

"Back to the hospital," she instructed the driver, who nodded.

But once I was seated and we reached the end of the driveway, I told him there was somewhere else I wanted to stop by first.

"The Touro Synagogue," I heard myself saying, marveling at this strange new habit—my mouth bypassing my brain and speaking all on its own.

"No problem," the driver said. "It's on the way."

Five minutes later, we pulled up in front of the synagogue. The moonlight settled around the building like a glimmering blanket, giving off a mystical awe.

"I'd like to get out for a bit, if you don't mind waiting," I said. The driver swiveled around to face me.

"Not a great idea," he said. I only now took note of him—a middle-aged man with a kind face and a fatherly air. "It's pretty safe around here, but it *is* after midnight."

I glanced at my watch. The driver was right; it was exactly 12:15. How could I not have registered the time? Why had I asked the driver to bring me here?

I nodded. "Okay. But could we just sit here for a moment?"

"Sure. No problem. I'll take you back when you're ready."

He turned off the engine and the world hushed. The sound of my own breathing filled my ears. And then, from behind the synagogue, I saw ghostly forms taking shape: people emerging, one by one, as if from a hidden cave—a few at first, and then more and more, swelling within seconds to become a small crowd. Shadow shrouded them, despite the brightness of the moonlight, in the hues of a black-and-white movie, multiple shades of gray. Squinting into the image, I saw that the people were dressed in shabby, old-fashioned garments, perhaps from somewhere in Eastern Europe, like Poland or Russia. An air of desperation hung around them. My eyes settled on a man, middle-aged, with hunched shoulders and piercing eyes. Holding his hand was a girl around my age with long black hair, her face dark with fear. And beside her—another girl, and how odd, I could see her fair hair, but her face was fuzzy, like a photograph in which the facial features are obscured. They made no noise at all.

The driver slumped forward in his seat, breathing the heavy breath of sleep.

"What do you see?" I blurted out in a voice louder than intended.
He started. "I'm sorry, what?" he asked.
I pointed out of the front window, jabbing the air.
"There! What do you see?"
"Why, the synagogue building, of course. What do you see?"
I blinked once, twice. There was nothing but the synagogue, hugging the muffled brightness of the moon close to its angular contours. No people, no living beings at all; only the driver and me, sitting in the taxi, peering out into the night.
"I'm sorry," I said. "I was just …" I let my voice trail off.
In the rearview mirror, the driver's face was creased with concern.
"Miss, are you sure you're okay?"
"I think I'm just very tired," I said.
I had no idea what was going on. Tears sprang to my eyes and I blinked them away.
"Let's go back," I said.
"Not to the hospital?"
"No. Back to the hotel."
We drove back in silence. The streets peeled away, their sleeping buildings in rapid retreat, as if the whole world were silently reeling while I sat stock-still, frozen beneath the eye of the moon.

* * *

Back at the hotel, I fell into a troubled sleep, punctuated by the clanking of the ice machine, which appeared in my dreams first as slaves trudging along muddy paths, their legs linked by heavy chains, then as a huddled crowd crushed up against a chain-link fence.

I awoke to the sound of the door being carefully opened, and the looming shape of Papa carrying Billy, asleep, in his arms. The soft early-morning light peeped through the crack in the curtains. Mama told me everything was okay, that Billy had a double ear infection but was on strong antibiotics and no longer had a dangerously high temperature.

"He's going to need to rest," Mama said. "They gave him so much Tylenol, he'll be out like a log. Papa and I need to sleep for a while. It's been a long night. But let's do something fun this afternoon, just you and me. Papa can stay with Billy."

I could hear the strain in her voice and appreciated Mama's effort to put a good face on the situation.

"Is he going to be okay?" My voice came out sounding choked and I realized how sick with worry I'd been about Billy all night.

Mama put her arm around me. "Of course, darling. Those high fevers are scary, but he always recovers quickly. The doctor told us not to worry. The antibiotics do wonders. He'll be back to his old self in no time."

I spent the morning reading, and in the afternoon, Mama and I went out for a late lunch and then visited the Newport Art Museum. We spent an hour looking at paintings by Helena Sturtevant, a renowned Rhode Island painter. Her landscapes pulled me in; one showed a country lane with bushes on one side and towering trees on the other, a soft sun in a bright sky thick with texture. I felt the path under my feet where the sunlight lay like butter in the dirt. And there was a painting of the Touro park as well as of the synagogue! I saw from the plaques that Sturtevant had been born in 1872 and died in 1946; seeing these places I'd just seen myself through her eyes excited me, as if history were shimmering, like sunlight on water. I closed my eyes and had the strange feeling that I could lift up my feet and climb into that sunlit water and perhaps float backward on its gentle tide.

Something stirred within me—something new that was tantalizing, confusing, and just a bit frightening. An image crystallized in my mind's eye: a patch of river, a rocky bank presided over by a single tree, and dust colors, the sky settling to a glossy peach, quietly alight with the day's end. I snapped open my eyes to find Mama looking at me, her eyes searching, and a faint smile on her lips. She said nothing, only took my hand, and we continued our slow stroll around the gallery space. Painting after painting, all by Sturtevant; it was as if everything she ever noticed and cared about and loved were springing up all around us—her world, her vision, her mind and soul and heart.

And then, a painting made my heart leap so intensely, it scared me. There, before me, was the *exact* image I'd visualized only a moment before, in the privacy of my own mind. That same piece of river, the rocky shore, the sky, hanging in glossy patches on the water's surface, flecked with gold. I could hear faint birdsong coming from the tree, where a few dabs of yellow paint showed the light glowing through, and a scuttling in the foreground, a little family of lizards, I imagined, where flinty rocks glinted like jewels in the scruffy grass. How was this possible? *What was happening to me?*

"What's wrong, darling?" Mama asked.

"I don't know, that painting …" I said, staring closely at the scene. It was titled *Paradise.*

"Beautiful, isn't it," Mama said. "There's something about the light in the sky."

"It's just that …" How could I tell Mama what was happening? That my *mind* had shown me this exact scene before my *eyes* had actually seen it?

"What do you think the painting is about?" Mama asked. I wondered if she sensed my terror and was sidestepping it.

"What do you mean?" I could hear the tremor in my voice.

"I don't mean the obvious subject—the landscape. I just feel the painter was trying to tell us something. Something else, besides showing us the beauty of this particular scene of nature."

I closed my eyes again for a moment, and the image from earlier reared up again. That same scene, vivid and real—not a painting at all, but an actual river! I could see the ripples on the water moving in silent, gentle time with the imperceptible touch of a breeze. How was it possible that I could have seen this exact view *before* we actually saw the painting? My mind lurched back to the eerie image of last evening, when I sat with the taxi driver in front of the Touro Synagogue. The girl with dark hair and the man with hunched shoulders, her father perhaps, walking silently, gray with dread. I had not told my parents about that strange adventure. They'd had enough to worry about, with Billy ill and spending the night in the emergency room. That vision had also been intensely *alive*, as if I were looking straight at *reality.*

"I think the painting is about time," I found myself saying. "Not only that the painter has captured a moment in time—this river at sunset—but that this little stretch of river captures the nature of *time itself.* What time is all about—"

I felt overcome by confusion and inexplicably, the urge to cry. Before I could choke them back, tears spilled down my cheeks. I looked at Mama and saw that the worry in her eyes had vanished; her face shone with love.

"I bet Helena Sturtevant would have been happy to know what her work made you think. And feel."

This was a comforting thought.

"Expression and connection," Mama said, "that's what art is about for me. The landscape she painted brought something alive for her— ignited her artistic imagination. And now her painting has done the same for you."

"Yes," I said. "It's like a chain, passing from person to person, across time. More than fifty years after she died ..."

In that moment, I knew why the painter had called her painting *Paradise*. Not just because it showed a scene of beauty and peace—it went beyond that, I felt certain.

"I feel like I can see her, standing there, on the bank of the river. Almost like it's me, seeing the water myself, hearing the sounds of birds, watching the sun set. But for the painter, that moment passed. And she knew it would pass. Other people would stand there one day and look at that river. In real life, but also looking at her painting, the way we're looking at it now. All of it—I don't know, timeless. That river is still flowing today. Both in real life and right there!"

I pointed to the painting, as if that would explain everything, as if my finger were an exclamation point that would settle this once and for all.

* * *

By next morning, Billy was feeling much better, though he was still weak and a bit woozy. After breakfast, we packed up the car. There was no talk of staying for the Friday night service at the synagogue; that idea seemed to have dissolved in the worry about Billy. Though eager to go to the service, I didn't want to bring it up. Mama and Papa seemed to have a lot on their minds, and I didn't want to divert them from their plans. I felt sad as we left town, taking the exit back onto the highway, and looked back over my shoulder, images of the Touro Synagogue flickering through my mind's eye—what I had seen when we'd visited as a family, what I'd imagined on my strange late-night adventure, and also the memory of Sturtevant's lively depiction of the synagogue painted almost a hundred years ago.

Billy stared out the window, blinking under the influence of the antibiotics and Tylenol, which always knocked him out. I reached for his hand. He turned to me and smiled. "Don't worry, Sis," he said, "you and me will go to *synigig* one day. At home in Brooklyn. We have one of those there."

I guess he'd been thinking about missing the services, too.

"Yes, let's do that, when we get home to Brooklyn. Take a nap, now, little guy." I patted his hand.

Billy sighed, and drifted off to sleep.

Mama turned from the front passenger seat, took note that Billy had fallen asleep, smiled my way and reached her hand out for a quick squeeze. She turned back and began talking to Papa in a low voice, so as not to disturb Billy, I supposed, though I wondered if there was something more to it. Papa nodded slowly a few times.

I looked out the window, where an enormous dock unfurled, hoarding a village of boats, from small sloops to larger cabin cruisers, bobbing on the water. The road hugged the water, whose languid expanse was held in place by the shimmering horizon. I felt a plunging sadness that made no sense, given the beauty of the landscape—heard, again, the faint birdsong and reptilian scuttling that had echoed from the thick paint dabs in Sturtevant's *Paradise*.

The journey after that was a blur. While Papa concentrated on the road, Billy and I filled the long hours in the car playing games, with Mama officiating from the front seat. The never-ending Great Count was Billy's favorite; he was speedy with his estimate of head of cattle whenever we saw a field of grazing cows, shouting out with conviction. "Sixty-eight!" or "Ninety-two!" and, once Mama introduced him to the concept of a dozen, "Two dozen! Eight dozen!" I wrote down everything he said, "Word for word, Sis," according to his instruction. We stopped at diners and other roadside eateries for lunch and dinner in whatever new town we found ourselves in. We wandered down main streets, once taking in a movie in a dilapidated movie theater, and another time visiting a churchyard where we wandered among old tombstones, trying to make out the names and dedications, feeling sad when we found a small grave whose dates showed that the deceased had been a child.

* * *

I fell in love with NASA the moment we saw the massive rectangular vehicle assembly building rise from the flat surrounds, the painted American flag on the left and the NASA symbol on the right like two enormous mismatched, far-seeing eyes. Billy erupted with excitement as we walked through the exhibits in the Kennedy Space Center; I myself felt like jumping for joy, confronted with the magical details of space travel, the unimaginable-impossible rendered real. The sounds of Cape Canaveral boomed as we sat in the little theater, watching the Apollo launches, one after the other. And then, the historic Apollo 11 liftoff: *Three ... two ... one ... zero, all engines running, liftoff, we have a liftoff, thirty-two minutes past the hour.*

"They landed on the moon, right, Sis?" Billy said. "Let's go *there* one day, on 'nother *crosscrountrytrip.*"

"That would be a cross-milky-way trip, Billy," I said, tousling his hair.

"Milky way?" he asked. "Astronauts got their mamas too, giving out candy on the trip?"

I explained about galaxies, and that the candy was named after our own, and Billy nodded seriously, his face alive with the wonder of new knowledge.

We ate at the Rocket Garden Cafe, where Billy ordered from the junior astronaut menu, a three-item selection, convinced that while in space, astronauts must eat only pizza, chicken nuggets, or "uncrustables," all served with apple slices.

Mama allowed us each to buy something from the gift shop; Billy chose a baseball cap and I chose a backpack, both emblazoned with the NASA logo. We were a little surprised, since Mama had been telling us since we were little that we were not a family who "endlessly buys things in gift shops," emphasizing that we visited places for the experience, not to waste money with "mindless consumerism." Mama handed her credit card to the cashier—and this time, there was definitely something different about her, something big and worrisome, though I could not put my finger on what.

* * *

"Why not stay here?" Mama put it to Papa, her eyes full of fun.

We'd just come from a wonderful Nashville lunch of hot chicken and biscuits slathered with gravy and were pulling into the parking lot of the famed Belle Meade Plantation. The plan had been to do the tour and then head back to the Hampton Inn.

"Why not, indeed?" Papa said, patting Mama's arm.

I loved the look that passed between them, the silent language they had. But there was something else—a flash in Papa's eyes of pain, and then Mama replying with a calm look and a reassuring stroke of his arm.

We were amazed at the splendors of the mansion, with its high ceilings and massive fireplaces, intricately carved period furniture and tall windows with heavy silk drapes in vivid jewel colors—garnet, amethyst, jade. *Greek-revival style,* the tour guide explained, pointing out which bits were added on when, and recounting stories about the wealthy Harding family who'd owned the plantation through several generations. They'd built a vast enterprise that included a cotton gin, grain mill, and most famously, the breeding and racing of thoroughbred horses.

Historically, the plantation drew an illustrious crowd of visitors, including General Grant and President Grover Cleveland and his wife. Though the Civil War interrupted operations, the plantation continued to thrive through to the end of the nineteenth century.

Later, however, the vast fortune dissipated and eventually, the plantation and its grounds were sold. I was struck by how common this story was: a great rise to success and riches, followed by an equally dramatic decline. But then, of course, the reverse was equally common; I was familiar with the stories my mother had told of her many childhood friends, growing up in Melbourne, Australia, who were children of Holocaust survivors. Often the lone surviving members of large families murdered by the Nazis, thousands of these concentration camp refugees had started from nothing and taken whatever jobs they could find. They built businesses, entered professions, had families of their own, beginning a new chain of history—against all the odds, from the terrible ashes of destruction and despair.

Our friendly tour guide was relaying the plantation's history in her singsong southern twang. Her face darkened as she began talking about the workforce at Belle Meade—the *enslaved people* was the term she used—who had worked the land and served the family.

When she talked about how Harding brought in enslaved workers as horse trainers and jockeys, Mama muttered under her breath, "Slave jockeys. My god."

Billy chose that moment to raise his hand. The guide fixed him with a friendly, indulgent smile.

"What mean 'slaved people?'"

"Enslaved people," the woman began, enunciating carefully, as if it were important that Billy know how to correctly pronounce the term. "This was a long time ago, we're talking about history."

"History," Billy repeated. Mama spoke again in that frustrated half-whisper, under her breath, "Not that long ago, really."

"Back then, some people were bought and sold, they were made to work. They were denied their freedom and lived in very hard conditions."

The young woman seemed flustered, like she'd never been directly asked this question before.

Billy nodded, but I could see the confusion in his face and imagined he had no idea what the guide was talking about.

Later, in the gift shop, Mama took a stab at answering Billy's question.

"I know it's hard to understand," she said. "Our country had a very bad time. Our guide was trying to explain to you about slavery. White people were in charge and they stole people from their homes in Africa, in countries very far away. They took people away from their families and put them on ships and brought them to America. And they made them work very hard for no money, and they hurt them very badly. Very, very terrible."

Billy's eyes grew round. "Did they see their families again?"

Mama shook her head. "No, they didn't."

Tears filled Billy's eyes. "People can't steal people! Why did they do that? Why were those people so bad? Did they say sorry?"

Mama's mouth was tight and grim.

"No, they didn't say sorry. They still haven't said they're sorry. I don't know why they did it. People do very terrible things, Billy. They were cruel and wrong."

"Why don't the police put them in jail?"

"You're right, Billy," I said. "They should have put them in jail. But they didn't."

I wanted to offer Billy words of comfort, but there were no words to offer. The truth was unspeakable, but it had to be said.

Mama took Billy's hand and we walked around the gift shop.

I heard Mama lean over and say to Papa, "This place—doesn't look quite so beautiful now."

Papa nodded, his eyes directed toward the ground.

"All of this," Mama said, gesturing toward the window, through which we could see the mansion and glimpse the wide sweep of expansive grounds, "built on the backs of slaves."

A startling image came back to me, one that had haunted me since reading Toni Morrison's *Beloved:* the chokecherry tree on Sethe's back, the knotted clumps of scar from repeated whippings she'd endured as a slave.

We walked toward the rear of the gift shop and Mama stopped by a large rack that held local artwork on display for sale. She stood for a while, examining the offerings. She spent several long minutes examining a series of photographs, lost in serious thought.

"Hey, kids," Mama said after a time, holding one of the enlarged photographs out for us to see, "this looks very pretty, doesn't it?"

Billy and I peered at the photograph; it looked like the main living room of the mansion we'd just walked through with the guide. But the photograph had been double-exposed, a second, translucent image superimposed over the lush draperies and elegant furnishings.

"Trees inside!" Billy said. "How'd they do that?"

"Look more closely," Mama said. I scooted around Billy to take a look as well.

"It's the slave quarters," I said.

Mama nodded. "Interesting, isn't it," she said, almost to herself. "The photographer, her name is Annie Hogan—oh, how interesting, I see she's Australian!—well, she had the idea of superimposing an image of the reconstructed slave cabin over the interior of the mansion living room."

The image was beautiful; light poured in through the high windows, fanning out to a broad gleaming swath on the parquet floor. Trees in full leaf from the second image cut delicate shadows from the fallen light around the ghostly outlines of the slave cabin, also shown to us by the guide, which hung suspended in the middle of the frame, vague and heavy.

"Built on the backs of slaves," I said.

Mama reached out her hand and rested it gently in the middle of my back.

We had hot chocolate and cake in the visitors' restaurant. Mama tried to act cheery, but her mood had clearly changed.

"I don't know, maybe we should just go back to the Hampton Inn," she said.

"I hear you," Papa said.

"What?" I asked. "What do you hear?"

"This kind of place really isn't my cup of tea, I guess," Mama said with a weary smile.

"Does this have something to do with the slave quarters?" I asked.

"Yes, I suppose it does," she said. "Now how about giving me a taste of that carrot cake? It looks delicious."

That's when it clicked. Behind Mama's slightly forced smile, her face was gray, and her usually bright eyes were dulled to a smoky yellow. It all came together in my mind—the growing knot of fear within me, the dark shadows I'd seen crossing Mama's face and sometimes Papa's, and the most telltale sign of all, Mama's awful pallor. *Mama is ill—and it's something serious.*

* * *

Back at the hotel, Papa took Billy and me down to the pool. Mama said she was tired and needed to rest. The pool was packed to capacity, kids jumping in and out, playing with pool toys, the room ricocheting with happy shouts and the slap-splash of water. Billy found a boy his age and they did doggy-paddle races along the edge; I watched their bobbing heads inch along the side of the pool. Billy's face was like a cartoon rendition of joy: ear-to-ear grin and flashing eyes. Reaching the steps, he climbed out of the pool then hurried over to where I was hanging on to the pool's rim, kicking my legs underwater. Billy's new friend swam to the other side of the pool and also got out, walking slowly toward his parents, as if reminding himself of adult instructions to be careful on the wet tile.

"We both won, Sis!" Billy shouted with glee.

"You mean it was a tie," I said.

"No. Both of us got there at the same time. We both won."

He leaned down, came close up to my face and whispered loudly. "He's my new friend," he said. "His name is Connor. And he isn't a slave."

I jumped up out of the pool, took Billy's hand, and walked him over to where Papa was sitting by the table where we'd left our things.

I leaned down to look Billy directly in the face.

"What do you mean? About Connor?"

"I saw the pictures." He pointed through the window. "At the big house. In the gift shop."

"I have no idea what you're talking about."

"Of the slaves. They have black skin. I asked Connor if he was one, and he said no."

"Billy! That's a terrible thing to say. You shouldn't have said that!"

"Now, kids," Papa said, "what's going on?"

"Papa! Billy asked that little boy if he was a slave!"

Papa's face went pale. Carefully, kindly, Papa asked Billy to tell him what he'd said. He wasn't able to get much more out of him. Resolve in his face, he took Billy by the hand.

"Come on, son. We're going to go and talk to Connor and his family."

Connor was on the other side of the pool with his mother and a girl of about my age. They greeted us in a friendly way when Papa introduced us. The girl was Connor's sister—her name was Monique.

"Look, I'm sorry to say, my son said something rather odd to your son. Perhaps Connor told you about it?"

"Actually, no," Connor's mother said. "He told me he made a new friend and had a fun race and that they both won!" Smiling warmly, she leaned down a little. "Billy, right?"

Billy nodded, very serious, now.

"I shouldna ask him if he's a slave. I'm really sorry, I didn't know."

"I'm so sorry," Papa said, looking mortified. "We've just come from a tour of the Belle Meade Mansion. Billy learned about America's terrible history. He didn't know about slavery … I suppose we … well anyway, it made a big impression."

Connor's mother let out a little laugh.

"Well, kids do say what's on their minds," she said. "It's a lot to take in. Really, don't give it a second thought."

Papa looked relieved.

"Listen, Connor only learned about slavery this past term, in pre-K," she said. "Let's just say, the teacher is very, well, passionate. She did this exercise—I thought it was a bit strange, especially for kids that young. She had all the kids wearing colored sneakers go to one side of the room. And for a couple of hours, they weren't allowed to do anything fun and they had to sit still and not speak. She was trying to demonstrate racism, and then she told them about how people were enslaved here, in our own country."

"Challenging way to make a point …" Papa said.

"Well, Connor came home pretty upset. *It's so terrible what happened to black people,* is what he said. *I feel so bad for them.* I told him, Honey, you're black, too, and then he said, *I know I'm African American, is that the same thing?*"

Papa shook his head sympathetically.

"Actually, my husband and I talked about taking him out of the school—it's a private school. The population is not at all diverse. There's only one other black kid in his whole grade. We worry that if he stays there, he's not going to know who he is."

I was taken with Connor's mother's directness.

"It's a complicated world, isn't it?" Papa said.

"Sure is." Connor's mother gave a wry smile. "Especially for kids."

The two boys had jumped back in the pool, and now she looked over at them wistfully.

"Maybe their generation will make a better go of it."

* * *

The phone call came the next morning as we sat in the hotel breakfast room eating waffles. When Mama saw the incoming number on her cell phone, she gave Papa a knowing look, then jumped up and walked out into the lobby to take the call. Papa stood as well.

"Keep an eye on Billy," he said, his voice flat.

I watched them through the glass partition; Mama was staring into the middle distance as she listened to whoever was talking on the other end of the phone. Papa's arms hung down loosely as he waited, his eyes fixed on Mama's face. The call over, she leaned into Papa and said a few words. I saw him grit his teeth and clench his eyes shut for a moment. Then, he took Mama's hand and caressed it. In that moment, I realized the *something serious* must have been going on for some time. They just hadn't told us about it, though I was certain that this was about to change.

Back at the table, Papa launched right in. "Kids, I have some news that will come as a disappointment. We have to return home. We're not going to be able to continue our trip. And we need to get back quickly, so we'll be flying instead of driving."

"Oh boy, a plane!" Billy said, though I could see anxiety in his eyes. Even Billy knew something was up.

"What is it?" I asked. "What's happened?"

Papa told us Mama was ill. Cancer, he said. They'd been waiting for final results, something to do with what kind of treatments she'd need. The news she'd had on the phone was clearly not good. I didn't know the precise details. I only knew that Mama was ill and that our big adventure had been snapped in two.

Billy piped up. "But what about our car?"

"You don't need to worry about that, Billy. We'll take care of the car."

We packed in awkward silence. No one tried to make light of the situation. I could see Mama was struggling with that. She was always the one with a funny take on things, looking on the bright side, cajoling one or the other of us out of a cranky place. Now and then she gave either Billy or me a hug. I felt like the world had given me a great punch to the stomach. I'd never been faced with a situation that my family wasn't able to cast in a positive light; I'd had drilled into me the notion that glitches and difficulties were part of life, were always an opportunity to learn or "build character," clouds had silver linings, and that coming together as a family to face hardships could actually be one of life's bountiful gifts. Now, there was no sign of any of this kind of talk. No mention of silver linings or exciting challenges. Only gray, gray, everywhere gray, roiling in the air around us.

* * *

On the plane, Billy asked, again, about the car. Papa mustered a quick reply in his best reassuring voice.

"We found a nice young man who's going to drive it back for us."

"Do we know him?" Billy asked.

"Well, we met him. We know him now."

"A stranger," Billy said, persistent. "If he's a stranger, how do you know he's nice?"

"Son, trust me, you don't need to worry about the car. The car will be okay."

"What about Mama, will Mama be okay too?" Billy asked.

"Why yes, Billy," Papa said with a forced smile; his eyes were not smiling, though, only his mouth. I don't know if Billy had heard it, but I had—the instant of hesitation before he answered, a quick breath of silence.

Mama always told me that mothers sleep with their ears open; I suspect she could also see through walls. She knew things about my brother and me that normal eyes or ears, asleep or awake, could not possibly have known. Like exactly when either of us was about to wake up, or when I was harboring a troubling secret or when one of us was especially sad.

But daughters, I've discovered, also hear and see in unusual ways when it comes to their mothers. In the past, my mother had occasionally felt far away—when her work piled up or when she had to deal with a troublesome situation. But since returning to Brooklyn, she had a new kind of faraway—not the sort she'd snap back from; no promise that a tale from my day or a joke or scene recited from a school play would alter that staring, pained look in her eye. I was unable to bring back the sparkling smile that made her dark eyes dance and her face flicker with joy. The faraway place had a grip on her and there was nothing I could do to change that.

We were home for less than two weeks when Papa took us for Italian ice and told us that Billy and I would be going to Australia to spend time with our grandmother. The treatments for Mama's cancer, he said, were going to be harder than they'd thought. Mama needed to focus on staying strong, and he needed to focus on taking care of Mama.

"But we can help!" I said. "We can help you take care of Mama."

Papa took my hand and held it the way he'd done when I was little. Something plunged within me as I realized that I still felt little—that I still *was* little! The lump in my throat didn't let me say anything. I concentrated on the word *treatments*. Tried to think of a mountain resort with hot springs, where young women lie about getting mud wraps and massages and gossiping while waiting for their nails to dry. Then pushed my mind to picture teams of friendly medical professionals, determined to hunt down every offending cancer cell in my mother's normally strong body, never resting until they could resolutely declare my mother cured.

"We bought the tickets," Papa said.

"But I don't want to go! I want to stay here with Mama!"

"We need you to be strong," he said. "It's going to be a hard time."

I looked at my uneaten ice, a slush puddle in the soft paper cup. My brother's ice was dripping down his chin and onto his shirt in pink-and-blue rivulets. What was Papa trying to tell me? That we would be in the way? Or maybe that Mama didn't want us to witness what she was going to have to go through?

"We won't be in the way, I promise!" I said, trying to dampen down the desperation rising into my chest.

"We've given this a lot of thought, sweetie. This will be best all around, really. You'll be helping by taking care of Billy on the plane, and helping Grandma take care of him when you get to Australia. Plus, this way, you can have another big adventure this summer."

"I don't want another big adventure," I said, staring at the melted slush with despair. "I've had enough adventures this summer. Don't want any more."

There was no point arguing. My parents had made up their minds. The tickets had been bought. I threw my dripping paper cup of melted ice into the trash can on the street. I opened my mouth to speak but the big lump in my throat squeezed my voice to nothing.

"I'll be taking you to the airport tomorrow afternoon," Papa said.

Tomorrow. I tried to wrap my mind around it all.

"There's a quick, easy change in Los Angeles—you'll have no trouble with that—and Uncle Michael will collect you at the other end."

I nodded, grabbed hold of my brother's sticky little hand, suddenly feeling very small and alone.

"How 'bout that, little guy," my father said to Billy. His face was deadly serious. "An adventure with sister, just the two of you."

Billy turned his bright face upward toward me and grinned a rainbow-ice grin. "How 'bout that, Sis! You and me!"

Back home, I told Papa I'd be up in a minute and sat on the second top stair of the stoop, one of my favorite places to think. The late-June weather was glorious, the sunlight buttercup-yellow, and the air warm and still breezy, before the humid heat turned the city into a grimy, muggy hothouse. But for me, the dryness felt mournful, as if my beloved Brooklyn had been reduced to a parched gulch; in my head was a whistling wind that only I could hear. An elderly neighbor passed by, leaning on her cane, her tread heavy and uneven. She froze as a little kid whizzed by on a scooter. Our street was lined with towering trees, each holding a hundred years or more in their branches; I looked up through the needles of the giant pine in our neighbor's front yard that spread over our stoop, listening to the riotous birdsong. I had always loved sitting here, watching the world go by. But now, everything looked different. I didn't know the old woman leaning on her cane, or the little kid whizzing by—they weren't neighbors from my block—and the birds seemed raucous, as if our sweet little sparrows and thrushes had been replaced by scrappy, caterwauling seabirds. Even the squirrels had a feral look. I'd never thought of them as related to the sinister rats we'd seen scuttling along the trash-strewn subway tracks; now, their rodent nature seemed starkly revealed.

I could not have known what an extraordinary adventure I was about to embark upon. Though perhaps part of me knew, the part of a person that pulls little puzzle pieces from a day and turns them into dreams.

After dinner, I went to my room to pack. My limbs felt heavy and my mind felt like sludge. I had to keep reminding myself that in Melbourne, it would be winter. I couldn't for the life of me remember where I'd put my winter gear. My gaze wandered to the wall above my bed where I'd displayed the art museum postcards Papa always brought back from his work travels, where he gave lectures and attended academic conferences.

My eyes settled on the oversized postcard depicting Rembrandt's painting of Jeremiah, elegant in his despair as he lamented the destruction of Jerusalem. Papa had told me about the Rijksmuseum in Amsterdam where dozens of Rembrandt paintings and drawings hung, this one included. The deep pain in the prophet's face broke my heart anew; in the distance, the city of Jerusalem burned, the flames' thick ochre smudges lapped at the giant dome of the temple, dissolving upward into heavens that were dark with destruction. The prophet rested his head on his hand, eyes cast downward, a few gleaming treasures beside him, likely rescued from the burning temple—religious objects of silver and gold. He had prophesied the destruction, but no one listened. His sense of helplessness flowed into the room, joining my own.

Mama appeared in the doorway.

"Can I help?" she asked.

"I can't find any of my stuff!" I said.

Mama pointed to under the bed.

"Remember? Last year we bought those plastic bins ..."

I crawled under the bed and dragged out the bins, which were heavy, filled as they were with winter boots, coats, sweaters.

Mama sat on my bed as I packed. Her smile seemed effortful, as if she were posing for a photographer who was taking too long to snap the picture. She suddenly looked thin and frail, lost in the large black cardigan she'd pulled around her; it was warm, but she seemed to be feeling chilly. She looked like a teenager wearing her mother's clothing. I stopped what I was doing—the half-folded T-shirt dangling from my hands—and searched her face. Still that gray tinge to her skin and her eyes ringed with black circles. She tightened her smile, as if that might be more convincing.

I thought of the other mother I knew much better than this one: sparkly and zany, with a rippling laugh. The one who once pretended to chide Billy and me for splashing wildly in our oversized tub, then climbed in, clothes and all, and splashed along with us. Who took me, when I was five or six, to the Plaza Hotel for tea, and when I said "Yuk!" at the smoked salmon sandwiches on their silver plate, responded in a false, uppity voice, "Now, dear, the correct thing to say is: *That's disgusting and it makes me puke!*"

I looked at the stiff woman-child on my bed and wondered where my mother had gone, wondered if she were ever going to come back. That strange stretched smile was still on her face, but I saw that her eyes were welling; I watched as a tear rolled down her cheek. I dropped the T-shirt and climbed onto the bed, then put my head in her lap.

"You don't have to try to smile, Mama," I said. When I looked up, I saw that the unfamiliar, taut smile was gone: sadness—and some relief, I think—had taken its place.

"I'm going to do my very, very best," Mama said. "I'll be the best patient, ever. Promise."

"I know you will," I said. I did not have words to say what was in my heart, so I said nothing more.

The next morning, Mama rose early with all of us and shuffled around the kitchen, making pancakes. Little beads of perspiration gathered on her forehead as she whisked the batter. I wanted to tell her not to worry about breakfast, that we would grab a bagel at the airport, but seeing her effortful movements, the grim determination of her jaw, I stopped myself. She was making the pancakes because she wanted to, because she needed to. She was making them to tell us she loved us, to tell us she was sorry she was not coming with us, to tell us she was sorry she was ill.

At the door, our bags already packed into the car, Billy gave Mama a big hug.

"I *love* you, Mama," he said.

"I love you too, silly goose," Mama said, with a trace of her old buoyancy.

Then, it was my turn. I took my newly thin mama in my arms and gave her the best hug I could. When we drew apart, she looked at me deeply and long.

"Take care of Billy," she said. Then, she pointed to my heart, and whispered: "I'll always be here. Remember that."

* * *

Our flight to Australia was agonizingly long. Twenty-three hours, to be exact. Billy was a dream, perky and funny and joyous, as he has been since he emerged from that sleepy newborn twilight, six weeks into life. I remember when he was an infant—four months old, on his first trip to Australia—how when Mama put him up on Grandma's kitchen counter in his bouncy chair, he beamed warmly at the tiles. I guess he just loved life.

Being responsible for him felt terrifying. What if something went wrong? What if he got ill or scared? Every now and then, throughout the long flight, Billy asked, "Where's Mama?" or "Where's Papa?" My heart would lurch and I'd have to stop myself from thinking about the fact that we were thousands of feet in the air, two children away from their parents, alone above the wide, dark, impossibly deep ocean. Even glimpsing this thought sent terror shuddering right to the seat of my soul and I'd grip little Billy's hand and mete out one of my small store of answers— "Papa's taking care of Mama so that she'll get well," or "We'll be there soon," or "We're going to see Grandma!" Billy seemed content with my responses, which I backed up each time with a few purple Skittles, his favorite, that we'd bought at Dylan's Candy Bar, where you could buy the colors separately.

After what seemed like forever, the plane finally began its approach for landing. I held Billy's hand—"The plane is going *fast!* We landing, Sis?"—and then there it was, that Australian light: intensely white-yellow and somehow ringing with sound.

"Where we going?" Billy asked.

"To see Grandma," I said, discreetly wiping my eyes. For a moment, looking out at the tarmac, I felt the world swoon, as if everything around me were doing a slow, eerie slide.

"Oh boy, Grandma!" Billy said. He looked out the window. "Will Mama be coming soon?" he asked.

"We're going to see where Mama grew up," I said, shaking my head gently in the hope of setting the sliding world to rights.

"Where Mama grew up," he repeated. Billy probably didn't remember the last time we were in Australia, when he was only two.

"Where Mama was a little girl," I said, aware of a dryness in my throat.

"Oh, where Mama was a little girl," he whispered back.

Uncle Michael was at the gate.

"Hey, kids. Welcome to Oz!" he said in his broad Australian accent. Uncle Michael was tall and athletic and loved kids and dogs. In past visits, he'd taught me to play backgammon, gin rummy, and spit.

"Got the games out for you lot," he said as he swung Billy up onto his shoulders and then took charge of our bags. "Took them to Grandma's. She made you a giant chocolate cake."

"Wow! A giant!" Billy said. I imagined what he was picturing—a massive cake formed in the shape of the ferocious creature depicted in his *Jack and the Beanstalk* storybook.

"It's a big cake, Billy. That's what Uncle Michael means."

"Oh, a big cake," Billy said, adjusting his expectations with a shade of disappointment.

"But hey, Auntie Liora's there too; I shouldn't tell you this, but she got you guys a whole lot of prezzies!" Auntie Liora had the kindest smile and always seemed to be doing everything for everyone. She had a knack for knowing exactly what would delight us and gave us the loveliest things. How exciting that I would see her soon!

On the drive from the airport, I silently greeted the towering eucalyptus trees that flanked the highway, with their slender, willowy branches and droopy dusty-olive leaves. As we got closer to the city, I watched out for the view of the city skyline—sleek towers and regal, angular colonial buildings, interspersed with swatches of leafy parks. Turning off the highway onto the wide city streets, we passed by rows of beautifully restored Victorian houses. The footpaths, as they called the sidewalks here, were filled with people heading to work, as well as some families—parents dressed in business suits wheeling strollers, likely taking their children to day care. It was a mild, wintry day—the opposite season here, being on the other side of the equator—but the light was as splashy as ever, as if pouring from the heavens in golden bucketfuls.

Grandma and Auntie Liora were standing in front of the house when we pulled into the cul-de-sac. Grandma's face had a funny look about it. I could see she was happy to see us, but she was also upset. I suppose she was thinking about Mama, back home in New York, who was probably this moment crumpled up on her bed enduring the terrible waves of nausea brought on by her cancer treatment. Auntie Liora put her arm around me at once and drew me close.

"My darlings!" Grandma said, opening her arms. Billy shyly submitted to her embrace. "How was your flight?"

"We were on a *very* big plane, Grandma!" Billy said. "Oh—and lots of clouds. A million!"

"And did you count every one?" she asked, her smile filling the whole of her face.

"Emily, did you sleep on the plane?" Auntie Liora asked.

"Not much," I said.

"You look a bit pale. You're probably just tired. Let's all have a cup of tea. And Grandma's chocolate cake. I know Uncle Michael is dying for a piece."

Though Grandma was almost seventy years old, her eyes shone with childhood. I loved the way she got excited about everything.

Like the time we stopped for half an hour to watch a tiny army of ants making their way across the sidewalk toward their anthill on the nature strip, many bearing loads that looked a hundred times their size. I loved that she carried small gardening shears in the pocket of a big cardigan she wore when she went out for her daily walks, so she might clip a bloom when its beauty called to her. Once, she told me mischievously, she'd climbed over a tall fence to get to an extravagant camellia bush.

I had never known my other three grandparents; two of them died long before I was born, and Papa's father died when I was a baby. I don't think Grandma quite realized how significant it was to be a child's only living grandparent.

We all sat around the kitchen table. Billy gripped onto my hand, stealing shy glances at Grandma and bolder ones at Uncle Michael and Auntie Liora. He happily tucked into his cake and soon had a chocolate mustache and beard.

After Billy washed his hands and face, Grandma showed us around, to refresh our memories of the house. My mother had told us many stories of her own childhood in this house; we called it "The U House," as it was shaped like the letter *U* around the back yard, which contained the swimming pool we'd always envisioned with such awe, being New York City kids. We loved our tiny cement patch in back of our Brooklyn house, a luxury among city dwellers, and could hardly imagine a yard sizable enough to contain a swimming pool.

Daredevil Uncle Michael told us how when he was twelve, he'd climbed onto the roof and jumped from there into the pool.

Auntie Liora shook her head. "Don't be like Uncle Michael," she said. "He was such a naughty boy."

One length of the *U* was a long hallway with floor-to-ceiling windows on one side and doors to the bedrooms on the other. Sunlight slanted in and marked the varnished cork flooring in bright parallelograms that Billy jumped into and out of. Looking into the back yard, I could see the pool cover sag in the middle, where rainwater flecked with leaves had gathered. A lone silver birch towered above the gray brick patio, holding the sky with its bare arms, its papery white bark hanging in places on the trunk in enormous vertical curls.

Outside Grandma's room was an unusual bench I'd always liked, made of a wooden frame and thin leather thongs woven crisscross to form a seat. Grandma had brought it with her when she and Grandpa Jack emigrated from South Africa, when Mama was a baby. She told us it was made of a now-extinct South African tree named *stinkwood*. Billy leapt onto it with glee, as I had done, the first time I'd visited Australia when I was exactly Billy's age.

"Stinky stink, stinky stink!" He bounced up and down on the leather thongs.

"He's discovered the *bankie*," Grandma said, using the Afrikaans word for this kind of bench, one of the few relics she had from her South African childhood.

She leaned down and whispered in my ear: "I have something special earmarked for each of you to take home with you when you're grown-up. You always liked the *bankie*; it has your name on it."

What a happy thought! That Grandma wanted, one day, to give the *bankie* to me.

"I loved this bench myself as a child," she said. "My happiest moments were spent sitting on it—dreaming of my future. Or playing with the dolls I used to make out of mango pits. I'd scrape all the fiber off the pit except at the top. That was the doll's hair. Then I'd paint on eyes, nose, and mouth. I used to play with them for hours."

Auntie Liora and Uncle Michael left, and Grandma showed us to our room, which she'd set up for our arrival. The shelves had been cleared of her books and were now filled with toys and games and children's books she'd rummaged up from when my mother and aunt and uncle were young. There were bright posters on the walls: Winnie the Pooh and his Hundred Acre friends over Billy's bed, and a Monet print over mine—a garden with a little bridge.

Back in the living room, my eyes fell on the large samovar, sitting in its special place on the sideboard. Last time we were here, I'd asked Mama what it was; she'd explained that it was the pride of my great-grandmother's household when she was a child in Lithuania, a symbol of warmth and hospitality, the communal tea drinking at the heart of family life. The name had evoked something formal, imperial, and military, like a hussar in full regalia, with epaulets and brass buttons, a sword swinging from his hilt.

"Grandma, have you ever used the samovar?" I asked.

Grandma turned to look at the cylindrical samovar, about a foot and a half tall, made of brass, with elaborately carved feet and an ornamental crown. It was polished to a bright sheen. I recalled seeing Grandma rubbing at it with a chamois cloth.

"Yes. Well, no. Not for a very long time. We used it on special occasions in South Africa, when I was a child. It must be decades ..."

She paused. "Come—let's take it to the kitchen and clean it out."

Together, sharing the weight of it, Grandma and I carried the samovar into the kitchen. Billy followed behind us, with his usual, "Can I help? Can I?" I moved aside, and he placed his hands beneath mine, his face eager.

In the kitchen, Grandma removed the ornate top and rinsed the inside with water.

"Look," she said. Billy climbed up on a chair and we both peered inside. "That's the heating chamber." A wide tube ran down the middle of it. "They used to fill it with dry pine cones which burned nicely and cost nothing."

"Let's go out and get some!" Billy said.

"I'm not sure we'd find any," Grandma said, smiling. "Coal works just as well. I have a box under the sink. I use coal sometimes in the fireplace."

Grandma rinsed out the inner chamber and filled it with fresh water and together we carried the samovar over to the kitchen table, where she placed it on a metal tray. Grandma broke two small bricks of coal into pieces, placed these in the central cylinder, then put pieces of torn newspaper on top.

"Emily, why don't you light it?"

I took a long kitchen match and held it to the paper. We waited for the coal to catch.

"They used to have little bellows that were made especially for samovars to keep the fire going," Grandma said, "and a special teapot that sat right here, on top, and stayed hot. The tea concentrate was made in that. They'd pour a little into a cup and then fill it up with the boiling water." She pointed to the dainty faucet at the bottom of the samovar.

"I bet my Japanese teapot will do fine for the concentrate," she said, and went to the cupboard to get it.

While we waited for the water to boil, Grandma told us a little about what life was like for her mother, Sarah, at the turn of the twentieth century in Lithuania. They'd lived in Dusiat, she said, a small town on the Sventoji River. The Jewish shtetl accounted for the majority of the population. The family lived traditional Orthodox Jewish lives, which revolved around Jewish practices and festivals. While Grandma talked, she packed tea leaves into the teapot, added a little water, then removed the crown of the samovar and set the teapot into the indentation above the heating channel.

"The water is ready," Grandma said after a time. "Can you feel the heat?" She held her hands six inches away from the brass surface. "You have to be careful or you'll scald yourself. You probably already feel you're drowning in tea, but you've got to try this. It tastes quite different, you'll see!"

Grandma took three elegant cups and saucers from the cabinet— my great-grandmother's wedding china. The cream-colored china, decorated with a heavy, old-fashioned design of burnt orange and gold, was covered in fine little cracks, like the delicate face wrinkles of the very old.

How extraordinary, I thought, the way these objects—some hefty, others fragile—had followed my mother's family in their intergenerational journeys, from Lithuania to South Africa to Australia. Perhaps one day, some would find their way to my home in America. *We're wandering Jews,* my mother had once said of her family. *Never really had a chance to put down roots.* I hadn't known what she meant at the time, though I sensed something ominous behind her words. My knowledge was patchy, but I now knew enough of Jewish history to understand what she'd meant—the exiles, the fleeing, droves catapulting from one continent to another.

Grandma filled each cup with a little of the tea concentrate, and then held it under the samovar nozzle and turned the handle. A stream of steaming water poured down.

She placed a tiny silver spoon and cube of brown sugar on each plate and then passed the tea around. She filled Billy's cup only partway so that the tea would quickly cool.

I dissolved the sugar in the cup and then lifted it to my lips, expecting something exotic and fragrant. Instead, the hot mouthful tasted like old rusty water.

"Yuk!" Billy said, spitting his own mouthful back into the cup.

Being older, and more secure in my manners, I politely swallowed the rusty mouthful.

Grandma pulled a face.

"You're right, Billy. It is yukky. Sorry, children. I didn't realize the samovar was rusty on the inside."

I could see that Grandma was disappointed. "Never mind," she said, "it was fun to give it a try."

She looked at me with that mischievous look and added: "And if ever anyone asks you to make tea in a samovar, you'll know how!"

A great tide of sleepiness overcame me suddenly, like a sledge-hammer blow to the head: that druggy jet-lag exhaustion that comes with flying long distances. I felt Billy's hand loosen in mine and turned to see he was slumped against the cushions, fast asleep. I pressed the heels of my hands into my eyes.

"I think you need a nap as well. Heaven knows how long it's been since you left New York," Grandma said.

I became aware of a dull ache in the back of my head. "Yes," I managed to say, my voice thick and far away. "I'm not feeling so well."

Together, we roused Billy so that he was able to toddle down the hallway, Grandma and I each supporting an arm. I changed into my pajamas, flopped onto the bed, and fell into a blank sleep.

The room was pitch black when I awoke. When I'd lain down, the sun had poured through the window, bringing to life tiny beads of dust that danced in the sunbeams. My headache had worsened; the pain felt like a silent, dull roar. I crept out of the bed, stepped into the hallway. A slice of dim lamplight from the door of Grandma's room cut through the darkness. I tiptoed in its direction, just as Grandma's old clock rang out. I paused to count the chimes. One, two, three, four. Four o'clock in the morning. Why was Grandma still up?

"Grandma?" I whispered. I thought I heard the sound of nose blowing and a few quiet gulps.

"Come in, darling. I was just reading."

Grandma was lying in bed; hastily, she picked up a book without realizing she was holding it upside down.

"You've been asleep for hours. The jet lag will do that. Are you hungry?"

I shook my head, no. My stomach felt like it was filled with mud, and my head full of lead.

"It zaps your appetite, too, doesn't it …"

Grandma's eyes were red from crying and, though she tried to put on a brave smile, her face was very sad. Perhaps she'd been speaking to my mother on the phone; given the fourteen-hour time difference, this would be a good time to catch her.

"Mama's going to kick this thing, you know," I said.

Grandma nodded, acknowledging what I'd seen. "She's strong, that's for sure," she said. "And brave." She reached for a tissue from the side of the bed and wiped her eyes.

Something ached within me to think of Mama having to be brave.

"Now, why are you up?" Grandma asked.

"I have a terrible headache—I think it woke me."

"I know you don't feel hungry but eating might help. Bread and jam and hot milk. That should do the trick."

We walked in our slippers to the kitchen. Grandma put some milk in a pan on the stove and then set some thick slices of fresh wholewheat bread on the table, along with gooseberry preserves and a slab of butter, which in Australia is a deep yellow color.

"The long trip must have been hard, alone with Billy," she said. "I'm not surprised you're all topsy-turvy."

I sat quietly, taking small bites of bread and jam and sipping the hot milk. Grandma had not drawn the blind; through the window, I could see the sky, ablaze with stars. It made me think of the night before we left New York, when we'd all gone into the postage-stamp-sized front yard of our Brooklyn brownstone to look up at the sky. We'd stood there for some time, Mama with one arm around me, the other around Billy, and Papa behind.

Billy had been the first to speak.

"I'm looking at the stars' shining faces," he'd said.

"Oh?" Mama said.

"And they're looking back at ours."

There was wonder in his face, and something inside me squeezed tight as a fist.

"Look, Sister. The stars are pretending that *we're* stars, too."

Now, looking out through Grandma's window, I was aware that far away in Brooklyn—ten thousand three hundred miles away—this same sky was wearing daytime: deep blue, I imagined, with no sign of cloud. I thought of Mama, pictured her curled up on her bed, hoped, at least, that she could see the sky through the window.

I looked up to see Grandma with a soft look in her face.

"I spoke to her, not long ago. Your mama."

I nodded.

"She's not feeling the best. But she's battling on." I could hear the crack in her voice, though her face looked determined and strong. "She's a good soldier, your mother. Always has been. If anyone can lick this thing, she can."

I found myself playing that game in my head that seemed to be becoming a habit. A kind of algebra that involved my own behavior—past, present, and future—and the probability of my mother getting well. How good a daughter had I been, really? And how good a sister? What small and large crimes had I committed in the course of my fourteen years? And what if I pledged to be the perfect child from now until forever? To do everything cheerfully and well, never to whine or complain, always to keep jolly spirits, never a word of irritation or gesture of anger? Was I in any way responsible for my mother's illness? Were there things I had done or said—or failed to do or say? And if so, how stringent were the requirements to set things straight? Just how perfect did I have to be to have my mother go on living?

"It's a funny thing, mothers and daughters," Grandma said. There it was again—Grandma tuning in to my thoughts. "Wait a moment, darling. I'll be right back."

She left the kitchen, then returned a few minutes later, something cupped in her hand. When she sat down, she handed me a little woolen wad: pink baby booties, hand knitted, faded and worn.

"My mother made these," she said. "My sister wore them before I was born. My mother and I were never close the way you are with your mama. I always blamed her for that ..."

I felt my eyes well up as Grandma talked. I reached for a napkin from the copperware napkin holder Grandma had brought back from her exotic travels.

"Once I was a mother myself, I revised my view. There were so many years that I walked around in a fog of exhaustion. I had help, though, and no money worries; your grandfather was a wonderful provider. And yet I was tired all of the time and worried about everything. Now, it seems silly. What did I have to worry about?

"My own mother had nine children. She and my father had no education. They ran a little general store in a town the size of a peanut, in the middle of a wasteland: South Africa's Orange Free State."

Grandma's voice took on a bitter edge. "Believe me, there was nothing *free* about it. I saw more oppression and unkindness growing up there. But that's another story. The point is, for my own mother, there were problems and more problems. Within the family, and also in the awful society around her."

Grandma paused to think, and when she spoke again, her voice was low.

"By the time I came along, my mother was worn out. She simply had nothing left to give. And there was something else. You see, I was brought into this world to replace another little baby: Rose, who died when she was not yet one year old. After seven boys, only my mother's second girl. In her grief, she wanted another baby—to replace Rose. But when I came along, I was a constant reminder of her loss. And of the terrible mistake my mother had made that had caused Rose's death."

"What terrible mistake?" I said.

"Rose was allergic to cow's milk, so my mother fed her with goat's milk. She had to take a long train journey and took along goat milk. There was a woman on the train who had no milk for her baby, who was screaming with hunger. Rose was asleep, so my mother gave the stranger her goat milk."

Grandma shrugged. It was a strangely uncharacteristic gesture.

"When Rose woke up, of course she was hungry. At the next station, my mother bought cow's milk to give her, since goat milk was hard to come by. She probably hoped that just one time, it would be okay."

Grandma reached over and touched the pink booties, which smelled faintly of mothballs and hand-washing detergent. I imagined her taking them out of storage from time to time and washing them in the laundry room sink.

"On top of everything, the cow's milk was spoiled. Rose got very sick. She died a few days later."

So many years ago—almost seventy—and yet Grandma's voice had the ring of fresh pain.

"When my mother was dying," she said, "I traveled to South Africa to visit her. That was when she gave me these." Grandma's eyes glistened. "It was her way of saying she was sorry. I'm certain of it."

"Sorry?" I asked.

"That she'd been unable to love me as a mother should. She looked so frail—like a child herself. And I understood something for the first time in my life."

Grandma was nodding, as if I must have understood something as well, but I didn't know what to make of her sad story.

"What did you understand?"

"That my mother had done the best she could. Which is, in the end, all that any of us can do."

52

She was looking at me as if she could see right into my soul.

"You see, Emily," she said, "it's all shadows. The truth of the world. Patterns of light and dark. *Chiaroscuro.* Perhaps you know the word; it's used in the study of art. The shading that gives form to life's mysteries. It's the medium of some of the greatest painters in Western Art—Caravaggio, Goya, Rembrandt."

In fact, I did know this word. My own mother had told me it was *mine*—that this word somehow belonged to me.

"It's also the medium of life, my darling. Though perhaps you're too young to really understand this. Don't young people hate being told this! Parents and grandparents can't help themselves. We were all young, once, but we oldies have the rolling years of experience. We can't help but try to pass some of it along. Though chances are, you're going to have to figure it all out in your own way, in your own time.

"What I'm trying to say is that it's impossible in this life not to experience the shadows."

Grandma let out a gentle sigh. "I know what a great big scary shadow your mama's illness is. And you—with your far-seeing eyes. You have only to look around you to see so much in this world that warrants sadness and regret. That's simply the way things are."

There was something of hope in the way that Grandma was looking at me.

"I think you should have these," she said, gently sliding the booties across the table.

I cradled them in my hand, tried to imagine my great-grandmother, though I had no idea what she'd looked like. I tried to picture her sitting by a fire in a simple wooden house, pregnant, knitting these booties. But no image came to mind; it was all a sad blank.

I said nothing, just looked across the many years into Grandma's face. Then, concern crossed her features and she reached a hand to my forehead.

"You're hot," she said, as if to herself, "and you're not looking yourself."

My eyelids were beginning to droop. I wondered vaguely what Grandma meant—that I didn't look myself.

"Time to sleep," Grandma said, her own voice weary. "It's very late and tomorrow's a new day."

I walked with Grandma down the hallway to my room, aware of a weakness in my knees, steadying myself with one hand against the wall. I climbed into my bed—Billy was sound asleep across the room—and Grandma leaned down and kissed me on the forehead. She turned and left, and I listened to her retreating footsteps, muffled by the thick Persian rug. The hallway light was flicked off, leaving a diffuse illumination coming from Grandma's room; it washed over me as I drifted off to sleep.

* * *

I was awoken again by the chimes of the old wooden clock. I counted the clangs: one, two, three, four. Darkness all around: the blind heart of the night. Coming out of the fog of sleep, I was confused. The same four chimes I had awoken to earlier, and yet I felt as if I had slept for a very long time. How could that be? I could not possibly have slept through a full twenty-four hours. I rolled over to see Billy curled up like a puppy, his hands cupped together, a somber expression on his face. It was always surprising to see Billy's face without a smile.

In our many family photo albums, I doubt there's a single shot of Billy with a serious face; the boy with the wide grin and no visible lips, that's what you'll find. I, on the other hand, peer out, page after page, with grave eyes. One picture comes to mind: not yet two, I'm in diapers, you can see them peeking out from one side of my ruffled pink bathing suit. Mama would sigh when looking at that photograph, though I knew she especially loved it.

"So wise," she'd say. "Not yet two, and yet already more than grown-up." It made *me* sad to think that that picture of me made *her* sad.

I took this to mean that being a grown-up meant having those heavy feelings I'd sometimes get, feelings that were like a woolly shadow that would come out of nowhere and cover things up, making the bright yellow sunlight turn greeny-brown. When I was older, Mama started calling these my "Big Feelings." She told me I had a big soul to go along with them—that this was who I was, and I should embrace it. And that one day, I would make good use of those feelings.

I closed my eyes and conjured up my mother's face—not the thin, pale face of recent months, but her bright, cheerful face from the past. I let the memory fill me—smelled her warmth, nuzzled into the cradle of her arms.

"My little chiaroscuro." That was when I'd first heard this word. "You see it all. The sunshine and the shadow." I could feel her hand, stroking my arm. "True vision is a gift. It's the sound of your soul." As she spoke, her face had been as soft and glowing as her voice.

But now the memory fuzzed over and shifted. I opened my eyes—and yet I was still in that moment. No longer a memory. Happening now. How was this possible? How could the past have leap-frogged into—now? How could Mama be here with me, in Melbourne, in the middle of a long, dark night, when I knew that she was, in fact, at this moment, in Brooklyn? Far across the oceans, and not robust and youthful as she was in my memory, but exhausted, thin, and ailing, suffering from the effects of aggressive chemotherapy?

I clutched her hand—yes, I was holding her hand! It was here, right here, and pulsing with life.

"But what does it mean, Mama? What should I do?"

"Rivers speak the same language," she answered, her voice so rich with love it made me want to weep. I had no idea what she meant. "Like us, they all come from the sea. And like us, they are turbulent, always in uneasy—but beautiful—motion."

I peered up at her, squinted to try to make sense of what was happening.

"Find a river you love and spend time with it. Watch it and hear it and listen to what it says. There, you will find the answers you seek."

I looked down; my hand was still curled, as if holding another, but it was empty. The room held a stillness that seemed as vast as a desert night. Nothing made sense, nothing at all.

I rose, as if in a dream—was I in fact dreaming? Could that explain all of this? I tiptoed over to Billy's bed and kissed his cupped hands. I stepped into my slippers and out into the hallway. The blackness was there, too—no halo of light, this time, coming from Grandma's room.

I felt my way along the wall, squinting into the darkness. My body felt heavy, as if someone had draped me in sandbags, and my head ached with a throbbing pain that was sharp and dull at the same time. Every step felt like a mighty effort, time lurching fitfully with my feet. Fragments of images, sounds, and thoughts hung about me, mixing in with the stories Grandma had told me in that other thickness of night that now seemed a long time ago. In the black space of the hallway, I could feel the flickering images of the past, again as if they were all happening *right now*, just as Mama, moments ago, had materialized from nowhere. An eerie feeling filled me with excited dread. What if the past *could* suddenly rear up into the present?

I peeked in on Grandma, who was sleeping, the blanket pulled up to her chin against the brisk air coming in through the window. Grandma always kept the window open, even in winter; she loved the fresh air.

Back in the hallway, I felt as if my knees were about to buckle. The pain in my head intensified, as if a web of metal wires were tightening around my skull, sending sharp, reverberating pain shooting in every direction. I sank down onto the *bankie* and closed my eyes.

The darkness was no different with my eyes closed: that same flickering mixture of shadowy background and backlit image fragments that had made me swoon only a moment before. I realized I was still holding the pink baby booties I had clutched in my sleep.

The next chime came at the precise moment that the air was rent by a thunderclap so loud my hands flew to my ears. My first thought was for Billy, who feared only two things: darkness and storms. He would surely awaken in terror. I made to rise, intending to go straight to our room and take Billy in my arms, but I found myself strangely frozen. Another loud thwack from the skies. Again, a chime from the clock—One, Two, Three, Four. Impossible! Clearly, the clock was malfunctioning. But I had no time to worry about such things; Billy was all I could think of. I needed to get to Billy. Again, I tried to leap from the bench, but it was if I were cemented there; I could flail my arms, but I could not raise myself to standing.

Suddenly, the storm was indoors, here, in Grandma's hallway. A zigzag of lightning cracked against the wall, followed by another thunderclap so close to my head it sent a wave of pain through my ears. Rain pelted down in stinging needles: icy on my face, soaking my nightdress through.

I felt myself being flung forward, as if a giant had picked up the bench and hurled it. A wind screeched so fiercely it burned my face, and I tumbled, a heavy, slow movement through a menacing endless darkness of a kind I'd never before known. Fear gathered inside me until I thought I might explode.

It was just at the point when I felt I could bear it no longer, when I felt as if now, I must give up the fight, that I heard the voice. At first, I could not make out what it was saying, but then it became clear. It was Mama! Mama was speaking to me through the storm!

"There will be guides—you will find them." My head was exploding; my hands were two tight steel fists. *"Just keep your eyes open."*

* * *

As suddenly as it had come upon me, the violence ceased. My breath returned, my eyelids became unglued, and I opened my eyes.

I was back in my bedroom at Grandma's. Shafts of dawn light streamed in through a crack in the aluminum blinds. Strange: Grandma had curtains, not blinds! Once again, the old wooden clock chimed out. One, Two, Three, Four, Five, Six, Seven.

Seven in the morning. What had happened to the three hours left of the night?

I sat up and looked about me, my confusion growing. The same room; *not* the same room. A different feel to the light. I looked over to Billy's bed. It was then that my stomach gripped in panic. Not the little mound made by Billy's sleeping form, but someone else. Older—about my age. A girl, her long, dark hair making a wavy curve on the blue floral pillowcase.

I knew I was in Grandma's house, and yet it was all so different and strange.

Who was that girl, lying asleep in the other bed?

CHAPTER TWO

Y ES, I WAS CLEARLY STILL in Grandma's house. But everything looked different. The walls were no longer painted white, as they had been when I'd gone to sleep, but covered in light blue wallpaper, crisscrossed with white lines and adorned with little daisies. In place of the polished wooden floorboards was plush beige carpet.

I sat up in bed—one of those old-fashioned foldaway beds, low to the ground, a thin foam mattress set upon a creaky metal-and-spring frame. The room was the same one I'd been sleeping in with Billy not long ago, only now it contained just one regular-sized bed, up against the far wall.

The chimes, there they were. I counted them again. Six, seven, eight. I'd been lying here, in this familiar-unfamiliar room, for an hour. It must be a weekend morning, I thought, or else surely the figure in bed—I had been staring at her, now, for quite some time— would be up getting ready for school. I was aware of a weird feeling inside, something jumpy and unpleasant, which made me think of a goblin. Who could this be peacefully sleeping, in this oddly trans- formed room?

I was afraid to move, to make any noise, afraid I would wake up the girl. I wracked my brains for some explanation. Could Grandma have invited the granddaughter of a friend so that I'd have someone to hang out with? Could I have been ill or something—I'd had an awful headache before I went to sleep; maybe I had a violent flu and somehow slept through it all? The girl arriving, then going to sleep? But that wouldn't explain the changed wallpaper and carpet, the fact that there were now blinds on the windows instead of curtains.

Or maybe I was sicker than I realized—delirious, even. Imagining the blue wallpaper, and that the beds had changed, that Billy sleeping in that bed over there had doubled in size and grown a mane of black hair.

The girl rolled over and let out a sigh. I froze.

I shook my head, opened and closed my eyes several times very forcefully: if it was a delirious vision, perhaps I could shake it loose. But no, there she was, stretching her arms above her head and blinking sleepily. I watched as she emerged from sleep, watched the cloudy expression clear, found myself looking into eyes that were so unexpectedly known, I let out a gasp of surprise. No, it was unthinkable! Surely, I had sunken into some kind of delusional state.

You see, the girl whose eyes I was looking into, who looked to be about fourteen, had a face that was more familiar (and yet, being so young, also suddenly strange) than my own: the very first face, in fact, that I ever saw.

The storm, the dreadful, exhilarating, terrifying storm, must have been not a storm of weather—but of time! Somehow, I had tripped through a portal and been thrown backward more than three decades! I had no idea how to think about this. It was as if the storm had been a wave—a time wave—that had deposited me in the childhood bedroom of my very own mother, who was now sitting up in bed, fully awake.

I heard a voice ring out—a strong man's voice, full of vigor and good cheer. I knew immediately who it must be: Talia's father—my Grandpa Jack! Mama's beloved father, a surgeon, who had died long before I was born. An image flashed in my mind—the photograph my mother kept high on a shelf in her study of a surgeon, his face covered by a cloth surgical mask, bent over an operating table, a light attached to a headband on his forehead. As a small child, I'd never known who it was or what the person was doing, it was just a picture almost out of sight in the study where my mother spent hours each day, writing her children's books. One day, it occurred to me to ask.

"Who's that, Mama?"

"Who's who?" she'd asked; she was busy working when I'd entered the room.

"That," I said, pointing emphatically up at the framed photograph. She put down her pencil, her eyebrows raised quizzically.

"Why, that's Grandpa Jack, of course!" she said. "Didn't you know?"

I shook my head.

"All these years that picture's been up on my shelf, and you never knew who it was?" She let out an incredulous laugh. "For heaven's sake! That's your grandfather!"

"You never told me," I said in a small voice. For some reason, my mother's response had filled me with shame, and I found my lip trembling.

"Darling, don't be upset!" Mama said, drawing me near. "It's my fault! I can't imagine why I never thought to tell you."

That was really the first time I'd heard in any detail about my grandfather. He was a surgeon, who'd saved people's lives. Mama told me about how when she was a child, it was not unusual for her to see her father walking into the house as she was leaving for school, bone-weary after having operated for ten, twelve, even fourteen hours straight. She'd ask him what he'd done that night and he'd say something like—"Oh, it was a vascular transplant. But we ran into trouble." Or: "Kidney transplant. Cross fingers it won't be rejected." She'd felt awed and proud. He'd kiss the top of her head and then go in to sleep for an hour or two before showering and returning to the hospital to conduct rounds.

I could hardly believe that I was about to meet him! And then, the most wonderful and startling thing happened. Bounding into the room was a man of impressive height, with a handsome, youthful face and a shock of silver hair. He entered the room with a feeling so strong you could almost hear it—like an invisible jazz band in full swing.

"It's up and at 'em, Talia!" he said, his voice as luminous as his presence. "How about going up in the plane? I was thinking of Broken Hill."

The girl—*my mother*—looked over at me and her eyes fluttered with confusion as she met my gaze; at the same time, her father also seemed to notice me for the first time.

"I'd forgotten you had your friend sleeping over. You'll join us, of course. For a day trip to Broken Hill. Ever been in a small plane?"

Behind Talia's face was now an unreadable flicker. "Funny, I'd sort of forgotten you were sleeping over myself. I must have been having a ripper of a dream." She offered me a warm, if sleepy, smile. "Jasmine— I'm so glad you're here!"

Jasmine, I knew, was my mother's favorite flower.

I followed Talia's gaze to a shelf across the room; it held a silver vase from which a sprig of jasmine hung. Now, I placed the sweet scent I'd been vaguely aware of since waking up in this altered time-space. I did the math quickly in my head; if my mother was about my age, fourteen, then the year must be—1974.

I looked at Talia's father. *Grandpa Jack.* The larger-than-life fig-ure who'd bounded through the world full of passion for everything he did. And he did do *everything*—from devising new surgical tech-niques, to flying small aircraft, to collecting ancient coins, to raising prize-winning cattle as a weekend "gentleman" farmer.

It hit me then. I knew this look, this energy—the electric exu-berance and infectious spirit that flashed through the room. Billy! My mischievous five-year-old brother! His soul was there, spreading across Grandpa Jack's face. Or—should I say—Grandpa Jack's soul had fired from the heavens beyond, long after his premature death, into my little brother, Billy.

My face must have revealed some of what I was thinking as Grandpa Jack—Talia's father—was eyeing me oddly. I'd been about to throw my arms around him and hug him with all my might, but instead drew my arms around myself and held on tight.

"I'd *love* to come," I said, jumping at the sound of my own voice, which resounded, surprisingly, with an Australian accent.

"Well then, I'll leave you girls to get dressed."

Talia sat up in bed and stretched. "Why don't you call your mother and ask if you can sleep over again?" she asked. "We won't be back until after dark."

Her face held a strange, secretive look—as if she knew the idea of me calling my parents made no sense but had decided she needed to go along with the charade: as if we were in a play and there were some audience we needed, together, to convince.

"They'll be fine with it. But I'll go give them a quick ring."

I headed toward where I knew I'd find the kitchen. Luckily, no one was around. It was early, still, and I figured that Grandma—how fun it would be to see her before she was in fact *Grandma*!—was still asleep.

In the kitchen, I walked over to the phone, picked up the receiver, and dialed our New York number, recalling the necessary pre-number codes, having memorized them before leaving New York. I don't know what I expected, but I found myself feeling jittery as the phone rang. Who was at the other end of this line? Where was this phone sitting, on the other side of the world, as it rang on and on? It could not possibly be ringing in our Brooklyn brownstone—as there was no house belonging to the woman I knew as my mama, since she wasn't yet a woman; she was, in fact, the girl I'd just been talking to in the other room!

For that matter, where was Grandma—the Grandma I knew, not Talia's young mother, who was still asleep in her room here, in this different-though-still-the-same house? And where was *I*—the *me* of *my* time? Had I disappeared from the house I knew as Grandma's house, ahead in the future? Was Grandma frantically searching for me? Had she alerted my mother and was she, too, distraught that I was lost? My head was spinning; my thoughts felt like leaves in a cyclone, whipping around and around. A feeling of unbearable bewilderment overcame me. I willed the thoughts to slide away.

Playing along with the strange charade, I talked into the empty echo of the ongoing ring.

"Hi, Mama? It's—um—ah, Jasmine. Is it okay if I stay over at Talia's house again tonight? Yes? Great! I'll see you tomorrow, then.

Around noon." I hung up, aware of a chilly feeling all over, and noticing little goose bumps up and down my arms.

I walked back to Talia's room.

"My mom said it would be just fine," I said. And then, I realized a frightening truth: if I were not to sleep here again, tonight, where would I, in fact, have gone?

Talia's face broke into a smile—a smile I knew intimately and yet did not know at all. She sat up abruptly and threw a pillow at my head.

"Why the serious face? Get dressed. We've got a plane to catch!"

It was a cold, windy day. We put on our jeans and Talia handed me a heavy woolen sweater. "Here," she said. "You'll need a jumper." Jumper—the Australian word for sweater.

We went to the kitchen and fixed ourselves a sandwich to eat on the way—cheese and tomato on whole-wheat bread.

"Where's your mom?" I asked.

"She has trouble falling asleep, so on weekends, she sleeps in."

"Oh," I said, disappointed, as I'd been hoping to meet this different younger Grandma. I pictured her sparkling, fun-loving eyes—and felt a spear of intense yearning for her, though of course here, she'd not yet become a grandmother! Here, she was just Talia's mother.

"Can we wake her?" I said, feeling foolish the minute the words were out.

Talia looked at me oddly.

"Why would we do that? She works hard all week—she deserves a little rest! You *are* a silly thing!"

My heart squeezed tightly. I wouldn't be seeing Grandma, at least not for now.

Outside, the air was crisp, and the sun was dishing up its usual bounty of light. We got into Grandpa's white sports car. Above the silver bumper I read: *Datsun 240Z*. He pulled out of the driveway, accelerating quickly to an impressive speed.

We drove through thoroughfares presided over by older versions of the bright green-and-yellow trams I loved that ran on silver tracks and were guided above by triangular electrical wires attached to their crowns. The trams seemed both lumbering and sleek, like large zoo animals—lions or tigers—bulky at rest but able to spring to graceful action. Grandpa Jack drove with the windows down; I shivered a little at the inrush of cold air. We turned onto smaller streets, lined with old-style Edwardian houses half hidden by overgrown English gardens—lots of dark green shrubbery and heavy hanging foliage. Here and there, we came upon a shopping strip that was already alive with shoppers.

As we progressed into the outer suburbs, the houses became more uniform—rectangular and built of orange brick, with strips of green lawn bordered by neat flower beds, each with the same kinds of flowering plants.

"I love those rhododendrons," Talia said. "Like old ladies dressed up as clowns. Do you know how they get those zany colors? Blue and purple—look, there's one that's hot pink. They pour food coloring into the soil. The roots suck it up and it goes to the blooms."

I liked the pansy borders: mostly bright yellow flowers with patches of black, though there were other colors, too—hot pink, iridescent blue, and white with light purple fringes. Like moth colonies, hovering above the ground with outstretched wings.

Finally, we turned onto a road with a loose-stone surface that ran alongside the small airport. We passed a series of simple hangars: makeshift affairs each consisting of a wooden hut with a light aircraft parked alongside. Grandpa Jack slowed as we approached the security gate; the sign read Moorabbin airport. The guard, sporting a friendly grin, raised the beam.

"G'day, Prof," he called out as we sailed by.

"G'day, Bazza," Grandpa Jack said, raising his hand through the open window.

We pulled up to Hangar Number Five and came to a halt by a small blue-and-white plane: *Cessna 172* was painted prominently on its tail.

"How's my girl!" Grandpa Jack said as he leapt from the car. Talia turned to me with a sheepish smile.

"He only just bought this plane," she said. "It's the latest love of his life."

She gazed proudly over at her father, who was walking around the plane, eyeing it appraisingly.

"My dad collects interests. Did I tell you about his farm? He raises cattle in his spare time—his steer actually win prizes. He also has a passion for ancient Greek and Roman coins. He started an International Numismatic Society. But flying is his number one. Mum hates it. These dinky little planes scare her—and she vomits terribly, every time she goes up. But Michael and I love it. Not sure how Liora feels—I guess she thinks it's okay."

"Where are your brother and sister, anyway?" I asked. What fun it would be to see Uncle Michael as a boy and Auntie Liora as a teenager!

"Michael's sleeping at a friend's house. Liora's away at camp. I thought I told you that already ..."

Talia looked at me again in that sideways manner, as if wondering something, frown marks between her hazel eyes.

"Of course," I said. "I just forgot."

Talia brightened. "Come on! Don't you want to get going?"

We jumped out of the car. A wiry young man carrying a clipboard emerged from the hut, and Grandpa Jack greeted him with the same exuberance he seemed to have for everyone. They exchanged pleasantries, Australian style: *G'day Mate, 'Ow's it goin'?* And Grandpa Jack asked after the man's wife and baby. Then it was all flying jargon—longitudes, latitudes, headwinds, tailwinds. Grandpa took the clipboard, then climbed into the pilot's seat and immediately began checking the instruments and fiddling with dials.

We climbed into the four-seater plane after him. I'd never been in an aircraft so small. As we wedged our way into the back, I was struck by how flimsy it all seemed. The windows opened outward with a silver lever, like old-fashioned car windows. The smell of new leather mixed in with the repulsive odor of airplane fuel.

"Okay, kids. Are you ready?" Grandpa Jack asked.

"Ready for takeoff, Dad!" Talia said. Grandpa Jack hand-signaled to the young man waving triangular flags on the ground, then began to turn knobs and pull levers. The engine whirred to life.

Soon we were taxiing down the runway, which was much shorter and narrower than the commercial runways I was used to. The body of the plane rattled, the engine roared and the propellers whirred. As the plane lifted from the ground and we glided up into the air, the rattling diminished. The intense smell of airplane fuel sent a wave of nausea through me.

"Don't worry, it gets better!" Talia said over the roaring engine. I could see Grandpa Jack's strong, handsome profile from where I sat diagonally behind him; he had a marvelous look in his face—a combination of intelligence, concentration, and joy.

The landscape unfurled beneath us. The boxy orange-brick houses soon gave way to countryside: a raggedy mix of brush, undergrowth, and towering eucalyptus that opened out into an uneven patchwork of cultivated fields in rich shades of browns and greens.

The little plane rode low over the fields. I could see all kinds of detail: trucks and cars crawling along dirt roadways, farmhouses and outbuildings dotting the fields, even miniature people, going about their business.

We flew for some time in silence. The nausea lifted and I was able to enjoy the feeling of speed. Talia looked intently out the window. The fields spread out beneath us in seemingly endless supply, as if the whole world were fertile ground, freshly tilled and sown.

"Hey," Talia said, her voice now audible over the grinding hum. "Let's play a game!"

"Sure," I said, wondering what kind of game we could play up here in the noisy, vibrating plane.

"Let's do Where, What, With Whom." Talia was wearing a mischievous expression I of course knew well—open, fun loving, and a bit outrageous.

"I'll start. Let's use the first letter rule."

"Hmmm," I said, though I had no clue what she was talking about.

"Go on, you galah, give me a letter!"

Galah. A word Mama had used in jest ever since I was little.

"*M*," I said, entranced by the fun in Talia's face.

"*M*," she said, then without missing a beat: "'Merica, Manuscript-maker, Mind-worker. There! Now the questions."

"'Merica doesn't count," I said. "You can't just drop a letter like that to make it work!"

"Yes, I can," she said. "Truth rules—and that's the truth, I feel it. As long as you can shoehorn the truth into the parameters, you're golden." She gave a quick wink. "Kind of like life, don't you think?"

The truth, I thought. America, Manuscript-maker—a writer. That was on the money. Talia—my mother—would move to America and become a writer. As for the *With Whom*, which I took to mean the person who was to be one's life partner, she'd uncannily gotten that right as well. Talia was going to marry a professor—mind-worker was a perfect descriptor!—the man I knew would be the *love of her life*, the words my mother had used when she told me how she and my father had met, perhaps my favorite of all my mother's personal anecdotes.

"Mind-worker … what exactly is that supposed to mean?" I asked.

"You know, someone who earns their living with their mind."

"A thinker, then," I said.

"Bingo. I don't know—a professor, maybe?"

There was a quick reversion in Talia's eyes to opacity, as if she were looking inward. Her face grew serious. "Yes, it's right. I can feel it—I'd be willing to offer a guarantee. You can call me one day to congratulate me—I don't know ten, maybe fifteen years from now! Course, it will be long-distance, so you better have a career that throws up lots of dosh. Other questions?"

"How many kids? What sex? What will they be like?" The words shot out of my mouth before I had time to consider.

"Two. A girl and a boy. The boy will be quirky—funny, a bit of a rogue. The girl, well, she'll be more serious. An artist of some kind." Her smile had turned soulful; she eyed me with an unwavering gaze.

"Kind of like you, Jasmine," she said, grabbing my hand and giving it a squeeze. "I hope so, in any case. Your turn. Letter *Q*."

"No fair … " I said.

Talia let out a ripple of laughter. "Come on, give it a go!"

"OK. Quebec—I don't have much choice about that. What other

place is there? Queen of the Artists, as you suggest. And Quintuplet-maker. There, I'll be marrying a fertility doctor! You've boxed me into Quite the future!"

Below us, the richly colored patchwork melted away, replaced by long stretches of dry yellow grass and clumps of grayish-green vegetation. We flew in silence, aloft in clear blue skies streaked with foggy cloud.

Looming ahead, I saw the rise of stony brown mountains.

I turned to see that Talia's face was alive with excitement.

"This is my favorite part," she said. "Heading toward the Barrier Range."

I craned my neck to take in the impressive sweep of the landscape, which now showed true desert of the most extraordinary color—bright orangey-red, with outcroppings of similarly colored rock. Along one ridge were the signs of a small city, its patches of green a startling interruption to the aridness all around.

"There it is. Broken Hill," Talia said, pointing to the town.

Grandpa Jack began a burst of renewed activity at the controls.

"Coming in for a landing."

A landing strip appeared, at the side of which stood a tall pole with a large wind sock that thrust out forcefully in a horizontal direction.

"We've got a strong headwind!" Grandpa Jack said. "I'm going to circle around and come in from the other side."

The plane swerved in a U-turn; I clutched onto the chrome handle above my seat.

"I'm bringing her down!" Grandpa Jack said. The intense rattling resumed, the propellers increased their whirring, and the engine heightened its roar. There was another sickening blast of fumes. My stomach lurched, and I grabbed for the sick bag in the seat-back pocket. Talia smiled sympathetically as I heaved into the bag. She reached over and held my arm.

"The first time is the worst," she said above the noise.

Then, we were bumping over the tarmac. The engine shut down, the whirring stopped. I crumpled up the sick bag and listened to the sudden, intense silence.

"Great flight, girls. What do you think?" Grandpa Jack said with a grin. "Sorry about that, Jasmine," he added, nodding toward the sick bag I was holding. "You've been inaugurated. It will only get better."

We clambered down, to be greeted by another man, this one older than his Moorabbin counterpart.

"G'day, Prof. 'Ow's it goin'? J'ave a good flight?"

"A beauty." Grandpa Jack clapped the man on the back.

"Welcome to New South Wales!" the man said, helping us down from the plane.

There were three rickety taxis waiting at the large wooden hut that was the Broken Hill Royal Flying Doctor Service airport. We climbed into one of them and headed for the town. I marveled at the redness of the desert soil as we drove—even richer in tone than it had seemed from the sky. The clumps of dry vegetation were subtle shades of mauve and dusty green.

We drove through the residential outskirts—simple fenced-in houses with sparse, rocky front yards—and entered the commercial district, passing several hotel pubs boasting the impressive Victorian wooden and wrought iron balconies I'd seen in Melbourne. In front of each were several horses hitched to posts. We decided to have lunch in one of the pubs and then head toward the Miners Memorial.

After a lunch of hot meat pies, an Australian specialty, followed by a bowl of vanilla ice cream, we set out along Federation Way toward the Line of Lode, the central mining location. It seemed that from anywhere in the town, one could see the towering structures of the mining industry, some rusty and ancient, others modern and new.

I asked Talia about Broken Hill's history; having flown here many times with her father—I had to keep reminding myself that he was my Grandpa Jack!—she had lots of facts at her fingertips. She told me the structures were called "dumps" and "headframes," and that it had been here, in the mid-nineteenth century, that Australia's mining industry was born. Part of the country's leap from a largely agricultural society into the industrial age.

"Did you know that the eight-hour workday came into being right here, in Broken Hill, New South Wales, Australia? The rest of the Western world has us to thank for that."

Beneath Talia's enthusiasm, however, I sensed a sadness, which I found a little confusing. It was a lovely day—hotter, here, than it had been in Melbourne—and there was much to see and do; to me, it was a grand adventure. Perhaps she was a little bored with the place, having been here so many times, though I sensed there was more to it.

At the end of Federation Way, we stopped to examine the Miners Memorial. Talia rattled off the local history; every now and then Grandpa Jack jumped in to add some point of interest.

I realized what was troubling in Talia's descriptions. She lacked the pride that was clear in the voice of the taxi driver as he described the sights, or in the manner of the man at the airport who'd welcomed us to New South Wales. For all her knowledge of the place, Talia sounded like a tourist—as if, like me, she were merely a visitor from some foreign place and time. As if all the things she was talking about were just facts from a history book with little to do with her.

Grandpa Jack went off in search of a men's room; Talia and I sat on a bench, watching the other visitors to the memorial as they milled around, enjoying the early-afternoon warmth.

"You know an awful lot about this place," I said.

Talia shrugged. She was watching a group of children playing tag ahead on the path.

"Dad likes to come here. It's an easy flight from Melbourne. Mum's sick of going with him and my brother and sister are always busy—he plays sports, she does music and dance. So, I come along."

"I noticed something earlier," I said. "It struck me as a little strange."

"Oh?"

"It was like you were talking as a tourist."

71

"I am a tourist, really. I don't live here, after all."

"No, I mean like you're not—I don't know, an Australian."

"Well I'm not Australian. Not really." She looked a bit startled, as if her own words had come as a surprise.

"But you've spent your whole life here!"

"We're immigrants. You know that. I was born in South Africa and came here as a baby."

The children she'd been watching wandered off; Talia cast about a distracted gaze. "You seem to know a lot about my family," she said, a flash of confusion in her face.

"Only what I've learned from you," I said, thinking of the times my mother had talked to me about her early life.

"It's funny, being a Jew. I always feel somehow like we're, I don't know—well, temporary."

Two enormous black-and-white magpies plopped from nowhere onto the path in front of us, and set about their nonchalant, hoppy bird-walk.

Talia's face relaxed into a faint smile. "Quirky little chaps, aren't they," she said, watching the magpies poking about in the clumps of scraggy greenery at the edge of the path.

"I suppose it's silly of me ... World War II is already history ... it's weird ... but I feel like I have to be on guard ... "

I didn't fully understand what Talia was talking about. And yet I recognized something—the dark brooding that came over her, along with a familiar shadow of anxiety in myself.

"My brother got beaten up one time—not badly, but still. And someone in a pastry shop once told me to *Go Home*. I said—where? Where should I go?"

Talia gave a forced, humorless little laugh. "Hardly counts as serious anti-Semitism. But it kind of bites into how you feel about a place. Do you know what I mean?"

I didn't really know what she meant, so I remained silent.

"It's nothing compared with the racism here. It makes me sick the way the First Australians are treated. As if they don't count at all."

I knew that look in Talia's face—I'd seen it in Mama's. Talia—it hit me afresh: *Mama as a girl!*

"The Jews have been exiled so many times," she said, her voice far away.

I tried to remember what I knew—the Babylonian Exile, the expulsion from Spain, decades of pogroms, the Holocaust. It was all jumbled up in my mind. Not only exiles, but murder, mass murder, genocide. How little I knew about any of it—the child of a Jewish mother, and yet I knew almost nothing about Jewish history.

"It doesn't make any sense, does it," she said. "White Australia is all about exile—not just criminals, but poor people who might have stolen a bit of bread for their kids. Sent away—*Beyond the Seven Seas*—forever, forbidden to return to England, their home. I should feel a kinship with that. I don't know ..."

Talia was staring at the magpies with an intensity I recognized; I was here with Mama, after all, though she was not yet my mother ...

The magpies flapped their wings then lifted off; Talia followed their movement with her gaze, her face softening into an expression of appreciative calm.

"Hey," she said, brightening. "Wanna race?" She jumped up, scanned the surrounds. "Okay. Over to that tree, around it five times, across to the pub with the veranda, up and down the steps three times, then back over here."

Not waiting for a response, she crouched to a racing preparation position. I assumed the same position then repeated the instructions she'd just given.

"Ready ... set ... *Go!*"

I glanced across to see Talia's long, dark hair flying behind her, heard the rippling laugh I knew deep in my bones, though the tone was lighter, the pitch of a girl's voice. A raw feeling of joy took hold of me, intensified by the sheer pleasure of rapid motion. My legs pumped beneath me and all thought fell away; in my vision were blurred swatches of faded color against bright blue and cloud, the rusty color of dessert clay, and people turned to fluid streaks.

We arrived back at our starting place and collapsed, laughing.

"Incredible," Talia said through soft gasps. "Dead heat. You'd think we were twins!"

I tried to return her broad, unselfconscious grin, but found myself constrained by pangs of longing: for that different-same person—my mother, as I knew her—who was both here and not here. Just then, Grandpa Jack returned.

"Sorry, girls. Got carried away talking to a nice chap—he's also a pilot. He told me about a different route to Melbourne; might be fun to have a change of scenery on the way back. Let's go visit the base of the Royal Flying Doctor Service, first. It's not far."

He paused, looking at our reddened faces. "What've you girls been up to?" he asked, tousling Talia's hair. "Shenanigans, ey? Flying around in your own way."

Another pang—a wish that Grandpa Jack would tousle my hair, too. A moment later, he did.

My mother had told me about the famous "flying doctors" of Australia, who responded to emergencies in the Outback. Grandpa Jack, himself a surgeon, had visited the base many times and knew people there.

We took another jalopy of a taxi and sat in silence as we bounced along the road. Looking out the window, I felt a kind of visual hunger—like I'd been starving for these colors, for this rocky-red clay earth, for the sage-and-olive hues of nature's green, here, so different from what I was used to back home.

At the base we were welcomed with the good-natured cheer that was as bright and abundant here as the light. Everybody seemed to know Grandpa Jack, who had an impressive ability to remember people's names and those of husbands and children and wives. There was lots of backslapping and arms flung around shoulders. Talia seemed to enjoy it all and showed me around the base as she'd shown me around other parts of Broken Hill.

We were invited to join a group for tea; by this time, we were hungry again and happily tucked into scones with strawberry jam and clotted cream, and lamingtons—cubes of yellow sponge cake soaked in chocolate sauce and rolled in coconut. The teapot seemed like the treacle jug in an Enid Blyton story my mother read to me when I was little: magically and endlessly full. I must have gulped down five cups of the strong, sweet, milky brew.

"Good Lord!" Grandpa Jack said, looking at his watch. "I had no idea of the time. We really must get going. I don't relish the thought of flying in the dark."

Out the window, I saw the light fading and the sky streaked orange and pink.

We made quick business of our goodbyes then climbed into the car of a guy who offered to drive us to the airport. By the time we got to the hangar where Grandpa Jack's Cessna awaited us, the sun was bobbing down behind the mountains and the air was hazy with dusk.

"We've done this hop at night before, eh Tal?" Grandpa Jack said. "It's always gone without a hitch."

Despite the casual sound of his voice, I could see a shadow of anxiety in Grandpa Jack's face.

He turned his concentration to the instruments. Talia and I sat silently in the back seats, looking out at the darkening shapes of the mining structures that crouched above Broken Hill like protective, watchful beasts.

The engine started up: whirring, rattling, the sickening wafts of diesel fuel. We lifted from the ground and were airborne. Gone, now, that carefree thrill I'd felt upon taking off in Melbourne, when we'd found ourselves high up in a sunny sky, with its weightless blue freedom, the landscape spread out cheerfully before us. Now, we flew into dark shadows that swallowed our sight as if we were entering a cave, the whirring propellers like flapping bat wings in my ears.

I focused on my breath, tried to still the rapid pounding of my heart. We were silent, as if clenching our mental strength to help Grandpa Jack navigate the dark skies and bring us safely home.

All of a sudden, I realized that we were turning around in a large arc. Something in the atmosphere of the plane seemed to have changed; I felt it, pure anguish coming from the pilot seat where Grandpa Jack was engaged in a new burst of activity at the controls. Then, I heard his voice. Quiet, low, but what he said was unmistakable.

"Shit! I've taken a wrong turn." He paused, busy at the controls. "Sorry about the language, girls. Don't worry, it'll be fine." There was something ominous in his tone.

We circled again, another wide arc, which seemed to go on forever. As the propellers ground away at the increasingly dark night air, I could feel my heart pounding with panic. For a moment, we went into an eerie, slow descent; we seemed to hover for an instant, as if the plane were taking a quick, short breath and holding it in—and then, a sudden blast of acceleration.

Something was happening to the wind; the whistling turned to a howl, and the windows shook wildly.

"Don't worry, girls!" Grandpa Jack shouted again from the front seat, but his voice was unconvincing. And then something further I couldn't make out.

This was probably just typical when flying in a small aircraft, I said to myself, searching for calm. They must have been through this kind of thing many times—and Grandpa Jack was so brilliant and knowledgeable, surely he knew what to do. I looked over at Talia, expecting her to shoot me a reassuring smile, to reach over and pat my arm. Instead, her face was ashen and there was fear in her eyes. She reached over, but instead of patting my arm, she gripped my hand and held fast. The panic rose in me like pressurized steam. *Oh my god,* I thought. *I might die here, in the Australian Outback! Without even having a chance to say goodbye to Mama and Papa and Billy!* The plane was now thwacking about, as if the air outside were pummeling it. My head banged against the window, wrenching my neck. I felt a jolt of pain wrap around my skull.

"We're coming in for a landing!" Grandpa Jack shouted above the racket of the propellers. He was no longer trying to sound nonchalant.

"But Dad! There's no airstrip!"

"It's pretty smooth ground. There's a strong tailwind and there seems to be something wrong with one of the props. Tighten your belts!"

I reeled as the plane tipped sharply, and Talia and I were jammed up against each other. I gripped her as she'd been gripping me, our panic turning to terror. I yanked hard on the seat belt flap, which had been comfortably loose across my lap, then glanced at Grandpa Jack, who was battling the steering control, his face clenched with concentration. Another dip, this time in the opposite direction, and then a forward slant.

Now we were tipping even farther forward—not quite a nose dive, but definitely heading in a direction that didn't seem right for a plane: directly down. Grandpa Jack's face was white. Talia's was mottled grayish-green. My stomach plunged and I let out a thin scream. I realized that Talia was doing the same, calling out "*Maaaa-maaaa,*" in a panicky voice.

In a flash, we were hurtling toward the ground. The earth thrust up toward us, trying to meet us halfway. A series of powerful jolts shook the plane; I heard a horrible crunching, and then an unnerving, smoldering stench filled the cabin. The whirring propeller suddenly ceased.

Then, we were bouncing along the ground. Talia was still gripping my arm and we were slammed first against one side of the plane and then against the other. I closed my eyes tightly and a picture of Billy's pixie face appeared in my mind, nose crinkled and eyes twinkling. Then Papa: elegant, thoughtful, kind. And Mama. Not tired, thin Mama, but funny, lively Mama, her face shining with love.

For a moment, we were off the ground again. I opened my eyes and looked through the window to see that we were sailing over what seemed to be a small hill. The wing and propeller on my side of the plane were no longer there. The plane—what was left of it—tipped ninety degrees, and we came to a sudden halt, in a position that had all three of us, still strapped into our seats, perpendicular to the ground.

There was a long and echoing silence.

"Girls. Are you alright?" Grandpa's steady voice came from the front seat, where he was struggling to unlatch his pilot's harness.

I heard Talia's voice from beside me, shaky and weak.

"Okay, here, Dad. Jasmine?"

"Okay, too." My own voice sounded as shaky as Talia's.

"Quick, girls. Out! The tank might blow!"

My seat belt snapped free. I reached above my head to where the door now was and managed to hoist myself up and push the door upward. One by one, we climbed up and out of the cabin. As we scrambled from the plane, I could see, in the moonlight, that the cabin was all that was left of Grandpa Jack's spanking new blue-and-white Cessna. Wings, tail, propellers, and nose had all been ripped clear—by trees?—in our crash landing. It was a miracle that the cabin had remained intact, and that we were unharmed.

"Holy moly," Grandpa said, a great weight of relief compressed into the sound of his whisper.

As we hurried away from the plane, I could see that Talia was limping. I took her hand and we crossed quickly—some two or three hundred yards, picking our way through undergrowth that included thick, dry branches and crackly old leaves. Here and there, bits of twisted debris from the plane shone dully in the moonlight. We stopped under a tall eucalyptus tree, crouching beneath its leaves.

Grandpa Jack was very still, and serious. After a time, he said: "I don't think the tank's going to blow. I'm going back to the cabin to fetch some supplies. You stay here."

He strode back toward the cabin and clambered up the wreckage, disappearing into the hole below the open door, which looked like the stiff, outthrust wing of a dead bird. Talia lowered herself to the ground. Only then did I notice the tear in her jeans at the calf, and the dark stains growing on either side of the tear.

"Talia," I said, trying to keep the panic out of my voice, "you're hurt."

She looked down, placed her hand by the wound.

"God, I didn't even notice."

"Does it hurt?"

"I guess so," she said, her face going pale. "Now that I'm paying attention to it."

Grandpa Jack's head had reappeared above the open door of what was left of the plane, and I saw him place several objects on top of the cabin. He re-entered and again reemerged, his arms full. It took him two trips to get all the stuff back to where we were sitting under the tree. He set everything down.

"Talia's injured," I said.

"Darling, what's wrong?" he asked, kneeling beside her, his brow furrowed.

Talia pointed to her calf. "I don't think it's serious," Talia said.

Grandpa Jack grabbed the first aid kit he'd brought back with him from the damaged plane, also the flashlight, which he shone close to the wound.

"You're right," he said. "Not too serious, but you will need a few stitches." He sounded relieved, but I could see that his face was still hung with worry. Carefully, he lifted the hem of Talia's bell-bottomed jeans and pulled it up to the knee. Then, he cleaned the wound with a disinfectant wipe and applied several butterfly bandages, pulling them tightly across the wound. He added several dabs of antibiotic cream, then covered the area with a wad of gauze and first aid tape.

"That will do for now," he said, casting a glance around, taking in the surrounds, the tall eucalyptus trees, clumps of grayish-green vegetation and rocky outcroppings in the rust-colored soil.

"Jasmine," he said, eyeing me closely, "you sure you're okay?"

My head was in fact aching where it had banged against the window, and my wrenched neck felt uncomfortable. There was no cut, though, or anything he might tend to. I didn't see the point of worrying him further.

"I'm fine, truly," I said. I reached up and touched the spot on my head that hurt to find a large, tender bump, but no wetness that would suggest blood.

"Okay," Grandpa Jack said, all business now, "let me show you what we have.

We turned to examine the supplies he'd brought from the plane.

Two warm, lightweight blankets; the first aid kit; an emergency box that contained a compact lantern, three flashlights, spare batteries, flares, and a Swiss Army knife with all the extras; a fire-making kit—lighter fluid, several gas cigarette lighters, and a compressed material that functioned as tinder; and a carton of food supplies—dried beef jerky, several cans of tuna, a box of tea bags, six large bottles of water, dried milk, sugar, three packets of Marie biscuits, and four large bars of Cadbury milk chocolate.

There was also a "billy" drinking tin. And a lightweight tent folded into a pouch, with several retractable aluminum poles shortened to a length of about six inches and attached to the pouch with a clip.

Surveying our goods, the reality of what had just happened hit me and I started to shake—from the top of my head down through my fingertips and all the way to my toes. I could hear my own teeth chattering. Talia must have heard them too.

"Jasmine. You're shaking like a leaf!" She wrapped a blanket around my shoulders.

Grandpa Jack eyed me with concern. "We're very lucky, you know, girls. That little plane sure took care of us."

"It's like it decided to take all the hits, and spare us," Talia said, glancing toward the wreckage strewn for several hundred yards around us. The moon, which had been mysteriously absent during our doomed flight, was not very bright, but we could see fairly well by its light.

"All these trees helped," Grandpa Jack said. "Once we got close to the ground, they broke the speed."

The plane had careened through the trees, which in ripping off the wings, the propellers, the nose, and the tail, had brought the plane to a halt.

"I can't believe the cabin wasn't crushed," I said through my chattering teeth.

Grandpa Jack nodded. "I know. It's a good plane, that Cessna. Look, girls. I'm going to go for help."

He glanced again at Talia's calf. "It's fine for now, don't worry. But I do want to get that leg of yours seen to. I'm not sure exactly where we are, but you can see that we're well out of the desert, at least. You should be all right through the night. It's cool, but it shouldn't get too cold. You have the blankets, and it's safe to make a fire in this clearing, if you want; it's not too dry."

He explained how to use the flares, then picked out a few supplies to take with him: one flashlight, extra batteries, a bottle of water, a package of biscuits, and one bar of chocolate.

"Just stay put. I'll get back as quickly as I can."

He gave Talia a hug and kissed her cheek. Then, he turned to me.

"How about a quick hug for the road," he said, enveloping me in his arms.

The shaking in my body stopped. Tears sprang to my eyes. I realized that all my life, I'd longed for my grandfather—longed for the three grandparents I'd never known.

He whispered one last thing to Talia, and then was off, loping into the bush with his forthright stride. I was hoping Talia would tell me what it was he'd said, but I didn't want to intrude by asking.

"Good old Dad," Talia said. "He'll be back sooner than you think. He has a way of making things right."

I thought of Papa, back in New York, or should I say, ahead in New York. It suddenly occurred to me: here, it is 1974, which would have made my father—not, of course, yet my father—a boy of seventeen. Was he at school, now? Sitting in a classroom? Kicking a soccer ball around a field? I thought of the permanent furrow that creased his brow, etched there by years of worrying that seemed imposed on him by his nature. I thought of the way he looked at me from beneath that furrowed brow, his blue eyes filled with affection.

"My father has the oddest expressions. Just now he said: '*Give it a tonk, Tal!*' That's what he says when I have some challenge to face, like a difficult exam."

"Is he always so cheerful?" I asked.

"Pretty much. I bet my dad just popped out into the world with a grin, then went scooting about in search of anything and everything to be interested in and love."

Talia could have been describing Billy! His temperament must have come directly from Grandpa Jack. The thought of her father seemed to energize Talia, lifting her concern.

"I may as well get a fire going," she said. "Why don't you figure out the tent? It probably just springs up somehow and then needs the poles stretched out and inserted."

"You okay to do that? Your leg …" I said.

"It's nothing, truly. I'm fine," Talia said, rising and testing her weight on the leg. I watched her head toward the little eucalyptus woods, favoring the good leg.

Talia was right. The tent did spring up, once I unfolded it and pulled here and there on the flexible wire frame. I unfurled the aluminum poles and found the narrow pockets into which they slid. Fifteen minutes later, I was admiring my work.

"Home sweet home!" I announced.

Talia, busy over the pile of twigs and logs she'd gathered, turned toward me and grinned. "Who needs civilization?"

Then, I saw her freeze. The next instant, I heard what she'd heard. A crackle and snap. There was a pause. Then another crackle and snap. Talia carefully laid down the lighter and phial of fluid she'd been holding, put a finger to her lips and made a barely audible "Sssh." I froze, too, and listened. There it was again. The crackle of dry leaves, the tiny snap of a twig. Crackle again, no snap this time. The sound of a heavy tread. Not a small animal, or even a large one. It was the sound of a person, someone who was carefully choosing each step to avoid making too much noise.

I crouched, peered through the foliage. I thought I saw the bottom of a pair of pants—blue jeans.

"Hello?" I said, without thinking. "Who's there?"

A man emerged from the clump of bushes, barefoot, taking in the scene. The blue jeans had frayed bottoms and tears in both knees. A football shirt of some kind completed his outfit; it was black with a diagonal red stripe. His eyes were wide set and dark; his long, stringy hair was light brown and streaked blond. Pursing his lips, he let out a low whistle.

"See you had big trouble with your plane, eh?" he said. "I never liked planes myself. I like to get about on these," and he slapped his thighs.

"You barrack for Essendon?" Talia said. The man's face relaxed into a grin. "Nope, Collingwood. Me mate gave me this as a joke. But I don't go in for footy much anymore. Not since I left town."

He tossed his head in Talia's direction. A small flame had leapt up from the little pile she'd built.

"You wanna keep that goin' or you'll lose it. You girls got a billy? I could use a cuppa myself." He reached behind him and tugged at something around his waist. His hand reappeared and I saw he was holding a tin mug.

"Jimmy's the name. Walkabout's my game. Sorry if I scared you."

He strode up toward us and hunkered down near the fire, which was spurting to life.

"Nice fire," he said, looking into the flames, which were beginning to dance blue and yellow in the dark night air.

"Only kidding, about the walkabout." He pointed to our faces. "*Gubba* think we Kooris are always goin' walkabout." I figured that *gubba* was an Aboriginal word for *white people*. "We do, now and then. Sometimes, though, we're just goin' from one place to another, like anyone. I got work down in Menindee." Jimmy pointed again, this time toward the plain stretching out beneath us. "Down there, by the Darling River."

Jimmy looked back in the direction of the plane wreckage. "So, what happened, anyway?"

The inflections of Jimmy's voice intrigued me; his Aussie accent was broader than Talia's and Grandpa Jack's. I was also wondering whether or not to be scared. There was something disconcerting about Jimmy, though I couldn't put my finger on it. I felt in my gut though that he meant us no harm.

Talia gave a brief account of our misadventure.

"Your dad will be back here, one two three," Jimmy said, eyeing Talia as she picked up one of our bottles to pour water into the billy. "Hang onto that, you'll need it. The Darling's got lots of little creeks and stuff. They're like her granddaughters. Nice, sweet water. Just have to know where."

Jimmy reached over, took the billy and disappeared back into the scrub.

Talia and I looked at each other.

"What d'ya reckon?" Talia said.

"I don't know," I said. "He seems nice and like he wants to help. But there's something odd about him." I pulled the blanket tightly around my shoulders.

Talia nodded. "I know what you mean."

"His face is smooth, but he has the eyes of an old man. No, a child. I don't know, it goes back and forth, like he's young and old at the same time."

We were both quiet for a while.

"I've never met an Aboriginal person before," I said.

"There aren't a lot of Aboriginal peoples in the city," Talia said. "Not in Melbourne. I knew an Aboriginal girl, Alexi, when I was in third grade. She lived in the orphanage. I went there a few times to play with her. She slept in a dormitory with the other girls, and they were all like sisters. But the housemother was horrible. The kids were scared of her."

Talia poked among the sticks on the ground in front of her.

"I never asked her what happened to her parents. Why she was living in the orphanage, not with relatives or something." Her voice was grim, her face looked tight and closed. "I've thought about her a lot lately. With all the news stories about *the stolen generations*. I can't believe the terrible things our government did. This is their country, their land. Imagine! Stealing children from their homes. Destroying families. Decimating cultures. Makes me want to run away to some-place else. But where would I go? It's not like there's some perfect place where peoples have never been mistreated."

I thought of Billy, asking that little boy in Nashville if he was a slave: thought of our own terrible history, in all its brutality. Of the countless injustices that still prevailed in so many areas of our society.

"After I left primary school, I never saw Alexi again. I always felt like there was some awful secret going on. I can't explain it, but I felt it. And it was *true!* There *was* an awful secret!" Talia's eyes filled with tears. "I want to—I don't know, say sorry to her."

This seemed to make Talia remember something. She sat up bolt straight. "You know, the Aboriginal people have asked the Australian government to apologize for their terrible brutality. For stealing children. For destroying their culture. And the government won't! They're too afraid of having stuff taken away from them—the land that they stole in the first place!"

I remembered so clearly the day, a few years ago, when Mama excitedly showed me the video recording of the new Australian prime minister finally issuing the long overdue apology to the First Nations. *Way too late, and way too little,* Mama had said, but still, she had smiled through her tears as she watched. I closed my eyes and again saw in my mind's eye the prime minister, reading from his notes, heard again his words—so clearly, as if he were speaking right into my ear. *"To the mothers and fathers, the brothers and sisters, for the breaking up of families and communities, we say Sorry. And for the indignity and degradation thus inflicted on a proud people and a proud culture, we say Sorry."*

I wanted to take Talia's hand and tell her that one day, many years from now—thirty-four to be exact—Prime Minister Kevin Rudd would finally issue the apology to the First Nations, though of course this would do nothing to undo the unforgivable wrongs that had traumatized the Aboriginal peoples.

So much had happened in the past day, I found myself feeling confused trying to take it all in. Before I could sort my thoughts out, Jimmy reappeared, holding our billy, filled to the brim with water.

"That was quick," Talia said. "The river must be nearby. Funny, I don't hear the sound of water."

Jimmy set the billy down on the string Talia had rigged up, tied to two long, sturdy sticks, above the thriving flames of the fire.

"It's just a creek," he said. "I hear it. But my ears are from around these parts. You girls from the city, yeah?"

We both nodded.

"Here—look," Jimmy said, walking a few yards to where the bush thinned a little. He gestured to us to follow. Rising, my knees creaked, and my ankles wobbled. We followed Jimmy and then all three of us crouched down by a bare patch in among the bushes. Jimmy pointed through this opening. I saw a glimmer and, a moment later, heard the faint sound of moving water, as if my glimpse of the creek had brought the sound to my ears.

Jimmy smiled, as if he'd just sighted an old friend.

"*Gubba* give some real stupid names to things," he said. Then caught himself, adding: "No offense. But I like that one—the Darling River. She *is* a darling. She's my mother's sister."

We walked back together to the fire.

"You girls hungry?" Jimmy asked. "I've got some bush tucker."

"Yes, please," I said. We'd not eaten since our afternoon tea at the Flying Doctor Service base. Talia nodded, too. Jimmy opened the canvas satchel that was slung across his chest and drew out a bag of sliced white bread—what we called, in America, "Wonder Bread"—a jar of mayonnaise, and a package wrapped in wax paper and tied with twine.

"Dried 'roo meat," he said, untying the twine and pulling some reddish-brown strips from the wax paper. I let out a little involuntary groan.

"No worries," he said. "Tastes just like chicken." He proceeded to coat three slices of the white bread with a thick layer of mayonnaise then placed a single strip of dried meat on each. He handed one open sandwich to Talia, the second to me, then placed his own on a large dried leaf in front of him.

The water was beginning to boil; Talia put a teabag in each cup, filled them with hot water, and added a teaspoon of dried milk and sugar.

Jimmy bowed his head in what looked like mock prayer, a little smile playing around his lips.

"Rub a dub dub. Thanks for the grub. Yay, Lord!" How amazing! That was the funny grace Mama had taught us when we were little, the one Billy loved to say. An Aussie thing, poking fun at everything. I was surprised, though, that Jimmy just happened to know it and trot it out now.

"Grace," he said through his mouthful of sandwich. "Learned that from my *gubba* mates at school."

Jimmy was beginning to see, I think, that neither of us seemed to get his jokes very well. I didn't know how Talia felt, but I was a little nervous. Here we were alone with a man who was a complete stranger.

Jimmy put down his sandwich, chewing thoughtfully.

"You very safe, here," Jimmy said, his smile gone. He had read my mind! That seemed to keep happening here, on my strange journey. "This is friendly country. We're happy to have you here. I'm gonna wait with you till your dad comes back. I will tell you about this country, if you like. I will introduce you, very serious."

Now, he looked directly into my eyes. "I'll even tell you secrets— some secrets of my people, of this land."

The kangaroo meat tasted surprisingly good—Jimmy had been right, it was like chicken, with a gamey aftertaste. And it went surprisingly well with the white bread and mayonnaise. Maybe I was just so hungry I'd have found live witchetty grubs delicious!

For a moment, I recalled seeing the kangaroos at the Melbourne zoo on two past trips to Australia with my parents. But then I reminded myself that for farmers, kangaroos were pests—like rabbits could be in America. In parts of the country, kangaroos had over-multiplied and needed to be controlled to maintain the ecological balance.

The fire quickly warmed our hands, feet, and faces. It also provided additional light, by which I could make out the contours of the bush around us. As I looked around, the dark shapes of the unusual variety of bushes and trees started to seem like appealing creatures that might soon uproot themselves from the dusty brown soil and join us around the fire.

Jimmy had finished eating and was drinking his tea, his face glowing in the firelight. He turned toward me and I saw that his eyes had changed once again. No longer young-old but timeless, like water or sky.

"You want to know about my people?" he asked, his eyes brushing over me like a breeze.

I nodded.

"I want to know, too," Talia said.

"When the *gubba*—white man—first came here, you know, real long time ago, he said to his boss, no man owns this land. No fields ploughed, no houses or churches. Okay, no owners, we take the land. They was wrong, of course. My people was here. Many peoples, all one people.

"Even today, a lot of people say Kooris never ploughed, never grew wheat, never planted apple trees and orange trees. We never had to. Our mother, the earth, she gave herself freely to us. And because we respected her and loved her, we never had to go and do all them other things. That would have been harming our mother. So we just took what she gave us.

"You see, this land, it is my father's land, my grandfather's land, my grandmother's land. I am related to it, it give me my identity. That's why I left town and came back to live on the land that is the land of my grandfather and grandmother."

Jimmy looked at me again with airy eyes—like he was looking right through me.

"Our story is in the land … it is written in those sacred places, that's the law. Dreaming place … you can't change it, no matter who you are.

"This is what Kooris—Aboriginal people—believe. I believe it is true for all peoples, *gubba* too. Just they don't know it. So, like I say, this is my Mother." Jimmy reached down with one hand and stroked the ground at his feet—lovingly, as one might caress a baby.

"Mother to my people. We are the Yuin Monaro. We live here a very long time, all the way back to the Beginning, to the time of the Dreaming."

Jimmy paused. He seemed to be thinking something over. Again, he looked at me—singling me out, I felt, which made me a little uncomfortable. Talia did not seem to notice.

I had the uncanny feeling that Jimmy knew me, or had known me, long ago.

"You are interested in water, no?" Jimmy said to me with that faint and private smile. "Our Darling River. My people have depended on it since the Beginning. I will tell you how the waters came to our Mother. I will tell you about the creation of Toonkoo and Ngaardi, in the Dreamtime.

"When Darama, the Great Spirit, came down to the earth, he made all the animals and the birds. He gave them all their names. He also made Toonkoo and Ngaardi. One day, Toonkoo said to Ngaardi that he'd go out hunting. He went out hunting kangaroos and emus, while Ngaardi stayed home and got some bush tucker. She was waiting and waiting, but Toonkoo never came home."

I was getting used to Jimmy's way of speaking; now I could understand everything he said. He was lost in his story, staring into the flames, which sent light and shadow dancing across his features.

"Ngaardi started worrying. Then she started crying and as the tears ran down her face, she made the rivers and creeks come down that mountain. She waited there all day for him to come back with the food, but he never came back.

"As Toonkoo was out there hunting, he chucked a spear and got a kangaroo. Then he walked a bit farther and he looked up and saw Darama, the Great Spirit, up in the sky, watching him. He chucked a spear up to the sky, up to hit Darama, but Darama caught it, bent it, and chucked it back. As it came back it turned into a boomerang. That's how we got our boomerang."

I thought of the boomerang my mother had bought me at the Sydney airport when I was five, on my first trip to Australia, sitting in its pride of place on my bedroom dresser. I saw again the smooth wood with the splashes of color in the center, a lizard painted in traditional Aboriginal dot style, then in my mind's eye looked around my bedroom: the bookshelf packed with my books, the windowsills and shelves mounted on the walls filled with mementos—shells from the beach, pretty rocks and stones I'd foraged during our many family trips. There was the door, leading out onto the hallway, across which my parents' room was to be found.

I turned my attention back to Jimmy's story.

"Toonkoo was out hunting and he was still wild with Darama, so Darama took him away and put him in the moon. As the moon was coming up, Ngaardi was still crying. As she saw the moon coming up over the horizon, over the sea, she looked up into the full moon and there she saw her man, Toonkoo.

"She went to the mountain and she laid down. She said to herself: 'If ever he should come back, I'll leave my heart on the mountain for him to find.' Today, her heart is the red flower called the waratah."

Jimmy's gentle voice cast a spell. I looked over to Talia; to my surprise, she was fast asleep, curled up by the fire, wrapped in a blanket.

Jimmy stared into the dwindling flames. He picked up a stick and poked at the embers.

"You liked the part about the boomerang, yeah?" he asked, still staring into the flames. I sat very still. Had Jimmy *actually* read my mind this time? Could he have known that my thoughts had turned to my own home, so very far away, as his Dreamtime story explained the origin of the boomerang?

I nodded, slowly.

"Boomerangs. They go from the earth—our Mother, our home. They fly up and across, very high. Toonkoo—he sent it all the way into the sky, where the spirit people live. But they come back. They always come back to your country, to your Mother."

I was beginning to understand the special way Jimmy used certain words. For him, the words *country, people, mother, land, earth,* and *home* seemed to all mean more or less the same thing.

"But that's only one message of the story," Jimmy said. He put down the stick and turned to look at me. "And for you, not the main one."

Jimmy's eyes held the reflection of the flames, though he was no longer looking into the fire.

"The story tells of the origins of water in this land. Our land is very dry, which makes water even more precious. The Dreaming story tells us that water—it comes from crying. But it is life."

He looked back into the flames of the fire.

"You know about water, don't you? Anyway, what is your name?"

I almost said Emily but caught myself. "Jasmine," I said. "My name is Jasmine."

Jimmy smiled. "You are a flower. You need water to blossom and grow. You are not red, like waratah, heart flower. But Jasmine: white. Like a star. You are Star Flower. You travel in the sky, but you search for your place. Where you can put in your roots. Find the water of the land. Blossom and grow."

I had begun to tremble again—not from cold, this time, as it was warm by the fire, but from the way Jimmy had reached right in and touched my soul.

How did he *know* all this? About my strange, impossible journey? About *me*?

Jimmy leaned close toward me, placed one hand on my arm.

"You will find your country, your Mother," he said, his hand patting the earth again, as he had done before. "She has cried her river for you and you will come to settle on its banks."

I glanced up at the black sky. The stars shone fiercely.

"Yes, but how do I find it?" I whispered back. Jimmy extended his hand. Tentatively, I reached for it. His palm was smooth and dry.

He put his lips up to my ear, as a child does when telling a secret. "You will hold their sadnesses in your hand," he said, "but you must also be touching their *land*. Then you will tumble, and in your tumbling, you will find what you are looking for."

What did he mean? The thought of the pink baby booties Grandma had given me flashed across my mind; I had forgotten all about them. I stuck my hand in the pocket of my sweater. They closed around the soft little wad. Here they were! They had been with me all along! I clutched onto them. *You will hold their sadnesses in your hand. Then, you will tumble.* I had been holding these booties when the storm had hit in Grandma's house. *You must also be touching their land.* I had been sitting on the *bankie* chair, that beloved object from Grandma's own childhood home, made of rare South African stinkwood, which she had brought to Australia from South Africa—her home, however troubled a home it might have been.

I closed my eyes. The pain in my head had thankfully receded, though my neck still ached. Exhaustion poured through my limbs. The warmth of the fire felt soothing, lapping against my body like hot, feathery waves.

The sound of rumbling wheels snapped my eyes open. I jumped up, Jimmy jumped up; our hands flew apart.

"Your dad. He's back," Jimmy said. In one quick movement, Jimmy had his mug tied around his waist, and his satchel packed. He leaned down, took me by the shoulders, looked at me straight with his deep and changing eyes.

"Remember," he said, "the Dreaming happened long ago, it is happening still, it will always be happening."

His eyes flashed with humor and warmth. "You have a white face, but you are like my people. You must go walkabout to find yourself. Follow the water, it will take you home."

And he was off—a streak in the dark. I stared into the bushes. The leaves, in their small fluttering motion, shuddered and shook a little, and then were still.

Over by the fire, which must have flickered out while Jimmy was saying his goodbye, I saw that Talia had opened her eyes and was looking at me sleepily.

"I hear a motor," I said.

Talia jumped up. On the other side of the spent fire, where the plain stretched out, I could see an open Jeep, bumping along the rocky ground. As it got closer, I saw Grandpa Jack's silver-white hair flying around his handsome, youthful face.

"Look! It's Dad!" Talia limped surprisingly quickly in the direction

of the approaching Jeep. I stayed put, watching as the distance between them closed. The Jeep slowed, then stopped, and Grandpa Jack
leapt out and wrapped his arms around Talia. They stood there like
that for some time. Another man was at the wheel—an Aboriginal
person somewhat older than Jimmy. Soon, Talia and her father were
back in the Jeep heading toward me.

"Jasmine! Talia's been telling me about your visitor. Where is he?"
The Jeep came to a halt. Grandpa Jack climbed out; he put out an arm
and drew me to his side.

"I don't know," I said. "He took off when he heard the Jeep coming."

"Too bad. I would have liked to thank him for taking care of my
two girls."

My heart leapt at this: *my two girls*. Grandpa Jack smiled down
at me. Looking into those welcoming brown eyes, I felt overcome by
a feeling of calm joy; for a moment, the ache of missing home—of
missing Mama and Papa and Billy, my house, my neighborhood, my
friends, my school—vanished. Here, in this foreign time and place,
looking into eyes that were strangely familiar, I was, for an instant,
also home.

"How's the leg, Tal?" he asked.

"Hurts a bit, not too bad," Talia said.

"There's a clinic, about two hours away," Grandpa Jack said. "I'm
exhausted, though. Need a bit of sleep, first. So does Mick, I think.
Give us an hour, then we'll get going."

The man in the Jeep nodded. Both of them did look very tired.
I suddenly noticed that the sky, at the horizon, was faintly streaked
with gold and pink.

"You've been gone longer than I realized," I said.

Grandpa Jack grinned. "Four solid hours of walking in this bush
didn't go so fast for me." He yawned widely.

"I see you've set up the tent. Why don't you girls go in there and
grab some sleep. I'll cuddle up to this rock here."

Talia and I insisted that Grandpa Jack take the tent; he was the
one who'd done all the walking, not to mention the strain of battle-
worthy piloting, before our terrible—but miraculous—crash landing.

With a little coaxing, he agreed. The driver, Mick, stretched out on the back seat of the Jeep and in a moment the sound of his quiet snoring reached our ears.

Talia and I sat back down by the spent fire.

"What happened to Jimmy?" she asked.

"He finished his story and then, when he heard the Jeep, he just took off."

"He didn't say goodbye?"

"Well yes, he did, as a matter of fact. But it was strange—like he was leaving me with a puzzle."

"A puzzle?"

"Something to solve. Something important."

"I missed the ending of the story," Talia said. "I got to the part about Ngaardi crying tears that became the rivers and lakes. Didn't he have a wonderful voice? I was so tired, though. I couldn't help falling asleep. Like someone hit me on the back of the head and knocked me out." Talia sat up, shook off the blanket. "What sort of puzzle did he leave you with?"

I hesitated before I spoke. "He seemed to think I was on some kind of journey. As if I was looking for—"

"For what?"

"For my people. For my home."

"Well, are you?"

Above the mountain in the distance, the sky was lighting up with dawn.

"I don't really know," I said. "Yes, maybe I am."

Talia reached up and fiddled at the back of her neck. When she drew her hands down, she was holding something, which she passed to me.

"This is a Star of David," she said. "I wear it underneath my clothing, so you've probably never noticed it. It was my grandmother's. She brought it with her to South Africa from Lithuania when she was about our age. They had to flee the pogroms."

"Pogroms?"

"I wish I knew more about her, about her life. I hardly knew her, really."

Talia gave me that look again, the sidelong glance.

"You're not Jewish ... Why do I not know this?"

"Actually, I'm half Jewish," I said in a halting voice. "My mother's Jewish, my father's not."

Talia shook her head, as I'd seen her do, now, several times, as if she was trying to shake something perturbing away.

"It makes no difference. This Star of David is special. I can't explain it. And I don't know why, but I have this feeling ..."

"Yes?"

"I have this feeling that it belongs to you."

Talia waved her arm in a semicircle, bringing it to rest with her hand pointing at the plane's cabin some three hundred yards from where we were sitting.

"We might have lost our lives, here. It's like we were spared by the gods. Given a second chance. I know this is going to sound really weird, but I sense that you being here with us is what saved us."

Talia looked down at the necklace she was holding, and when she spoke, it was as if she was talking not to me, but to the little Star of David.

"Jasmine," she said, "who *are* you?"

Then, she looked up at me. The frown appeared again only this time, instead of confusion in her eyes, I saw inklings of a troubled realization. Was the truth dawning on her? That the girl sitting with her, the girl she thought of as her friend Jasmine, was in fact a person from her own future—the child she would one day name Emily? *Her very own daughter?*

Talia blushed. "I'm sorry, I must be going mad. The crash, hardly any sleep. It's been such a long night. I don't know, being here, in the bush. I think it's all been a bit too much."

I could see the distress bubbling up; Talia's face crumpled a little, as if she was about to cry. She did not, after all, know the truth, and yet my presence, here, was upsetting her. I felt I owed her an explanation, though I had no idea what I could say that would make any sense.

"I've often wondered," I found myself saying, "how you can tell where a river begins and where it ends. It seems to me that in the end, it's rather arbitrary. The labels we give to things."

Talia's face relaxed. She seemed relieved. "I love such riddles myself," she said.

I lowered my voice to a whisper. "In answer to your question, the truth is I'm not sure I quite know. Who I am."

Something my mother told me once came back to me. "Isn't that what the Sphinx said was the ultimate point of life? To *know thyself?*"

We both looked soberly at the gray ashes of what had been our cozy little fire.

Talia nodded. "I think I know what you mean," she said.

"Jimmy *was* trying to tell me something," I said in a whisper, almost to myself. Watching the dawn light diffuse the remaining shadows of night, it occurred to me that perhaps Jimmy was my guide. Isn't that what Mama had said to me, through the terror of the squall, as I was hurtling back through time?

There will be guides to help you. If you keep your eyes open, you will find them.

I looked over at Talia. Now, she smiled.

"Here, take it," she said, handing me the Star of David.

There it was, that mischievous, fully alive smile: my mama's smile. I felt a ballooning happiness.

"What a night," she said. "I feel like we need some kind of ceremony. I know! I'm going to say a blessing—a Jewish prayer. I don't usually go in for stuff like this but—I don't know, it seems right.

"For religious Jews, this prayer is the most important one of the day. They're supposed to say it every morning, when they wake up. The English translation goes like this: *Hear O Israel, the Lord our God, the Lord is One. Blessed be the Holy Name of the Lord, King of the Universe forever.* Okay, now in Hebrew."

Through the pain in my eyes, which was rising in gloomy crescendo, I looked at the necklace she'd handed me: the fine gold chain bearing a small gold star with two Hebrew letters in the center, which of course I did not know how to read. I closed my fist tightly around the star. We both stood: I felt the firm land beneath my feet, breathed in the rich scent of the bush, strongly tinged with eucalyptus, and closed my eyes.

"*Shemah Yisroel, Adonai Elohenu, Adonai Ehud,*" Talia said. The words sounded so foreign to me—if it had been Hindi, they would have been no more familiar—and yet they slipped from Talia's mouth like a native tongue. "*Baruch Shem K'vod Malchutoh L'Olam Va'ed.*"

But then, Talia winced and she sat back down. Her hand reached for her calf.

"Okay?" I asked.

"Wow—"

"What?"

"Dunno, like someone just stabbed into it."

"Let's get your dad," I said, the panic returning.

Talia shook her head. "No, let him sleep. Mick, too. We have a long drive. I'm just going to take a quick look."

Talia reached down and removed the tape and the gauze.

"Here," I said, flicking on the flashlight and directing the beam to the wound.

It looked awful, nothing like the clean, dressed cut of last night. Her calf was swollen and the skin around it was mottled red. A sliver of something yellow shone in the beam of light.

"Pus," Talia said. "This isn't good."

My head was getting worse by the minute. I looked over at Talia. Something shifted in the atmosphere, something peculiar, as if the air were being sucked away.

"Hey," Talia said, glancing over to the ruined cabin of the plane. "Did you tell your mum you were going up in a small airplane?"

I shook my head, no.

"We should have gotten their permission," she said. "They're going to be upset. We shouldn't have brought you, not without their permission."

An abrupt dread poured into me, leaving a chalky feeling in my mouth of doom. I looked at Talia. Her skin was tinged green. What if my being here at all was undermining everything? What if *I* had somehow been responsible for the crash? What if the infection in Talia's leg had turned septic? I knew about septicemia. Knew that one day, Grandma would end up in a coma for a month with a raging case that almost killed her. The pain in my head was now excruciating. I reached up to find the small bump on my head had grown to the size of a large plum.

"Jasmine, are you okay?" Talia asked. "You're doing it again—shaking all over like a leaf."

I couldn't speak.

"We'll call your mum as soon as we get to town. We'll—"

A terrible loneliness filled my veins. How lost I was! How far from everything I'd ever known. From home, from my family—but no! *She* was my family! It was impossible, but—

"Talia!" I said, almost shouting. "Don't you see? Don't you know *who you are?*"

"What are you talking about?" she asked, looking afraid herself.

"I can't *tell my mother* anything! Not unless I *tell you!*"

Grandpa Jack popped his head out of the tent.

"Girls, is everything okay?" he asked.

I could see his head there, at the opening of the tent, but everything was pitching, turning sideways. I tried to speak, but no sound came out. And then, something erupted in Talia's face, a look of horror that was the most frightening thing of all. The ground was sliding. Talia's hands flew out to steady herself, as if she were trying to take hold of the ground and set it to rights.

What if I'd done something terrible! What if Talia was going to get really, really ill, even die, so that—so that—how could that be? Then I would never be born?

I had to tell her! Had to tell her everything—that she'd grow up and leave her home, that she'd raise her own children far from her family, that she'd hardly see her parents and siblings as the years poured by, that her father—Grandpa Jack! How vital he was! So utterly alive!—would die way too young, when Talia was not yet out of graduate school, that she would herself get very sick when I was only—well, the exact age I was now, with Billy, her darling little boy, only five years old. That—

Her face was a mask of fear as the earth slid and she slid with it, down into the dark shadow that had abruptly opened up in the sky and plunged down to where we were sitting on the ground.

And then, my whole body tipped. My eyes slammed shut, I tried to open them but they were glued tight, and the spinning began. All around me, a shuddering cold: I was tumbling again. I stretched out my arms—tried to howl—*Talia! Grandpa Jack! Come back! Don't leave me! I need you!* The words stormed in my head; I tumbled into the cold, whipping wind, a motion crazier even than the motion of the first storm. Inside, I was shrieking. *Mama! Mama!* I recalled Talia's desperate cry as the plane was crashing through the trees, bouncing every which way, filling us all with the great danger of what was happening, with the dreadful awareness that perhaps our lives were about to end.

In the midst of the terrible cold and wind, the tumbling that sucked away my breath, I heard it again—the calm, loving voice of my mother. Not Talia, the girl who would be my mother one day, but my grown mother, who was at that moment very ill, far away in Brooklyn.

"Stay brave and you will return. I am here, waiting for you."

With the sound of her voice, the panic within evaporated; suddenly, I felt I was on a calm sea. I opened my mouth to respond to my mother's voice—and found that my lips were no longer sealed, nor my eyes, which now opened.

* * *

Gone, the Australian bush. Gone, the plane wreckage. Gone, Talia—Mama, as a girl. Gone, Grandpa Jack—the grandfather I'd never known, who had died before I was born. A surge of grief took hold of me, but then also, a feeling of gratitude. On this strange journey, I had finally met my Grandpa Jack.

Now I was walking on a dirt road in an utterly unfamiliar land-scape. Dry grass all around, but of a different color than in Australia: washed-out, wintry browns and greens. All around me, rather than wild bush, were crudely cultivated fields. In the distance, I could see a small colony of mud huts, with roofs of thatched straw. I looked down to see unfamiliar shoes on my feet—old-fashioned leather boots with worn soles and badly scuffed toes. Someone was walking beside me. A girl. She was talking in a beautiful, melodic voice. And with a different accent from Talia's broad Australian tones. Much more English sounding. I turned to look at her, and as I did so, before I actually saw her face, I realized with a jolt where I was, realized what had happened. Understood, with astonishment, with whom I was walking.

CHAPTER THREE

MY FEET AND ANKLES ACHED; we must have been walking for some time. I found myself slowing down. "Camellia, we're going to be late!"

My name, then, was to be Camellia in this new place. Why, of course! Grandma's favorite flower! Just as I had been Jasmine—my mother's favorite flower—in Australia.

I knew her immediately, this girl hurrying beside me: there was something about the feel of her, more than anything physical, as she looked so different from the Grandma I knew. Something dramatic must happen to the way people look once they move into that shady time-world of being *old*. As beautiful, dynamic, and alive as Grandma in Australia was, I had to search the face of this pretty young girl— thin as a rake and with a mop of curly, dark hair—to find her. Yes, there was that spark in her eyes, which revealed delight in the world, but also something wary.

And here I was, in faraway South Africa, very likely somewhere near the tiny town of Koppies—*a one-horse town,* as she'd always de- scribed it—where Grandma had grown up.

She was not, of course, yet *Grandma,* but Darlene. I picked up my pace to match hers, stumbling on the loose stones of the unpaved road. All around us, stretching endlessly, were bleached fields, dotted here and there with enormous haystacks. The mud-hut village was behind us, and I could see another up ahead on the horizon. The sky showed the cautious light of a new day and, already, it was hot. The cotton jacket I was wearing—faded blue, slightly too large—felt uncomfortably heavy.

We hurried along in silence, drawing closer to what had looked like an old barn but that I saw, as we approached, was a schoolhouse standing in a field and encircled by wire-mesh fencing. To keep out animals, I imagined—sheep, goats, maybe donkeys.

Behind the schoolhouse was a tar macadam yard on which the remains of a white diamond were still visible, though the paint was old and peeling and in certain places altogether gone. Clusters of children of all ages gathered in front of the schoolhouse on the patchy, yellowed grass, some crouching over marbles, others playing a game with a ball and stick, and a number just milling about. We slowed to an amble as we entered through the gate.

I glanced at Darlene and saw that her jaw was clamped tight. She seemed to have suddenly grown an inch or two—her neck elongated and back held very straight. She did not approach any of the little groupings and greeted no one. As we passed among the other children, I saw heads turning our way; their faces held unpleasant, sneering expressions. There was a look to those kids, especially the boys, I'd not seen before: angry, hungry, abandoned.

When we were halfway to the steps of the schoolhouse, a boy of about fifteen made a beeline for us. He was gangly and tall, with sandy hair and freckles, and a grim, fierce expression. When he was almost upon us, Darlene reached into her satchel and drew something out. As he passed us, Darlene casually, surreptitiously, handed him whatever she'd taken from her satchel.

"What is it—?" I said, my voice heavy with a South African accent.

"Ssshh," Darlene said. "I'll tell you later."

After that, I followed Darlene's example; I stopped stealing glances around me and instead looked straight ahead.

Inside, the schoolhouse was larger than it appeared from outside. It consisted of four comfortably sized rooms, two on each side of a wide bare hallway lined with old wooden cubbies in ramshackle condition. Darlene paused by one: the shelf and hook were missing, and the wood on the sides was split. She removed a notebook from her satchel and placed the bag on the floor of the cubby. Then, she took off her jacket, folded it neatly, and laid it on top of the bag. I did the same—finding I had a similar notebook—placing first my satchel and then my folded jacket into the adjoining cubby.

The hallway was buzzing with movement and noise as children hurried here and there. An earsplitting bell clanged and everybody, suddenly silent, filed into their classrooms.

Darlene slid into the bench of a desk in the back row. I slid in beside her. A few minutes later, an older man with a military bearing strode into the room. Tall and powerfully built, he had pure white hair that was slicked to his head with oil. His gray eyes glinted with malice.

A hushed fear filled the room. Not one rustle, not a murmur or whisper or cough: all eyes were directed at the schoolmaster.

"Open your books," he said. "History, page ninety-eight."

There was a flurry of turning pages.

"First, an announcement. The troops of the Third Reich are battling the Communists on the Eastern Front. We send a prayer for their victory. We pray for the slaughter of all enemies of the Third Reich."

The man was speaking an ugly, guttural language I'd never heard before that sounded a little like German. I realized it must be Afrikaans; I knew from my grandmother that this is what white people of Dutch descent spoke in South Africa, and that all her schooling had been in this language. Darlene and I had been speaking English; Grandma had told me she'd spoken English at home, as Jewish people did. Oddly, I understood every word the teacher said and, looking down at the textbook in front of me, I discovered I could also effortlessly read the strange-looking words.

The lesson was about the Boer War. We began to read aloud, together. Many of the students stumbled over words; some seemed barely literate. Sitting in front of me was a scruffy boy with greasy hair whose neck was caked with dirt; he seemed only to be moving his mouth, rather than actually enunciating words. We were reading about the *brave Boer soldiers* and how they *marched toward victory*. I didn't know anything about the Boer War; the textbook copy, though, sounded like propaganda.

After four pages of laborious group reading, the teacher abruptly called for a stop. He then launched on a summary of what we had just read, embellishing even further on the *just cause of the Boer freedom fighters*.

But then, he broke off, mid-sentence. I looked up to see that he was glaring at Darlene, who was studiously focused on her book.

"Is there a reason you're staring off into space, Darlene?" the master said. "Are my words, in your view, not worth attending to?"

"But sir," Darlene said, "I was following the story in the book."

"Don't answer back, rude child!"

The master raised his hand. Everything suddenly altered, as if transformed to slow motion. Something gray and oblong flew through the air toward Darlene. I heard a thud and turned to see Darlene's skin, just below the hairline, split open, then watched as a trickle of blood made its way down her forehead and settled in her right eyebrow.

"I'm listening, sir," Darlene said. "I heard every word."

She sat immobile, stifling the instinct, I imagined, to reach up and touch the fresh wound on her forehead.

"Well then, might I trouble you to return my blackboard duster?" the master said with mock courtesy. I dared not look about me; I did, though, hear several semi-suppressed snickers escape from the mouths of other children.

Darlene bent to the floor to retrieve the blackboard eraser, then stood and walked toward the teacher with that same stiff-necked dignity I'd observed earlier. She handed back the offending object. The teacher made a sudden movement with his hand toward Darlene's head. I thought he was going to cuff her on the ear and I let out a little involuntary gasp. He didn't hit her, though; he only grabbed her arm and drew her close. He leaned down and whispered something loudly in Darlene's ear. I saw her face redden.

The teacher turned and looked at me. "And if Miss Camellia has anything to say, she can stand up and bestow her intelligent remarks on the classroom."

The master made no attempt to mask the scorn in his voice. He reached for a long wooden ruler that was lying on his desk and tapped it gently on his palm.

"Is that what you wish to do?" he said, glaring at me. "Come to the aid of a *Jew?*"

I looked from the teacher to Darlene, whose dark eyes seemed frozen, but also fearless. I could feel her willing me to remain silent, willing me not to bring down on myself the same fury we'd all just witnessed being directed at her.

The Nazis will be defeated! I wanted to yell. *Three months from now, Hitler will put a bullet in his head and the utter madness will come to an end!* I felt myself adding something else, for myself—that it would never be *over*, that humanity could never recover from such evil. Instead, I simply said: "No, sir. I have nothing to say."

I did not, though, hide the hatred in my eyes, the way Darlene had clearly learned to do. The master seemed to notice this. I saw a flicker of spite in his face; slowly, he crossed the classroom to where I was sitting. He stood by my desk for a moment, tapping the ruler against his palm.

"Hands out straight," he said. I lay my hands flat against the desk. He raised the ruler and brought it down hard across the knuckles of both my hands, once, twice, three times.

"Next time, you will keep your gasps to yourself."

I placed my hands under the desk and nursed my smarting fingers.

The lesson continued for what seemed an age, if you can call the tedium of reciting dull facts and copying out pages of propaganda from a textbook a lesson. I followed the instructions automatically, as Darlene seemed to do, marveling every now and then at my fluency in this strange language. I watched with amazement as the words flowed from my pencil across the lines of the page.

The raucous clang of the bell split the silence. The teacher announced recess.

Everyone rose. My hands still burned and ached and my knees trembled so badly, I could hardly stand. Somehow, I managed to keep my balance and file out with the rest of the class.

Inside, I was jangling with questions. I bit my lip to stop myself blurting them all out in a mad rush. Darlene grabbed something from her satchel as we passed the makeshift lockers, and then made her way out the back entrance of the school, heading toward the far corner of the school yard.

I took Darlene's hand.

"Are you all right?" I asked, looking at her forehead, where the blood had dried.

Darlene gave a curt little nod.

"Can I help you wash up?" I asked.

She shook her head. "Let it stay," she said. "How are your hands? Hope he didn't give you the *burn whack*."

"Not too bad," I said. "Don't worry."

We sat beneath a tree of a kind I'd not seen before. It had a skinny trunk and gnarled branches that stretched crookedly skyward, here and there sprouting sparse bunches of misshapen brownish-green leaves.

"What did you give that boy this morning?" I asked. "When you took something from your satchel, before we went into the school house?"

"Oh. Just a sandwich. I give him one every day. Schmaltz and salami on rye."

"Why on earth? He didn't exactly look like a friend of yours."

"Protection. That way, no one will beat me up. They hate us Jews, but they like our sandwiches."

Darlene opened her hand. She was holding something wrapped in a piece of wax paper. She withdrew two sugar cookies, handed one to me and took the other for herself, and then carefully folded the paper and put it back into her pocket.

"Joel gave me an extra one for you," she said. I didn't know who Joel was, but I had the feeling I'd find out later.

"Please thank him for me," I said. At the sight of the cookie, my mouth watered. Once again, I realized how hungry I was. The opportunities for eating on this strange journey of mine were few and far between.

"Doesn't that bother you?" I asked. "Having to give that awful boy your sandwich every day?"

"I'd rather go hungry than get beaten up," Darlene said, taking a tiny bite of her cookie. "Besides, he needs it more than I do."

"Is he very poor?"

"He's from the St. Augustine Orphanage. A lot of the kids here are," she said, gesturing toward the playground where the groups had gathered again to resume their games of earlier. "Most of their parents are in the army, up north."

"Up north?"

"Algeria and Egypt, mostly. But you know this as well as I do, Camellia." Darlene gave me a hazy look. "It's true, they're just awful, but you only have to look at them to see how unhappy they are. There's no one to take care of them. They pretty much raise themselves."

Darlene's gaze drifted across the school yard. I turned to see what she was looking at. On the far side of the yard, beyond the wire fencing, was a group of dark-skinned children—barefoot, ranging in age from tiny infants, held in the arms of the older children, to about twelve or thirteen. Each child was wearing either pants or a shirt, but not both; bony legs or thin chests showed below or above the faded scrap each wore. Flies swarmed around their noses and eyes. Some of the children held onto the wire, pressing their faces right up against it.

"It's all relative, though, isn't it," Darlene was saying. "The St. Augustine children at least get the chance to go to school. To use the *Whites Only* entrances and facilities. To eat most of the time, even if they don't love the food."

Darlene had stopped nibbling at her cookie. She glanced at my own cookie, which I'd not yet bitten. I passed the cookie back to her and she rose, walked to the far end of the yard, and passed both cookies through the fence. She paused there, talked, for a moment, to the children on the other side.

As she walked back toward me, Darlene discreetly brushed her hand across her eyes.

Hunger gnawed at my stomach. I pushed it from my mind.

Darlene was back. She sat down beside me on the hard dirt.

"I was wondering," I said. "What did the teacher whisper into your ear?"

"Oh, nothing much. The usual."

"What's the usual?"

"That Hitler will win. That he'll make good on his promise to rid Europe of the Jews. That then it will be our turn here, in South Africa."

"Oh," I said, not knowing how to respond.

"Mr. Van Graan hates Jews, like pretty much everyone here," Darlene said, pronouncing his name with the same heavy Afrikaans accent the teacher had. "You sort of get used to being hated."

I saw in Darlene's face that same peculiar look I'd seen on Talia's face back—well, back whenever that was in Australia (years ahead, though for me, it was some kind of yesterday).

"But why am I telling you this?" she said. "You know about it just as well as I do!"

The sudden clanging of the bell saved me from having to respond. We both jumped up and hurried back to the schoolhouse.

The rest of the day passed in a fog of tedium. School for me had always been exciting and fun; the drudgery in that hot, dusty, horrible schoolroom, half a world and more than half a century away from the home I knew, bore no resemblance to education as I knew it.

When the school bell finally clanged, signaling the end of the day, I felt immense relief. I followed Darlene out of the classroom. We grabbed our jackets and satchels and then bolted from the schoolhouse, tearing across the yard. We didn't stop running for about a half mile, by my calculation. It was only then, having slowed to a normal walking pace, that the discomforts assailing me rushed full force into my awareness. My feet ached in their tight boots; I could feel angry blisters blooming at every point where my skin came into contact with the leather. In my stomach, the fiercest hunger I'd ever known sent a wave of nausea through my body that found its way to my head as a pounding headache. And the heat! It bore down on my uncovered head like a vise. I looked over at Darlene. Surely, she was also suffering in the same miserable way. And the wound on her forehead, on top of everything!

She didn't complain, though. She was walking calmly beside me, a faint smile on her lips.

"Do you hear that lovely warbling?" she asked. "Red-breasted robins! Don't you adore them?"

I was awed by how Darlene was able to muster cheerfulness after the hellish day she'd had.

We walked for a time in silence. The dry landscape was becoming familiar. Here we were again passing the mud huts of the African village, some distance from the road; the burning sun turned their straw roofs to gold.

"I'm going to leave this place, as soon as I can," Darlene said.

"Koppies?" I asked. "The Orange Free State?"

"South Africa. The whole country, it's rotten. Rotten to the core."

"Where do you want to go?"

"It depends on my husband. On where his career will take us."

I gave a little laugh. "Do you already know who your husband is going to be?" I asked.

She looked impatient. "Well no, not exactly. But the day I finish high school—three years and forty-three days from today—I will take the train to Johannesburg where I will live with my brother and attend the college for nursery school teachers. It shouldn't take more than a few months to meet my future husband."

"Oh, really?"

"Johannesburg is full of nice Jewish boys looking for nice Jewish girls. They want someone who is pretty and sweet, and who is clever at all the things they need to be clever at. It would be a bonus for me to have a certificate in teaching. That will make me a better mother.

"All the most intelligent men go overseas to study, especially the doctors. I imagine it will be England, though we might end up in America! I'm not too concerned about where. But we'll go. And, I'll make certain that we never come back!"

Darlene could not have known just how close to the letter her plan would work out. How she'd meet my grandfather, Jack, a medical student, at a Jewish singles dance. How two weeks later, she would open the door of her older brother's house where she was living to see Jack snazzily dressed, holding a bouquet of roses and looking nervous but happy, knowing that he intended to propose to Darlene that evening, over dinner. How she would, in fact, travel across the world, but to Australia, where she'd build a new life, far from her detested homeland.

We came to a crossroads, which appeared to be the tiny heart of the town. On one corner was a petrol station, on another, a ramshackle building with a faded sign declaring it to be the Koppies *Poskantoor*, which I knew from my sudden proficiency in Afrikaans meant Post Office. Diagonally across were a clothing store, its window boasting three mannequins dressed in farming clothes, and another store bearing the sign *Deegwinkel*—Pastry Shop. We crossed the road; Darlene paused before the window of the pastry shop and looked longingly at a plateful of napoleons.

"Don't they look delicious?" Darlene said. "I've always wanted to try one. But I've never had more than five cents of my own. That was a present from my brother Barry, when he came home from army training."

My heart flew out to Darlene; I was filled with a burning desire to help her. To put things right. I could hardly believe that, with all the hardship she clearly faced, this girl would one day become my lively, talented, and supremely capable Grandma. I thought for a moment about the lifetime of struggle and striving that lay between this lonely girl—who many years from now would give birth to my mother—and the grandmother I knew.

Those napoleons did, indeed, look delicious, so creamy and flakey. We hadn't eaten all day, and had walked miles and miles, and now my stomach growled angrily. I would have given a good deal for one of those pastries. The thick layer of yellow custard made my mouth water.

I leaned over to Darlene. "One day," I said, "I'll buy you a great big plateful of napoleons. I promise."

Darlene nodded almost imperceptibly. I saw that she was biting her lip. She reached over and took my hand and together, we walked away.

"You know, we had a traveling salesman with us for two weeks," Darlene said. "Now that everyone but my brother Harold has moved out, my mother rents an extra room whenever she can. Well, this man was a prince! Mr. Krige. I'll never forget him as long as I live. He gave me the most beautiful present—a china tea set. I'll show it to you when we get back home. We can have a tea party with my dolls!"

By the time we turned into the front yard of Darlene's house I was limping—and so thirsty, I'd have lapped at a pig's trough, had one appeared.

The house was a rambling old farmhouse in a state of disrepair. The red roof tiles were missing in patches; in one section, the brick was crumbling, and there were cracked or missing windowpanes. The damage seemed confined to one side. I imagined the family lived only in the well-maintained section.

Darlene took off at a sprint. "Come on!" she said, running around to the back of the house. I limped behind, following her into the kitchen in time to see her greeting a tall, middle-aged black man, a beatific look on her face.

"Look, Joel. Camellia's here! She's my cousin's cousin—all the way from Durban. She's going to sleep over. Isn't that glorious?"

Joel had kind, far-seeing eyes. When he greeted me, he seemed to be looking right into my face but also somehow gazing at a distant horizon.

"Hello, Miss Camellia," he said. His voice was as warm and rich as his eyes.

I was hit with an aroma so enticing, I almost cried out with joy.

"You girls must be hungry," Joel said. "I have your dinner ready early."

The spring suddenly back in my feet, I followed Darlene to the kitchen sink, where we washed our faces and scrubbed our hands with a coarse bar of soap. The dust from our long walk home had entered my pores and seemed stubbornly determined to stay there. I did the best I could, and when I was finished, I almost bounded over to the wooden table and sat down before one of the steaming bowls Joel had set there.

"*Mealie pap* and chicken casserole!" Darlene said, tucking in.

"And a custard trifle for dessert," Joel said.

I dug in, too. The stew was pungent and extremely flavorful. It sat in its thick gravy on top of a mound of steaming cornmeal that had been cooked up into a chewy porridge.

I couldn't remember when a meal had tasted so good. I swallowed the last mouthful, trying to stem the disappointment I felt at the sight of the empty bowl—I was still so hungry, as if I hadn't eaten at all! But then, Joel appeared beside me with the pot and ladled another helping of the *mealie pap*. A moment later, he returned with some more stew. I ate more slowly, this time, relishing each mouthful.

Joel went into the laundry room off the kitchen and as we ate, I could hear the sound of water filling a trough, followed by great swooshings. I pictured Joel at work, perhaps washing the family's linens.

Once the large meal had given chase to my ravenous hunger, I was able to pay attention to the room, which was spacious and had a certain rough elegance. Across from us stood an enormous glass-fronted cabinet containing an assortment of dishes and glassware. Beside this was an ancient pot-bellied stove, which gave off intense heat. On the floor beside the stove was a straw mat, rolled and tied loosely with twine, along with a large metal bowl. I brightened at the thought that Darlene perhaps had a dog.

"Do you have a dog, then?" I asked.

Darlene shook her head. "I wish we did, but no."

She followed my querying gaze to where the mat and bowl sat on the floor by the stove. Her face dropped and when she spoke her voice cracked with pain.

"That's Joel's mat. He sleeps there, during the week. The bowl is his toilet. On weekends, he goes home to his village. It's not that far— an hour and a half by foot."

Her words fell like soft blows to my ears. I thought about the gentle, dignified man in the back room, from which I could still hear those loud swishing sounds and felt a cold rage rising within as I imagined him settling at night on the hard floor while his "masters" slumbered comfortably in their beds.

"That's just awful!"

Darlene nodded, then looked away.

I saw again that photograph we'd looked at in the Belle Meade Plantation gift shop, heard Mama's heavy words, *Built on the backs of slaves.* What country was free of horrors? Was there no society on earth where justice and kindness truly reigned? Even this sorry farmhouse, in the middle of a nowhere that included vile, bigoted teachers who threw chalkboard erasers at children's heads, was built on the backs of servitude—on the very back of the kindly man who seemed like a father to Darlene, and yet bore the title of *servant.* The rude word ricocheted in my mind. I recalled the faces of the children in scraps of clothing, pressed up against the wire fencing around the school yard. Layer upon layer of cruelty—I didn't know what to do with all the feelings that surged violently within.

Just then, a familiar chime rang out, and I almost jumped out of my skin. Grandma's clock! The clock given to her mother—my great-grandmother—on the occasion of her marriage! The very same clock I had awoken to—gosh, an age ago—in Melbourne. The clock had been given to Darlene's mother, Sarah, as a wedding present; much later, Darlene would bring it to Australia. Perhaps one day, I thought, I would pack it into a velvet box and take it with me to New York. It gave me goose bumps to think about this clock, chiming up through the decades, marking the hours, days, weeks, years, of so many lives that came into being and then drifted away.

"The chimes startled me," I said.

"I love that clock," Darlene said. I wanted to say *I love it, too!* However, I kept silent, aware of the eerie secrecy I felt bound to regarding the truth of who I was and where I came from. But looking at Darlene, I realized something else: that I was also in some way discovering new truths, laying claim to something lost.

At that moment, Joel returned, carrying a large earthenware dish. "Here's the trifle."

Darlene jumped up. "I can serve it up."

"Thank you, Do-Do," Joel said, and returned to the laundry room.

The trifle was heavenly: layers of pound cake, strawberries, and thick yellow custard, topped with heavy clotted cream. We each ate a large serving while drinking several cups of steaming brewed tea, to which we added frothy milk and lumps of brown sugar.

When we finished, we took our plates to the sink, then grabbed our satchels and passed through a long hallway to Darlene's room. She hung her school bag on a hook, removed her shoes, and placed them neatly by the foot of her bed. I did the same.

"Here," Darlene said, reaching under her bed excitedly and retrieving a sizable wooden box. Her fingers were shaking with anticipation. Only now did I notice that the nail on her right pinky finger was very long and sharpened to a point.

"Why do you have such a long pointy nail, and only the one?" I asked.

"Oh, that!" She laughed. "That's my weapon."

"Your weapon?"

"You'll see," she said. "But look, have you ever seen such a lovely tea set?"

The box opened on two impressive brass hinges to reveal the tea set Darlene had told me about; each item was nestled in its own special section lined with velvet. The miniature dishes were made of real bone china, decorated with an elaborate pattern: rose clusters, joined by lengths of twirled vine with delicate green leaves. Darlene removed each piece, one by one, and arranged them carefully on the table beside her bed.

"Let's prepare a tea party for my dolls."

I cast a glance around, looking for her collection of dolls, sighting only a crew of rough-hewn creatures fashioned from mango pits sitting squatly on the chest of drawers. This, along with a tiny wardrobe and Darlene's bed, completed the furnishings of the room.

Darlene gathered her mango-pit dolls. "The Smithson family is coming to visit the Harrisons for tea!"

Just as I was beginning to wonder why a girl of fourteen would still be interested in playing with a tea set and dolls—and mango pits, at that—Darlene's game took an interesting turn.

"The Smithsons are a family of famous anthropologists. They've spent years in Mexico, studying the Indigenous people, who the Smithsons have discovered are incredibly kind. They adore children. They carry their babies in slings on their backs—the mother or the aunt or sister, it doesn't matter. Children are never left alone and as a result, they are never sad and almost never cry. Even the Smithson children have been involved in the family research. They know how to speak the native languages and they talk and play with the Indigenous children.

"The Harrisons are art historians. They know the history of European Art backward and forward. Their children have little reproductions of the world's most famous paintings all over their bedroom walls. At night, before they go to sleep, they recite the names of important painters, starting with Cranach and ending with Picasso."

Darlene's cheeks were flushed with pleasure. For a moment, I thought she'd forgotten me, but then she turned and clasped my hand.

"Come on, Camellia. You can help me figure out what they're going to talk about over tea. Maybe the Smithsons will tell the Harrisons all about the art of the Mexicans: their pottery and beautiful embroidery. Or perhaps—"

Darlene froze mid-sentence. While she was chattering away, she'd carefully placed the china pieces on the wooden table by her bed, except for one plate, which remained in its felt-lined partition. I was startled by the sudden change that came over her. The look in her eyes—terrified and fearsome, both.

"What have we here?" I heard someone say. I turned to see a handsome fellow of sixteen or seventeen leaning against the door jamb.

"Two little girls, playing with dolls and a tea set. Wouldn't you say you're a mite old for such babyish games?"

It was impossible not to note the malice in the boy's face.

"Hey girls, want to see what dear old Mr. Krige gave your brother Harold, here?" He gave an oddly impersonal smirk.

"A wonderful new baseball. All the way from America. Ever seen a baseball, girl? They're hard. *Really* hard."

A flurry beside me told me that Darlene had sprung to action. She was trying to gather up the pieces of her tea set, having realized her brother's intention. In her panic she fumbled, though in any case I imagine she would have failed. The boy was simply too quick. Besides, he had the advantage of a predator who has cornered its prey.

The ball whooshed by my head. Darlene snatched her hand out of harm's way at the very moment the ball smashed into the china. A delicate tinkling followed the crash, as shards flew from the table onto the ground. Not a single piece remained intact. Out of the corner of my eye, I saw Darlene's hand steal toward the felt-lined box on the ground and stealthily remove the single remaining plate. She was able to slip it under her skirt without her brother seeing.

"*St-r-iiike!*" He called out.

Harold crossed the room to retrieve the ball then walked back to the doorway. He stood for a moment, looking over at where his sister sat ramrod straight on the floor, then he disappeared.

A moment later, Joel appeared at the door. He surveyed the mess, then looked sympathetically at Darlene.

"Let me clean this up for you, Do-Do," he said.

Another tread approached. A heavy-set woman, whose dark brown hair was streaked with gray, appeared in the doorway.

"And what may I ask is going on here?" she asked, in a surprisingly husky voice.

She crossed the room and pulled Darlene up by the arm from where she knelt over the shattered fragments that minutes before had been her new tea set.

"What a clumsy girl," she said. "You don't deserve nice things."

Only now did she seem to notice me.

"You should be ashamed, in front of your friend. No supper for either of you. Clean this up, then straight to bed."

She let go of Darlene's arm, which glowed pink from where her mother had gripped her. Darlene's face had turned stony. She uttered not a word in her defense, but simply set about carefully picking up the shards from the floor.

Darlene's mother walked briskly from the room. For someone of her heft, she moved with surprising grace.

Joel and I both knelt down to help Darlene clean up the broken pieces.

"I'll fetch the broom and dustpan," Joel said. He disappeared and returned carrying the broom and pan. When we'd finished cleaning it all up, Darlene sat down on the bed; she was biting her lip, struggling to hold back tears. Joel again approached her but stopped a small distance away, as if deliberately positioning himself just out of arm's reach. He stroked one of his own arms with the flat of his other hand, as if he meant to be stroking Darlene's but was making do with his own. He uttered something in a loud whisper in a language I did not understand—Zulu, perhaps?—then repeated the phrase twice more.

Darlene nodded, returning Joel's intense gaze. He leaned down and whispered something to her, then left, carrying the broom and dustpan full of broken china pieces.

Darlene rose. "I'm sorry about all of that," she said, giving a weak smile. "Joel just reminded me that tonight is Mother's bridge game. She lives for bridge. That's a lucky thing, or I'd be more skin and bones than I am. Joel always sneaks me food when I'm punished. Usually, it's just a piece of bread and a hard-boiled egg, something Joel can hide in his pocket. But on bridge nights, I can sit in the kitchen and eat a proper supper. She doesn't leave until nine o'clock, though, so we have a few hours to wait. It's a good thing Joel gave us our dinner early."

We opened our satchels, took out our books, and set about doing our homework. The work came easily; I had a strange knowledge of what I was doing, even though I had been in class only the one day.

We labored through several columns of sums. Then, we filled three pages with text we had to copy from a geography book. There was an essay question, too, and it was only halfway through regurgitating the information recited earlier by the teacher about the Boer War that I realized I was writing in Afrikaans!

I looked up from my work.

"The Afrikaners hate the English, don't they?"

Darlene looked up from her notebook, wearing the same quizzical-patient expression of earlier.

"Of course. The Afrikaners hate everybody except for themselves. And the Nazis, who in their view, have the right idea about things. Why do you ask?"

"I guess I just wanted to be sure," I said, fearing that in my ignorance of local realities, I'd given myself away.

I wondered about this odd feeling I'd had now several times since finding myself on this journey. This fear of *giving myself away*. Was I afraid that Darlene would discover I was from another time and place? And what if she did? Or did I fear something else; that Darlene would discover I was not who *I* thought I was?

I put down my pencil.

"Darlene, why didn't you tell your mother the truth? That we weren't being careless. That Harold deliberately smashed your tea set."

"She'd never believe me."

"Why not?"

Darlene also put down her pencil. Again, that patient look in her face.

"Harold is my mother's favorite. When my father was alive, they would fight about him. They each had different favorites; my father's favorite was Barry. If my father hit Harold, my mother would hit Barry. My father would do the same—threaten to beat Harold if she struck Barry. In a way it was lucky for me, being no one's favorite. Mostly, they just ignored me.

"But if I ever say anything against Harold, she'd take notice. I've learned to keep as quiet as I can—and stay out of her way."

From the kitchen, we heard the sound of boisterous laughter: Harold and his mother, enjoying the supper from which we'd been banished. It was a couple of hours since we'd eaten Joel's hearty meal, and as I'd eaten so little for days, my stomach was already rumbling again.

Darlene looked down at her nail "weapon."

"Once, when Harold was hitting me, I tore a strip of skin from his cheek with this."

"Weren't you afraid he'd tell your mother?"

Darlene shook her head. "He'd never admit he'd been hurt by a girl, let alone by *me*."

We turned again to our work. Through the window, I could see the light fading. In the distance, small rain clouds gathered, further blotting out what remained of the day.

After a time, Darlene put her notebook and pencils back in her satchel and I did the same.

"She'll be gone, by now," she said. "My mother."

"And Harold?"

"Oh, he'll be in town with his friends. He never stays in after supper."

We made our way to the kitchen where Joel had set two places on the counter by the sink. We sat side by side on wooden stools and Joel placed before us each a boiled egg in a wooden eggcup, two thick slices of brown bread slathered with butter, and a bowl of steamed vegetables. After finishing the first egg, we each ate a second.

When we'd polished everything off, Joel pointed to a plate on a shelf by the stove that was covered with a cloth napkin. "I saved you some cake," he said.

It was dark brown honey cake. It went wonderfully with the cup of milk Darlene poured for each of us from a jug.

Darlene smiled warmly at Joel and said goodnight. I was struck by the way they communicated; it occurred to me now that there was never any physical contact between them. I recalled the way Joel had stroked his own arm after the tea set had been destroyed, as if comforting Darlene by proxy, and how he later caressed her with his eyes, as if enfolding her in a protective embrace.

I also said goodnight and Darlene and I made our way to the bathroom where we washed our faces and hands in the cracked porcelain sink. She shook some white powder onto a toothbrush with raggedy, worn bristles and scrubbed at her teeth. There was another toothbrush by the sink; I assumed it was mine. I also sprinkled some of the powder on the brush. It tasted soapy and left an unpleasant, filmy feel in my mouth.

"Why don't you ever hug Joel?"

Darlene turned to me, her face hung with surprise.

"You know perfectly well why," she said.

"Actually, I don't."

Darlene's eyes wavered and when she next spoke, her voice sounded odd and far away.

"Because it's against the law for a black man to touch a white girl. He would lose his job. Maybe even be sent to prison."

"Yes, of course. I know that," I said, overcome with confusion.

"Then why did you ask?"

I paused, aware of a peculiar shiver traveling the length of my spine, and then, unable to come up with a suitable answer, simply said what I felt. "I don't know."

Darlene nodded, something curiously knowing in her eyes, as if this was a satisfying answer—the answer, in fact, she'd been expecting.

Back in her room, Darlene took something from the back of her top drawer and handed it to me—a solid little chunk wrapped in aluminum foil. I opened it to find six squares of milk chocolate.

"I was saving this for a special moment. And now, here it is!" she said.

I broke the joined pieces into two even sections and handed one to Darlene. I bit off one of the squares and let it melt on my tongue and Darlene did the same, folding the piece of foil and replacing it in her top drawer. She seemed to save everything.

When we'd finished eating the chocolate, Darlene changed into a nightdress, offering me a simple cotton shift. She insisted on making up the cot that was to be my bed. She took great care with the sheet and blanket, smoothing them until they were tight as a drum, then gave me her one feather pillow, on top of which she placed a lace doily she'd crocheted herself. It was clear that Darlene owned very little: a single dress hung in the wooden armoire, alongside two carefully pressed blouses and an old blue cardigan, all of which looked like hand-me-downs. Her tiny chest of drawers seemed to hold equally few items.

I slipped in between the sheets of the cot and lay down on my side. Darlene retrieved something from between her mattress and the wooden bed frame—an envelope. She kneeled down by the bed, closed her eyes, then put the envelope to her lips. She seemed to be muttering a prayer. When she had finished, she rose.

"What's that?" I asked, nodding toward the envelope.

"It's a letter my mother got from her brother and his family in Lithuania, more than two years ago. It was the last time we heard from them. They asked us to pray for them."

"What happened to them?"

For a moment, Darlene's face went blank. She sat on the end of my cot, then opened the envelope and pulled out a sheet of paper. She spread it open and began reading—in yet another new language, which I think was Yiddish. Miraculously, again, I understood every word.

Dearest Sarah,

You can't imagine what's happening here. We scarcely believe it ourselves. Nazi soldiers are everywhere. People are being taken away. They just disappear—we hear terrible things about shootings in the forest. We have to leave our house, it is being taken, like the property of all Jews. We do not know where we will go. We will bring Chaya's mother, who is eighty-three. How on earth will she survive?

We don't know what to do with Latka, our dog. He's been a member of our family for five years. Lord knows how, but we've managed to keep him fed in these dreadful times—bits of fat and bone—though he is very thin.

I do not know if this letter will reach you. I will try to give it to the postal clerk. We were friends, once.

Pray for us. Think of us.

In love, sadness—Dear God, in fear—

Your loving brother Josef, and Chaya, and the children

Darlene refolded the paper and put it back into the envelope. "We've not heard from them since."

Sarah's voice had gone flat. The name *Josef* rang a bell, but I couldn't place it. My mother had told me stories about her relatives, but they jumbled together; having grown up without extended family, they seemed more like storybook characters than real people.

"We know what the Nazis are doing to Jews over there," she said. "We heard about it on the radio broadcast. Some American journalists were trapped in the region when the US entered the war—they were exchanged for Germans who'd been in America. They wrote about what they had seen; one said there was an 'open hunt' on the Jews. Hundreds, thousands at a time. Rounded up and shot into pits."

I knew that before the Nazis came up with their more efficient methods—gas chambers and crematoriums—they had the Jews dig the pits themselves and enlisted local collaborators to help with the shooting. My heart pounded in my throat. I tried to stifle the terrifying images that leapt into my mind's eye, flowing from the words—*an 'open hunt' on the Jews*—

Darlene returned to her bed and slipped the envelope back beneath her mattress.

"I said a little prayer for you, too, Camellia," Darlene said in a small voice.

"Oh?"

"I prayed that you would find what you are looking for."

I didn't know what to say.

"Thank you," I finally uttered. And then, "Good night."

"Good night. And Camellia—" She took in a sharp breath. "I'm glad you're here."

I lay back and looked up at the ceiling, thinking about how very far away I was from my own world. The cracks on the ceiling arranged themselves into animals and clouds. If Billy were here, I'd snuggle him into my arms and spin the characters that were appearing on the ceiling into a story to help him settle to sleep. How was he getting along without me? Surely all of them were sick with worry. What must they be thinking?

Darlene's breath slowed to the rhythm of sleep. I rolled over to see that she was curled into a ball, the sheet pulled tightly around her. I thought again with sadness about what a lonely, sad girl she was—and yet so giving and warm, and tilted toward joy.

I tossed and turned for some time; sleep would not come. My limbs were so restless—I had to get up and walk around. Quietly, I stepped from the bed, tiptoed past Darlene and then carefully opened the door.

In the hallway, I squinted into the near darkness and took a few steps. I trained my ears on the stillness and realized I could hear a faint crackling. Out through the window, a handful of stars sent haloes of light into the night sky. I stood still and listened; it was as if the crackling were coming from the stars.

A beam of light at the end of the hallway spilled from a slightly open door onto the floorboards. On cat's feet, I made my way down the corridor and came to a halt outside the door. The crackling was coming from within the room; it was a radio, the volume turned down low.

I flattened my back against the wall beside the door jamb. Carefully, I leaned around to peer in through the crack in the door. I found myself looking into the bedroom of Darlene's mother, back from her bridge game. She was seated at a small dressing table, leaning over something spread out before her. It looked like a map; yes, she was studying a map. Now I could hear the voice of a newscaster talking about the battles being waged in the various theaters of war, rattling off victories and defeats. A small lamp burned on the shelf above the dressing table; in its weak illumination, Darlene's mother, pencil in hand, was making marks upon a map. A trail of tears glistened from her eye to her chin.

The newscaster barked his news—of deaths and danger and city upon city destroyed by bombs—and Darlene's mother continued to put marks upon her map, the tears streaming down her face. Quietly, I turned and walked back down the corridor to Darlene's room and crawled into bed.

* * *

Sleep engulfed me—the kind that is exhausted and blank, no dreams, no experience of any kind. And then, breaking through the emptiness was the awareness of a sharp prodding at my shoulder. I shook the dreamless sleep from my head and opened my eyes to see Darlene sitting at the end of my cot. A very bright half-moon filled the room with light and lent an eerie glow to everything.

"Camellia, I'm sorry to wake you, but I have something I must ask you."

I sat up; even in the heart of the night, the heat was oppressive. I could feel a layer of sweat covering my entire body.

"This is going to sound odd, but I sort of jolted awake with this feeling that I don't know where you've come from."

"I beg your pardon?" I asked, rubbing my eyes.

Sleep hung fuzzily around me. Moonlight washed the floorboards white, hazing everything to immovable, ghostlike precision—the folds of Darlene's blanket like carved marble, impossibly rendered, the dresser turned to mottled salt, and Darlene herself a china doll with perfectly painted features and glossy, lifelike hair.

"It's funny—I know certain things about you. That you are my cousin Gloria's cousin from Durban, and that you're staying here because Gloria has the measles. But they're just facts—not things I understand, if you know what I mean. I'm confused. I've known you such a short time. So how come I feel I *know* you deep down? And how did Mr. Van Graan know your name? It doesn't make any sense!"

Darlene had clearly intuited something of the truth of my strange circumstances; perhaps it had come to her while she slept. I yearned to blurt everything out. To tell her about my ill mother in New York—Darlene's own future daughter! To tell her about the extraordinary trapdoor in time I had tripped upon. How maybe this time travel had something to do with my own mother's sadness and hope. I had an even stronger urge to tell Darlene how her life would unfold—that her dreams would sustain her and carry her halfway around the globe into a wonderful life, far away from this backward, bigoted place.

And yet I felt a compulsion—as if it were a command from on high—*not* to reveal these truths; I had the distinct feeling that to do so would be to disrupt history. How could I tell Darlene that in the future, she would be my grandmother? If I revealed her destiny—the reality of how her life did, in fact, unfold—would I not be opening the possibility of changing history? I would be changing the unknowable unfolding of the future into the undoable, fixed facts of the past, and I sensed that to do this would involve a serious danger of cosmic proportions. Darlene might find herself tempted to live things differently; she might not marry Grandpa Jack. My mother might not be born. Which would mean I would not be born—and not be here to alter things in the first place! Yes, that's what must have happened in Australia, on my last adventure with Talia! It was when I blurted out the truth—that were I to tell my mother anything, I'd be telling *her,* Talia, *not* my classmate but my *future mother!*—that the earth tipped over and the world fell away. That's how I lost them—Talia and Grandpa Jack. It had been a terrible mistake, allowing my fear and loneliness to get the better of me. But how was I to know what was right, here, and what constituted a mistake? Without any clear rules, no guidance of any kind?

My head reeled. But I did sense one thing, deep in my gut: I could not tell Darlene the truth.

I could, however, tell her how I felt.

Darlene was looking down at her lap. "You think I've gone crazy," she said. "I'm sorry, it's just that every now and then, since we were walking to school yesterday, I find myself feeling puzzled and wondering—"

"Yes?"

"Well, wondering, *who are you?*"

That question again. Talia had asked me the same thing, an eternity away, in Australia. Darlene was regarding me with deep and slightly baffled eyes.

"I'm just a fourteen-year-old girl in search of something," I said.

Darlene seemed to be waiting for more.

"It's like there are shadowy worlds behind my life—worlds I know nothing about," I said. "Well, not in their details. But I *do* know what these worlds feel like. It's funny, but I feel like in a way, they are *part* of me—that they define who I am in some important way. And yet—and yet—"

Darlene gave a slow nod.

"I think I know what you mean," she said.

"You do?"

"I feel that way sometimes. Mostly when I play the piano or sing. Or sometimes when I listen to music."

She turned away, as if overcome with shyness.

"What's it like for you?" I asked.

"I've never told anyone this," she said. Her voice was hesitant, and yet there was something bold and strong in it, something I'd not heard before. "I don't know, maybe you'll understand it—"

"Give it a try," I said.

"It feels like music is—I don't know, a person. Someone powerful—like an emperor or empress, maybe even a god. This—let's call it a deity—breathes its life into the composer, and then, as I work through the piece and finally gain some mastery over it, I take up this same life-force. It becomes me and I become it. I feel frightened, but I also feel more alive—and less alone. Maybe not even alone at all!"

Darlene was suddenly glowing with light; her shyness had evaporated, her voice was strong and clear.

"And when I listen to a wonderful piece of music on the gramophone, it's a bit like what you're talking about. Like another world opens up right in front of me—" She gestured in front of her, cupping the moonlit air in her hand. "And all I have to do is close my eyes and tip myself into it. And there I am, far away from everything I know—from my family, from Koppies, from *this place*. But I'm also closer than ever to—" Darlene took in a little gulp of air and I saw that her eyes and her lips were trembling.

"To what?" I asked, my own voice trembling.

She closed her hand gently and placed it over her own breastbone. "I don't know, to here."

I remembered something my mother once talked about. She often sat on my bed at night and told me wonderful things she had learned. Now, I recounted to Darlene the story of Plato's Cave. The most famous of the early Greek philosophers, Plato had the idea that the world we lived in was really like a cave, and that the reality we knew was no more than the glimmering on the cave wall of images from another reality that we could never actually know. It intrigued me, though I couldn't say I fully understood what Plato was trying to say.

Talking to Darlene, I glimpsed what this might mean. I had stepped outside the cave of my own world to discover other realities that all along had been glimmering within my own reality—my mother's life, as she'd lived it, and now also my grandmother's. Reflections of other distant, shadowy worlds that were in fact part of the world I'd taken to be my own.

Darlene gazed right into me with her illuminated eyes, but also through me to a distant, unimaginable world that was wholly her own.

"I know just what you mean," she said. "I think I've felt the same way myself, though I'd never have been able to put it into words."

Darlene shook her head, the same way Talia had shaken hers in a similar moment between us.

"But look, there's something else—" Her voice was suddenly urgent. Only now did I notice that she was fully dressed.

"Darlene. Why are you dressed?" The chimes of the clock rang out. One. Two. "It's two o'clock in the morning!"

"I can't live here anymore. I've decided to—to—to run away!" she said. "I thought—well, I thought you might want to come with me."

I sat up in the bed. "Where will you go?" I asked.

"To Joel's. He'll help me figure out what to do. Maybe he'll even take me in himself."

"But isn't Joel here?"

"No. He had word yesterday afternoon that his grandson is ill. Joel's daughter, the boy's mother, is a servant in Johannesburg. My mother told him he could go last night, after we went to bed; she gave him tomorrow—I mean today—off to take care of his grandson until his daughter can get back."

"But Darlene. Do you really think this is sensible?"

"I don't care what's sensible and what isn't! I'm going—whether you come with me or not."

"Very well, then," I said. I was beginning to trust in the mysterious logic of this adventure; I had no place here other than with Darlene, no choice other than to go wherever she went. I threw aside the sheet, removed the cotton shift I was wearing and quickly got into my clothes. It was with some dismay that I looked at the ill-fitting, uncomfortable boots I'd had to suffer all of yesterday.

"Do you have any sticking plaster?" I asked. "I have awful blisters."

Darlene opened her top drawer, where she seemed to keep what few treasures she had and removed a small cardboard box. She carefully removed its contents—only three plasters remained—and handed them to me.

"Thank you," I said, and put them on the worst of the blisters. I stepped into the offending boots and laced them up.

Outside, the mild night air held a remnant of the day's heat. The semi-darkness made my senses keener. I breathed in the unusual, pleasing scents of dry grass and unfamiliar trees and trained my ears on the rustle of leaves, the scuttling of night creatures, the soft whooshing of insects in their hectic swoopings.

Darlene broke into a run and I found myself racing beside her across the dry grass on the slope behind her house. We reached a low wooden fence and Darlene helped me over before climbing over herself. We had no trouble seeing in the light of the moon; it bleached the landscape to shades of glowing gray. My legs felt strong and energized, though we ran for some time, and I could hear my breath coming in short bursts. It was a comfortable flight; I gave myself over to the smells and sounds, to the unearthly light and exhilarating feeling of speed.

After a time, we slowed to a brisk walking pace. We passed by fields and here and there, modest brick or wooden homes, sometimes in clusters and sometimes alone. We came to a small cemetery. Darlene turned toward the rusted gate and reached for the latch.

"This is one of my special places," she said, swinging the gate open. "I come here to think. It's especially perfect at night."

The cemetery was surrounded by open fields; in the far distance, almost at the horizon, I could just make out a small village of mud huts, much like the one I'd seen on our walk to and from school, though it looked to be a good deal larger. The same baked dirt walls, empty holes for windows, and heavy thatched-straw roofs. Darlene followed the direction of my gaze.

"That's Joel's village. We'll go there just now. First, I want you to see the Jewish graveyard."

We walked through the gate and Darlene latched it again after us.

"There aren't many Jewish families left in Koppies. There used to be more. And there are quite a lot of Jews in Vereeniging."

Darlene leaned down to the ground and hunted around. She found what she was looking for: two small, smooth stones. She handed one to me.

"Come," she said, and I followed her to a small granite headstone. There could not have been more than a hundred graves in all.

Darlene knelt and placed the stone on the granite and then gestured that I do the same with mine. As I leaned over to place my stone beside hers, I read the name and dates engraved in the tombstone.

Rose Selda Shapiro.
February 26, 1928–December 10th, 1928.

Below this were several rows of Hebrew lettering I could not decipher. I wondered whether the writing was Hebrew or Yiddish, then felt a pang of sadness that I didn't know the difference.

"My baby sister," Darlene said. "She'd have been my older sister, of course, had she lived. Maybe it's because she died as a baby that I think of her as little."

She knelt on the ground before the grave.

"I like to come and visit her. Nobody else does, as far as I can tell."

Carefully, Darlene pulled at some scraggly weeds that were growing around the edge of the grave.

"I feel like if I don't come, she'll be lonely. All she has is me."

"Doesn't your mother come? Or your older brothers?"

Darlene shook her head.

"No one wants to remember her. But no one seems able to forget about her, either. I feel like she fills up our home like a ghost. Don't you feel it?"

I imagined Darlene was talking about the heavy, cold atmosphere of her home: the anger her mother seemed to push before her, like a black cloud.

"It's because of how she died," Darlene said. In the moonlight, I could see that Darlene's jaw was clamped tight. "It was my mother's fault."

Darlene had no idea that I knew the story—of what had happened to Rose. She herself—not as Darlene, but as Grandma—had told me in her elegant home in Australia, far away from here in place and time. She could not know that she had given me Rose's little pink booties, crocheted by her own mother so many years ago.

A chill ran up my spine; I reached into the pocket of my jacket, trembling with anticipation. The woolen booties were there, having survived another enormous tumble through time, having survived the storm and the changes of clothing and the running from here to there. I let my hand close around the soft yarn, held the booties tight.

"Rose was allergic to cow's milk ... well, it's a long story, but all you need to know is that my mother ended up giving her cow's milk on a train journey. The milk had gone bad, which made it even worse. Rose died, and my mother never forgave herself. She's never said that in so many words, but daughters know their mothers."

Darlene turned to look at me, her face filled with pain.

"She has no idea that I know these things. My mother, I mean. But I do."

She reached up and touched the place on the side of her forehead where the wound from her tussle with the blackboard eraser was beginning to scab over. I recognized the gesture—Grandma had touched that place on her forehead in that very same way, that night we sat together in her house in a future far distant from this bright, moonlit night.

"It's all inside of me. Right here." Darlene placed her fist on her chest.

How could I not think of that oppressive darkness that sometimes smothered me? That felt as if it belonged—I don't know, to someone else?

We sat in silence. Something passed between us—something delicate and yet vivid, like a moth with somber markings, making its way in the dark.

Darlene rose and together, we made our way to the gate.

Back on the dirt pathway skirting the field, our feet again flew across the ground—that wonderful, effortless gliding that left me feeling lighthearted and free.

The wide horizon and open fields and huge bowl of sky above me spread out in all directions for what seemed an eternity. As we walked, I realized the village was farther away than it had looked from the cemetery. The feeling of light-heartedness and ease slipped away and I became aware once more of my aching feet and the places on my heel and toes where the ill-fitting shoes painfully rubbed. I looked across to Darlene, walking beside me, her face determined and grim. Her feet must have ached, too; her shoes seemed as badly fitting as my own. I had the feeling that Darlene was used to all kinds of difficulties and discomforts, and to suffering in silence—and alone.

Finally, we turned onto a small dirt roadway and found ourselves among the thatched-roofed mud huts we'd seen from afar. The pleasant, earthy smell of baked dirt and reedy straw mingled with an assortment of animal scents—chickens, perhaps, and pigs—along with the smoky aroma of spent ash. Cooking odors hung in the air: savory meat and the husky sweetness of cooked cornmeal.

Darlene made her way deftly down one pathway and up another. No one was about, but I was aware of the heavy feel of countless sleeping people. Finally, we reached a large hut at the end of a row. Darlene came to a halt. She rapped gently on the rough wooden door in what seemed like a signal: two slow, hard raps followed by three quick, light ones.

Moments later, the door opened to reveal Joel, dressed in a robe made of colorful fabric of the kind I had seen in Brooklyn many years ahead in the future.

"Dear Lord mercy, Do-Do. What in heaven's name are you doing here?" he asked, casting furtive glances up and down the pathway.

By way of answer, Darlene flung herself into Joel's arms. For a moment, Joel looked alarmed.

"Do-Do, Do-Do," he said, shaking his head back and forth. "Come in, before anyone sees you."

Not once had Darlene cried or expressed any real anger in the long day I'd known her, despite the many affronts and disappointments. On each occasion, she had gritted her teeth, seeming, in fact, to grit her entire being, a steely look fixed in her eyes.

Now, enfolded in Joel's arms, she wept.

"Come, come," he said, guiding her into the hut. I followed, closing the door behind me.

Inside, it was so dim I could make out only vague charcoal shadows, nothing but the suggestion of things. Joel stood and held Darlene, who continued her silent crying, her thin shoulders heaving pitifully. He stroked her hair, whispering in Zulu.

After some minutes, Darlene's tears were spent. She withdrew from Joel's arms and when she turned to me, I saw that her face was puffy and red. She reached into her pocket, drew out her frayed handkerchief, and discreetly blew her nose.

"Let me heat up some milk," Joel said. "How you managed to make it here all by yourselves, I'll never know."

Joel lit a candle and the inside of the hut sprang to view: a simple, bare room with clay walls and a dirt floor, swept clean. Joel crossed to the far corner, where I saw that a wood-burning stove was built into the hard-baked wall. He lit the tinder that was under a black pot then took a jug from the shelf and poured in some milk.

Across from the stove, on a large woven mat, five little children lay sleeping, all lined up neatly together. I watched the slow rise and fall of their chests. In the far corner was a wooden table with four chairs.

"How is your grandson?" Darlene asked Joel.

"His fever broke an hour ago," Joel said, nodding in the direction of the sleeping children. "Now, he's cool and sleeping with his cousins."

The children cuddled together, an arm curled here and there in embrace.

We sat at the table and Joel brought us each a mug of milk and a cornmeal biscuit. The milk was frothy and slightly sweet, the biscuit dense and delicious.

"Now, Do-Do," Joel said, "tell me what this is about."

Darlene's face took on a pointy look of determination. "I woke up feeling I just couldn't stand to live there anymore. I've felt this way before but somehow—" Now she glanced over at me. "I don't know. It just seemed different this time. Like I wanted to do something about it. Maybe because Camellia is with me—I had the courage to leave them, once and for all."

Darlene looked from Joel to me and then back again to Joel. Her lips trembled. "So, I decided to run away."

"You decided to run away," Joel said.

"Yes," Darlene said, trying to muster the steeliness that she seemed suddenly to have lost.

"Do-Do, you know you can't stay here."

"But Joel, you're my family!" Darlene glanced over to the children asleep on the mat. A fresh tear formed at the corner of her eye and slipped down her cheek. "Why can't you be *my* grandfather, too?"

Joel's face was kindly and sad. He shook his head.

"I can't take you from your own people," he said. "You belong with them. Besides, you know very well it would be impossible, even if I wanted to keep you here."

He pointed first to his own face and then to Darlene's. "Black. White," he said.

Darlene nodded.

"It's against the law. I'd be put in jail. Then where would they be?" Joel glanced over to his sleeping grandchildren. "They are my responsibility."

When he uttered the word *responsibility,* he drew out each syllable, making the word sound velvety with love.

Darlene looked down at her shoes. "Am I not your responsibility, too?"

"You are. But I can best help you in your own home."

Darlene said nothing; she only continued to look down at the ground.

"Your mother can be harsh," Joel said. "It is true. But she's not a bad woman."

Darlene's eyes burned. "Well, she's not very nice. Not to me."

"Perhaps not. But she loves you in her way. And she is your mother."

"I wish she weren't." Darlene's voice was rock-hard. "But she is.

What point is there in wishing the impossible? It's like a bird wishing it were a snake."

Joel looked down at his own arm and then held it up. In the flickering candlelight, I could see his roughened palm.

"Do you think I wish I were born white? That my children and grandchildren were born white? In a country where you know what it means to be born black—could such a thought not have crossed my mind? I am a man, like any other. A man who wanted his children to have opportunities and hope. A man who wishes more than a man can wish anything that his grandchildren might live a life of dignity."

Joel's rich voice made the word dignity sound like the most beautiful word in the English language—which perhaps, after all, it was.

"What choice do I have?" Now, he pointed to his chest. "I am who I am. I was given this life, in this body, in this time, in this place. What can I do but make the best of where I landed?"

Darlene's expression had softened; she listened as if in a trance.

"And you, Darlene, were given to this life in your body, your time, your place. You cannot change the family you were given into. It is up to you to make the best of what life has handed you. To make the best of who you are."

Joel rose from the wooden stool and motioned for us, also, to rise. We stepped out into the night. He seemed to have forgotten his earlier concern, as if something of greater importance had overtaken the worry that we might be seen. The bright half-moon hung above the village, a thick crescent of otherworldliness, smiling sideways at our earthly plights. We walked away from the other huts, veering off the dirt pathway and out into an open field. I drank in the cool country air. The field inclined; on the downward slope, we came to a halt.

"Look," Joel said, and he pointed to the horizon. "Do you see that?"

I squinted into the distance; there, a shimmering stroke on the landscape in the far distance.

"*Bloedrivier*," Joel said.

I understood the Afrikaans at once: Blood River. But what did Joel mean?

"You know the story, from school," he said.

Darlene nodded; she turned to me as if intuiting that I had no idea what Joel was talking about. And there it was again—that now-familiar, inscrutable look in Darlene's face.

"Camellia, Joel is talking about the Voortrekkers, the pioneers who crossed the veldt in their wagons. They fought back when they were attacked by Zulu warriors. It was suicide—five hundred Boers against more than five thousand Zulus. But they won—such slaughter, the blood of the Zulus turned the river red."

Now, Joel spoke. "My great-great-great-grandfather was taken from his mother's arms soon after his birth by one of those Boers. Raised as a slave in their household. They say he was a sweet boy, a cheerful boy. His master favored him. He was already a young man when the master decided to join the wagon Voortrekkers and cross into the veldt to escape from the British."

"The British," Darlene said, as if for my benefit, "who ruled over the Boers."

Joel picked up the thread of his story. "The Afrikaners were the only family my great-great-great-grandfather had ever known. Yes, they were his masters and he was a slave. But that was his life.

"When the Zulus attacked, I imagine he didn't think about it. He did what his brave, loyal heart told him to do. He fought for the people he called his own—his Boer masters. He fought bravely against the Zulu warriors that were attacking the wagon trains. He was defending his master and his own livelihood. Those were his loyalties."

Joel gazed off into the distance. The moon was losing the power of its glow in the glaze of early daylight, spreading across the sky.

"This is the story my mother told me when I was a child, younger than you," he said, turning to face Darlene. "I often used to think about that ancestor of mine, when I was a boy. I would see him sitting on the banks of the river, after the battle was over, his spear in his hand. I would picture this brave warrior crying into the river of blood."

"Joel, that's awful!" Darlene said, looking at Joel in horror. "Why are you telling us this?"

Joel continued to look off at the horizon. "Camellia asked about the river."

"Did she? I don't remember her asking."

"She may not have voiced the words, but I felt the question." As he said this, Joel placed his hand on his heart. Then, he turned to me, with eyes I recognized. My heart was thumping so loudly in my chest, the others must surely have heard it. Jimmy! That's where I'd seen the look in Joel's eyes!

"Your friend. She's very interested in rivers, I think," Joel said. "Water. The source. We all come from the sea, isn't that so?

"We must travel the river we're thrown into. Every river has its story. Their sources reach far, far away—and their destinations, well, those are the greatest mysteries of all."

Joel was trying to tell me something, I could feel it: to communicate an important secret. But I couldn't grab hold of it. It seemed to slip right through my fingers like—well, like water.

"We do not choose the river we are thrown into. All we can do is ride the current as best we can."

Joel shook his head slowly. "Do-Do, the older I grow, the less I understand about the heart of man. But I do know this. You cannot run away."

I felt so confused. I did not understand why Joel had told us that terrible story about his ancestor. What was he trying to say? I could see that Darlene, too, was struggling to make sense of what Joel was telling us.

"You must know your own river if you are to rise above its currents and swim your way home. Running away from your family, from the truth of who you are, is not the way."

Joel hunkered on the ground in front of us, his eyes deep pools of their own.

"I've lived with my great-great-great-grandfather all my life; he is here, in my own mind and heart." Joel pointed gently first to his temple, then to his chest. "He did not choose the circumstances of his birth any more than I did. His fate was a terrible one—far worse than either mine, or yours, Darlene. Nothing can change where you come from. But you can find a way to ride the river *away*: to travel upon it *toward* a place that feels more right for you.

"Miss Camellia, tell Miss Darlene to see reason."

"I can't go back," Darlene said, through silent tears.

"Joel's right," I said. "You *can* leave this place—when you're older, old enough to make your own life."

Suddenly, there before my eyes: an image of Grandma sitting in her beautifully appointed study, half a world away in Melbourne, Australia, a place my young companion Darlene could hardly have imagined. "Running away now—well, I can't see how that is going to help things."

"Your mother is surely very worried about you," Joel said. "You must go."

Joel walked us back to the dirt road leading away from the village and gave Darlene a tentative, brief hug. In her face, I saw wonder—to be finally experiencing the gift of his embrace. He turned to me, an enigmatic look in his face, and gave a brief, acknowledging nod.

"I'll see you on Friday," Joel said. "Now, Do-Do, be a good girl until then."

We turned and began the long walk back to Darlene's farmhouse. My strength had returned and I pushed ahead, trying to ignore the unplastered places on my feet where the skin burned against the tough leather. We walked almost the whole way in silence.

By the time we limped into Darlene's yard, our legs aching and fresh blisters on our feet, the day had arrived and the household was beginning to stir. A thin spiral of smoke coiled up from the chimney and disappeared into the pale sky. We entered through the front door and hurried to the bathroom, where we washed our hands and faces, brushed our teeth, and tugged combs through our hair. Then, we rushed to Darlene's bedroom and changed into our school clothes.

By the time we entered the kitchen, Darlene's mother was serving up bowls of porridge, apparently unaware that we'd been absent and not worried at all.

"I've saved the cream," she said in her husky voice. She seemed less grim than she'd been the previous day.

Darlene seemed excited at the sight of the thick cream sitting in a green bowl beside the porridge; it was clearly a special treat.

"Thank you, Mother," she said.

"There's a second bowl for each of you, if you'd like."

I followed Darlene's lead, sprinkling sticky brown sugar onto the oatmeal and watching it darken and melt before scooping a ladleful of cream into the bowl. Hungrily, we ate. The cream was delicious, like nothing I'd ever tasted before—silky smooth with a hint of natural sweetness. I'd have loved that second bowl, but we didn't seem to have time. We took our empty bowls to the sink, picked up the sandwiches wrapped in wax paper, and retrieved our satchels from where we'd left them by the door.

"Do well in school," Darlene's mother said.

"Thank you for breakfast," I said. Darlene's mother eyed me and gave me a nod. For the first time, I noted a look of vague curiosity in her face.

We raced out the back door and began the trek to the schoolhouse. The morning cool remained and yet I found myself feeling hot, as if the sun were already high in the sky. I reached a palm to my face and was surprised to find my cheeks burning.

"I expect you're looking forward to going home," Darlene said, throwing me a sideways glance.

Of course, I was looking forward to going home, though not to any home that Darlene could have imagined. I wondered, though, which home she meant. At the thought, I found myself feeling faint. My feet suddenly felt extremely heavy and I had to slow down. Darlene adjusted her pace to mine.

We came to the crossroads of the town, but instead of continuing on ahead toward the schoolhouse, Darlene turned left.

"I want to show you something," she said.

"But what about school?"

"Everyone needs a day off, now and then," Darlene said, a mischievous look in her eye.

A rooster crowed in the distance, way behind schedule. We were approaching a cornfield, dense with growth. The plants, which were about our own height, waved and rustled in the breeze. Skirting around the edge of the corn, we came to a hill. Darlene raced to the top; I followed as best I could, willing my heavy feet to speed up. What was wrong with me? I felt I was moving through molasses. I shimmied down the other side of the hill, coming to a stop by an unusually wide and gracious tree where Darlene stood smiling.

"I wanted to show you my favorite tree!" she said, grabbing hold of a sturdy, low-lying branch that stretched out almost horizontally from the thick trunk. "It has the most beautiful flowers in the spring. You must come back and see them—every bloom is perfect!"

Darlene's voice was so full of feeling I thought she was going to cry. She climbed to a branch halfway up and sat in the comfortable-looking V where the branch joined the trunk.

"Come on! It's stronger than it looks." She encircled the trunk with her arm and kissed the tree's rough bark.

Taking hold of the lowest branch, I gingerly hoisted myself up. I was not in the habit of climbing trees, being a Brooklyn girl. The awful pounding started up in my head; I did my best to ignore it. A few minutes later, I was up there with Darlene. I lodged myself in a second V made by another branch to the side of where Darlene was sitting.

"I've never had anyone else here with me," Darlene said, her eyes shining. "This has always been my own special place. Now it can be ours."

She reached into the pocket of her pinafore and drew something out.

"Here," she said, "I want you to have this."

Darlene placed something into my hand. I looked down to see the little china plate from her precious tea set: the sole surviving piece. The china felt smooth in my palm; I looked, for a moment, at the border of tiny painted roses.

"I told you that no one had ever given me such a beautiful present. When I opened the box, I couldn't believe my eyes."

I recalled the horror in Darlene's face when her brother had destroyed her treasure. Now, she was smiling.

"I've never had a friend my own age before. Having you is much more special even than the tea set."

I didn't know how to thank Darlene. The words got caught somewhere in my chest. As we smiled at each other, I noticed, for the first time here in South Africa, Grandma's distinctive dimple just beneath the corner of her mouth, off to the side. Her face froze in that expression and made me want to weep. The branches were waving around her in the rising breeze, and now, from the corner of my eye, in ghostly negative, the outline of a rough cabin with a brick chimney shimmered within and beyond the leaves. I turned to see another image, the interior of a vast paneled room with tall doors, elaborate ceiling moldings, and high windows, also transparent, laid over the sky and the trees, shimmering all around us. I recognized the double exposure photographic images at once—we'd seen them in the gift shop at the Belle Meade Mansion, a world away. Before I knew Mama was ill. Before the storms had whisked me away from everything I knew and loved.

Now, instead of the cabin slave quarters and the elegant room inside Belle Meade, I saw Joel's hut, with his grandchildren cuddling together in sleep on the floor, superimposed onto the outline of Darlene's schoolhouse, her classmates scowling in the school yard, and pressed up against the chain link fence, the faces of the village children.

Darlene was smiling, still, and she reached out her hand.

"I'm just so happy you're here," she said.

"I've come from very far away," I said, tears springing to my eyes, as self-pity gushed through me.

"Well, not so very far," Darlene said, squeezing my hand.

I shook my head.

"What?" Darlene asked.

"It's just—well, there are things I can't tell you," I said, the tears now falling freely from my eyes. "You see, I'm actually lost. And I'm so afraid—afraid that I'll never find my way—"

Darlene's smile fell. Her eyes were hard nubs of determination.

"I have a theory," she said. "*Everyone* feels that way. Well, anyone who has any heart and soul. If your eyes are open just a little bit, you have to see that human beings are just about the most awful species on the planet. I'd take the tigers and panthers and lions any day. Joel says you get one life and you don't choose which one you get given. But that doesn't mean you can't—"

"You can't what?"

"Do the best you can with it."

Her words held little comfort. I hung my head. A pang of anger spiked my heart and then fanned out and filled me. The world seemed such an awful place; you just had to touch the surface of it to feel the layers of suffering and injustice that went down, down, all the way down.

Yet here was Darlene, who had every reason in the world to feel angry and hard done by, her face alive with gratitude and joy! A little slug of shame crawled through me. Who was I to feel helpless? To give into self-pity? To allow anger to close me up and shut me down?

Darlene smiled again, the dimple popping back into place at an angle below the corner of her mouth.

"I have an idea," she said. "Let's remember this moment—let's remember it always! And make a promise! That in twenty years' time—no, let's make it longer! I don't know, forty years! Wherever we are in the world, let's write to each other! We can celebrate everything we've done in our lives. All the places we've visited. We'll have families of our own! And I'm going to travel all over—really see the world! And—"

My mind clicked with numbers. Forty years from now, Darlene would be fifty-four. She'd be a mother and a grandmother. In fact, that very year would be the year I was born. The year she became the grandmother of *me*.

"No, we won't write to each other!" I said, the feel of this perfect alignment of numbers like a plump little treasure in my hand. "We'll be together! I know it!" I remembered my mother telling me that one of the most precious experiences of her life was having her mother—Darlene, the skinny girl with the curly, dark hair sitting here in the tree with me—coming to spend a month with us soon after I was born.

"Grandma adored you from the moment she set eyes on you," Mama had said, showing me a photograph of me, a squishy newborn, lying on a mat with Grandma, whose arm was curled around me, her face glowing with the same expression of wonder and joy as I saw now in my friend Darlene's face!

"We'll be together, I know it," I said, smiling at Darlene through my tears. "I can see us, there, on the mat—"

The most perfect thought had formed in my mind like a crystal, shiny and delicate and rock hard, and I was about to say something else, but the words were whisked from my lungs with the sudden crash of wind as an awful vise grip seized my already aching head. My hands flew to my temples, just as I felt the great push from behind and found myself tumbling forward, somersaulting widely, a much greater distance than surely existed between the tree and the dry yellow grass.

The new day, which I'd been so enjoying, with its deepening blue sky and fresh country air, was suddenly eclipsed by a growling thundercloud. The thunderclap that followed slammed against my ears; I thrust the little plate Darlene had given me into my pocket and clamped my hands over my ears, though they were little protection against the sound's tremendous force. I closed my eyes, gave myself over to the tumbling, aware of tears welling behind my closed eyelids. I tried to keep Darlene's smiling face in my mind's eye, wondering what was happening back there for her. Wondering if she knew she had just lost forever her new—her one and only—friend.

Well, not forever, I suppose. If you could call the future, when I would come to her as her granddaughter, some kind of antidote for forever.

Is this why I'd always felt a special bond with Grandma—I wondered as the storm raged around me—because I'd known her in the past? Of course, this thought made no sense. How could I have known her before I was born—before *my own mother* was born?

My thoughts scrambled with the great cracking open of time. There was now only the heaving and spinning and pressure of darkness. I waited for the voice of my mother to pierce the terrifying blackness so that I'd know she was watching over me, so that I'd know she was showing me the way. But nothing came—no word, no feeling of care and embrace.

A great, aching loneliness welled up inside. I clenched my fists and prayed. *Please, dear God. Help me find home.*

CHAPTER FOUR

I AWOKE WITH A FEELING OF mind-numbing exhaustion—the way
you feel when you've come down with a nasty flu. All of me ached:
my muscles, joints, throat, eyes, and most of all my head. With
great effort, I heaved open my eyelids, which were crusted together
and felt unbelievably heavy.

I saw the shadowy form of a person moving slowly, too fuzzy to
make out who it was. A sound, like a rustling of clothing amplified
a thousand times, crashed against my ears, painful in its intensity.
And great, clanging thuds, the footsteps of the giant from *Jack and the
Beanstalk*, rattled the windows. I tried to lift my head; a searing pain
shot down my neck then on through my spine. For a moment, I felt
coolness, wetness, on my forehead. And then, a warm, soft brushing
against my cheek. A familiar, pungent scent burned my nostrils and
rose into my skull. So familiar, it tugged at my heart and made me
want to weep. Grandma! I tried to open my mouth but my jaw was
clamped shut. *Grandma!* The word ricocheted like a hammer banging
on the inside of my skull.

I blinked once, twice. Felt myself sinking, as if into warm water, a
new heat washing over me as the awful clanging vanished, sinking into
silence and calm. The pain in my head evaporated. I drew in a deep
breath; all of me expanded with lightness and relief. I blinked again
several times, and after a few moments, my eyes were able to focus.

I was in a bed, my face turned toward a wooden wall. The air was
heavy with smoke and crackled with the sound of burning logs.

"Finally!" I heard a cheerful young voice say.

I sat up. The voice belonged to a girl who was sitting across the room, poking with an iron at a small fire that was flaring to life in the grate of a broad red-brick fireplace. Hanging above the sputtering flames was a large iron pot, like the cauldrons in storybooks my parents had read me when I was little.

"I've been trying to wake you up for the longest time! Come on, we've got so much to do!"

What an interesting language! I found myself thinking. Guttural *ch's* and rounded, elongated vowels, *ouhs* and *aaihs*. It sounded like the German I'd heard on the trip I'd once taken with my father to Heidelberg. I understood perfectly well what the girl was saying, and knew from my recent experiences that, when I opened my mouth to speak, I would find that I, too, would be able to speak the language like a native.

I smiled at the thought of how easy it was, on this journey, to learn languages. If only back home in Brooklyn I could just open my mouth and find myself in full command of an utterly new tongue!

"Go ahead, smile if you want. But I don't see how me doing what's left of the work for *Erev Rosh Hashanah* is exactly funny! You promised to help me. *Sarah,* you said. *I'll do the lion's share.* That's why you came, isn't it?"

She didn't sound the least bit angry: only amused.

And I was grateful that she mentioned her name, and so quickly: no need to guess.

"Yes, of course," I said, pulling aside the scratchy blanket and swinging my legs over the side of the bed. "It's cold. You'd think the fire would take the edge off."

"Well, get dressed, you silly chicken," Sarah said, laying down the crooked fire iron and picking up a long wooden spoon. She stood to stir the pot and I saw that, though she was petite, she had a strong build; she looked as if she'd have no trouble wrestling me to the ground, if it ever came to that. Her light brown hair was pulled tightly into two braids that fell down her back to her waist. She stirred vigorously with the spoon and the starchy smell of some kind of porridge wafted across the room to where I was sitting. My stomach responded with a loud gurgle.

"The others won't be back for hours," Sarah said. "Between morning and afternoon prayers at the shul, they're having lunch at the Lubovskys. Let's eat breakfast. Yossele can eat when he's finished his game." She looked out into the yard; only now did I register the sounds of children playing.

"Yossele can't get enough of that game! He and Moishe from next door are at it every morning before cheder. Papa says it helps get the wiggles out so that he has *sitzfleisch* for Talmud."

I marveled at my instant understanding of all her Yiddish expressions: *cheder*—the school for Jewish children, where they taught the Old Testament—Tanakh—and the commentaries of the sages—Talmud. And *sitzfleisch*: the ability to sit still for long periods of time.

Sarah smiled. "And if you ever decide to get out of bed, you can start the samovar!"

She jerked her head in the direction of a wooden cabinet on which stood the beautiful, shiny brass samovar. *Grandma's samovar!* The one that sits in the display area of her wall unit, built especially to showcase it. How peculiar, that Grandma showed me how to use it just before—well, just before I began falling through time. The samovar that her own mother—*Sarah!*—managed to bring with her from Lithuania when she fled the pogroms and sailed to South Africa.

Sarah. *Grandma's mother.* It was startling, looking at this warm, lively girl, to think there was any way she would ever turn into the hard, unyielding woman I'd just left behind in South Africa.

A gray hessian dress was draped across the end of the bed; I pulled it on over the heavy cotton underclothes I was wearing that appeared to double as pajamas.

So, I had gone back yet another generation and now I was here, with Sarah in a small shtetl somewhere in the heartlands of Lithuania, at the beginning of the twentieth century. On the floor, beside the bed, was a pair of coarse leather shoes that looked roughly my size. I glanced over to see that Sarah was wearing similar shoes. I picked them up, noticing the neat little stitches joining the uppers to the soles. The leather laces had the same handmade look. I raised one shoe to my nose to smell the natural leather.

Sarah was serving porridge into two bowls; she looked over to see me sniffing the shoe and gave me an odd look.

"You've been wearing shoes made by my father your whole life," she said.

"I know." I felt the heat rise to my face. "I just like the smell, that's all."

"You are a funny creature, aren't you," Sarah said.

I marveled again at how this pretty, good-natured girl could have become the dour woman that had filled Darlene—and me—with fear. What lay ahead for her that might bring about such a dramatic transformation? I knew so little about her; Grandma had never talked of her, except in referring to the treasures she'd passed down—the samovar and the cuckoo clock, and the orange-and-black wedding china. I scanned the room, wondering if I might lay eyes on the cuckoo clock that I'd come to love; my heart leapt a little at the thought that I might hear again its familiar sound. But then I remembered it had been a wedding gift—and Sarah's marriage still lay some years ahead, in a future that was to me the distant past. *The distant past* ... What an impossible thought that this room, so vivid, in all its antique detail, as real as anything I'd ever experienced, in fact existed almost a century before I was born!

On my way over to the samovar, I paused to look out the window; the uneven glass, set within a lattice of crudely shaped lead, had a greenish hue, with little bubbles trapped here and there within. Beyond the window stretched a dirt yard, dominated by an ancient water pump and a long wooden trough. Beyond the yard stood other simple wooden houses much like this one, each with its own large patch of packed dirt, separated from each other by enormous gnarled trees. The early-morning light was diffuse, almost gray; I was reminded of sepia-toned photographs I'd seen lying in disorderly piles at the antique stores on Atlantic Avenue, back home in Brooklyn.

In the yard, two boys, seven or eight years old and dressed alike in simple brown trousers and rough-hewn shirts, both wearing peaked caps, were engrossed in a game involving short, pointed sticks. They took turns crouching on the ground and flipping one pointed stick over with a second, to see how far it could be flipped. As they ran to check the precise location of each flipped stick, they held on to their caps. I had a vague memory of some old photographs my mother had once shown me of her mother's family from Lithuania. A sepia image floated up from somewhere deep in my own hidden memory: serious faces, hair styles and clothing from another time, a grouping of people looking out from the past, wary, perhaps unnerved by the glassy eye of the camera.

"Always the daydreamer." Sarah's voice snapped me from my reverie.

"Sorry," I said. "I was watching the boys."

"You'd never think, looking at him, that Yossele is the star scholar at cheder. He's such a mischievous pup."

My heart clutched at the thought of my own brother, Billy, whose sixth birthday was coming up. Oh no! I thought with dismay. I'm going to miss his birthday! Another jolt overcame me at this thought; here I was, still thinking in normal terms about the passage of time— as if it made any sense to think that in a few weeks it would be Billy's birthday! I was a hundred years away from that date—and from Billy! What could it possibly mean to be one hundred years away from my brother? My head wavered, my knees felt weak, as if I was going to faint; it was all too confusing. Lost in time and space, away from everything—everyone—I loved.

"Anyone would think you want to go out and join the boys with their silly sticks!" Sarah's voice brought me back to the moment.

"No, I'm too old for that," I said, aware of how sad my voice sounded.

"You make growing up sound about as glorious as a funeral!" Sarah's voice rippled into laughter.

The surprise of it—Sarah! With humor bubbling out of her!—snapped me back into the moment of *here, now,* though I could feel myself fighting it, as if I wanted to stay sad, wanted to keep the thought of my little brother, Billy, close before me. I shook my head, allowed the feel of it all—of *the real me,* the lost me—to subside. But even as I allowed it to ebb, a tiny, fierce refusal did not allow it to disappear entirely; deep within, I could still feel the dull, aching throb of what I knew was my *real life.*

One last glance revealed Yossele and his friend, shouting with fun and rolling on the ground in a tussle.

I turned to the samovar. How lucky that Grandma had shown me how to use it—but also, how odd! Now, her words came back to me. After our failed experiment, which left us with the unpleasant taste of rust in our mouths, Grandma had said: *If ever anyone asks you to make tea in a samovar, you'll know how!* How prescient her remark was! Could she have in some uncanny way known that I would find myself in that exact situation—where someone, her own mother, in fact, would issue that very request?

I knelt to examine the dried pine cones in a wooden crate by the fireplace. I chose the smallest, driest ones and a few tiny, dry twigs for tinder, lighting one in the fireplace to get the fire burning. I spotted the little teapot on the shelf above the fireplace; beside this was an old, battered tin containing large, brittle tea leaves, very black and curled. I placed these in the teapot. When the water in the samovar was hot, I filled the teapot and set it to rest on top. I waited a good fifteen minutes to let it steep, and then prepared a cup of tea for each of us, using the concentrate from the teapot and topping it up with fresh hot water from the samovar, the way Grandma had shown me.

Sarah fetched two thick cubes of brown sugar, handing me one and placing the other between her teeth. I did the same and raised the cup to my lips, sipping through the cube of sugar. I braced myself for a bad-tasting mouthful but instead found the tea was fragrant and very strong—with no hint of rust!

After breakfast, we took our dishes outside and washed them in a wooden tub that we filled from the water pump.

"*Oy Gevalt!*" Sarah groaned as Yossele came bounding toward us; his face was flushed, his hair slicked to his forehead. He yanked off his cap and tossed it to Sarah, who caught it expertly.

"I'm late! But I was winning at *catchkus*—and I never win against Moishe! I didn't realize the time!" he said, cranking the pump and vigorously washing his face and hands. "Brrr! Could Hashem make it any colder?"

"And that was a clean shirt," Sarah said with a mournful sigh. "The other one's on your cot. Go on in and change it."

"You'll wash this one for me, darling Sister?" Yossele turned gleaming eyes to Sarah, his face lit with warmth.

"You're impossible," Sarah said with a smile. "I'll be in to serve you some porridge."

"No time! I have to get to Shacharis!" Yossele said as he ran toward the door. Before entering, he stopped short, fumbled in his pocket, then turned and ran back to Sarah. "Here, Sis. Take these." And he shoved something into Sarah's hand. "I've never seen such smooth, round ones. Tonight will be a triumph!"

Sarah slipped whatever Yossele gave her into the pocket of her apron as she watched her brother swivel around and disappear into the house.

"What did he mean—he'd never seen such smooth, round ones?"

Sarah laughed. "Oh, his little treasures," she said, reaching into her apron pocket and withdrawing two large walnuts. They were indeed unusually smooth and round. "He must have spent an hour going through the nuts," Sarah said. "It's for *palantes;* you remember how much fun it was to play that on *yontif* when we were little? I have a mind to borrow one of these and play myself! Yossele devoted all of last evening to sanding down the plank. These nuts are going to roll down so fast they'll leave all the others in the dust. Look—" Sarah stretched out her hand so I could better see them. "He's marked them, so he'll know they're his." Branded into the indent where the nut's stem had once been was a dark burn mark.

"Come on," Sarah said, pocketing Yossele's walnuts. "I want to make sure he eats something before he leaves."

In the short time we'd been outside, the filmy gray veil had lifted from the sky to reveal a cold, deep blue.

Inside, I heard the sound of whistling coming from behind the door to Sarah's parents' room, where I assumed Yossele had gone to change. At the happy sound, I was overcome once more with the sadness that had overcome me earlier, as I stood by the window watching Yossele and their neighbor at play. Before I could hide what I was feeling, I realized that Sarah was eyeing me intently.

"Hadassah," she said, her voice gentle. "What's wrong?"

Finally, I thought, my name—the name I was to carry here. I knew instantly that the name meant myrtle and tried to recall how a myrtle tree looked.

"It's just that—well, Yossele reminds me of someone." The words slipped out before I had time to think about what I was saying.

"Oh? Who?"

I was about to hedge, but the truth popped out against my will. "My own brother. Billy."

"*Bee-lee?*" Sarah repeated—the shape of the syllables awkward through her heavy Yiddish accent. And then, there it was: the furrowed brow, the gauzy look of confusion, the same kind of expression I'd seen first on Talia's face, and then on Darlene's.

"He's full of joy. For the longest time, we thought he had thin lips, because he's *always* smiling!" I tried to clamp down on the flood of words, but they rushed along heedlessly, as if I no longer had control of my tongue. "He's the sweetest boy in the world. And clever as can be! We're very close—like you and Yossele." My eyes welled with tears. There was nothing I could do to stop them; they spilled out in a rush. "Mama calls him *joyous boyous.*"

Now, the whole picture burst forth in my mind—all of us, the family, *my* family. Gathered around the breakfast table on a Saturday morning, Mama's face filled with expectation as we tucked into whatever breakfast she'd made—pancakes or French toast, or scrambled eggs.

"I don't know," I said. "I feel like I can see my brother in your brother. Something about the eyes—"

Sarah's face relaxed into a tentative smile—gone that troubled, mysterious questioning. "That's my Yossele. Little rascal, I'm going to have to wash his shirt and pants—and they were clean this morning!"

Yossele emerged from the bedroom, tugging on his jacket, which I could see was shabby around the lapels and cuffs, though scrupulously clean and brushed. Sarah disappeared into the pantry and returned with a piece of black bread slathered in congealed chicken fat.

"Now you be a good young man, Josef Anshel—so that you'll be worthy when it comes time for you to complete the minyan."

He took the bread and bit into it hungrily.

"Eat carefully," Sarah said, eyeing the clean jacket.

Josef Anshel. The name rang ominously in my ears.

Josef Anshel. I knew that name—but from where? Yossele, then, must be his nickname. I rifled through my memory and a sickening nausea crept over me. My head reeled. *Josef Anshel. Josef* ... my great-grandmother's brother. Which is to say Sarah's brother, of course. Grandma's uncle. Her *Uncle Josef,* whose story had haunted her whole life but whom she'd never met.

The memory snagged me: and there she was, my mother, in my mind's eye, her face unspeakably grave. Her voice rippled back to me; I clung to the sound—clung to the faint and yet steely connection *with her.*

"My grandmother was the only one who left," she said. "If they hadn't gone to South Africa ... " Her voice trailed off.

"And Josef? Your grandmother's younger brother? You told me they were very close—like me and Billy."

"Yes," Mama said, looking at me from some other place. "Like you and Billy."

For a moment, she seemed to forget I was even there; it was if in traveling back with her recollection into the past, I had ceased to exist.

"Mama," I said. "You were telling me about Josef."

"The Nazis dragged them into the street. The whole family. Josef, his wife, his three children." Her eyes were inward; I don't know who Mama was talking to, but it didn't seem like she was talking to me.

"They herded the whole village into the woods and made them dig an enormous pit. Then they shot them, one by one, right at the edge of the pit ... so efficient ..."

"How old were the children?" I asked.

"Seven, five, three," Mama recited, staring into unfathomable blackness.

Josef—*Yossele*. This sparkling, bright, mischievous boy who was the star of the cheder. That is what the future holds for him, I thought. And now I remembered something else: the letter Darlene— Grandma—pulled from beneath her mattress, written to her mother. Hadn't that been signed *Your brother Josef?* The family for whom Darlene had prayed, night after night, for who knows how many years. Maybe Grandma is praying for them still, for their souls—for the soul of this boy before me who could not have been more vivid and alive.

In my agitation, I found myself scratching hard through the coarse fabric of the gray dress.

"Hadassah, what's wrong?" Sarah said. "Is there something wrong with your arms?"

I felt Sarah at my side; her hands were on mine, holding them still.

"I don't know," I said. "It was just—something I could see."

I knew the instant the words were out that they sounded strange— that *I* sounded strange. A wild gulp rose in my throat. *Mama!* I wanted to cry. *I want my mama! And Papa! And Billy!*

"Sssshh." Sarah didn't query my odd words, just held my hands with hers.

I opened my mouth, the words on my tongue—*I want to go home!* But I choked them to silence. I had no home to go to—not here, not now.

Yossele was standing still as a statue, looking at me with intensity—as if he were trying to uncover my thoughts, as if he could sense my dreadful knowledge *about him* in the horrified depths of my eyes.

Frantically, I tried to break up the images in my mind's eye so I might hide them from him—as if I were cracking them into shards with an icepick.

Sarah noticed Yossele's strange look, and with a last, concerned glance at me, turned back to her brother.

"Remember, there's no other if you dirty this one," Sarah said, tugging Yossele's starched white collar into place. "Go on, you can finish eating that on your way."

"Gut yontif," Yossele said, averting his eyes, suddenly shy.

"Gut yontif," I replied. He glanced back up, and for the briefest moment, again held my gaze. This time, there was puzzlement in his face—and perhaps, I thought, just a shade of fear.

"Run along, for heaven's sake!" Sarah said, and Yossele spun around on his heels and was gone.

"We still have so much work to do," Sarah said. "We need to stay busy."

Sarah's words echoed hollowly in my mind. *We need to stay busy.* Another thought glistened its way through my agitated mind. *Mama*— always busy. Always doing something, in motion—Grandma, too. Everyone in a frenzy of action, never stopping, never stopping to—

"Come along," Sarah said. "We need to bring everything up from the cellar."

Sarah lit a candle that was in the kind of old-fashioned holder I'd seen in movies. I followed her through a small door and down steps made of hard-packed mud. The damp smell of the earth felt reassuring. The candle flame shot up thin and tall—no breeze, here, to make it shorten and flicker. It cast long shadows, making everything look mysterious. Deep shelves were dug into the mud walls and large sacks and wooden tubs lay neatly arranged on the floor. She pointed to a hessian sack.

"You grab that one," she said, all business, now.

The bag was too heavy to lift, so I dragged it across to the bottom of the stairs, then pushed and pulled it all the way up.

We made several trips down and back. Sarah was right—it was good to be busy. My melancholy thoughts receded; I found myself pleasantly absorbed in the physical labor.

I don't know how long we hauled things—I lost all track of time. Dragging a huge wooden tub of root vegetables across the kitchen floor, I paused, aware of the fatigue in my arms. I looked about at everything we'd brought up: carrots, turnips, onions, a dark leafy green that looked like kale, only more delicate. There was also a large earthenware dish filled with congealed chicken fat, the surface studded with little skin rinds.

"Don't forget to pick out the bits of skin for *gribenes*," Sarah said. The word was familiar; Grandma had made it for me on several occasions—a delicious, salty mixture of crispy fat rinds, onions, and carrot ends.

On our next run down to the cellar, I brought up a freshly slaughtered chicken; Sarah carried a thin, wide slab of beef. Back down, this time for a half-dozen scrawny dried fish that gave off a sharp odor, their eyes shriveled like raisins that nonetheless seemed to track my face with their dead gaze as I climbed back up the stairs.

We peeled and chopped and carted heavy pans back and forth to the fireplace cauldron or outside to the oven that was housed in a wooden hut behind the house. We kneaded the sweet challah dough until my hands ached and then set the dough under a cloth to rise in a little alcove in the wall beside the fireplace. Later, we would braid the dough and shape these lengths into two large rounds. I remembered this characteristic Rosh Hashanah shape from the bakery in Williamsburg that my mother took me to once around this time of year; she'd explained that the round challahs symbolize the wish for a year in which life and blessings continue without end.

I sat for a moment to rest. Over by the fireplace, Sarah wiped away a sweaty strand of hair, then dipped a wooden spoon into the chicken soup pot and brought the steaming liquid to her lips.

"Perfect," she said, a satisfied smile spreading across her face. She glanced at me then, the smile fading from her lips.

"Are you thinking about it all, too?" she asked.

I didn't know what she was talking about, although Sarah clearly assumed that I did.

I nodded.

"Are your parents also talking about leaving?" She set down the wooden spoon, her face alert with concern.

"Yes," I said, feeling what was becoming a familiar wave of sad confusion. Who were my parents here, in Lithuania, in the early part of the twentieth century? Where were they? And why was I here with Sarah—and at such an important time for this community, the Jewish New Year—rather than with them? I knew from the experience I'd already accrued on this strange journey that there was no point wondering such things. The stark truth bit into me: I was an orphan traveler, lost in time.

"Nothing's been the same, since the death of Yitzhak Baron," Sarah said, crossing to the table and sitting down beside me. "I was eight years old when he was murdered; I remember it all so clearly, though, like it was yesterday. He used to come with the other yeshivah students to take his Shabbos meals with us—the only time all week they ate anything besides potatoes and gruel."

Sarah's eyes shone with sadness. "I think about him all the time. He was a hero: the way he barricaded himself with the others in that house and threw stones at the czar's men."

Her expression darkened. "My father didn't want to crawl down into the cellar that night to hide. Lots of people did; they were the smart ones. But we ran. Ran and ran, through the streets. I'll never forget it—the Cossacks on their horses, holding flaming torches."

"How absolutely terrible," I said.

Sarah sniffed, then brushed her hand across her nose.

"You're right, of course you're right. It was terrible—the worst thing that had ever happened to me. It was also horribly confusing. We were in a panic. I'd never seen Mother like that, Father, too. They've always been—I don't know, calm, strong. Taking care of everything in our lives."

Sarah leaned toward me. "Did you know Father was once an important scholar? I used to watch him pack his cobbling tools away at the end of the day—just to see the happy look in his face, knowing he had all evening to devote to his books. Mother would serve us dinner, and then Father would go behind the curtain."

Sarah gestured to the thick cloth on the far side of the cabin. I imagined that perhaps there was a little alcove there, set aside for private study.

"His candle would burn for hours. Sometimes, I lay awake and watched the flickering shadows."

Now, finally, Sarah smiled. "I used to pretend that the shadows were the secrets of the Talmud, coming to life."

She looked a little embarrassed. "I sound like a fool!" she said, her eyes shining, but no longer with joy. "When Father gave it all away, it was a terrible thing—for all of us. For me! After that, I stopped running to his workshop at the end of the work day. I couldn't bear it!"

"What couldn't you bear?"

"The deadness in his face. As if the light of his soul had gone out."

"And that happened after the death of—Yitzhak Baron?"

"I never told you this … " Her voice trailed off, but then Sarah continued with resolve. "I saw Yitzhak's body. In the street. They'd done terrible things to him—too terrible even to say. He wasn't recognizable. I only knew it was him because my father told me so. Everything around us was burning. *Burning.* The butcher's shop, the cheder, our synagogue. It was summer—the vegetation was so dry. Do you remember that enormous yew tree outside the schoolhouse? It was on fire—like something from the Torah. Holding the flames in its branches, waving its arms around, making a horrible crackling noise, like it was a burning person."

Sarah jerkily shook her head, as if trying to dislodge the image of the burning tree from her mind.

"Even that didn't prepare me for the sight of the burning books. They dragged them from everywhere and stacked them up outside the schoolhouse. But you know all of that. Everybody does."

I nodded, trying to fix my features into a believable expression of horrified recall.

"Who could have known what books look like when they burn? Father said something to me then. Right as we were passing the huge bonfire of books."

"What was that?"

"He was quoting from some famous German poet. I don't know, maybe from a hundred years ago—."

She frowned, trying to retrieve the name. "Heine, I think." She fell silent.

"What was it?" I asked carefully. "What did the poet say?"

The words seemed stuck in Sarah's throat; finally, she gave them voice.

"*Where they burn books, they will also burn people.*"

A shudder ran through me as I recalled the terrible images I first saw when I was eleven years old: skeletal corpses, Jewish people murdered by the Nazis, being bulldozed toward the crematorium, hundreds, thousands, in order to be burned.

"And then, we were running again. Stumbling, tripping. It was so hot, all around us. Ash was flying through the air. I could taste it in my nose and in my mouth. Father must have snatched his tallises before leaving the house; he had two, they were his prize possessions. One was precious to him—passed down in his family for, I don't know, maybe a hundred and fifty years and given to him on his Bar Mitzvah. It had embroidery made out of real gold. The other one he was given on his wedding day by his wife's parents—that's the one he gave me to hold in front of my face, so I wouldn't breathe in the ash."

"Behind the tanner's, the stench got worse—maybe the cow skins were scorched. It was so bad—I felt like I had to vomit. That's where we found him. In the gutter."

Horror was etched into Sarah's features; she cast her eyes downward, as if she could no longer bear to meet my gaze.

"You have no idea ..." she said, but then caught herself. "His own mother wouldn't have recognized him. What they did ..." Her throat caught. "Father recognized his yarmulke. Imagine. His yarmulke. Father took his own precious tallis, the one he'd treasured his whole life, and laid it over Yitzhak's body. He kneeled down, and I kneeled down next to him, and he recited the prayer for the dead. Right there, in the middle of that nightmare. The smoke, the fires we'd left behind us, sucked up all the air. The awful smell was overwhelming. I felt like everything stopped—that there was only us and our words. I'll never forget the way the old cotton of Father's tallis slowly turned dark red, until there was no more yellow or gold at all."

There, in that rough, simple cabin was a stillness that felt as old as time. I don't know how long we stayed that way, but then, still visibly distressed, Sarah rose and moved aimlessly from here to there, as if trying to remember what task we'd left unfinished.

"I must have been mad," she said.

"Mad? Why?"

"The *trouble* died down. That's what the grown-ups call it. *The trouble*. I thought it was over, forever. That it was all just bad memories. But now ..."

"Yes?"

"Well, you know as well as I do!" It was the first sign I'd seen, on this strange journey, of impatience about my odd situation, about me. As if it was suddenly irritating to Sarah that I didn't know what I was supposed to know.

"It's all started up again! How are we supposed to make sense of that? How are we supposed—?" Sarah let her unfinished sentence dangle in the air for a moment. "Just the same as before! Burning Jewish stores and synagogues all around Ezerenai. It's only a matter of time before the looting and fires reach Dusiat. We'll never be safe, not *ever!*"

"The violence is still very far away," I found myself saying. "Besides, things have changed. I can't imagine the authorities will let it get so out of hand again."

I had no idea what I was talking about! Perhaps I was not too far off the mark, though, or perhaps Sarah was just desperate to put the matter from mind. Whatever the reason, after wiping away a tear, she nodded.

"Nothing's going to happen tonight," I said. "Tomorrow is another day. Let's bring in the new year with a spirit of happiness and peace."

Grandma had told me a little about her mother's life, how she had fled a terrible pogrom with her family, ending up in South Africa. I knew that Sarah was right—that her family was not safe in Dusiat. I also knew that they would escape, but that many of her family would not. I wanted to reassure her, but it was all so complicated. And in that moment, everything I thought I knew about Sarah from the little snippets I had heard from Mama and Grandma felt papery, like a story I'd once read long ago, not pertaining in any real way to the flesh-and-blood girl before me. What I knew was just a *story*, a fairy tale or myth. And yet I also knew that the plot of the story, which had been passed along to me by my own mother and grandmother, was, in a sense, *true*; those events had happened, they were what the future held for my new friend, Sarah, sitting with me here, now, her eyes fiery and afraid.

What if—what if I *could* say something now that would change that plot, that would make the future unfold differently? In some way that was better for Sarah and her family? The thought pressed on me with the weight of a millstone, leaving me feeling helpless.

Part of me felt there was nothing I could do, that history was unchangeable, that everything, in fact, had already happened the way it was going to happen.

Sarah, however, seemed to have been cheered by my words.

"You're absolutely right," she said, her mood brightening. "Come on, let's get back to work. Why don't you do the *tsimmes*? I want to get to the *taigelach*. It always takes longer than I expect—they're so fiddly."

Sarah got busy at the large wooden table with the *taigelach* dough, forming little balls and dropping them into a clay dish filled with honey.

I trusted I would know what to do, given the way I had so far been mysteriously endowed with whatever language or skill was necessary. I chopped carrots and turnips and threw them into a medium-sized pot, adding a generous cup of sugar. Then I added several handfuls of plums and raisins from one of the wooden barrels we'd brought up from the cellar. I placed the pot on a hook hanging down from a wooden beam over the flames in the fireplace.

Sarah drained the last of her *taigelach* from the pot of hot oil and plopped down on a wooden chair, giving a satisfied sigh.

"It's so much easier having you here to help! We might even have a chance for a real rest before the sun goes down. Mother made the *holupshas* and gefilte fish yesterday, so that leaves only the kugel and the compote. If we're lucky, Uncle will bring some of that dark chocolate from Vilnius that we had last year. He promised, and you know he's a man of his word."

We finished up our preparations in a flurry of contented activity. My stomach let me know with a round of crazed rumblings that we'd not eaten since breakfast. Once again, Sarah read my mind.

"No point stopping to eat now," she said. "Better to store up our appetites for the huge feast. Otherwise we'll never get through the meal."

Against the protests of my gurgling stomach, I nodded. The fabulous smells of all the dishes cooking in the house were a torture—though nothing compared with the excruciating temptation when I brought the steaming challah loaves in from the outdoor oven, my hands protected by thick mittens. It took every ounce of willpower to stop myself from tearing a piece of the glossy caramel-colored loaf and stuffing it into my mouth.

Finally, everything was ready: the table laid with the family's best linens, crockery, and silverware, the candles secured in silver candlesticks, the challahs on their special plate, covered with the white embroidered challah cloths Sarah's mother had ironed before sunrise.

Sarah boiled up a huge pot of water and poured it into the metal tub by the back door. A sheet hanging from the rafters gave us privacy; we stripped down and climbed into the steaming water. Sarah handed me a bar of brown soap that felt hard and smooth as a candle. I brought it to my nose; it smelled like honey.

"You're always sniffing things, aren't you," she said, smiling.

"It's just that it's all so—" I caught myself. I was going to say—*all so new and strange, living in another place and time.*

"Everything is so—what?" she asked.

"Fragrant, I suppose," I said.

Sarah cocked her head, gave me that look—the *look* they've all given me at some moment or other, in each of the worlds I'd visited. I steeled myself. *Here it comes,* I thought. *The question.*

"Hadassah, I was just wondering—" she began, faltering a little. "Yes?"

"Well I know it's a strange thing to ask, but it's just, well—who, exactly, are you?" Squinting at me through the steam, Sarah seemed a little taken aback by her own words.

"Why, I'm your friend," I said.

"I don't know—I feel as if I've known you forever."

"Well, we've grown up together, after all. So, in a way, you have known me forever."

"We didn't grow up together," she said. "You only moved to Dusiat recently. You were born and raised in Vilnius."

Then, Sarah looked right into me, as if she were trying to dig the truth from me with her eyes.

"I meant that we met at an important time in our lives—when we've grown from girls to young women."

I gave up trying to get any lather out of the hard, slippery bar; I slid it over my skin and then handed the soap to Sarah. She took it and let out a little sigh.

"I don't know," she said. "I have this funny feeling—" She seemed momentarily embarrassed.

"Go on," I said. "You can tell me."

"It's just a feeling—that you know things: about the future. That you know how it is all going to turn out."

"What do you mean—turn out?"

"The *trouble.*"

Of course, Sarah was right. I did know how it was going to turn out. I knew that what would happen to Sarah, to her family, to the people she knew, and later, to the Jews throughout Europe, was far, far worse than she could imagine.

"I get that feeling sometimes myself," I said, "that it's all preordained. That everything that is going to happen has already happened."

I recalled my father once explaining—in that excited way he had when talking about interesting ideas—Nietzsche's notion of the eternal return of the same: that everything in human existence and experience cycled around so that nothing, in the end, was ever really new.

Sarah smiled. "Yes, that's it, I suppose," she said. "It's a bit like that feeling I sometimes get where a memory feels like a premonition. I'll be thinking about something, remembering something that happened when I was a little girl, and then I get confused and think—no, that never happened, but I know that one day it will."

I nodded.

"Then—you've had *that* feeling, too?" Sarah asked, incredulous.

"Maybe not exactly the same, but I feel like I know what you mean."

Sarah leaned over the edge of the tub to place the soap in the metal dish on the floor, then jabbed her palm against the water, splashing it up into my face.

"Then I suppose you're not the only odd one after all," she said. "I guess we're just two of a kind."

"And we don't do half badly together in the kitchen," I said, splashing her back.

Looking across at this playful, generous, hard-working girl, flushed with the heat of the bath, my heart squeezed at the thought of what life held for her: the anguish and fear, the hardships of emigrating to an unforgiving place, decades of hard work and childbearing. The loss of her precious baby Rose. The piling up of disappointments, the hardening of her spirit. I tried to picture Darlene's mother—the coldness, even cruelty in her eyes, the bitterness that hung about her like an odor—but was unable to. All I could see was my new friend, laughing and splashing, her brown eyes shining and beautiful and full of life.

We dressed quickly into fresh underclothes and two almost identical dresses Sarah retrieved from her parents' armoire that were made of navy blue wool, with high necks, hems that reached to mid-calf, and sleeves that buttoned tightly at the wrists. Just as we were closing the last buttons, we heard the sound of heavy boots and voices.

"They're here!" Sarah said, hastening to the door.

A moment later, in they burst, Sarah's parents and four brothers. Her father was wearing a large black cap without a brim that looked like an oversized yarmulke, and a simple suit I imagined was his holiday finery. He wore a full beard streaked with gray, with short forelocks tucked behind his ears. The other men and boys also had short tufts of hair tucked behind their ears, along with similar kinds of brimless caps. Yossele was among them, his cheeks flushed with excitement. Sarah's mother wore a headscarf and a simply tailored woolen dress like the ones Sarah and I were now wearing.

"*Gut yontif!*" everyone called out to each other. Sarah's father kissed her on the head, then gave me a warm look, and smiled.

A bustle of conversation followed while coats were removed and taken into the parents' bedroom and the new arrivals warmed their hands by the fireplace. The talk was of the afternoon service at the shul, which Sarah and I had foregone, being busy with the holiday preparations. I understood that we would attend services with the others the next morning and found myself excited at the prospect of experiencing my first ever synagogue service.

I flashed on our visit to the Touro Synagogue in Rhode Island, pictured again the bimah and the heavy candelabra that hung down from the ceiling. I wondered how the synagogue in Dusiat would compare, recalling how Mama had wanted to go to the services before Billy's illness intervened. I also remembered how I'd found myself back at the synagogue later that night, where I'd been visited by that uncanny, remarkable vision of people dressed in old-fashioned garb, swelling around the synagogue, trudging about under some kind of unbearable weight.

Everything within me clutched, as had happened now so many times on my lonely, tumbling journey through time. Was it really possible? Had I in fact—sitting in the back seat of the taxi outside the synagogue in Rhode Island—had a premonition of *here?* An image of people just like those now swarming all around me? But wait, not just people, these were members of my own family! My very own relatives from long ago.

Mama, how I longed for her! How I longed to leap into her arms and shout: yes! You can go to the Jewish services—with me! Here, in our very own historical synagogue, who knows, perhaps older than the Touro. The synagogue of your mother and grandmother and great-grandmother, and all these other lively people talking and laughing and preparing for the grand feast. We could go together tomorrow! *If only you were here!*

My thoughts were interrupted by Sarah.

"Come on, let's heat the water. The sun is slipping down."

There was still an hour or so until sundown, when it would be time to light the candles. Sarah and I heated pots of water so that the rest of the family could bathe.

Sarah took the hot water out while I went to the well to fill the second pot which I then set on the fire to boil. I was grateful for the long minutes as the water heated; I was able to rest.

Yossele was the last to wash. "I don't need a bath," he said to his sister.

"If you promise to wash very carefully ... " Sarah replied, ruffling his hair.

"Promise!"

I sank onto the bench by the fire and allowed my eyes to close. My mind whirled with all the impressions of the day; images of *gribenes* and freshly baked challah and dried fish with raisin eyes danced behind my closed eyelids and I found myself sliding into sleep.

I was awoken by Sarah's mother, a plump woman with a pretty, but oddly vacant face, who was calling out: "They're here! The rest of the family is here!"

I jumped up to see a group of people cheerfully, noisily entering the house, taking off their coats, walking over to the fire to warm themselves. An uncle and aunt, Sarah later explained, with their three teenage children, as well as Sarah's two older sisters, one of whom was very pregnant, and their husbands. They made their way to the table, and everyone fell silent. Sarah's mother lit the candles; along with the other women, Sarah and I partially covered our eyes and recited the prayer. Then, Sarah retrieved a metal container with two handles and we traipsed outside to the pump. One by one, each person filled the container and poured water over their hands, first one and then the other, and back to the first, muttering the hand-washing prayer under their breaths. When everyone had had their turn, we filed back into the house in silence. The thin man at the head of the table—Sarah's father, whose angular face harbored interesting shadows—placed his hands on the covered challah and recited the prayer for bread. He peeled off the cloth, broke pieces from the challah and dipped them in honey, then passed them around the table.

I don't think I've ever tasted anything as delicious as that first bite of bread: so sharp was my hunger, so soft the bread, with its perfect chewy-smooth crust. A plate of apple slices was then passed around, along with the honey. I dipped my slice into the pot; the honey sheen glimmered like sunlight as I raised the apple slice to my lips. Those first divine tastes were the beginning of a magical evening. One course followed the next, served by the women; Sarah and I, who'd prepared and cooked most of the food, were released from serving. The food, from first to last, was exquisite. As each dish was served, the diners heaped compliments upon us, and every now and then, one or another relative would cross to where we were sitting and enthusiastically pinch our cheeks.

I'd always been a bit unadventurous in my diet, preferring to stick to familiar foods. But I surprised myself, tucking in heartily to everything that was offered—spreading salty, congealed chicken fat on my challah, sampling the chopped herring and chicken livers that arrived early in the meal. We all sipped heavy, sweet red wine from metal cups. Between courses, the entire table lifted their voices in song, delivering the ancient Hebrew prayers up to the heavens. The room flickered with a dozen candles placed in alcoves in the wall, making all the faces around the table glow.

Late in the evening, light-headed from wine and heavy-bellied with food, I looked around, suddenly detached from the proceedings. Here I was, celebrating my first ever Rosh Hashanah. I felt a sinking within my chest, as if my heart were being dragged away from its normal place.

The women and girls cleared away the food and resumed their places for the singing of the Birkas Hamazon, the lengthy, sonorous prayer sung after meals. Yossele proudly took the lead, lifting his voice high, closing his eyes, and swaying to the beautiful melody. He was singing from the heart; his youthful warmth, love, and commitment seemed to wash through the room, affecting everyone. As the prayer came to a close, I could hear Yossele's clear voice, drawing out the melody line so that it wove languidly through the air.

> *Poteiach et yadecha, umasbia l'chawl chai ratson. Baruch hagever asher yivtach badonai, v'haya Adonai mivtocho.*

I felt once more my mother's presence: it was as if she were coming to me in the sounds of the prayer rising in this simple wooden house. I could almost hear her voice, singing along with the crowd.

I closed my eyes. A faint memory tickled at me—the sound of my mother singing those same Hebrew words as I slipped into sleep. An even fainter recollection—whispered words in my ear: *That's a Hebrew prayer, darling. Doesn't it sound sweet?* How old had I been? Three? Four? My mother singing me to sleep—I always had trouble falling asleep—with songs from old-time musicals: *The*

King and I, Mary Poppins, The Sound of Music; perhaps having run out of things to sing she reached back into her own past for another song or two, retrieving the Birkas Hamazon she'd learned at Hebrew school.

I opened my eyes again to see the beatific faces around the table, transported by the ancient prayer to some place I did not know, and yet that did not feel completely unfamiliar. No one seemed to notice I was not singing. I felt a hollow ache in my chest and a tear leaked from my eye; though I often seemed equipped with the knowledge I needed on this remarkable journey, the Birkas Hamazon eluded me. How I wished I knew the words so that I might join in.

Why did my mother never teach them to me? How could I have reached the age of fourteen—a full two years beyond the age when Jewish girls back home in Brooklyn celebrate their Bat Mitzvah—without having celebrated a single Rosh Hashanah or Yom Kippur, or any of the other holidays that were central to my Jewish heritage? This surely came about by way of a well-thought-through and deliberate act—to cut my brother and me off from all of this; such a thing could hardly have been an accidental oversight.

It didn't add up. Sitting there, aware of the feeling of connection in this simple room—extending beyond the family to an entire people with almost two thousand years of history—I recalled something else. My mother: not as the grown woman I knew as *Mama*, but as a young girl named Talia, sitting in the little square in Broken Hill, talking sadly, with a kind of brokenness, about how she'd never really felt like an Australian, for the simple reason that she was a Jew.

Sarah's grown sisters and brothers-in-law took their leave, along with her aunt and uncle and their children, and her four older brothers, who lived in the dormitories at the yeshivah, where they studied. Yossele, happily exhausted, climbed the ladder to the alcove above his parents' room where I assumed a small bed of some kind awaited him. Sarah and I were left alone with her parents. Her father had shed a little of his sadness with each cupful of wine, and now he smiled as he congratulated us both on our cooking.

"Let's do the Torah reading together," he said, rising and taking a somber-looking book from the bookshelf at the far end of the room.

I glanced at Sarah, who leaned across to me and whispered:

"We still do the holiday reading together on holy days. It's one of my favorite things ..." Her voice trailed off; she watched as her father returned to the table, walking slowly, carefully, the large volume open in his hands, head bent in the flickering candlelight to peer closely at the small print on the page. When he finally sat, he removed his eyeglasses and turned his attention to Sarah, fixing hovering eyes on her face.

"I always think of the Rosh Hashanah reading as my Sarah-le's special passage," he said.

He turned back to the page—hunched his shoulders a little and began swaying gently back and forth in his chair, slowly, at first, increasing his speed by shades. He sang in a voice that was both joyous and sad: Hebrew or Aramaic, I could not tell, and yet once again I understood every word.

"*And God remembered Sarah as He had said, and God did to Sarah as He had spoken. Sarah conceived, and bore Abraham a son in his old age, at the set time of which God had spoken to him.*"

Sarah's father sang these words—straightforward enough in their meaning and sound—as if they contained within them deep wisdom and transporting beauty. He repeated the haunting chant once, twice, and then abruptly broke off and resumed in a spoken voice.

"She named her son Isaac—which means *will laugh* because, as Sarah declared, *God has made laughter for me, so that all that hear will laugh with me.*"

How strange, I found myself thinking; the man Sarah would marry, Grandma's father, was named Isaac.

There was silence in the wooden house, but for the sound of the scholar's voice. I wondered where Sarah's mother was; she had disappeared. *Absent,* I thought. Even when she was in the room, it was as if she wasn't there.

"And so, Sarah-le, may God bless you, too, with many, many reasons for joining in such laughter—the music of angels, the best music there is." He reached over and affectionately patted his daughter's cheek.

Could he have known that one day Sarah would give birth not to one or two children—but ten? One of whom would not survive— whose booties, knitted by Sarah many years forward in the future, Grandma had actually given to me! Sarah's father turned and fixed his gaze on my face; there was something unsettling about his regard.

"Sons, yes—may you have sons. But also daughters."

His eyes were boring into me, reaching for something—effortfully reaching for knowledge. Could Sarah's father have intuited—even if not consciously—that I was the grandchild of Sarah's future daughter? The daughter conceived to replace her precious, lost baby Rose? My grandmother the daughter she would tragically find herself unable to love?

"Daughters," he said. "God's sweet treasures."

He turned back to the book before him and seemed to slip into a trance; he remained very still, suddenly taller in his seat, as if an invisible cord were pulling him upward. Warmth suffused his features as he focused intently on the book in a way that was both gentle and fierce. I was gazing at an unknown landscape of emotion; he took me with him, and I felt he was taking Sarah, too. Now, he seemed almost to be emanating light. I squinted tightly; an aura of illumination appeared around his body.

My eyes suddenly felt almost unbearably heavy. I allowed them to close and it was as if a door slammed, taking away the cocoon-like world of Sarah's family home, leaving me stranded in a blank nowhere, curiously silent. And yet, the chanting of Sarah's father still filtered in, as if the life of that room were both happening and not happening at the same time. I felt sure of only one thing: the breath coming in and out of my lungs, the whooshing feel of it, feathery and light.

A vague and yet powerful memory of elongated shapes and forms came over me, flashes of color, taste, smell, floating in a sea of sound. An image swam into my mind: an enormous candelabra, its shiny gold stems coiled like snakes, the flames pulling up from blackened wicks to rise like hot ghosts to the ceiling. Light fractured into a hundred colors and spread across a vast space.

A single voice: a man's song loud in my ears. My own eyes blinking sleepily, my hands balled against something soft, oh! So very soft! Plush, a blanket. I un-fist my tight hands, stretch out my fingers— reach for the hot colored light pouring down over me, blue, pink, yellow, purple, broken into shapes by lines and curves of black. My eyes blinking, now open wide to see the stained-glass window above.

I turn my head; how different it all feels! My neck mushy, soft, my limbs circling, everything so different, *so different*, me and not me: someone else, but only me. I turn my head again and this time, the new sight slams into me, jolts me from this strange underwater domain: my mother, only different, *so different*, her face—what? Like Talia's? More like Talia's in any case—the Talia of so long ago, so recent for me, and still so far ahead in the future, not yet born as I sit here, at Sarah's table, listening to Sarah's father chant ancient words.

I am a baby in a baby carriage, the young, Talia-like Mama I glimpse in this strange, early memory is my mama from then, from when I was a baby.

And I place the memory. I had, after all, been in a synagogue, only long, long ago. My mother must have taken me when I was a baby, still in a carriage. The memory of it lost long ago, or never fully formed, and yet something about being here, now, snagged the hidden recollection and made it bloom to life.

My eyes snapped open; Sarah's father had finished his chant and was staring into the middle distance. Sarah, too, appeared to be in a trance. Finally, her father spoke.

"My dear girls. Now, it is time to sleep." He bent and planted a gentle kiss on Sarah's forehead. "May the Lord bless you and keep you."

Then, he looked at me and for a moment hesitated. I felt as if he wanted to plant a kiss on my forehead, too. It was as if he was wondering if I were indeed family, since then, it would be permitted. Physical contact with a girl outside of the family would be forbidden.

I am family! I wanted to call out. *I am your very own great-great-granddaughter, and I have traveled all the way from Brooklyn and back more than a hundred years ... impossible, I know, but it is true!*

He seemed to be listening to something, as if trying to make out the very words that were echoing in my own mind. Solemnly, he bent again, this time placing a kiss on my own forehead.

"And may the Lord bless you and keep you," he said, before turning toward his room, his rough workman's hands hanging heavily by his side.

Sarah watched him disappear behind the door. Silence, and then the authoritative sound of a small bolt being carefully moved into place.

"I'm not the least bit tired," Sarah said, turning to me. "Are you?" Her eyes shone in the light of the single candle still lit behind her on the alcove in the wall. "Why don't we go out and take a quick look at the river? Now's our chance!"

I glanced about to see if I could sight a coat that might belong to me. I found nothing like that. Just as I was thinking how cold it was likely to be outside, Sarah spoke.

"You take the blanket. I'll take Mama's heavy shawl."

I tugged the blanket up from the small bed, folded it into fourths, and draped it around my shoulders. It was incredibly warm. I reached to remove the candle from the alcove.

"We won't need that," Sarah said. "The stars are bright tonight—I saw them through the window. Maybe they know it is Rosh Hashanah and there is no moon—and they want to help us bring in the new year with the glory of light!"

We left through the front door, closing it slowly behind us.

* * *

The sky was indeed bright with what looked like ten thousand stars. They hung in endless layers, shimmering with unfathomable mystery. I looked up and down the dirt road to see small wooden houses, similar to Sarah's, modest in the white wash of light.

Sarah turned her head up to the skies.

"Can you believe how bright they are? And just after our holiday reading about Sarah! Do you remember the passage from the story of Abraham, Sarah's husband? From Genesis … "

"No," I said, "I don't remember."

"Well you know that Abraham and Sarah wanted children so badly. God takes Abraham outside and says to him, 'Look up at the sky and count the stars—if indeed you can count them. So shall your offspring be.'"

My mind flashed back to Billy and how much he loved to count everything. I imagined him craning his neck upward beneath this impossibly bright sky—could almost hear his little voice in my ears. *"Sis! How will we ever count all these stars! There must be a zillion, trillion, bajillion!"*

We walked toward the glimmering sliver in the distance, beyond the town: the river.

The brisk air chilled my cheeks and nose, though my body, under the thick blanket, remained warm. We rounded the corner onto a broad dirt road and came to a halt before a much larger building than any I had seen so far. It was a simple structure, almost like an oversized cabin, made of roughly hewn wooden planks, several stories high. The roof also seemed to be made of wood, with two odd little red-brick chimneys sitting on top. The imposing polished wooden doors seemed out of place, to belong more to a stately edifice of stone. Mounted above the doors was an oversized Star of David made of the same dark polished wood as the doors.

"Are you sorry you missed services tonight?" Sarah asked.

I was curiously choked up and unable to speak, so I only nodded. Sarah took me by the hand, such a simple, sisterly gesture, it brought tears to my eyes.

"We'll have our chance in the morning. Let's get up even earlier than everyone else so we can be the first ones here!"

We stood a moment longer, the light-pricked skies wide above us. The old wooden synagogue seemed weary, as if sagging on its foundations, and I had the odd thought that it was only managing to keep from collapsing through pride.

"Come on," Sarah said, tugging me away. I turned reluctantly from the synagogue, my anxiety spiking to dread. "Come *on!*"

We hastened along the road. Sarah seemed to be floating. I held tight to her hand and found myself floating beside her. Something had happened to her mood, I could feel it as if it were a ripple of heat—a delicate sense of freedom. We passed shops, shuttered in the starlight, Yiddish signs painted in bold calligraphy declaring their identities: butcher, grocery, bakery, ironsmith. The squiggly letters had a peculiar effect on me, rolling in my imagination with a physical vitality, as if tumbling against my palms. It all seemed—I don't know, so *solid*, as if these simple wooden buildings had been here forever. Countless children through the ages must have moved along this street in the depth of a night like this, generation upon generation of girls just like Sarah and me, sneaking out on a late *yontif* evening, hungry for adventure.

We walked at a brisk pace; after all that rich food, it felt good to be moving, the blood pumping through my veins. The streets were silent. The houses we passed were shrouded in darkness, the entire village slumbering, the villagers sated from their own Rosh Hashanah feasts, dreaming, perhaps, of the religious services that would take place the next day, beginning at dawn.

The street seemed to go on forever, and then, abruptly, came to an end, and we stepped off the hard dirt road onto a field covered in short brown grass, chewed down, perhaps, by sheep or goats. The land rose and then dipped; we broke into a slow run on the downward incline and I felt a rush of cold air in my hair.

The river was closer than it had seemed from the road; we were now only three or four hundred yards away.

The silence was broken by a strange rumbling that I felt as vibrations in my feet before the sound reached my ears. The sound grew to thundering: hoofs, pounding the ground. It was coming from behind us, beyond the village. I looked back to see a posse of horses being ridden hard by young men riding low, their hair streaming behind them.

"Cossacks," Sarah whispered. "They're training for Dusetos."

"Dusetos?"

"The races. On the shores of Lake Sartai. They couldn't be more than two weeks away."

We stood, frozen, watching the riders speeding along in the distance. Sarah glanced at me; her face was filled with fear.

"What is it?" I asked.

Sarah's lip trembled; she shook her head, looked away. "Come on, let's go down to the river."

We ran swiftly toward the riverbank, our cares whisked away by the cold air. My heart pumped wildly, my speeding feet seemed to lift from the ground; I was flying through space and time, released.

And then, there it was: the expanse of gray water, no longer a shiny band of metal, but a surface of choppy little waves, crumpled by the wind. We stood on the bank panting, then plopped down on the ground.

I turned, smiling, to face Sarah. To my surprise, I found that she was not smiling at all; her face was unhappy and pinched.

"I can see why they called the river Sventoji—whoever it was who named it."

In the starlight I could see a thin, shiny line starting in the corner of Sarah's eye and moving down her cheek, a tiny river all its own.

"*The Holy,*" she sighed. "That's exactly what it is."

She looked at me full on, her eyes burning. "But then, all rivers are holy, aren't they?" Her voice was thick and pained. "The source of life." She paused, lost in thought. "Helpless, too," she said, as if to herself.

"I don't know what you mean," I said, feeling helpless myself.

"This beautiful river—oh, how I love it! It has been my closest friend the whole of my life—but it's powerless to stop them from killing us. To stop them from *wanting* to kill us. How many centuries has it lain here, moving, always moving, toward the sea—*toward freedom*—while our own countrymen set fire to our homes?"

Sarah reached out and gripped my arm so hard I let out a little cry of pain.

"Those waters are dark! And I feel like I know something—some terrible truth. There is much more killing to come. I feel it here." And she freed my arm to place her open palm on her chest. "It's only going to get worse!"

The terror in her eyes spilled out, flooding over to me.

"What are we going to do?" I said.

"My parents have been talking about leaving. That won't come as news to you; your parents are probably talking about the same thing."

Did I imagine the shade of a frown in her face as she uttered the words *your parents*?

"So many people have gone to Southern Africa. It's almost impossible, now, to get into America. Ever since Kishinev ..."

"Kishinev ..." I said.

"It made no difference, did it," Sarah said, "that they found the murderer in the end. The government had already declared that the death of the Christian baby was a ritual murder, plotted by Jews. The peasants formed a mob—how efficient they were, burning, killing. With the full support of the government. As far as everyone was concerned, if they *said* that Jews did it, then they did it—even after a Christian relative of the baby confessed to the crime.

"I think that's what scares me most. That there's no reason to it. It's just pure hatred that has nothing to do with reality."

It was colder here, by the river. Despite the blanket, I began to shiver; the shaking seemed to reach all the way to my bones.

"Perhaps we ought to go back," I said.

Sarah wiped away a tear.

"Yes, I suppose we should," she said.

"It's a new year. Maybe everything will settle down. Blow over." The moment my words were out, I realized how hollow they sounded.

Sarah gave me a probing look. "I've always found hope in the bright spots of our history," she said. "The times our people have flourished."

Hearing her say that—*our history*—jarred; the history she was talking about, of *the Jewish people,* felt like it had nothing really to do with me. Yes, my mother was Jewish, and I had known that all my life, but since I'd not been raised Jewish, it seemed like a fact that did not really impact *me.*

"Such as …?"

"My favorite period is when the Jews were allowed to return to Jerusalem, almost fifty years after Nebuchadnezzar destroyed the First Temple. You know, when King Cyrus of Persia decreed that not only could they return, but he would provide funding to help them rebuild the temple. Did you know that Jews talked Aramaic in those days? Papa has taught me some in our studies together, since some of the Torah is written in Aramaic. I am so lucky, since most girls don't get to learn like the boys … I've always loved that passage about the edict; it comes right at the end of the Tanakh. I memorized it when I was a little girl:

So said Cyrus the king of Persia: All the kingdoms of the earth has the Lord God of the heavens delivered to me, and He commanded me to build Him a House in Jerusalem, which is in Judea. Whoever among you, of all His people, may the Lord his God be with him, let him ascend!

"Those last words fill me with hope—*let him ascend!* It means that one day, we *will* go up to the place we call home, where we belong, where no one will set fire to our houses or murder us just for being who we are.

"That period of the Second Temple lasted for six hundred years. Six hundred years! I know, there were still wars and all kinds of terrible things happening—that seems to be how history works. But it was a period mostly of peace and flourishing for Jews. I long for that—for our people to be *left alone.*"

I didn't know what to say. Together, in silence, we turned our backs on the river. The return journey seemed longer; the chill had sharpened, and though I held the blanket tightly around me, the frigid air crept in through the unavoidable crevices. By the time we rounded the corner onto Sarah's street, I was shivering uncontrollably. A bank of cloud dampened the starlight, sinking the house in shadow.

Inside, the house was dark—the single candle from earlier had sputtered out. I unfolded the blanket I'd been using as a wrap and spread it over the bed; we undressed in the near darkness and climbed in together.

"*Shanah tovah,*" Sarah said, reaching for my hand. Her voice seemed far away, as if coming to me through the wrong end of a telescope. I returned her grip, aware of a vaguely desperate feeling that I was clutching her hand to keep Sarah from slipping away.

"*Shanah tovah.*" My accent was as thick and natural as hers, as if I'd been uttering this Hebraic expression, "A Good Year," the whole of my life.

Within minutes I could hear, from the sound of her breathing, that Sarah was asleep. I felt exhausted, but at the same time alert and wide awake, as if I'd never sleep again. I lay there, listening to Sarah's deep, even breaths, my mind a whirl of images, impressions, tastes, and sounds from this very long day. I drew in some careful, steady breaths and tried to still the tumbling carnival of images. I found myself fixing on the disturbing conversation I'd had with Sarah in the midst of our marathon cooking session.

What was the name of that yeshivah student she'd mentioned—the one who, along with a group of friends, had fought back against the czar's men with stones, and was later savagely murdered? I had an urgent feeling—that I *must* recall his name. How could I let him lie there on the street in my mind's eye, brutalized, without remembering his name? I desperately wanted to say a prayer for him here, in his hometown, on this Rosh Hashanah evening.

It came to me. *Yitzhak Baron.* If Sarah was eight at the time, then that particular pogrom took place five or six years ago. And now, according to Sarah, the violence was again in full swing, though it had not yet reached Dusiat.

I pictured Cossacks on horseback holding firebrands, kicking children down in the street, drawing pistols and swords: knifing, shooting, attacking the men and women with whom we'd celebrated this evening. Wasn't the world meant to become less baffling as one grew older—not more? I longed for the feelings I'd had as a young child, lying in bed as my mother or father read to me, snuggly warm and safe, with thoughts only of Winnie the Pooh and the Magic Faraway Tree, filled with the certainty that aside from the villains in fairy tales, people were kind and good and righteous.

I curled up under the woolen blanket, suddenly woozy and aware of a crushing need for sleep.

* * *

The next thing I knew, I was sitting up in bed, coughing wildly. A thickness of black smoke burned my eyes and choked my throat. I shed the heavy blanket and stumbled to my feet.

"Sarah!"

She was lying in the bed, still asleep. I shook her body—she remained unmoving.

"*Sarah!*" I shouted again, and this time she stirred.

She leapt from the bed and ran coughing to the sideboard where the large jug of water stood. In a moment, she was back; she threw a soaked cloth to me and I caught it, then pressed it to my nose and mouth as I could see, in the wavering orange light, she was doing with a similar piece of rag. Sarah crawled on the floor to her parents' door and began pounding on it with her fist. A loud thud: Yossele, jumping down from the alcove and landing clumsily on his side. He, too, was coughing. I ran over to help him up. He winced as he righted himself but did not seem seriously hurt. Blinding smoke billowed through the space. The fire roared, attacking everything with burning claws.

The bolt, I thought, recalling how Sarah's father had bolted his door. At that moment, the door fell forward—whether her parents had axed it open or it had succumbed to the flames, I did not know— and Sarah's parents stumbled out. Sarah thrust wet rags into their hands and together we crawled along the floor to the back door.

Then, we were outside in the alleyway; the cool air rushed into my lungs with such intense relief, it felt almost like pain. Beside me, Sarah was gulping in air. She leaned close to my ear.

"Mama said it was going to happen," she said in a hoarse whisper. "She's been saying it all along." Her eyes were glassy and oddly calm.

We ran along the street. I looked back, keeping the damp cloth over my mouth and nose as the smoke billowed all around us. Row upon row of simple wooden houses I'd passed by earlier in the night were in flames. Beyond the houses, against the hills' silhouette, I made out a series of swiftly moving shadows: men on horseback, twenty or more, brandishing fiery torches. The powerful young men we'd glimpsed earlier in the evening, riding low on their horses, their jackets flying behind them. On their faces, I imagined a grim satisfaction as they turned back to look at the burning village, their eyes glinting perversely with pride.

I thought back to last night, when I lay in the wooden bed that by now was surely aflame, picturing a scene that was eerily close to what was happening now.

We ran on, joined by ever more people—men, women, children, pouring from the houses, running together, a burgeoning, frightened herd. I kept closely behind Sarah's father; I realized he was clutching something; a large piece of fabric was flapping in his hand. I squinted to make out what it was and recognized the crumpled piece of white silk, with its yellow-and-blue embroidery and shaggy white fringe. In all the commotion, surrounded by deadly, thick smoke and greedy flames closing in on their house, Sarah's father had thought to bring his tallis—the simple prayer shawl given to him on his wedding day by the parents of his wife.

What, I wondered, would I seize in such a situation from my own home—so very far away in time and place?

The street widened, and I felt a flare of intense heat; instinctively, I veered away from it toward the middle of the packed-dirt road. I turned my head to see the old barn-like synagogue furiously burning; only a few hours earlier, it had called to me in a sweet and welcoming way … There was something brighter about this fire. A horrible stench pressed through the rag I held to my nose: fumes, kerosene or some other kind of combustible fluid. The enormous wooden doors were aglow, eerily without flames. The illusion held for but a moment; an angry cracking, like the sound of logs being split, tore the doors apart, huge timbers chewed at by the devouring flames.

A loud creaking split my ears and I turned my face from the vile burst of heat that brutally punched the air. Time compressed, and though I continued to hurl myself down the street, along with the growing crowd, something inside me gripped onto the molten moment: the heat of the dying synagogue was inside me, like the energy in a giant coiled spring. Only a few hours ago I had longed for the morning, when I'd expected to pass through those enormous polished doors and into the sanctuary. Where I would join Sarah's family— *my family*—in prayer, the sinuous Hebraic words gliding from my own tongue, their meaning rich and plain as I rehearsed the service that my grandparents and their parents and all my ancestors down through two thousand years of history had uttered before me.

Now, it would never be; it would never come to pass.

Escape? But to where—and by what means?

Something in the heat that pummeled us, that flooded my being from within and tugged at my heart and soul, felt like a taste of what might have been, what would have been, if not for the Cossacks and their firebrands.

And then, it was snatched away—the sight of the burning synagogue, the houses all around. The street ended and we veered off onto open farmland, our collective feet muffled by the brown grass underfoot. We were off across the field, and then rounding a large copse of trees, moving farther and farther away from the village. Everything was suddenly dark, increasingly dense vegetation hiding the sight of the flames. No sounds but the thudding of our feet on the earth and the deep heavy breathing of hundreds of people—much of the population of an entire village, in the thick of the night, moving along carrying nothing, no possessions, only life—fleeing into the darkness with nowhere to go.

I looked up to the skies, which were darkening, swallowing the stars whose generous light had earlier allowed us to pick our way across the nighttime landscape toward the Sventoji River. We were now in dense forest; a small clearing opened up ahead and we all slowed, spreading through the space, quiet voices rising in ghostly chorus. Sarah slipped her hand in mine; we both waited for our breath to steady before speaking. I wondered how far we were from the river—wondered how long it would take us to reach, and whether there would be boats to sail us away from all this.

Sarah was studying my face and once again, for what felt like the hundredth time in the course of this very long twenty-four hours, I had the unsettling feeling that she was reading my mind.

"Father says there are going to be boats," Sarah said. "We don't know when they're coming—but soon. Small boats. They'll take us to the Baltic Sea."

"And then where?" I asked, scrambling to remember my geography. *The Baltic Sea,* how foreign that sounded, conjuring images of people and places I'd never imagined would actually involve *me.*

"They talked about the big boats, the ships. That sail to Southern Africa. We have people there. Distant relatives, from Dusiat. *They saw the writing on the wall,* that's what Papa says."

Sarah's eyes were shining strangely, the way eyes look with fever. Her voice, though still a whisper, vibrated with excitement. But my own heart sank; I knew that I wouldn't be going with them. I was

183

developing an instinct about my journey—and standing there, in the darkness, whispering to Sarah, I knew that I was about to leave her and find myself once again flung into some other reality.

Oh please, let it be home.

The wish was so intense, it felt like a crushing weight on my chest. But even as these words formed in my mind, I had a foreboding that my wanderings were not yet over. I felt an awful plunging within, as if my heart and stomach were sinking within me like giant stones.

"For now, we're going to hide in the forest," Sarah said. "Look—" She pointed into the darkness, some distance away, where a group of men were busy with shovels. Some were crouched on the ground, their bodies hunched, intent, busy. "They're digging pits," she said, her voice lowering to the faintest whisper, so soft I could only just make out her words.

"Pits?"

She nodded. "You'll stay with us." Her voice was tentative, the fevered shine gone from her eyes, which were now hollows of seriousness.

I said nothing. What remained unsaid, hung between us: *Where else would I go?*

Sarah gestured toward another group of men, huddled together within a dense grouping of trees.

"Yossele is going back with my eldest brother, Chaim. To Kovno. Things are calmer there. Chaim says the government will keep *the trouble* in check. He can join Chaim at the yeshivah."

No! I wanted to shriek. *Yossele mustn't go with Chaim!* The terrible image of Yossele's future reared up in my mind, bloody and awful; my hands trembled as I reached for Sarah's arm.

"Hadassah, what's wrong?" She searched my face.

My throat seized; I could not utter a single word.

I felt I was choking on time itself; I knew the future, which meant I had the power to *change* the future, to speak out—no, to *shriek*— Come with *us,* Yossele! So you might live in South Africa, not here, not in Kovno, where several decades from now a new band of evildoers will make the Cossacks' attacks seem pranks by comparison. So that you and your children might be spared the horror of succumbing to the Nazis' bullets. In South Africa, you will have a different wife, different children—and you will all survive!

But how could I interfere with the past? The past had already happened!

A voice threaded its way into my confusion. *Wait,* this inner voice said, *Yossele has nothing to do with your own past.* I struggled to make sense of this thought. Since Yossele was Sarah's brother, he was not in the direct line of my own family—only now did I make the actual connection that Yossele was in fact my great-great-uncle. His fate, therefore, had no impact on the fact of my own birth. Maybe I *could* say something now, to Sarah? Maybe I *could change history* after all—maybe I could save Yossele! That sweet boy, so clever, the intelligence shining brightly in his eyes.

How could I *not say anything?* I closed my hands into fists—could feel the immense power in my own hands and tried to squelch it. It all felt too much! But—but—how could I turn away from the chance to save Yossele from his fate? Yossele, his wife, his children! I was too panicked to run the logic—and who could believe in any case in logic when it came to this crazy topsy-turvy time and space journey I was on? Logic would say this: that if Yossele went to South Africa with his sister, Sarah, he of course would end up with a different wife, different children. The point was, I'd be saving *him.* And yes, even saving the children that would not in fact end up being born. My mind was scrambling. The crowd was pressing in, we were being pulled apart by this river of humanity.

"Sarah," I said, aware that the pressurized-steam panic rising within me was evident in my voice. "Yossele *must* go with you! You *cannot* let him stay here!"

She shook her head. "We've talked with him," Sarah said, pressing my hand. "Mama, too, and Papa. It's agreed. He'll be safe here."

"He won't be safe! I'm telling you—you cannot let him stay!"

Sarah let go of my hand. "Hadassah, what are you talking about? How can you possibly know—?" There, the furrowed brow, her eyes wavering with confusion and fear.

"If you don't—he'll be shot!"

Sarah's eyes went blank. "Hadassah, what's happening to you?"

She looked at me sideways, this time with a wariness that made me want to weep. It was as if the feeling between us was suddenly sucked away. All the closeness and togetherness of the past day evaporated.

I sank to my knees, limp with helplessness. History itself was bearing down on me, a dark river governed by the moon, thrusting forward, but tugged by a raging sea—the future, *Destiny*, bearing down on the moment, on me, with brute, unyielding force. I saw myself for the first time as the tiniest thing on earth, powerless as a mote of dust.

"Sarah," I said. "I'm sorry." I reached for her hand and she tentatively took it, and then the dark look in her eyes melted away.

And then, he was there beside me, Yossele; I had not heard him approach.

"I want to say goodbye," he said. Was I imagining it? An unbearably knowing look in his eye? "And wish you safe journey."

I'd never felt so hopeless. I looked at Yossele, tried to return his farewell but was struck mute, as if by some mighty, external force.

"It's all right, really," he said, raising his arm toward mine, as if he were going to take my hand, but then dropping it again.

He turned, then, and walked away. It all seemed so surreal—hundreds of us milling around under cover of the forest, the night heavy around us. Ordinary people, standing about in an ordinary way, and yet everything *extra*ordinary, not normal at all: the world turned on its axis, lives uprooted, ripped from their foundations, everything changed, forever. And yet—after all, just people whispering and talking and planning, under the stars.

How must Sarah's parents feel—leaving their young son here, perhaps never to see him again? No, not *perhaps*. I had to remind myself: I knew how this would all turn out. After tonight, Sarah and her parents would, in fact, never see any of these family members again: not Yossele; not the other six older siblings I'd met this evening—which felt like weeks ago, not mere hours; not their cousins and uncles and aunts and everyone else remaining behind.

Something seemed to be happening; a murmur passed through the crowd, and then the strange, silent feel of motion, as if we were all giant particles heating up. Now, we were moving again, more slowly, this time, as if we were governed by a single force—as a herd moves: many creatures, one mind.

But where was Sarah? A moment earlier, we were together.

"Sarah?" I scanned about me. "Sarah!"

A sharp pain erupted in my left temple, as if someone had landed a blow with an iron rod. Then, the same pain in my right temple. Panic engulfed me, the signal, yes, that had preceded each of my tumblings back through time. *I'm not ready to leave Sarah!* I wailed within. *And with no chance of at least some sort of farewell?*

But then, a rustle beside me and there she was—her eyes feverish.

"Hadassah! I mustn't forget to give you *these!*"

"What?" I said, disturbed by the agitated sound of her voice, by the mysterious, unreadable look on her face.

"*These!*" And she reached her hand out—we were being parted by the crowd, people swarming, moving more quickly now, coming between us. Her arm stretched and was knocked aside, then reached back out toward me. I stretched my own arm out too, felt the warmth of others brushing up against me, pushing Sarah and me apart. My head was now throbbing with alarming intensity, the pain clouding my vision.

"Yossele—he asked me to give them to you! I don't know why—but it seemed important to him!"

I couldn't speak; my throat was dry as sand. I reached for Sarah, but the distance between us was growing.

"And it's important, also, to *me!*" Sarah said. "*Here!*"

Through the crowd, around and between, our fingers touched—our hands slid together in a fervent, quick clasp.

Two hard, round, smooth little balls—the oddly polished walnuts Yossele had chosen with such pleasure, knowing they'd bring him victory at *palantes*. I curled my fingers around them; they felt solid and reassuring against my palm. For an instant, I was overcome by an unexpected calm, here, in the midst of all this chaos.

And then, Sarah was being pulled away from me by the crowd, a startled look on her face; in my ears, the faint echo of her voice, whispering my name—lyrically, the Yiddish sounds stretching, sounding the way they had looked to me above the shop windows of Dusiat, with their unusual angles and beautiful arcs: "Hadassah—remember me. And I will remember you!"

I opened my mouth to speak—to say *But I am here—with you! You don't need to tell me to remember you! Don't leave—Stay—*

But she wasn't staying, she was moving away, away, out of sight, joined with the moving crowd, as if she were floating down a swiftly moving river whose tide rumbled suddenly within me, a churning, roiling desperation, threatening to engulf me, overwhelm me, swallow me down, and crush the breath from my lungs—

The pain in my head ballooned, swallowing all thoughts, and then, the tumble into pelting rain and dreadful hurling through tempestuous darkness. Gone the bright stars, the danger of fleeing and flames, the thunder of running in a human herd, the feverish look in Sarah's eyes.

* * *

And then, a violent slapping—water so cold it stung. And salt spray, burning my eyes. Everything was in complete darkness; I remembered, suddenly, the story of Odysseus that my father had read to me when I was young. And as I tumbled deeper into the storm, I thought of the squall in that story that lasted nine days and nine nights. Of how Odysseus and his men had tied themselves to the masts to keep from being flung into the raging, wine-dark sea.

I had no twine, no anchoring mast; in the face of the violent seething, I felt helpless and unprotected. My body twisted and ached as the stinging rain lashed me. I closed my eyes against the salt spray and balled up my fists, as if to battle the tempest with my hands. I kicked and thrashed and screamed with all my might, though the sound was swallowed to nothing by the roar in my ears.

I found myself doing something I never did back home, in my *real* life, in Brooklyn.

Praying.

I prayed I might again squeeze Billy's hand: look again into those gleaming, impish, smiling eyes.

I prayed that I would see my parents, that we would be a family again. That my mama would recover and go back to being the mama I knew.

I did not see how I could survive. I don't know how long I struggled. I was clinging to the slimmest thread of hope as time catapulted me farther back.

"Em—i—ly." It sounded like the voice of a small child, trying to speak through tears. *No, not a small child—Billy!* I was sure of it! Billy's voice, coming to me from—where? Desperately, I tried to open my eyes, but they were glued shut.

The touch of a cool hand on my forehead, the sound of a soothing voice.

"My darling ... "

The light intensified; even through my closed eyelids, I cringed with the intensifying pain it brought on. More voices, a man, a woman, the sound of people moving and talking, not close by but farther away, I couldn't make out what they were saying. A soft clanking, and rustling, the distant sound of mechanical beeps. Now, a quick, sharp pain on the inside of my elbow. And then, the pain crushing my skull and shooting down my neck peeled away, the light disappeared, and the voices and sounds drifted off into the ether.

CHAPTER FIVE

WHEN I CAME TO, I was face down in fine, silky sand. Immediately, I felt the scorching heat; the hair on the back of my head burned from the sun. Through my loosely fitted garments, I could feel an intense warmth. I did not, however, feel hot. The air was dry, and a brisk wind rose and fell, whooshing with hollowness.

Rising to my feet, I looked around. Everywhere were fields of sand and above me, a vast blue sky without cloud, a bright orange sun directly overhead. I felt as if I were the only person alive; for a moment, I wondered with alarm whether I'd been catapulted far forward in time, rather than backward, to beyond the end of the human race.

Now I knew why the wind sounded strange: there was nothing to break its movement, no trees or houses or any living thing around which it might swirl and nestle. Only desert sands that shifted with the gust's whims, sliding with sluggish grace into new flattened curves. But wait—what was that up ahead, in the distance? Shielding my eyes with my hand, I thought I could make out an astonishing sight: a massive city with buildings reaching upward, high into the sky. And all around it, glinting waters that wavered in and out of view. I squinted and the fantastic image vibrated, seemed to vanish, then leapt back to view. Could it be a mirage? My throat was parched, hot tears sprang to my eyes.

I had the feeling I was being watched. I turned to see a young woman walking toward me, draped in white linen, her head wrapped in a turban, a sheer veil covering her face. Behind her I could see

camels: some resting on the sand, others beginning to heave themselves up, their enormous bodies lunging with awkward, fluid motions.

As she came closer, she raised her arm in a wave, and then, she
was upon me. She slid the veil from her face.

"No, it's not a mirage. Though it always seems that way when it
first appears," she said. "Don't worry, Shoshana. It looks farther away
than it is. We'll be there soon."

The girl's dark eyes gleamed with warmth; her voice was deep and
honeyed, and it took me a moment to register the guttural-sounding
language. I flashed once more on my mother, singing me to sleep
with the concoction of Jewish prayers recalled from her childhood. It
definitely sounded like the Hebrew of my mother's sleepy prayer singing. Now, I remembered what Sarah had said—that the Jews spoke
Aramaic in ancient times. Was it possible that this was the language
I was hearing? As I'd come to expect, I understood every word and
knew that as soon as I opened my mouth to speak, I would have command of the same language.

"Before you know it," she said, "we'll be able to see the river. How
beautiful the tower looks from here! You can even see the hanging
gardens. One can almost forget ... " Her voice trailed off. She shook
her head, as if to dislodge an unpleasant thought, and then smiled,
revealing a set of pristine white teeth; a dimple creased one cheek.
It was a distinct, radiant smile, which made me think at once of my
grandmother back in Australia. I felt a sharp pang of homesickness.

That unbearable feeling that had plagued me before now overcame
me again. I couldn't imagine what Grandma was thinking, so far away
in place and time. What had happened to everyone? *Where were they?*
A new thought derailed me ... what if I was *still* there but *also here?* I'd
heard of parallel universes, but never thought they could actually be
real. What if—what if—but I was distracted from the thought by my
new companion, who was looking at me quizzically, awaiting a reply.

"The tower, the hanging gardens, the river ..." I echoed what she
had just said, rolling the unfamiliar new words around in my mouth.

"I do love the Euphrates," the girl said, as if reminding herself of
something. "I go down to her banks, outside of the city, where the ·

grass grows so thickly, and I tell her my thoughts and dreams." She paused, then said, "In my own mind, I call her Mother Euphrates. There! That's a secret I've never told anyone!"

The Euphrates. I flashed on Jimmy, so far away—another universe, another time—patting the earth and calling it his mother.

A massive tower … the hanging gardens … the Euphrates River … Could it be? Had I landed in—Babylon?

"It's so exciting, isn't it?" the young woman asked. "We'd had hopes when King Cyrus ascended, but for it all to happen so quickly!" She grabbed my shoulders and gave me a quick, impetuous hug. "I can hardly wait to read the edict to Father. It was certainly worth the trip to the royal scribes to get a copy, don't you think?"

"Can I hear it, now?" I asked.

"That's a fine idea," she said. "Funny—I must have read the papyrus to myself ten times, and yet the words still feel like a surprise."

She reached into her garment and pulled out a piece of rolled papyrus tied with twine. After removing the twine, she unfurled the page and began reading in a ceremonial voice:

The Edict of Restoration.

Let it be known to all, the edict of Cyrus, King of Persia, at the end of his first year on the throne:

Concerning the house of God at Jerusalem, let the temple, the place where sacrifices are offered, be rebuilt and let its foundations be retained, its height being sixty cubits and its width sixty cubits, with three layers of huge stones and one layer of timbers. And let the cost be paid from the royal treasury. Also let the gold and silver utensils of the house of God, which Nebuchadnezzar took from the temple in Jerusalem and brought to Babylon, be returned and brought to their places in the temple in Jerusalem; and you shall put them in the house of God.

"There," she said. "Undeniable. We're to be allowed to return home!"

Why did what she read sound familiar? The name of the king—Cyrus—and the reference to Nebuchadnezzar and the temple. Someone had mentioned these things to me, and recently—even yesterday. *Yesterday?* What did the days mean, anymore? When was *yesterday* in this strange, new world? Back in Lithuania? Yes! That was it! Sarah had talked about this very period when we were down by the Sventoji River! Her favorite period in Jewish history—the return of the Jews from their exile in Babylon back to Jerusalem, where they would rebuild the destroyed temple, inaugurating the period of the Second Temple. Sarah's recitation of the last passage in the Torah that filled her with such hope rang in my ears—*let him ascend!*

I'd been flung back in time exactly to that period, Sarah's favorite! It was as if all the girls I was meeting—my maternal forebears—were scripting my journey as it unfolded! How was I ever going to make sense of any of this?

Now, this girl who, like my other recent companions—Talia, Darlene, Sarah—seemed to know me, and whose name had not yet been revealed, re-rolled the papyrus and slipped it back inside her robe.

"How long has your family been here?" I asked.

"Why, the same as yours!" she said, a furrow forming in her brow. "Since the expulsion."

"Yes, of course, I know that," I said, a little flustered. "I guess I mean I was just thinking ..."

The girl nodded. "Oh, I see," she said, as if intuiting some meaning in my words that was beyond my own reach. "The memories of home—they've faded. After almost fifty years, well, in some ways, they're not really *our* memories, but in other ways, they are."

Every time she said the word *home,* I felt an awful pang.

"Our great-grandparents hold some memories of our home, though I suppose they were still young children when they were forced to flee. But for their parents—*home* was alive in their hearts. Some of the elders still live—"

She was studying my face in that uncanny way. "Shoshana, have you doubt?"

"What do you mean?"

"About the return? Do you not feel the pull—of our ancestral home?"

My heart certainly ached with longing—for my family, for my own time and place. Was it possible that this girl felt those same feelings for Jerusalem?

She seemed suddenly to remember something, and gently took my hand. "We really must hurry. Deborah will have some sharp words for us, no doubt."

We headed back to where a few camels were still heaving themselves to their feet. I found myself gliding lightly across the dunes. The leather sandals I was wearing seemed ingeniously constructed for this terrain: the smooth soles skimmed over the surface, preventing sand from getting into the shoe.

We reached the camels and the group of people attending to them—about fifteen men and women, all dressed the way we were, busying themselves with the animals, attending to the goods and supplies draping over them every which way, adjusting the heavy, beautifully embroidered materials that served as padding and saddles and headgear designed to keep sand from the camels' eyes. A slender woman approached, drawing away her veil to address us. She was middle-aged, with refined features and gentle eyes.

"Rachel, I told you girls not to run off," she said, sounding like a mother indulging a young child. So, my new companion—certainly one of my ancestors—was named Rachel.

Rachel kissed Deborah on both cheeks. "All those hours on a camel—you know how restless I get!"

The older woman received Rachel's kisses with delight and then turned to me. "Here, Shoshana, you must be thirsty." She handed me an animal-skin container, which looked exactly like the kind I'd seen in movies set in ancient times.

I knew my name here was Shoshana, since Rachel had already called me that. A vague memory rustled up from one of our many trips to the Brooklyn Botanic Garden, where a little nametag labeled each plant, tree and bush. We'd read somewhere that in the Bible,

Shoshana meant lily, and Mama had explained that in modern times, the name was understood to mean rose.

I tipped the animal skin and drank greedily. As the water poured through me, I could feel my strength returning.

"The sun makes fools of us all. The city looks so far away—" Deborah said. "Come, your camel's ready."

She led me to a camel folded down on its knees; it gave me a funny look, half serious, half amused. Even sitting, it looked enormous, like a large hill I was now supposed to climb. The embroidered crimson cloth on its back was stiffer than it looked; I noticed ridges up one side and realized they were little steps I could climb to reach the saddle. In a matter of minutes, I was perched on top, surveying the desert landscape around me. I held on tight as the camel loped to its feet.

And then we were on our way. I felt a surge of excitement as we sailed along; suspended in mid-air, dipping widely and yet smoothly, up and down, I was overcome by an astonishing sense of freedom. The pale-yellow sand stretched out to a horizon that hovered in the distance like the lip of an all-encompassing sea.

After a time, the city that had wavered far away like a mirage solidified in the near distance, a glittering conglomeration of fantastic shapes: buildings of smooth stone, others that looked like temples, their gold and silver surfaces refracting the sun's rays. Rising to an impossible height was a massive structure of stepped terraces covered in a profusion of greenery, dotted all over with colored flowers. Could this be the famed Hanging Gardens of Babylon—a long-lost great wonder of the world? To the west of the gardens, a slim tower rose into the sky, reflecting multicolored beams of light, its tip buried in cloud. It appeared to be encrusted with jewels, glinting in broad swatches with gold-flecked blue, breaking the sunlight into bright flashing spears. Encircling the thin tower, a thousand steps snaked in an evenly described spiral. I only vaguely remembered the Tower of Babel from my Bible stories—recalled that the tower was called "Babel" because after it was built, God imposed a gaggle of languages on the people, who could no longer understand each other. The opposite, in a way, to what was happening to me—being miraculously granted the ability to speak and understand whatever language came my way!

My tongue felt suddenly sticky with all the languages that had come to me on this journey, as if from the tower itself before me—Afrikaans and Yiddish, and now most likely Aramaic, the language of parts of the Old Testament. I felt as if I were a vessel through which history was pouring itself—and yet at the same time, I also sensed a new stirring within that I was somehow getting closer to a mystery that had everything to do with *me*.

We sailed along on our camels amid the dunes that rose and fell around us like static waves. I was mesmerized by the city, with all its odd shapes and glittering colors, which drew us as though reeling us in. And then, the sand beneath us changed, becoming steadily more solid as clumps of olive-green vegetation appeared, and then some scraggly bushes with spikey branches and spindly leaves. I peered down from the immense height of the saddle to see solid ground beneath the camel's hooves, hard-packed soil that showed deep, jagged cracks, and up ahead, a little group of trees.

I was overcome by my first sighting of the Euphrates, which rose like an apparition from the horizon, wide as an ocean and dotted with waves.

The city had indeed seemed miles away, but all of a sudden, it lurched in all its enormity right up before us, dwarfing the enormous walls that bound it. We found ourselves before the massive carved wooden gate to the city, which was guarded by sentries wearing pointed metal helmets and elaborate breastplates. We dismounted from our camels and the guards ushered us through. We made our way along the winding canal sent by the Euphrates through the city, which shone darkly in the afternoon sunlight.

I could hardly believe the swarming crowds—such a variety that even a city girl like me, accustomed to the melting pot of New York City, was amazed. Bearded men in dark clothing clutched coiled papyri, their heads bowed; and by one fountain, a group of what I imagined were soldiers or fighters of some kind hung about—massive youths dressed in red cloth woven with gold, over which they wore chain mail and polished breastplates. A few women flitted in and out of the crowd, their faces covered by veils.

Rachel moved swiftly beside me, holding her veil tight. The din of sounds and unusual, abrasive smells left me faint and confused.

I felt a sudden sympathy for my older cousin from Australia, Natalie, as I recalled her first visit to New York when she was my age. We'd crossed the Brooklyn Bridge by foot, hitting Wall Street just as the crowd poured from the subway stations on their way to work, then wended through Chinatown and Little Italy, crossing to Tribeca and through SoHo into Greenwich Village. The sun was beating down by the time we reached Times Square and stood among the neon advertisements, tall as skyscrapers. It was a landscape I knew well, and I felt excited to be showing it to my cousin. She suddenly stopped in her tracks, her face hung with dismay.

"What's wrong?" I'd asked.

She turned miserable eyes my way. "Where does it all *come from?*"

"What?"

She passed a hand before her. "All these people, all this noise. I don't know, all this *everything.*"

I sent the Natalie of back then a silent nod of understanding. Now, hurrying along the streets of Babylon, I understood how she'd felt.

We came to a halt beside an imposing house made of white stone. Deborah reached into her robe, withdrew an enormous key, and put it into a large iron lock on the door.

We stepped into a high-ceilinged foyer, which gave off the same cold, pleasant feel and smell I always welcomed when entering an old church. We climbed a narrow stairway, several stories up, passing closed doors through which I could hear quiet sounds of human activity. At the top, we entered a long room: a patterned rug filled one corner; sheer fabric hung from the ceiling around it, creating a private little space in which I presumed Rachel slept. Several other rugs of more simple design lay about the room, almost completely covering the floor. Cubby-like shelves set into the wall held a collection of small bottles and pots; my eye was drawn to a little jar with a conical spout, glazed in pale, translucent green.

"Let's rest for a short while before we go to the bathing house. The sun is still hanging quite high—we have time yet."

Time for what, I wondered?

Rachel threw herself down on a rug in the middle of the room.

"I think I could eat an entire sheep," she said. "I'm famished!"

My own stomach grumbled in response, and Rachel let out a little laugh.

"I see I'm talking for you, too! You'll smell the roasting meat, soon enough. The servants have been up since before the sun, readying the pits. Anyway, hunger is said to be good luck."

"Good luck?" I asked, my tone casual.

Rachel colored a little. "You know … " She turned shyly away. "Before the wedding."

The wedding? Could Rachel be talking about her *own* wedding? Though she looked mature, she was surely no older than I was.

"Tell me again," I said, trying to sound convincing, "about your betrothal."

"You know the story as well as I do," Rachel said. If she believed I knew the story, she nevertheless seemed delighted to have the chance to repeat it.

"I was seven and he was seventeen when our parents arranged the betrothal. He was always my favorite cousin." Her voice held a delicate tremble. "And he still is."

"You've been betrothed for half of your life," I said, hoping to get a bead on Rachel's age.

She nodded. "Only it seems like *all* of my life. I can't remember when we weren't betrothed."

Rachel leapt up. "What am I doing still resting? Tonight's the feast! I have so much to do—and then tomorrow—oh! How can it be, it always seemed so far off, but tomorrow, I will be married!"

Our session in the baths, a short walk from Rachel's home, left me feeling calm and relaxed. Deborah had poured fragrant oils into the water, and now the reedy scent rose from my skin. Back in Rachel's room, I sat on the rug beside her, as she slowly brushed her long, dark hair, her breath rising and falling in time with the strokes.

A soft clapping broke the silence; it was coming from the other side of the door. Rachel slipped by me, opened the door a crack, and then whispered for a few moments to whoever was there. When she glided back beside me, she looked worried.

"I've had word that Boaz needs me," she said. Did she mean her fiancé? She had not yet told me his name. "My betrothed," she added, looking away. I was now used to this oddly responsive reality—being supplied with exactly the information I needed whenever there was something I didn't know or understand. How weird it would be if people continued to do this when I eventually return home to Brooklyn! It would be like living in a dream, things oddly organized around *me*.

My own thought echoed in my mind—*when I eventually return home*. What made me so certain that I *would* return home?

"Shoshana, did you hear what I said? We must hurry!"

"Boaz—?" My own voice came out sounding as if I were underwater. I almost expected to see bubbles rising up from my lips and disappearing into the air.

"Yes, you silly thing!" There was affection, but also exasperation in her voice. "He doesn't have what he needs—I must go get his extra instruments and take them to him."

Rachel grabbed a long piece of sheer fabric lying over a chair in the corner of the room. Beneath it was another similar sheer length, which I assumed was mine; it was soft to the touch, and almost transparent.

We hurried along a dark passageway. Rachel's hands rustled about her head, making an intricate head covering and veil of the long swatch of fabric. I found I had a similar skill, my own hands darted about my face and head—a bit more clumsily, but not without success. I was surprised just how well I could see through the sheer fabric.

At the end of the narrow street, we threw ourselves into a throng of people crowding a small square. Jumbled sounds assailed me from the morass of animal life wherever I looked—donkeys tied to posts and strapped with sacks of all sizes, goats tripping along with panicked eyes, herded by shepherds in raggedy robes, unusual birds in rough cages, displayed on wooden benches—along with the guttural tones of languages different from the one I was speaking with Rachel.

The street turned to shallow steps and we found ourselves in the thick of the market. On either side I glimpsed small cave-like rooms, crammed with goods: sharp-smelling cheeses, vats of olives, pastries that smelled of honey. Fruits—apples, pears, figs, grapes, overripe plums. Also nuts and spices—cardamom, cinnamon, cloves. Onions and garlic, acrid-sweet wine, and a yeasty, syrupy odor like sweetened beer. I stumbled a little, made dizzy by the smells, which were now inviting, now off-putting. My stomach somersaulted between unsettling nausea and the rumbles of deep hunger.

One little cave-room, well-lit by a roaring wood-burning oven, gave off the smell of freshly baked bread. On a wooden rack in the front of the store were dozens of crusty rounds; the upper shelves held loaves in remarkable shapes—some like the conical hats I'd seen, others like human heads, ears, and hands.

We came to the top of the stair-like pathway and ducked into a doorway, which gave on to a steep rise of steps. I was breathing hard as I tried to keep up, following behind Rachel, who bounded up the steps effortlessly. Soon, we were before a narrow doorway so low we had to stoop to enter. Inside was a windowless room; in the corner, a woman crouched before a stone hearth ablaze with fire. A putrid scent wafted over from a pot, furiously bubbling over the flames. She turned as if by instinct; she could not have heard anything over the roar of the fire. The woman's face was deeply wrinkled and streaked with soot. When she wiped the sweat from her brow, I was surprised to see that her hand looked quite youthful.

"Rachel, beautiful bride," the woman said, smiling.

"My new mother," Rachel said by way of greeting, her own face relaxing into a warm smile. "Boaz sent me for his instruments."

The woman's face went serious again. A wordless communication passed between them; the woman wiped her hands on her apron, then crossed to the far corner and retrieved something from a wooden chest. She emerged from the shadows back into the blazing light, and it was then that I saw how beautiful she was; her dark eyes burned with intelligence. She handed Rachel a large leather pouch, which Rachel slid into what must have been a hidden pocket of sizable proportions on the inside of her robe.

"Will Boaz need to fumigate?" The woman asked, glancing toward the cauldron. "The potion needs still a quarter day to meld."

Rachel shook her head. "He said nothing of fumigation. He only asked for his instruments."

The two women leaned into a quick embrace, and then Rachel turned and left the room.

I searched the woman's face; I saw wariness, but also interest in her eyes.

The way back down was easier.

"How does it feel, having a new mother?" I asked, curious to know more about the woman, whom I assumed was Boaz's mother.

"She has taken me into her family as a daughter," Rachel said. "Since I am orphaned of my mother, as you know, I am especially happy. She helps Boaz in his work, making the fumigations and other medicines."

"When will the fumigations be ready?" I asked, fishing for information. I was so curious, but also aware of not wanting to give away the fact that I knew so little about—well, about everything.

"They're better when they're richer," Rachel said. "Boaz likes to leave them boiling for close to the full day. Sunrise to when the first shadows fall. Then, when he pours them over the hot coal, the smoke is thick and has an oiliness to it. It's easier to breathe in the thick smoke, that's what Boaz says. The medicine works better that way, and faster."

Free of the market, we found ourselves on a dirt road so heavily trodden it felt like smooth tarmac beneath my feet. The buildings grew steadily shabbier. Soon, we were passing structures made of mud mixed with straw. I glanced into one every now and then: they were little more than hovels.

At one point, I turned to see that Rachel had loosened her head covering to expose her face, twisting it cleverly along her forehead to make it into a headscarf. I reached up and with a few deft movements achieved the same effect. The air rushing over my features felt wonderful! My eyes darted to an open doorway, through which a troubled sound floated—a rasping cough, high-pitched and desperate. I came to a halt and peered through the smoky light. Within, I saw a painfully thin woman, clutching a small child whose hollow eyes shone with despair. There was an aching moment of silence, as if the world had screeched to a halt.

Tears sprang to my eyes. I turned to see that Rachel's face was grim.

"Come, Shoshana," she said, taking my arm. I opened my mouth to speak, but she only shook her head sadly. Without uttering a single word, she communicated what she needed to convey: *We can't stop here, there's a whole city of such scenes. People who need our help, people who need saving. We must go on. There is nothing we can do.*

I wanted to protest her wordless message—*We can't help everyone, that's true. But perhaps we can help this one child, this one mother?*

Rachel took my face in her hand, as if to steady my thoughts, to make me see reason.

"Come, we need to go," is all she said. I offered the smoky doorway one last glance. Sensing my attention, the mother turned her head and our eyes met; in her face, I saw utter hopelessness. She didn't expect me—or anyone—to help her.

A dry wind sprang up. We hurried along and soon broke free of the winding cobblestone streets and found ourselves in more open territory, where the roadway was wide and flanked by grand stone buildings. I found myself thinking about other wide boulevards I'd once seen in Paris, with my family: Montparnasse, the Champs-Élysées, Bonne Nouvelle, Montmartre. To think, that wonderful city was possibly modeled on this ancient one!

We turned a corner, and Rachel came to a halt before a colossal temple topped by a massive golden dome. Beneath the dome was a grotesque statue of a creature that seemed part human, part monster; it had a cruel mouth and enormous ears. Rachel turned pale.

"Eater of babies," she said, her eyes glowering. "How I hate his greedy mouth."

Eater of babies? What could Rachel mean?

"I hate him, too," I said.

"There's no place I loathe more in all the world then this Esagila. The Temple of Moloch."

Raw emotions passed across Rachel's features: disgust, fear, pain.

"But we have no choice. Boaz is waiting for us."

"Where are we going?" I asked.

Rachel looked surprised, as if she'd assumed I knew exactly what we were doing, as if we were one mind joined together, parceled off into two different people.

"We had to get Boaz's surgical instruments from his mother. A baby is hurt."

"Where?" I asked.

"In the temple," she said. "Below."

She spoke with finality, as if that was all she was willing to say.

The streets around the temple were eerily empty; where had the throngs of people gone? Rachel scanned in both directions, up and down the street, as if checking for something.

"They're all inside," she said, addressing the question that had sprung to my mind, "and everyone else knows well enough to keep away."

We ducked into a side alley so narrow we had to turn sideways to inch our way down. The walls were moist and oily; I used my palms to push away slightly so that my face would not rub up against the unpleasant surface. Rachel did the same, and together we sidestepped our way away from the light of the street and deeper into what felt like a horizontal tunnel. We seemed to be burrowing into some terrifying place, away from everything I had ever known.

Rachel came to a stop. "Help me," she said in a low and formidable voice. I saw she was pushing hard against the wall. I did the same, throwing the full weight of my body against the oozing stone. Something gave. A panel slid open and we fell into the darkness as the stone quickly slid back into place behind us. An unpleasant odor made me feel sick and I let out a little groan.

"Shhh, you have to be very quiet," Rachel said. Her voice still held its fierce tone, even at the pitch of a whisper. I had no idea what we were doing or where we were going. A hundred questions buzzed in my mind, but I knew it was impossible to ask them now. I had no choice but to put myself in Rachel's hands. I moved quietly beside her, my full attention focused on trying to tread in her exact footsteps. She, at least, seemed to know where she was going.

Again, she came to a halt. I heard a soft creaking. A door opened, releasing a glow of hazy orange light. We moved into a small room and the unpleasant odor became almost unbearable. In the corner, lit by a halo of light thrown down by a torch placed high on the wall, a man crouched over a bundle of rags. As we moved closer, I saw that it wasn't a bundle of rags, but a baby. It lay splayed on the floor, its limbs at odd angles. My heart pounded with fear. Could the baby be dead? But no, its eyes were wide, staring at the man, its face contorted in pain.

I was desperate to ask Rachel what was going on. Why were we here?

We crossed to the corner and Rachel crouched down beside the baby, her face filled with sadness.

"This is what they do to their babies ..." she said. The man, who I assumed must be Boaz, put his hand on Rachel's and silently nodded.

"Three, tonight," he said, his voice deep and low. "The ceremony is still going on. There will likely be more."

"Boaz, how did you manage?" Rachel asked.

"Nahum inserted himself. He managed to catch this baby before he went into the flames."

This must have been what Rachel had meant earlier, when she said that Moloch was an "eater of babies."

"Two had already been sacrificed," Boaz said. "Everyone was in such ecstasy, no one noticed Nahum. He put the baby in his robes and brought him here, to me. The child seems to have some broken bones ..."

Just then, a man emerged from the shadows. Something seized within me, as if I'd been struck in a strange and beautiful way; a quiet gasp escaped me as I struggled to make sense of the peculiar whirl of feelings that had suddenly taken hold. I could not take my eyes off this stranger. I realized, then, that he was staring at me; perhaps he felt it, too.

"That is Nahum," Rachel said.

"Nahum." The name fell from my lips. In a moment, he was beside us. He spoke quietly to Rachel, glancing at me every few seconds, his eyes tender and concerned.

Finally, he turned to me. "Are you all right?"

I'd never heard a voice like that before—deep, serious, but also touched with humor. I found myself gazing into eyes of a crystal green I'd never encountered before, like tinted glass and yet filled with warmth.

The most absurd thought sprang into my head: *I want him to be mine!*

Why on earth would such a thought cross my mind? This man was a complete stranger—I knew nothing about him!

In a flash, I remembered the story my mother had told me since I was little, my favorite of her large collection of personal anecdotes: the way she'd fallen in love *at first sight*, as she always put it, with Papa. "It was just like in a storybook," she'd say. "Violins playing, thunderbolts striking, the whole deal." I knew the words by heart; how many times had I asked her to repeat it? She always said the same thing: "My heart raced like a jackhammer, I could feel I was bright red in the face. It made no sense at all, and yet all the sense in the world. There he was, the most handsome man in the whole world, crossing the room. I'd never laid eyes on him before, and yet this was the thought that popped into my mind: *I'm going to marry that man. I'm going to have his children.* You could have blown me down with a feather! But that feeling was the strongest thing I've ever felt." My favorite part came next. "Life has its ups and downs, to be sure. But that feeling has never wavered for me, all these years. Not once."

Could that be what was happening to me? *Love at first sight?* Here, deep beneath the ground in some awful cave, filled with a disgusting smell. More than two millennia before my own time, in the biblical land of Babylon!

The man reached out a hand, which I took, in a daze, allowing him to help me to my feet.

"It is disorienting down here, is it not?" he said. There, again, that strange mixture of kindness, strength, and humor.

From the corner of my eye, I could see that Boaz was removing the horn stopper from a large animal-skin container. He poured dark purple liquid over the patch of stone next to the baby. The tawny, deep scent of wine wafted toward me. Gently, Boaz slid the baby onto the cleaned patch, and the little boy let out a tiny high-pitched mewl.

"What is he going to do?" I asked.

"I do not know," Nahum said. "Perhaps the shoulder is dislocated, and he needs to put the bone back into the joint." He paused, seemed to be thinking.

Boaz had turned his attention to the pouch Rachel had brought him. He loosened the leather-thong ties and carefully unfolded it. Inside, arrayed in a series of wide pockets, were metal tools. They glinted in the fluid light. Boaz's face transformed; it seemed eerily still, and his eyes glowed with concentration.

I was reminded of someone else, far away in time, with just this kind of expression. It took a moment to place, and then the image came clear: I saw again the photograph my mother had in her study, up on a high shelf—black and white, enlarged, in a thin gold frame— of her father, Grandpa Jack, decked out in surgical gear, bent over a patient in the operating theater.

Now, the details of the picture came back to me so vividly it was as if I were looking right at it—the strong lines of my grandfather's forehead, the straight nose disappearing behind the surgical mask, the eyes holding that very same expression I was seeing not twenty yards away in Boaz's eyes, as he examined his instruments.

The memory of Grandpa Jack, as I had known him for the first and only time in my life, back—I mean, forward—in time, in Melbourne, and then on our adventure to Broken Hill and farther into the Australian bush, now came leaping back. I felt suddenly weak-kneed and, alarmingly, found myself sliding to the floor. Nahum caught me and guided me into the shadows by the wall, where a thin rug was set on the floor. He gestured for me to sit. Gratefully, I sank onto the rug, which was comfortable and soft.

How Grandpa Jack would have loved being here with me. My mother had conveyed to me how passionate he'd been about his work. He'd kept a sense of wonder about surgery, about medicine, through a thirty-year career, cut short by an early death. And here was Boaz, that same sense of wonder marking every inch of his being.

He chose several instruments: one that looked like forceps, and a short, narrow blade, setting them aside. Then, he began, very carefully, to remove the baby's wrapping. Rachel joined me where I rested in the shadows. I covered my eyes. I couldn't bear to look.

"Boaz has given the baby some wine," she said. "That will help him. He will feel little pain."

The baby was surprisingly quiet. Every now and then, I heard it whimper.

I counted the minutes, closed my ears to the sounds, closed my thoughts as best I could and tried to be as still as a statue. I was aware of Rachel's warm hand in mine.

Finally, sensing it was all over, I opened my eyes. Boaz was approaching; over his shoulder, I could see that Nahum was wrapping the baby, who seemed, miraculously, to be asleep.

"Is the baby going to be all right?" I said, before Boaz had a chance to say anything.

"The baby will survive, God willing," he said, a faint smile at the corner of his lips. "I'm happy, finally, to meet you, Shoshana. Thank you for helping Rachel fetch my instruments."

"But I did nothing—" I said. Boaz stopped me with a gesture of his hand.

"You are her friend. There is nothing more important in life. Speaking of friendship, I see you have met Nahum."

There was something so decisive about each of these three young people, Rachel, Boaz, Nahum; you could see it in their faces. I wondered—is this what it was to feel in the grip of one's destiny?

Now it was Boaz who seemed to be studying me—perhaps wondering about something that was *lacking* in *my* face?

"Rachel tells me you're thinking of joining us," he said, "on the banks of the Ahava. Ezra has decreed that Zerubbabel will lead us; he is a fine choice, I'm sure you'll agree."

He paused, seemed to be trying to gauge the effect of his words. "But you must excuse me."

He leaned down and said something to Rachel, then returned to Nahum, who handed him the baby. The two men exchanged words and then Nahum glanced in my direction. He turned and walked toward me.

I rose; we stood facing each other, Nahum peering into my face. His piercing gaze seemed to strip away my veil. *It's as if I've known you all my life,* a strange little voice whispered inside my head. *And as if I will know you always.* This peculiar murmuring should have frightened me. And yet it didn't. Looking into Nahum's eyes, I felt the terrifying frenzy of the day recede; it was as if we were suddenly, wonderfully alone together.

"Zerubbabel will be at the wedding ceremony tomorrow evening," Nahum said. "You will meet him then and make your decision." He said this with quiet conviction, as if my decision to accompany them had already been made.

"Though perhaps now is not the time to discuss such matters." Nahum glanced across at Boaz, who was carefully rocking the baby. "That poor child ..."

"You saved him," Rachel said.

Nahum nodded.

Rachel turned to me. "Have you ever seen a ceremony?" she asked.

I shook my head, no.

"It's not a good idea," Nahum said.

"She should know," Rachel said, her mouth grim. "Then, maybe, she'll understand."

She took my hand. "Come. We should leave Boaz and Nahum. They need to take the baby to his new home."

Nahum moved aside. Whatever Rachel had in mind for me, Nahum had clearly decided not to protest.

"I'll see you at the wedding," he said, with that same intense gaze, "and then later, on the banks of the Ahava River ..."

We left by way of a small door that opened onto a corridor dimly lit by firebrands placed high on the wall. Immediately, I noticed the odd sound: a muffled but terrifying roar. We moved quickly, reaching a long, narrow staircase that wound down like a spiral. Rachel paused at the top and gave me a meaningful look.

"Prepare yourself," was all she said.

* * *

I took in a sharp breath, and we descended into darkness as the light from the torches on the walls above us receded. The air felt increasingly damp. Down, down we went, this time burrowing deep beneath the surface of the earth. The roar intensified and soon I could hear a din of voices, blaring in unison, wailing and high-pitched screeches, shouts and calls that were chilling. We reached the very bottom and Rachel pushed on a huge wooden door. The moment it gave, a deafening sound blasted through—a hundred times louder than it had been. I slammed my hands over my ears, but this did little to protect me from the awful, gut-wrenching explosion of noise. It took a moment for my eyes to adjust to the murky light which rose and fell and left giant shadows moving around the cavernous space. We were in a massive pit, a great underground stadium. I craned my head trying to estimate just how far down the pit extended; below was an enormous bonfire spitting up flames that arced and roared. Hundreds of people were writhing, dancing, and stamping on the mud steps curving all the way up the sides of the pit. With increasing horror, I realized that many of the hoard were stark naked; others were scantily dressed in what looked like bits of rag, haphazardly tied to parts of their bodies.

Rachel was trying to communicate something. Of course, she made no attempt to speak—I'd never have been able to hear her—but she was gesturing, pointing into the pit. I peered down, straining the muscles of my neck, and then I saw it: the enormous statue with the terrible grin, teeth bared, arms raised, its monstrous claws extended as if for attack. The same frightening figure fixed to the top of the temple that had caused Rachel to halt in disgust.

Moloch.

Flames erupted from the statue's mouth, and then poured from its eyes. The statue was literally spewing fire. A sudden, even more deafening sound erupted: a thunderous beating of drums that sounded like the pounding of a thousand bongos.

Rachel gripped my arm; I turned to see her nodding in a different direction, closer to where we stood pressed up against the sweating mud wall. I followed her gaze. An unnaturally tall man towered above the crowd, dressed in scarlet robes embroidered all over with gold thread. He was so tall he looked like he was standing on stilts. Beside him, a woman was throwing her body about in hysterical movements, her eyes rolling back. She was holding something—her mouth was twisted in a grin, making her look like one of those awful Punch and Judy puppets that used to scare me as a child. She threw whatever she was holding to the man. Was he some kind of priest? Expertly, he caught it. I could hardly believe what my eyes were telling me, but there it was, undeniable: little arms and legs flailing as the infant flew the short distance from the woman to the man.

I couldn't bear to watch what was certain to happen next. I covered my eyes and felt a sob burst from my throat. "No!" I shrieked and turned, frantic to find the door through which we had entered. Everything reduced to only one thought: I had to escape! I found myself pushing and pulling and then I was back in the near-darkness, leaping up the curved stairs, charging my way out of there, fleeing with all my might. I didn't care if Rachel followed me—all I cared about was leaving this ghastly place. Round and round, upward, the muscles in my legs almost seizing with the effort, lungs aching as they labored against the thick air.

Finally, after what seemed an age, I burst from the hard-mud stairwell back out into the corridor, where the mild light flickered all around. I collapsed, panting and sobbing. I felt as if I had come to the end of the line—the last possible place on earth, through time, that I could bear. I felt I simply could no longer go on.

The hard-packed dirt of the floor was cool against my face; I breathed in its earthy scent. A terrible pain ballooned in my head, shooting down my neck like knives. And then, a voice as gentle as could be, but saying the most awful words. It was Rachel. She must have been following me.

"It is true," Rachel said. "They give their babies to the priest, to throw into the flames."

As I found my breath, I realized I was crying.

Why? I heard the voice in my head call out. *Why would a mother do such a thing?*

Rachel seemed to be able to carry on the conversation without me having to utter a word.

"They are pagans," Rachel said. "That is what they believe. They are told by the priests that they must sacrifice children to Moloch to calm his fury, and they do it willingly. They get themselves into an ecstatic frenzy—you saw them. They're no longer human."

The disgust in Rachel's voice was gone. Now, there was only sadness.

"You see, the return to Jerusalem is not only for us. I know it sounds impossible—but it is for the world. We need to restore not only the Temple, but *the way* of the Temple. That is a sacred duty of our people."

I sat up. My breath steadied and my tears subsided, and then Rachel handed me a square of cloth she pulled from the hidden pocket of her robe.

"Now, do you understand?" she asked.

I had no idea what she meant. I wiped away my tears with the soft piece of cloth.

"Do you see why this place could *never* be home? No matter how many generations of our family are born here? When I say *we're going home*, I don't only mean Jerusalem, the city. Home is finding out where you belong."

Something wavered in Rachel's eyes.

"We were cast out of the country of our forebears. Here, we can only ever be outcasts. Now, it is time for us to journey back, to rediscover who we are." Rachel was looking at me in a curious way.

This was all too much. I felt so very tired. I could not make sense of what Rachel was saying. She seemed to be talking in clever riddles. I didn't want to hear anymore, see anymore; I only wanted to go home myself. Not the kind of home Rachel was talking about, some idea or concept having to do with her political and religious convictions. No, I wanted *my* home: Brooklyn in the early twenty-first century. I wanted my mama's arms around me, the soothing sound of my papa's voice, the feel of my little brother, Billy, in my arms as I told him everything was going to be okay.

But it wasn't going to be okay. I was here in this terrible place, so far from everything I knew and everyone I loved. I had never felt so completely alone.

* * *

By the time we got back to Rachel's house, I felt numb. So much had happened in the course of this overwhelming day. I'd reached my wit's end. We lay quietly on the rugs in Rachel's room. I closed my eyes. Moments flashed in my mind all mixed up, tumbling over each other: some unbearable, and others just confusing. Then, an image of Nahum coming out of the shadows emerged from the chaos and I felt suddenly calm. I closed my eyes and that feeling welled up again. I'd never felt anything like that before. *Destiny.*

I had no idea what destiny meant, not really. Everything seemed to be slipping from my grasp. But then, what *had* made sense on this journey of mine? Nothing! Absolutely nothing!

I opened my eyes to see Rachel rising from the mat. She walked to the window; a small clay pot on the windowsill held three red roses with long stems and little green leaves. I joined her by the window.

"They're perfect," I said, leaning to smell the roses.

Rachel plucked a stem from the pot and held the bloom to her nose. "The smell of paradise," she said, breathing deeply. "Deborah's an angel. She knows I love them. Sometimes, she brings me lilies. They're my favorite. But it is a far walk to pick them where they grow by the river."

Her face broke into a smile. "Like your name!" she said. "I never made the connection. Same as my favorite flower!"

It made me nervous, hearing Rachel point this out. I was always named this way—after my friend's—my relative's—favorite tree or flower. But this was one of my secrets; Rachel realizing this felt dangerous.

I suddenly remembered the poor little infant! How could we be talking about flowers?

"How's the baby?" I asked, my voice so tiny, I might have been a baby myself.

"I didn't see signs of bruising or bleeding. Boaz is certain he will live. He will be given to a childless Jewess, who will raise him as her own."

Plucked from the flames, I thought: reprieved from a pagan death to be brought into the Jewish fold.

Together, we looked out of the window. Several men in tunics walked abreast, filling the space of the roadway. Behind them, a stooped man urged two donkeys forward with a stick, and a line of women carried clay pots on their heads, likely filled with water.

"Are you going to miss all this?" I asked.

Rachel turned startled eyes my way.

"I never thought about that," she said, absently taking a rose petal between her fingers.

"I just wondered ... You've been here your whole life," I said.

The petal drifted to the floor. She took hold of another, which also came loose, and then another.

"We've always talked about returning. On fast days, we turn our hearts to Jerusalem, and our hunger and our longing for our home are one and the same."

The door opened. It was Deborah, carrying a large urn of warm water and a basket of dried lavender sprinkled with cloves. She left and returned a moment later with a small basket from which a tantalizing scent wafted, placing it beside the urn. I could see the basket held a mound of little round cakes as well as some plump dried fruits that looked like figs.

"Let's just have one or two," Rachel said, reaching for a cake. "To take the edge off our hunger."

I reached into the basket; the cake was still warm! I bit into it and heavenly flavor filled my mouth. The cake was filled with a purplish paste, a kind of fruit I'd never before tasted. I savored every bite, had to stop myself from gobbling down the whole basketful.

We stripped down to our cotton underclothing, then dipped squares of linen into the water to wash our faces, arms, and hands. I breathed in the wonderful lavender-clove scent, hoping the dreadful images from the underground cavern beneath the temple would loosen their grip on my mind. We sat on the stone floor to wash our feet and legs.

"Are you nervous?" I found myself asking. Rachel gave me an uncomprehending look.

"About what?"

"The wedding, of course!"

Rachel let out a little laugh. "What a strange question!"

How could she have thought my question strange? Surely, it was the most natural question in the world to pose to a fourteen-year-old girl on the eve of her marriage!

"I told you, Boaz and I have been betrothed forever! A week hasn't passed in all my life in which I haven't seen him. Ever since I can remember, I was told that Boaz and I were to be married. Now, it's happening!

"And I am excited about the return. To answer the question you asked—no, I don't think I'll miss—this place. We're finally going home, after all these years. Can you imagine? Fifty years ..."

There it was again—that look of absolute faith in Rachel's face.

I suddenly remembered the expression on Talia's face (my mother!), a face not filled with light, but hung with shadow, Talia standing on the pathway in Broken Hill, talking about how she'd never felt as if she'd belonged.

Something struck me like a bolt of desert sun. Perhaps *this* is what Talia, my mama as a teenager in Australia, had been longing for! Unshakable belief, a solid feeling of belonging. I wondered—had Mama ever found what she was looking for?

My mind's eye suddenly filled with other images of my mother from the time of my earliest memory. Mama smiling, laughing, singing us songs, turning even the most mundane activity into play; Mama looking at Papa with love, even adoration—no trace of the achy longing I'd seen in Talia's face at Broken Hill. Somehow, she'd made her peace with whatever was troubling her that day we flew over the Victorian landscape in Grandpa Jack's plane, gazing down at the rocky outcroppings and scraggly savannah vegetation. Whatever my mother's journey had been, I felt certain she'd found her own sense of home.

My own heart squeezed. Would I ever make it beyond—this? Would I find *my* true place in the world?

"Shoshana?" Rachel's voice broke through my reverie. It was still there—that blindingly bright look in her face, her eyes like strange, beautiful jewels.

Deborah had draped some lengths of white cloth over a block of wood by the basin; now, we used these to dry ourselves.

"Don't you see? Returning to Zion, to Jerusalem, will make us *whole* again."

"What do you mean?" I asked, stepping back into my dress.

Rachel crossed to where a piece of colorful fabric was hung on a rod and pulled it aside to reveal an alcove, filled with clothing and other objects—blankets, pillows, and a wooden shelf full of trinkets. I made out a few little sculptures and what looked like necklaces and other jewelry hanging on a rack.

"Being in exile—it was like we were broken. A people torn apart."

Rachel chose a pale blue robe from a pile of clothing arranged on a large pillow and returned to where I was sitting on the rug.

"But Rachel, everything I've seen—" I passed my arm before me in a wide arc, to indicate the magnificence of what I had encountered here, in Babylon: the splendor of her existence, the unearthly gardens reaching up into the sky, the glistening tower studded with gems. "How could all of this have anything to do with a broken people?"

Rachel pulled the robe over her head then sat beside me.

"I know you know the difference," she said, "between visible beauty and invisible suffering."

She swept her own arm about the room, though her movement was agitated, as if her intention was to wipe it all away.

"You were there with me, with Boaz." She paused. Was she about to say *and Nahum?* And oh—there it was again! My own cheeks burning merely at the thought of his name!

"You went with me into that dreadful pit. You saw what this place is *really* about …"

When she spoke again, her voice was hard.

"You're wrong. Whatever beauty there is here is ruined. Underneath everything is—well, the pit. Not the kind of beauty I could ever believe in. Or give my life over to."

I knew exactly what Rachel meant, recalled again that moment—so far away, now—at the Belle Meade Mansion, surrounded by splendor, Mama muttering to Papa, *built on the backs of slaves.* And the haunting photograph in the gift shop, the expansive living room with its high windows and elaborate ceiling moldings, etched with the ghostly outlines of the superimposed image of the slave quarters. My mind's eye trembled now with images from my journey, cycling one after the other: Talia, my mama as a girl, talking about her little friend who lived in the orphanage, taken from her family, *stolen!* The very idea of a child being stolen filled me with grief. And Joel, my grandmother's beloved friend and protector, pointing to the color of his skin, the anguish in his eyes as he spoke of the reality facing his grandchildren who lay sleeping, curled up together on the packed-mud floor of his hut. And the glowing light of a thousand flames, devouring the village of Dusiat, the thunderbolt crack as the synagogue doors succumbed, the great burning timbers collapsing inward as the fire spewed outward. Fire leaping back through the centuries, down into the vile pit we'd just fled that was burning still. My whole body felt filled to the brim with grief, as if the hellish fires throughout history were blotting out all hope, all belief in the goodness of humankind.

And yet, Rachel's eyes were glowing with something else: belief, faith, hope. There was something mesmerizing about the light that shone from her and seemed to lift to the heavens with a message, as if her entire being was what was meant by the word *prayer.*

"Don't you see?" she said. "We're meeting on the shores of the Ahava precisely because we're ready—and, praise be to God, finally able—to throw off the chains of all this *beauty* and return to our true heart ..."

I desperately wanted to feel what she was feeling, to join her in the bottomless reservoir that was her sense of home. But I felt shut out, as if there were a thick pane of glass separating us. Despair leapt to my throat like an ugly toad.

"But you've never *been* to Jerusalem! Nor have your parents—or your parents' parents. Isn't *this* your home? How do you know that going there won't be—I don't know, a new kind of exile?"

My exasperation only seemed to deepen Rachel's calm and resolve.

"It's hard for people to leave everything they know," she said. "I understand that. That's why so many refuse to leave. I can't blame them. They're comfortable here. They have a routine, everything they need. But if that's all a person knows, if that's all they care about or want—well, then it becomes dangerous. That's what I've been trying to tell you. That if you forget where you're from, if you forget your home, you are lost. No matter how comfortable your house is, how much food you have to eat"—she picked up one of the fruit cakes and threw it back into the basket with distaste—"captivity is *captivity*."

Rachel fell silent. I found myself tuning in to sounds I hadn't realized were in the background: delicate chirpings, tinkly and hesitant, as if an entire army of baby birds were opening their mouths for the first time.

How easy it was for Rachel to make light of other people's connection to where they had lived the whole of their lives. What did she know of homeless wandering? Of being cast far away from everything and everyone you had ever known and loved? She talked of the terrible *captivity*—of her great-great-grandparents being flung out of their beloved Jerusalem, of being strangers in someone else's land. But she'd been born here! She'd always lived in the impressive stone home her father had himself been born and raised in, with its colorful wall hangings and comfortable sleeping rugs and daily gatherings and feasts. What did Rachel *really* know of exile?

Rachel went back to the window and I followed. "Look, the roadway is full of workmen, returning to their homes."

The roses, now, were drooping; a handful of petals had fallen to join the few Rachel had absentmindedly peeled from the buds. I stooped to retrieve the velvety scraps, bringing them to my nose before placing them on the windowsill. Through the open square in the wall I could see men of all ages parading silently down the street, their heads half-turned toward the sky.

"Think about *your* home," Rachel said, her voice soft and sweet. "The home you've known and loved all your life. Close your eyes. Go there in your mind."

I felt a renewed surge of grief. That was the *last* thing I wanted to do; it was just too painful. And yet, I found my eyes suddenly heavy. I tried to keep them open, but they closed of their own accord, as if under the power of a hypnotist. Images flashed across my closed eyelids, fleeting, intense, and red-tinged: Billy on the swing in the playground, energetically pumping his legs, his face alive with pleasure; Mama standing over the stove, watching for the moment to turn the pancake, an attentive look on her face as she listened to my chatter; Papa embarking on one of his careful explanations, as we strolled arm in arm along a Brooklyn city street. The creamy yellow walls of our house—and motion, climbing the stairs, family photographs passing me on the walls, the creak of my bedroom door. Safe in my precious room: the smell of my pillow, lavender, from the drop of sleep oil Mama put on it at night, the porcelain angels hanging up near the ceiling, beneath the moon we bought at the Museum of Natural History. My art museum postcard wall, and stack of playbills from musicals and plays, and snapshots of friends—here, at the beach, there at a party, in the lunchroom at school.

What was Rachel thinking? Why was she doing this?

"I know what you see," she said.

How could she *possibly* know what I was seeing? Rachel, who had never seen an electric light bulb! Or a car, or photograph, or computer! She didn't even know that any of the things I saw in my mind's eye—any of the things in *my* world—existed! I felt a surge of anger. What did she know about *anything*? Why should I listen to *her*?

"And whatever it is you are seeing—that is only the beginning. A kind of map that will point the way to the most beautiful home in the world. Your *real* home. The home where we truly—and for all eternity—belong."

I wanted to rip away her ignorance. I wanted to close my eyes again and have her—and everything around me, this confusing, alarming Babylon, the vast Euphrates River, the markets and hanging gardens and the ghastly Temple of Moloch—just disappear. Slide away forever. And in its place—*in its place* ... I could hardly bear the longing that overtook me, the longing for my mother and father and brother, for the familiar places, my home and neighborhood and school, all the people I knew and loved. I only wanted *home*. Not some abstract place of religious worship, drenched in *historical* longings and aches. Not that, no: I wanted *my* little place in the world. Real, solid as stone. What I wanted was *my* home.

I shook my head, pure misery coursing through my veins, and made no attempt to staunch my tears. In that moment, everything became strangely transparent. It was as if I could suddenly see the shape and texture of Rachel's emotions shimmering through her skin. Her passionate understanding of a *true home*—a place she'd never actually seen, but had only heard of, through stories and lamentations and songs, in the words of sages and prophets and aged family members; her inspired vision about what was false in comfort; her commitment to history—to *her* history, her people, the past.

A vision took hold of me: I was looking directly at Rachel, but I was seeing an odd and yet beautiful home built of delicate colors, intangible as a rainbow. The home that she had built with her heart, her imagination, yearning, knowledge—and toward which she was finally, on behalf of her parents and their parents and their parents' parents, preparing to journey.

Maybe I had been wrong about her. Maybe she *did* in fact know how I felt! Perhaps our journeys were not, in the end, so very different, despite the unimaginable chasm lying between her experience and mine. I clasped her hand and looked into her eyes.

"I am going home, too." I was hardly aware of what I was saying.

"So then—you will come? You will meet us after the wedding tomorrow at the river Ahava?"

Her eyes were alive with so much: sadness and excitement and anguish and hope.

I found myself almost gasping with joy. My mother! She was there, right there, in Rachel's expression! My mother of long ago, before she was ill. Rachel ... Sarah ... Darlene ... Talia ... *Mama.* And then I felt something equally wonderful and unexpected: a feeling that perhaps my own eyes were shining with that same expression: that all of *them* were not only *in me,* but just, simply ... *me.*

Rachel cocked her head, seemed to be listening for something; she nodded and smiled, as if I'd said something she'd been expecting to hear, though I hadn't said anything at all. Then, she leapt up, and ran to the door.

"All right, then. I must go! Deborah is calling for me to come and have my hair braided. They have honeysuckle to put in my hair, all the way from Egypt! I will see you later, before the feast? By the waters?"

With that, she was gone.

With the closing of the door, my own moment of joy also slammed shut. How completely Rachel had misunderstood me! What I had felt in my moment of euphoria was that I, too, would be going home—*really* home, back to Grandma, and then soon after that, back on a plane to New York, where Billy and I would be reunited with our parents. Had I been deluded in thinking that Rachel had miraculously understood this? That she had magically intuited the truth about who I was and where I came from?

Rachel had clearly understood nothing of the kind. She had taken my declaration to mean that I was coming with her and her revered leader, Zerubbabel, back to Jerusalem.

I couldn't take any more of this! Yet *another* journey, this one by foot, across countless miles of desert sands to a place I had no desire to be. Even the thought of Nahum did not comfort me. It was true, I'd been hit by a small thunderbolt; what was surely meant by *falling in love*, though it was less of a fall than a plummet. But there was another truth. Nahum was a stranger to me, a stranger in a place in which I was hopelessly stranded.

I collapsed, devastated, on the rug.

The tears returned with a vengeance.

I don't know how long I lay there, curled in a ball, pouring my tears into the woolen rug. Each second crawled. I felt condemned to remain there, on that spot on the rug, coiled and alone, forever.

I must have fallen asleep. When I awoke, the room was in darkness. The torch lamps on the wall had burned out, the oblong opening cut into the wall now showed a navy patch of sky, allowing in the sounds of a crowd. People calling to one another, children laughing and playing, their feet scuttling in the dirt, while clangs and other noises suggested the preparation and setting up of food. I pictured servants laying tables in the square below Rachel's room, bringing platters of roasted lamb meat and bowls brimming with dried nuts and fruits—pomegranates, ripe figs, glossy purple grapes—and dense, crusty rounds of bread, steaming fresh from the wood-burning oven.

The basket of cakes was still sitting in the near-darkness of the room where Rachel had placed it on the shelf above me. I took a piece and bit into it. This one was rich and chewy, dense with something that tasted like carob, and absolutely delicious. I was so hungry, I polished off three of them, as well as several figs that were sticky and sweet as honey. I sat back with relief, the hollow in my belly for the moment sated.

I slipped on my sandals, grabbed the headscarf I'd worn earlier, and headed quietly down the stairs. I had every intention of joining the festivities, but once I got outside, I couldn't bring myself to take the alleyway leading around the back of the house. Instead, I found myself gliding swiftly down the stepped roadway. My feet seemed to have a plan of their own and for some reason my mind shut down, simply refused to think, allowing my feet to determine my movements. It was an immense relief; I was sick of thinking, sick of feeling so lost and filled with grief. *Go ahead,* I said aloud—I was talking to my sandals! *Take me wherever you think I should go.*

I turned onto an unfamiliar road; my feet took me this way and that, through streets that grew more crowded as I went along. As before, the crowd was made up of such unusual people: a group of tall, thin men with regal bearing and handsome dark-skinned faces, dressed in white robes. And across the path, what looked like a large family of men, women, and children, arguing in a sing-song language that included bird-like trills. Farther along, foraging in a pile of garbage, were a dozen or more urchins, their bare feet covered in sores.

The air filled with a pungent odor that brought to mind wood rot and slime, and unwashed bodies; moments later, the street opened out to a very wide section of river, clearly a port. Ships of all shapes and sizes crowded the waters, which sloshed muddily around sterns and bows, giving up oily froth. One massive vessel stood out; its elaborately carved bow was in the form of a dragon, the stern taking the shape of the dragon's tail. Dozens of enormous oars hung at angles from the sides like splayed limbs, empty of the slaves who would engineer the ship's motion across the seas. The upper deck swarmed with men dressed in ceremonial military garb; swords and scabbards hung from their sides.

I hurried along the teeming banks, holding my scarf close to cover my face, hoping to attract no attention. Soon, I was running. I could hear the sound of my own labored breathing; my chest felt tight, like someone was pressing down on it, but I only pushed myself harder. All I wanted was motion, the faster the better. The air whooshing past me felt like the breath of freedom. The world raced by, no longer distinct: vague and shifting shapes and colors, fading before my eyes.

Something caught my attention and brought me to a halt. I looked slowly around as my eyes refocused. To my surprise, the city buildings and streets had disappeared. I was surrounded by scruffy desert vegetation, clumps of reedy grasses and bushes low to the ground. In the distance, the dunes shimmered, lying up against the horizon like the humps of sleeping camels. Beside me, tall grasses and spindly trees spiked the grayish soil of the riverbank. An enormous moon bore down on the scene with unnerving glare. A glance behind me confirmed my suspicion: the walls of the city were not all that far away, perhaps a mile or so. It all seemed flat and unreal, as if it existed only in my imagination.

The river was wider than I'd yet seen it, giving it the character of a lake; the opposite bank seemed a distant shore.

The grass by the river looked silver-gray in the moonlight and gave off a cool, earthy scent. I sank down, pressed my face into the grass and inhaled. A haunting feeling overcame me; it was as if the earth itself were speaking—through time, through space, across generations. I squeezed my eyes tightly shut. Behind my closed lids I saw little flashes of light, which organized themselves into a single dim glow, faint, at first, and then growing stronger. My heart slowed, my breathing slowed, everything within and without seemed to grow very, very still. Slowly, I sat up, opened my eyes, found I was looking at the glassy surface of the river, also still, so very still. The air, too, had been cleared of wind. It hung around me, unstirring.

A tune came to my ears, and words: a song I'd sung with Mama as a round when I was a little girl. I realized that the quiet singing was coming from my own lips:

By the waters, the waters of Babylon
We lay down and wept, and wept, for thee Zion
We remember thee, remember thee, remember thee Zion

Here I was, sitting by those very waters, the famed river of Babylon! Was this a sign that I was never to return home, to *my* home, but was to go on wandering, my next and final journey back to the Zion of the song? The place Rachel and her parents and grandparents had sung about and remembered and hankered for the whole of their lives?

Gingerly, I inched closer to the river's edge, where the grass gave way to a slim band of dirt. A breeze had arisen, setting the waters into gentle, eddying motion. I gazed down at them, troubled, realizing I'd hoped to find my own reflection. Rather than reflecting my image back to me, it seemed to offer something altogether different, and dangerous; I had the terrible feeling that these waters could suck me down and make me disappear.

A crushing tiredness took hold of me.

I had no way of knowing how long I'd been away from Grandma's welcoming house in Melbourne. All I knew was that it was an eternity away. And even longer still since I'd seen my mama—since I'd held her, all the wrong way around, tiny and frail in my arms, a galaxy from here.

In all this time, across all these dimensions, I had done my best to keep strong. Now, I tried to reach for that strength, to find the steely strand within and clutch onto it tightly so that it might take me from here to where I longed to be, so that it might wing me back to my own little spot in the world, the one that was completely and totally mine. I closed my eyes, tried to reach for it, but found it was gone. Nothing to grab hold of: only the swirling, choppy waters traveling nowhere but down, down, tugging me into a terrible place from which I feared I would never escape.

Mama.

I heard my lips whisper her name. My sad, very sick mama appeared, in my mind's eye, as if I were looking right at her, here, now. Even frailer than when I had left her, even more pallid, more defeated. Weak, so very weak on her bed, she could barely open her eyelids, and when she did, her eyes were milky, as if she could no longer see into this world.

Mama?

Now, the sound coming from my own throat was a plea. I opened my eyes to see that the waters before me, these waters of Babylon, were settling, working their way back toward calm.

Where are you, Mama? Are you leaving this world?

The waters were steadying. I watched in a trance as they frothed and then ceased their movement altogether. The river was calm again. I leaned over its newly flat surface to catch just the briefest glimpse of the sky, a deep, dark bowl, its bright moon flashing back at me from where it lay on the smooth mirror of the water's skin.

My hand stole into the folds of my desert-linen garment, found the hidden pocket, curled around those precious objects I'd forgotten were there: Talia's Star of David on its delicate chain; Darlene's little tea-set porcelain plate; the two unusually smooth, round walnuts that Sarah had handed to me before we were separated by the surging crowd. And the tiny woolen booties that had kicked off the whole crazy adventure, given to me by Grandma in the deep dead of that Melbourne night long ago—and also millennia ahead of here.

I felt a sudden panic; Rachel had not given me any such object! The others had all done so—handed me something that held a special meaning for each of them, and that was maybe also a symbol of our togetherness. Wasn't that the key to setting off the storm? The storm that had been ripping me through time? I grasped the objects tightly and more tightly still, as if I might squeeze from them some kind of answer.

And then, something squeezed my head, an agonizing blow. That awful, vicious migraine stabbing and throbbing that erased all thought. I found myself staring again into the suddenly still waters at—me. My own image.

Me, my own self—not lost, abandoned, alone, but there before me, vivid and unmoving on the surface of the Euphrates, distant relative of all those other rivers with which I had had contact: my reflection, an image made up also of Talia, Darlene, Sarah, Rachel, all of us swirling together, *together*, in the river of time.

It came to me then—that this time, perhaps it was not my hand that would hold the parting gift, Rachel's contribution to my seemingly endless journey. My *eyes*, this time, *not* my hands—as Jimmy our friend in the Australian Outback had advised—were to take hold of the precious bequest. The meaning and the gift were there in the now-glassy surface of the water, together with the sky and the supernatural white globe of the moon—not in layers, but all one surface, one depth, one wholeness.

Mama, I said again. And this time it was not a word, but my own silent heart, filled with sadness.

Please, Mama, don't die. Not yet. You can't leave Billy. You can't leave Papa. And Mama, you can't leave me …

I watched the shimmery me that was one with the reflection of the deep dark sky and bright white moon. Watched as a tear slid down my cheek and dropped into the river, shattering, for an instant, and in only one tiny place, the calm mirror of water.

That one tiny tear set the world to roaring; a tremendous lightning bolt split the sky, followed by the loudest thunderclap I'd ever heard. My hands flew protectively to my ears just as the stinging rain pelted me from above, turning to hail that pummeled me all over, as if a small crowd were assaulting me with stones. Within the maelstrom, my head this time remained clear: no return of the awful throbbing, the vise grip of pain throughout my skull.

Why was it different, this time? Clearly, I was in the midst of the time storm. For once, I didn't try to resist—and astonishingly, I did not feel afraid, but exhilarated. For as mighty as the thunderclap had been, as blinding as the jagged spear of lightning that had wrenched the heavens in two, something even more intense was tearing through me: the conviction that this tumbling through time would be the last, that this storm was the tempest that would take me back—back to my time, my place, which I finally knew with a conviction as unshakable as Rachel's was my own true and precious home.

CHAPTER SIX

WASHCLOTH.

The word swam slowly up from murky depths, foreign at first, its meaning opaque.

Something warm and damp brushed across my brow, moving down to my eyes, working gently at the sealed-shut lids.

I struggled to open my eyes; my head, an immovable boulder, sank into a soft substance, the bottom of a riverbed perhaps, the water surrounding me weightless and breathable like air. Sounds reached my ears, undecipherable and yet familiar: a language I once heard long ago, in a dream.

A lyrical voice, someone singing.

No, not someone: *Grandma!*

And then, as if a trapdoor had sprung open in my brain, the indecipherable words being sung yielded up their meaning—not a foreign language after all but English, *my* mother tongue! How long had it been since I had spoken English? With great effort, I managed to wrench open my eyes; I found myself looking into Grandma's face. I glanced around, aware of a bewildering feeling that I'd just been born, that I was seeing everything for the first time. There was something miraculous about Grandma's face, something miraculous about the fact that I was back—back in my own time.

Mama, I found myself thinking. Is she all right?

Or had she ... had she—I could hardly bear to even allow the thought—slipped away?

Grandma's face suddenly relaxed into a relieved, ebullient smile.

"Darling!" she said, her eyes hovering with love. "You're awake! Thank the heavens! You've been so terribly ill."

Ill? What was she talking about? There was still that awful throbbing in my head that I'd fought each time I tripped back through time, only now, it was duller, much more bearable. I raised my hand to my temple.

"The doctor said your head would hurt for some time," Grandma said, "but you're no longer in danger. You're going to be all right."

Danger? What could Grandma be talking about?

I tried to speak, but my throat was parched, as if it were coated with sand.

"Here, have a sip." Grandma raised my head with her hand and brought a glass to my lips. The water tasted unbelievably delicious.

What was wrong with me? How long had I been ill?

"Don't try to talk now," Grandma said. "It's going to take time to get your strength back. You've had meningitis. You've been delirious for two weeks—that's a very long time."

Two weeks. Meningitis. Grandma had answered my questions without my having to ask.

This time, when I opened my mouth, I managed to find some words.

"Two weeks?" I asked, my voice gravelly and unfamiliar.

"Darling, you've been very, very ill." Grandma was biting her lip. There was a catch in her voice. "You've been in the hospital. We only brought you home this morning."

I was hearing Grandma's words, but nothing was really making sense.

"Very ill?" I asked.

Grandma nodded, and her eyes welled with tears.

"You've no idea ..." A grave shadow crossed her face; I could see that she had been beside herself with worry.

"You've been sleeping most of the time; I'd say about eighteen hours a day. The doctor said that was normal—that your body was exhausted from fighting the infection and you needed to sleep it off. And when you were awake—well, you weren't yourself. You were delirious—slipping in and out."

Grandma took my hand and looked at me closely.

"You don't remember any of this?"

"I had a lot of very strange dreams," I said. "I remember those. But they didn't feel like dreams—"

"No, I mean the conversations we had. The books I read you. We even took a slow walk in the hallway. You were attached to an IV—I wheeled it for you."

I shook my head. There was a lump in my throat that felt like the size of a golf ball and my throat and mouth were so dry, I could hardly swallow. My eyes fell on the glass of water on the bedside table; Grandma, observing my every motion, reached again for the glass and brought it to my lips.

"Take small sips," Grandma said, tipping the glass only very slightly. "The doctor said that would be best. You've been getting most of your liquid through the IV. It's all going to take time ... And it doesn't matter what you remember." She smiled faintly. She seemed worn out; her face was drawn, with dark circles beneath her eyes.

"It's just so wonderful to see you awake. Now darling, don't be frightened when your head starts to hurt again. The doctor said that it will hurt on and off for some time. You had a shot before you left the hospital." Grandma checked her watch. "Next dose is still two hours away. You'll be able to take the pain medication by mouth, now that you're awake. You're still quite hot, though. I'll take your temperature later. Now, you must rest."

Her eyes traveled the length of me, careful, assessing, as if making sure that all of me was still there. Her gaze caught on something on the bed beside me. The little pile of objects. My hand absently stole across and closed over them.

"Funny, I don't recall ..." Grandma said.

My eyelids felt heavy and closed of their own accord, shutting me back into a private space, opening me mystically to the feel of the objects beneath my fingers. Two little baby booties—that's where the journey had begun! Grandma's gift from her own past, given to me here, in this very house. And the little Star of David on its chain, given to me by Talia. My fingers were moving carefully over each treasure, pausing now to mark the shape of the miniature porcelain plate, the single remnant of Darlene's precious tea set; and though my eyes were closed, I could see in my mind's eye the delicate rose pattern around the edge. Finally, the two smooth, almost round shapes, the walnuts given to me by Sarah. No object from Rachel—but something else flashed within, a different kind of gift bestowed by that journey, something that came from *me*.

How could any of it have been only dreams! I had the proof right here, beneath my palm, that everything I could now remember so vividly, had *actually happened!*

With those walnuts tightly in my grasp, a sense of the most powerful treasure of all rose within me; not an object my fingers could touch, but something else: the recollection of my own reflection in the surface of the Euphrates. A face that looked like mine but was layered with the spirits of the girls I had known only briefly but had come to love. How many more had there been—between Sarah and Rachel? The sudden thought of dozens, maybe hundreds of young women— swirling through history in their lifetimes of adventure and suffering, panic, and joy—made me feel faint.

I opened my eyes to find Grandma regarding me with wonder.

"What do you have there?" she asked, a stillness in her voice that reminded me of the glassy surface of the wide Babylonian waters.

My fingers slid away. Grandma held out her hand; I passed her the objects, one at a time, feeling as if I was in some kind of trance.

"Funny ..." she said again, fingering first the star, then the little plate, then the walnuts. "How could you possibly ... ?"

Words failed her. She examined the objects in her hand as if they were tiny planetary bodies, miraculously dropped from the heavens.

Long minutes passed. Something changed in Grandma's face; it was like watching the weather move across the sky.

And then, she simply handed the things back to me—carefully, as if they were fragile.

"You'll want to put these someplace safe," she said, avoiding my eyes. We sat, for a moment, in silence, the air seeming to heat up between us.

When Grandma spoke again, she had returned to her normal state; the mystical feeling in the room had vanished.

"I've made some porridge," she said. "Billy's sitting at the table, waiting for you."

Billy! I had missed him *so much*! I tried to jump out of bed, but my legs were weak and crumpled before I was up and out.

"Easy does it," Grandma said. "He's not going to disappear."

Grandma helped me put on my bathrobe and held my arm as I walked down the hall; I stumbled a little, my legs felt weak and my breath was short from the effort. As we passed by the living room, I caught sight of the samovar in its place on the sideboard. I paused to catch my breath.

"Grandma," I said, "I've been meaning to ask—how did your mother's family get the samovar out of Dusiat?"

I felt it on my own tongue before I heard it—the way I said *Dusiat* in a perfect Yiddish accent. At the sound of the word, Grandma did a double take.

"That's the Yiddish way of saying it," she said. "And how do you know the name of the village my mother came from? I don't remember telling you that."

I could feel myself reddening.

"Mama told me," I said. "She also told me how to pronounce it that way."

"That's odd," Grandma said, more to herself than to me. "I wonder how your mama would know the Yiddish way?"

"I think she did research," I said, surprised at how easily the lies were coming. "You know, family tree ..."

"Yes, perhaps so," Grandma said, still with that faraway voice. "Well, to answer your question. As you probably know, my mother's family left Lithuania because of the persecution ... You know about the pogroms—?"

I nodded.

"Well, there was a nasty incident in Dusiat right around 1905. My mother was about fourteen—your age, as a matter of fact. A crowd set fire to the synagogue, and to many houses and businesses. A good part of the shtetl was lost. My mother's house was badly damaged. They could no longer stay there. A number of Jews from nearby towns had emigrated to South Africa; they took their chances going there too. It must have been terrifying—not speaking the language, and Africa being so different, so far.

"They had relatives in Vilnius who were also leaving who raised the money for their passage. At the last minute, while my mother's family was at the dock, waiting to board the ship, my mother's aunt rushed onto the platform, carrying the samovar. She had rescued it from the damaged house. It was terribly impractical, of course—look at it!"

We both looked over to the shining brass urn, which stood about a foot and a half tall and had a girth of about thirty inches.

"But my great-aunt was adamant—they were to take the samovar with them. So, they exchanged it for a suitcase filled with linen and clothing. They could only take so much onto the boat. They wrapped the samovar in a blanket. That's how they took it, all the way across the ocean to a completely new, unimaginable world."

In the kitchen, I forgot all about the samovar once I saw Billy's bright face. He jumped up and flung himself into my arms.

"Sister! You're awake!"

I squeezed him so tightly he called out for me to stop.

"I came to the hopsticle and sang you lots of songs when you were sick, didn't I, Grandma?"

"Can you sing me one now?" I asked.

Earnestly, sitting there with smudges of strawberry jam around his lips, he began: *Doe, a deer, a female deer*—and sang through the entire song, his voice clear and beautifully pitched.

Grandma had made porridge, spiced with nutmeg and cinnamon, just the way we liked it. She served me a bowl with brown sugar and milk. My hunger was overpowering: that same grinding hunger that had plagued me on my journey. But I only managed to get down a few spoonfuls; though I still felt ravenous, my stomach also felt uncomfortably full.

"It's going to take time to get your appetite back," Grandma said. "You've lost weight, your stomach has shrunk. They gave you intravenous fluids when you were in the hospital. It will take a little while until you can eat properly again. Don't worry, though; you'll be back to normal in no time. Here, take a few sips of juice."

Grandma had squeezed fresh orange juice. As I sipped, I thought again of my mother, who loved orange juice. *Liquid sunshine*, she called it.

"How's Mama?" I asked.

Grandma went quiet. "Thank heavens, she's doing much better, too."

My heart fired to thumping. "What do you mean—thank heavens?"

"She had a reaction to the chemotherapy. Right about the time ..."

"Right about the time ...?"

"... that you also took a downward turn, while you were in the hospital. She was in the ICU for two days."

I waited, the sound of my own breath loud in my ears.

"She stabilized quickly, thankfully. They started her on a new regimen—a two-month course. One week on, one week off. And she's tolerating it well; the doctors are optimistic. She's been very worried about you, needless to say. I waited until she was doing better before I told her you were so sick ... I had to tell her, of course ..." Her voice trailed off.

Grandma checked her wristwatch. "I called her this morning, after Doctor Barter left. He told us you'd turned the corner. I can't tell you how happy she was! I also spoke to your papa."

Papa. I saw his face before me, filled with relief. "He's been so worried about Mama," I said. More than worried, I thought. More like devastated.

"Is she ... going to be ... okay?"

"We all have our own versions of prayer, don't we," Grandma said.

I nodded.

"It can be a very powerful thing, all that prayer. Your Mama has a lot of people in her corner."

She went quiet for a moment.

"You know," she said after a time, "your parents are very lucky to have found each other." She seemed to be speaking more to herself than to me.

Nahum's face flashed before my eyes and my heart lurched.

"What is it, darling?"

That confusing little voice reared up again inside—*Mama and Papa, destined for each other,* it said. Then: *was he your one and truly?*

"You look as if you've seen a ghost!"

"It's just that—I met a man once—" I said, but then cringed at how absurd I sounded.

"A man?" Grandma smiled a slightly bemused smile.

"A boy, I mean," I said, hot tears of confusion springing to my eyes. "You know, Grandma, girls my age used to marry, back in biblical times."

The smile fell from Grandma's lips. "I'm sorry, darling. You're right. Love can come at any age. It's silly of us oldies to make light of it to young people."

She waited, perhaps to see if I'd say anything further.

"What happened? To the boy, I mean."

I shook my head. It was terribly hard to speak. A tear spilled from my eye.

"That feeling will come again," Grandma said. Her face was grave, but her eyes shone with feeling. "I know it, darling. You'll find your soul mate, just as your mama found your papa."

Grandma's eyes were like rays of hope; I felt, in that moment, that I would in fact find Nahum again some time, some place. He would look different, his name would not be Nahum, but there would be something—some clue, some sign—that would let me know that this man, whoever he turned out to be, somehow shared in Nahum's soul.

Grandma was consulting her watch. She counted under her breath. "It's the middle of the night in Brooklyn now. We'll call her later, and you can talk with your mama yourself!"

The thought of that—of talking with Mama—made me so happy, I could hardly stand it! I grabbed hold of Billy again and held him tight.

"Stop, Sister! You're hurting me!" Billy called out, but he was grinning ear to ear and hugging me back.

* * *

After three days of careful feeding and slow walks around the house, I started to feel my strength return and I was able to stop taking the heavy-duty pain medication. I still felt unsteady on my feet and had bouts of nausea and dizziness, though the most difficult persisting symptom was a sensitivity to light. Lamps and overhead lights were the worst; they made my eyes ache and triggered a return of the dreaded pain in my head. Grandma gave me a pair of her sunglasses, which mercifully reduced the effect. Billy thought my wearing them indoors was great fun.

"Sis is a movie star!" he said. "You gonna wear them outdoors, too?"

"Yes, I think I will."

"The paper-ratzy gonna come take pictures?"

Grandma smiled. She loved Billy's little-boy malapropisms.

"Who told you about the paparazzi?" I asked, reaching out my arms. Billy nestled close, taking care with his movements. Grandma must have primed him to treat me gingerly.

"I saw it on TV. Lots of people with cameras. *Flash, flash flash!* Grandma told me the word. Did I get it right?"

"You sure did, little guy. Did you wonder why they call them that?"

Billy fiddled with his finger.

"Yeah, but I don't wanna make a mistake."

"Well, it isn't actually anything to do with paper and rats," I said, stroking his arm. "It just sounds that way. It's from an Italian movie by a famous movie director named Fellini. He had a character called Paparazzo who was always taking pictures. That's where the word comes from."

Billy nodded. "I see," he said, trying to sound grown up.

"I tell you what. I think we should go out. I'm starting to feel cooped up."

"Cooped up?" he asked.

"I'll explain in the car. What do you say, Grandma? I feel like we should go out—to celebrate! I haven't been out in the longest time!"

"That's a grand idea!" Grandma said. "Where shall we go? But let's not make it too ambitious. It's early days yet."

"How about that lovely pastry shop on High Street? They have little tables—we can have a real Australian high tea!" Though my stomach felt achy from my few spoonfuls of porridge at breakfast, it grumbled at the thought of pastries, which I especially loved.

"Excellent. Anything that might help you put a bit of weight back on."

I washed my face and hands, brushed my teeth, then slowly dressed. I felt very draggy; everything was an enormous effort and seemed to take forever. Billy hovered outside first the bathroom door, then the door of our room, chattering about this and that, clearly not wanting to be too far away from me.

Grandma appeared in the doorway.

"You look almost as good as new!" she said.

She offered me her arm and we walked down the long hallway. By the front door, I paused to get my breath. I was already weary from the exertion. I turned to see a vase on the sideboard, holding fresh flowers.

"Camellias," I said, examining the four velvety pink blooms, nestling against sturdy, shiny leaves so perfect and bright they didn't look real.

"Divine, aren't they," Grandma said, the light in her eyes shining like distant stars.

"Your favorite flowers," I said.

"That's right!" She gave me a querying look.

"*Grandma's favorite!* Mama always says that, whenever we see camellias."

Camellia. The name felt newly sweet and heavy on my lips; it had been my name—the velvety pink beauty that seemed to come straight from Grandma had, for a strange but crucial day, actually been part of *me*.

I saw again Joel's eyes—Joel, beloved by Grandma in her childhood and youth, whom I'd actually met!—also deep with velvety beauty: kindness and suffering shining together like the glimmering of a still body of water in moonlight. Heard, again, his voice. *Camellia asked about the river. She may not have voiced the words, but I felt the question.* He'd heard my soul's echo even before I'd noticed it myself. I hadn't known what I'd been looking for—I only knew I was on a terrifying, though also exhilarating journey; all I knew was that I was *searching*.

Perhaps that *was* the point: that the journey, in fact, was about the search. Joel's wise words swam back into my mind. *We must travel the river we're thrown into.* How lucky I was, I remember thinking as he was speaking, to have been thrown into the river that was my very own life. To have the warm and loving family I had, and so many opportunities and freedoms. Though my heart squeezed around the knowledge of how many people, even in my own wonderful country, the United States, were still subjected to suffering and injustice. *Every river has its story*, Joel had said; I heard his voice again in my mind's ear. *Their sources reach far, far away—and their destinations ... well, those are the greatest mysteries of all.* That mystery stirred within me; it gleamed and beckoned, filling me with an uncanny feeling I could not name.

"Come," Grandma said, "let's get going."

We climbed into the back of Grandma's small red car; Billy sat close beside me and put his hand in mine.

"I love you, Sis." This was the third time he'd said this since I "came to," as Grandma put it, as if his repeated declarations might be necessary to keep me from slipping back into illness.

We drove some fifteen minutes through Melbourne's wide streets. I silently greeted each tram as if they were my own personal pets.

We pulled up to an open parking space in front of the pastry shop.

"Look, they kept us a spot!" Grandma said. "They must be expecting us!"

We got out of the car, then stood for some time before the window, surveying the offerings. Beautiful chocolate cakes, each boasting shavings or frills of real chocolate; fruit cakes, with visible chunks of nuts and dried fruit; a huge tray of cupcakes topped in brightly colored Sesame Street characters rendered in cream. Delicate lace-like cookies dipped in dark chocolate; shortbread sandwiches filled with red preserves; ball-shaped nut biscuits dusted in sugar. And smack in the middle of the window, a tray of enormous napoleons, with their layers of flakey pastry and thick custard cream.

For a moment, the cakes in the window seemed to waver, as if readying to collapse. I leaned against the windowpane, feeling woozy.

"Darling, are you okay?"

A wave of incredible exhaustion washed over me. "I'm tired," I said, my voice sounding weak and far away.

"Let's go in," Grandma said, taking my arm.

Billy chose a free table up close to the counter. He tried out each of the stools, which had padded orange seats and the marvelous advantage of making 360-degree rotations.

Four middle-aged women sat at the next table, talking and sipping tea. I sat down and closed my eyes. The dizzy feeling lifted; when I opened my eyes again, the world had stopped wavering.

"I'll go and order," Grandma said.

"I'll come with you," I said, slowly rising.

I pointed to a chocolate cupcake with white frosting and sprinkles. "One of these for my little brother, please," I said to the woman behind the counter, "and a plateful of those." Now, I pointed to the napoleons on the shelf in the window.

"A plateful?" the woman serving me said.

"I don't know, four or five," I said. "However many will fill up a plate."

The woman behind the counter turned toward Grandma expectantly, as if to say—*Surely you don't need a whole plateful! Just two of you, after all.* But Grandma nodded decisively.

"Thank you. A plateful sounds just grand." She turned to me and whispered, "Whatever we don't eat, we can take home."

We ordered hot chocolate for all three of us, then rejoined Billy, who was engrossed in the thrilling phenomenon of the rotating stools.

The server brought our pastries and hot chocolate. I placed the largest of the napoleons on a plate and handed it to Grandma, then took one for myself.

"Funny, I didn't know you liked vanilla slices," Grandma said, taking as dainty a bite as anyone can manage with such a large, flakey, custardy confection.

"In New York, we call them napoleons, and yes, I love them," I said.

Now, that same questioning perplexed look I'd seen in each face of all the girls I'd encountered in my journey passed across Grandma's features. When she spoke again, she seemed to be talking to herself.

"That's what we called them in South Africa as well."

I spoke before thinking. "I know."

"I often wished I could have one of these when I was a child," she said, "but I never got the chance."

"I know," I said again, in a voice as quiet as hers.

"You do?" That flickering look in her eyes ...

"Yes, I do."

"Did I tell you that? Or perhaps it was your mama ...?"

"No," I said, "it was you. A long time ago." My voice dropped to a whisper. "Before I was born."

I leaned across to Grandma and whispered in her ear. "We were standing together by the window of that little pastry shop in Koppies. I promised that one day, I'd buy you a whole plateful. Remember?"

Grandma patted my hand. I drew back and looked into her face. Her eyes were spiked with tears and she was biting a little at her lip. She just nodded again then looked for a while down at the white tablecloth. I wondered if it was possible both to *know* something and *not know it* at the same time

I looked at Billy, whose face was smeared from nose to chin and across both cheeks with frosting and sprinkles.

"You little monkey," I said. "How do you manage to get it over so much of your face? That's quite a talent, don't you think, Grandma?"

"Yum yum *yum!*" Billy said.

Grandma had collected herself; now, she smiled at Billy.

"Little monkey is right," she said. Now, she turned to me.

"Emily, you're going to have to take it slowly. For the next two weeks, we'll stay close to home. After that, we can do some of the things we had planned. I know Billy will just love the planetarium. Do you remember what you said the time I took you there, when you were Billy's age?"

I shook my head, no. "I remember that we went, but I was so little ..."

"Well, when they put up the night sky, you could hardly believe it. 'Our sky in Brooklyn looks different!' you said. 'It has trees in the way. Big ones. With squirrels!'"

"That's true!" Billy said. "Our trees have got squirrels! Here, you got possums. And magpies. And kangaroos!"

"We can go and see the kangaroos at Healesville. But that's a long drive, we'll have to wait until your sister's feeling better."

Billy's face went serious. "Yes, Sis has to get better. Poor Sis."

"We still have two whole months—we're going to have so much fun!" Grandma said.

* * *

Every few days, we got to talk to Papa, who told us that Mama was "a trouper" and "hanging in" and that she loved us so much, too much to ever convey over the telephone. Two weeks into my own recovery, Mama felt well enough to speak on the phone. The sound of her voice was like jolts from heaven. I was so choked by tears, I could hardly speak.

"Mama, I miss you so much," I said.

"I've been thinking about you, darling," she replied, her voice echoing a little on the long-distance wire.

"I know," I said, my own voice an echoing whisper, "and I've been thinking of you."

"Silly goose, getting so sick."

"You're a silly goose, too," I said.

"Yes, I am."

"I'm much better," I said. "Grandma says I'm almost back to my old self."

"I'm doing much better, too," Mama said. I didn't hear anything forced or unnatural in her voice—I felt certain she was telling me the truth. And I heard something else, something so forceful, it almost came to me as color—rosy, warm, the incarnation, somehow, of health.

"Yes, I can hear it," I said.

"What can you hear?"

And now, pure joy coursed through me, a sunny feeling glowing and thick like honey.

"That you're going to be okay." The words fell from my lips without my fully realizing what I was saying. "I feel as if I know that, in my bones."

Mama had gone quiet.

"Mama?" I asked.

"Yes?" I could hear from the sound in her voice that she had tears in her eyes, I could almost see them spilling down her cheeks.

"We know things, don't we," I said.

"Yes, darling, we do."

* * *

Two weeks later, I was pretty much back to normal. My eyes were still very sensitive to light, and most days, by late afternoon, I'd find I had a dull headache. But I was well enough to go out and do fun things with Grandma and Billy as well as with Uncle Michael and Auntie Liora and her children, my cousins. But the best thing of all was the phone calls with Papa and Mama, who was tolerating her treatments so well.

When Papa told me the doctors "were pleased with her progress," I could hear the hope and relief in his voice.

I didn't want to ask them too many questions, so I asked Grandma instead.

"I think the term is 'guardedly optimistic,'" Grandma said. The full smile on her face told me what I needed to know—that my mother was doing better than expected.

* * *

The days began to gallop. And of a sudden, it was time for us to leave. On the day of our departure, Uncle Michael arrived at Grandma's house early. Auntie Liora also came by to say goodbye. We sat around the kitchen table for the obligatory tea. Grandma had stayed up late the night before to make two cakes: Billy's favorite—chocolate, of course—and mine, an apple cake baked in an oblong Pyrex dish, topped with a rich crust sliced diagonally and filled with apricot jam.

How I'd miss these Australian tea ceremonies, I thought, making a mental note to carry on the tradition, which Mama had let slip, back home in New York.

"No goodbyes, my darlings," Grandma said as Uncle Michael packed our suitcases into the trunk of the car. I could see Grandma was fighting back tears. "After all, I'll see you again so very soon!"

Grandma had already booked her ticket to come and see us in New York, six months from now.

"By then, your mama will have a new head of hair!"

* * *

The engines did that lurching roar that comes before the taxiing, when you know that the plane is about to take off. We were both buckled in, but Billy managed to press up close by my side, as had become his habit. He craned his neck up to whisper in my ear.

"We're going home, aren't we, Sis?"

"Yes, Billy," I said, pausing to plant a kiss on his cheek, "we're going home."

Billy gave me his highest-wattage, full-nose-crinkle smile, then looked out the window at the fast-moving tarmac. The engine went into full throttle and I, too, leaned back as the plane tilted upward, lifting first its nose, then its full length, up from the earth.

I wondered if I would ever again encounter the Storm. For now, I felt perfectly happy at the thought of staying firmly put in my own time and place.

Looking at Billy lost in the magic of our liftoff, and feeling his trusting hand in mine, I was suddenly baffled at the thought of my own recent grief—as I sat weeping, lost and alone, in my final adventure by the waters of the Euphrates. Yes, I'd been crying for home, but there was something else, too. An ache I'd felt when each companion had asked—*Who are you?* I thought about the girls I had met on my journey, the girls I had listened to and accompanied, with whom I'd eaten and traveled and learned—with whom I'd fled and cried and hoped. I marked them off again in my mind. *Talia* in Australia. *Darlene* in South Africa. *Sarah* in Lithuania. And finally, in Babylon, *Rachel*. Four girls whose question I'd not been able to answer. Not only because of the strong feeling that it would be wrong to tell them I came from the future, but also because I did not really know, within myself, how to begin to offer a reply.

We both drifted off to sleep. I awoke suddenly as if an alarm had gone off, alive with dream fragments, iridescent shards from other worlds that were yet an intimate part of me. Billy was cuddled up asleep beside me, breathing slowly and gently; how peaceful and trusting he looked. I edged the window shade up halfway; we were suspended in a black sky. The red glow from the wing light pulsed in short little bursts. I peered into the night, black and flat and close up against the double pane. As my eyes adjusted, I was able to see faint pinpricks, hundreds of them, poking through the darkness, opening the flat sky into a depth of heaven. The cosmos surrounded us: a proliferating of eternal space, vivid and vast.

One pinprick drew my eye—faint, yes, but somehow more piercing than the rest. A single star in the heavens, I thought, calling me to take note. Since Grandma told me that my mama's treatments had been successful, I'd walked around feeling like I was clutching a tiny and priceless treasure that made me gasp with gratitude. I stared and stared at that star. My thoughts washed within like a slow tide, and then a single thin voice emerged. I knew it immediately; I was remembering Jimmy, in the wild Outback after our terrifying crash landing with Grandpa Jack.

I heard him again, talking about the waratah, the red heart flower from his story, heard him say that I, too, was a flower that needed water to blossom and grow—but of the sky, not of the earth. *Jasmine: white*, he'd said.

Like a star. You are Star Flower.

Was that tiny white star in the sky somehow mine?

You travel in the sky, but you search for your place, Jimmy had said.

How little I knew then of the journeys I was yet to take! And now, here I was, traveling through the sky. What else had he said? I struggled to recall his words, scrabbling in my mind through the impossible adventures I'd recently had. Something about roots—yes, Jimmy told me I was looking for a place to *put in my roots:* a place with water and land, so that I might *blossom and grow.* Talia, Darlene. Sarah, Rachel. I closed my eyes and their homes rose in my mind's eye, each one nestled on its unique little parcel of land spanning our globe, Mother Earth, and more years than I could make sense of— Australia in 1974, South Africa, 1943, Lithuania, 1905, and all the way back to biblical times, in Babylon. Staring into the night at the one star I felt certain was *mine,* Jimmy's words spun a silky web of meaning. In each adventure, I'd been led to a river. Could it be that each of those wonderful girls—my forebears, mothers, all of them, who in a precious flesh-and-blood daisy chain had led to *me*—were my land? For Jimmy, the word *land* was the same as the words *mother* and *home.* All the lands of my foremothers … my foremothers themselves … were *they* my country? In knowing them, had I been led back to— and found—a new, true place of *home?*

The last two hours of the long flight were a blur. And then, after landing at JFK Airport and disembarking, we caught sight of our beloved Papa, whose shining blue eyes were electric with love and joy. We waited impatiently for the luggage, then loaded up the car, pulling out onto the Brooklyn-Queens Expressway, watching the city unfurl alongside the highway in all its variety, finally catching sight of Manhattan, beside us, accompanying us in our approach to home.

Finally, *finally*, we were making our way beneath the BQE along Hamilton Avenue, alongside the side streets of our neighborhood, brownstone Brooklyn. First the smaller, more ramshackle two- and three-story buildings, some built of wood, veering off at an angle. The houses became stately and more uniform: four- and five-story townhouses with their distinctive brownstone facades.

Somehow, against all the odds, I had made it back home.

Here we were, the three of us, standing in front of the beloved house in which I'd so far lived this life that is mine—this moment in the river's passage.

In my thoughts, I turned silently, for one last moment, to all the fourteen-year-old girls I had met on my journey—the girls who would become the women who were my ancestors. At last, my vision was clear—I could see my way toward an answer to their recurring, disorienting question. The answer I could not, on my journey, give them suddenly glimmered in my mind, vivid and mercurial, like a quick-moving silver fish in crystal waters.

I am all of you.
I am part of the river.
I am myself.

I glimpsed, for an instant, another girl in another time yet to come: a slender girl, about my age, with an unfamiliar, and yet mysteriously known face. My own future daughter? Or her daughter, even further ahead in time? Would I ever have the experience of wondering if a new friend I was meeting was in fact *my own future daughter or granddaughter*, having herself traveled backward in time, on her own strange river journey, having come looking for me, as she searched for her origins, searched for herself?

Billy's eager, piping voice drew me away from the future and back to the present.

"Mama! I want to see Mama!"

He could not keep still; he was literally bouncing up and down on his little legs. "Come *on*, Sister. What are we waiting for?"

"Nothing!" I said, taking tight hold of his hand, which was sticky, as always, with something he hadn't got around to washing off.

"Come on, you little monkey!" I said, and together we bounded up the stoop steps. With my free hand, I pulled open the metal outer door and waited for Papa, who was striding up the steps behind us, to unlock the front door. Then, I knew, we would run even faster up the long staircase to the second floor, where Mama awaited us.

EPILOGUE

I STEPPED INTO THE SHOWER AND turned my face to the hot stream of water, exhausted from telling Ray about that summer half my life ago, depleted from reliving it all through the long night, yet also filled to the brim. It was five-thirty in the morning. We had to leave for the airport at eight.

Grandma's words from last night returned to me. That she'd remembered everything from when she was young. I'd had no idea what she meant, yet her remark triggered my memory, taking me back to that summer, and way, way back beyond that, as the whole impossible adventure swam back into my consciousness.

I had to see Grandma one last time.

I dressed in a hurry. Since we were packed, we were out the door in no time. We pulled up in front of the nursing home at six-thirty.

"I'll be back at eight," Ray said, leaning over to give me a kiss.

We gave each other a lingering glance. It had been an extraordinary night. At around one in the morning, I'd decided not to think about how crazy it all sounded but rather to just tell the story that was pouring from me in such vivid detail. I told myself to trust in our faith in each other, in the vows we had made long before our wedding day. When I was recounting my meeting with Nahum, something wavered in Ray's eyes—the same expression I'd seen on the faces of all the girls I had been with on my impossible adventure. I didn't know what to call that look, I only knew that it cut to the deepest mysteries of human connection, that it spoke to how much we *don't* know about life, as much as it also captured what for me felt like one of the greatest truths of all. Now, in the car, about to see Grandma one last time, Ray and I looked even more deeply into each other's eyes. Ray, who I felt I knew so wholly, though of course we were also just at the beginning of what I hoped would be a very long life together. But also—Nahum … it was as if he were also right here in the car in Melbourne, Australia, millennia and oceans away from Babylon. Nahum was Ray, and Ray was Nahum, one person, as if through all of time—my *bashert.*

Visitors were not allowed before nine, but Michelle at the front desk knew I was leaving this morning and buzzed me in.

"She's waiting for you," Michelle said. "She said you might drop by on your way to the airport. I guess she read your mind!"

Grandma was propped up in bed, her hair neatly combed, a little lipstick dabbed on her lips.

"I was expecting you, darling," she said. "I'm so happy to get the chance to say goodbye properly."

The lump leapt into my throat. She was saying it so casually— *goodbye*—but we both knew there was nothing casual about it. This would be our final farewell. The doctors had said she was failing fast.

"Grandma, I remember everything," I said. "I was up all night with Ray. It came back to me as I was telling Ray all about it. But Grandma, something you said to me last night has been going around and around in my mind. You said that after I left that summer, *you* remembered things too."

She nodded. "Yes, Emily, I did say that."

"What did you mean?"

"I told you many things over the years, about growing up in Koppies."

"Yes," I said, "you did."

"Sometimes I think I told you too much. That maybe it weighed on you …"

"No, Grandma! I wanted to know everything."

"Yes, you were a curious child, and with such a lively imagination. Just like your mama. Well, there was one thing I never did tell you—of course I would have, if I had remembered it. About my cousin's cousin, who came to stay with us from Vereeniging. The peculiar thing is, I forgot about it. Not in the usual way of forgetting. As if some strange force of nature had erased it from my memory entirely. When it *did* come back to me that summer you had meningitis, after you'd gone back home, part of me thought I must have imagined that it had even happened! And your mama was recovering, my mind was on other things ..."

I glanced at my watch. It was almost seven. I felt a sudden panic that I wouldn't get to hear everything Grandma had to tell me. I only had one more hour!

"Do tell me, Grandma. What you finally remembered. I really want to know."

"You know that Koppies was a tiny little place."

"A one-horse town ..." I said.

"Yes, that's what I always said, didn't I! You know I felt suffocated there. So much smallness—in every way. Tiny town, narrow minds, narrow lives. So, it was a real event when this lovely girl came to stay. Her name was—"

"Camellia," I said.

"Yes, Camellia." Grandma's brow ruffled, but she didn't ask how I knew.

"None of it was very clear, the memory jumped around, the way things do in dreams. At the same time, it all seemed—well, normal and right, the way the most outlandish things seem normal and right in dreams. Well maybe that's not the best way to put it ..."

"You mean—inevitable?" I said.

"Yes, that is what I mean. Inevitable. I knew it all *actually* happened. That it *wasn't* a dream. Because of how I felt here." And now Grandma placed a hand over her heart.

"Please go on," I said. My own heart leapt about inside my chest. I had the feeling it was all going to slip away before I had the chance to grasp it. To lay my hands on what felt like an important treasure.

"Camellia and I hit it off straight away. This was so unusual for me. I didn't have friends growing up, not outside of the occasional cousin who would come to visit. Meeting Camellia was one of the shining moments of my life. Those first deep connections—they can actually determine the course of a young person's life. Feeling seen, heard, and seeing and hearing—really knowing another person, with whom you share so much. It can become a blueprint for how you live your life.

"My cousin in Vereeniging got the measles while her cousin Camellia was visiting them from Durban. Camellia couldn't stay there, so they asked if she could come to us for a few days. We were both delighted, of course. She wanted to come to school with me, so we went together. It was an awful day for me, but so much less awful as I had a friend with me, my new friend, Camellia."

Grandma looked at me with such love—and gratitude—that it made me want to weep.

"We visited Joel," I said. My voice was a whisper. The room went silent. "In his village."

Grandma nodded.

"We sat in your tree."

A tear trickled from Grandma's eye and she nodded again.

"And much later, when you were my Grandma, after I was so terribly sick, we went to buy pastries. A whole plate of napoleons."

"Just like you promised," Grandma said, her voice as shaky as the smile on her face.

I took her hand. "We've always been so close, haven't we," I said.

"Yes, my darling. And how lucky I have been to have you in my life."

"And how lucky I have been to have you in mine."

Grandma's eyes fell on the Star of David sitting in the cup of my throat. Until last night, I'd had no memory of my mother giving me the necklace; I knew it came from her side of the family, but that was all. I would wear it on occasion, aware of a vague confusion, since it was a Jewish symbol that had no real connection to my own experience. Last night, as I was telling Ray about the plane crash in the Australian Outback, I remembered that at the last minute, before leaving New York, I'd grabbed the necklace from my jewelry box and put it in the satin jewelry pouch Grandma once gave me for my birthday. I retrieved it to show Ray; he placed it around my neck and fastened the clasp.

Grandma smiled. "Your Mama gave you that."

I nodded.

"I remember how puzzled I was, after we brought you back from the hospital, to find that you had it, along with those other items ..."

My hand flew to the little star.

"You know, my own mother gave that Magen David to your mama when she was young, on the one trip she made from South Africa to visit us in Melbourne."

"Yes, she told me," I said.

Grandma let out a long sigh, as if her exhaustion were crushing her.

"One day," she said, her voice weak and so tired, "you can give it to your own daughter. One day, you can give it to Rose."

I gasped. No one but Ray and I knew about the name we'd chosen for our baby.

Grandma's eyes drooped, as if she could no longer keep them open.

"I'm sorry, darling. I'm just so tired. I wonder when I'll stop feeling this exhausted."

My heart squeezed, knowing she would never again feel energetic. It was a miracle she was still alive at all; for four and a half years, she had defied the statistical odds for living with terminal pancreatic cancer. She was finally succumbing to the lethal illness.

"Grandma, I don't have to leave for nearly an hour. Why don't you sleep. I'm going to sit here and hold your hand. We'll still be together."

"Thank you, darling. I'll just take a little snooze."

She closed her eyes; her breathing slowed. Just as I thought she was fast asleep, her eyes snapped open—fully alert, urgent.

"Your mama is going to lick this thing, just as she did before. She's a fighter."

This was the second time my mother's cancer had returned. Both times, my mother had done well on the chemotherapy and the doctors were optimistic; they'd caught it at the first sign.

"Yes, Grandma, just like you!"

"She's the best mama in the world. Just as you're going to be the best mama in the world."

"And so are you, Grandma. The best mama and grandma in the world."

There—that radiant smile I loved so much, fully animating her face.

"Rest now, Grandma. I'll be right here."

She fell asleep, her breath at first even and deep, and then slipping into something more shallow and troubled.

I sat beside her, the tears flowing down my face. I couldn't keep my own eyes open, having stayed awake the whole night. I leaned back in the chair, holding Grandma's hand, and with great relief gave over to sleep.

Images flashed within, feeling both like memory and dream.

There, again, that beautiful green-eyed girl I had glimpsed in my mind's eye on the long flight over, a girl with skin halfway between the color of Ray's and mine, with light brown hair that fell to her shoulders in a cascade of curls. She was laughing—and now it was both of us, girls together, running down the stairs of the house I grew up in in Brooklyn, then down the stoop and onto the street. Headed off somewhere together, both of us fourteen, I knew this, filled with the giddy, almost fragrant excitement of an age when the future lay ahead in all its promise.

"Rose! Not so fast!"

She slowed down, then reached out a hand to grab mine.

"Slowpoke, come on! We're going to miss the fun!"

Someone rapped at a door.

The Brooklyn street broke apart as the knocking repeated; I cracked open my eyes to see Grandma sleeping fitfully in the bed beside me. The door opened.

It was Michelle. And beside her, Ray.

The clock on the wall showed a few minutes before eight.

Ray crossed the room, put his hand on my shoulder.

"Time to go, my love."

"Just give me a minute."

I struggled to lay claim to the dream—it felt like something of great significance was being pulled away from me and buried. I squeezed my eyes shut. Nothing but the reddish darkness of the inside of my closed eyelids.

I let out a little sigh.

Ray stroked my shoulder. "Em, we really should get going."

I nodded.

Grandma lay in her bed, asleep. I leaned in close to her.

"I love you, Grandma. I will always love you, as you have always loved me. Go in peace."

I withdrew my hand from hers. Ray put his arm around me and we walked to the door. I glanced around the room, taking it all in—the samovar, the portrait of Grandpa Jack and of my great-grandmother Sarah, and the paintings and little sculptures Grandma had invested with a lifetime of love, and the display of framed photographs, which included her parents, her own husband—Grandpa Jack—long since gone, her children and grandchildren at various stages of life. My gaze returned to my beloved Grandma, sleeping in the bed, her brow smooth, her beautiful hands resting by her side, her chest rising unevenly with the fitful movement of her breath.

I turned, grateful that Ray was supporting me with his arm. The door closed behind us. The latch echoed as we walked the hallway, then crossed the lobby to the double glass doors that led back out onto the street.

Notes

Chapter Two

The story of the creation of water is a direct quotation taken from the Australia Museum website, with material produced by Aboriginal Nations Australia. I reproduce here the full text of the story which is told by Warren Foster, in his own words. The title of this story, on the website, is "Toonkoo and Ngaardi."

Quotations:

1. *It is my father's land, my grandfather's land, my grandmother's land. I am related to it, it give me my identity. If I don't fight for it, then I will be moved out of it and [it] will be the loss of my identity.*
  Father Dave Passi,
  Plaintiff, 'Mabo' Case in 'Land Bilong Islanders,' Yarra Bank Films, 1990.

2. *Our story is in the land ... it is written in those sacred places, that's the law. Dreaming place ... you can't change it, no matter who you are.*
  Big Bill Neidjie,
  Gagadju Elder, Kakadu,
  'Australia's Kakadu Man Bill Neidjie,' 1986.

3. A Land of Plenty

A lot of people say Aboriginal people never farmed the land ... never ploughed the land and they never grew wheat and they never planted apple trees and orange trees. We never had to. Our mother, the earth, she gave herself freely to us. And because we respected her and loved her, we never had to go and do all them other things. That would have been harming our mother. So we just took what she gave us.
    Paul Gordon, Language Officer, Brewarrina, 1996.

The above quotations were taken from the website www. IndigenousAustralia.com.au.

Chapter Three

I would like to credit Colin Tatz's excellent book *A South African Childhood,* for some of the descriptive details pertaining to Darlene's school experience. The "protection sandwich" incident is taken directly from his account, as is the remark: "They hate us, but they like our sandwiches." The moment in which Darlene's mother sits marking a map, while listening to the radio, is also borrowed from an incident he describes.

Acknowledgements

I'm THANKFUL to Odette Sara Vaughan for directing me to Guernica, and to Michael Mirolla for giving this book such a fine home.

It was my good fortune at Guernica to work with Margo LaPierre, who generously brought to the manuscript the force of her talent as a poet, along with superb editorial acumen and finesse. I appreciate all I have learned from her as well as the pleasure of her attuned literary companionship.

I would like to thank several people for their valuable feedback: my sisters Ilana Nayman and Michele Nayman, who were enthusiastic readers, and also pointed up some factual errors; Michelle Caplan, who helped me rethink a key issue; and Yitzhak Ajzner, whose meticulous reading provided crucial religious, cultural, and historical details, and numerous important corrections.

My gratitude to the Hadassah-Brandeis Institute for a grant in support of this book, and also to The MacDowell Colony for a fellowship that afforded precious writing time and newfound community.

And I am deeply grateful to my family, near and far, for the collective experience of our ongoing lives.

About the Author

SHIRA NAYMAN is the author of Awake in the Dark, The Listener, and A Mind of Winter. Her work has appeared in magazines and journals, including The Atlantic Monthly.

MIX
Paper from
responsible sources
FSC® C100212

Printed by Imprimerie Gauvin
Gatineau, Québec